Ab

Susan Carlisle's lo... she made a bad gra... TV until the grade... with books. Turning... writing romance, she pens hot medicals. She loves castles, travelling, afternoon tea, reads voraciously and hearing from her readers. Join her newsletter at www.SusanCarlisle.com

Sarah M. Anderson won RT Reviewer's Choice 2012 Desire of the Year for *A Man of Privilege*. *The Nanny Plan* was a 2016 RITA® winner for Contemporary Romance: Short. Find out more about Sarah's love of cowboys at www.sarahmanderson.com

Sandra Steffen is an award-winning, bestselling author of more than thirty-seven novels. Honoured to have won The RITA® Award, The National Readers' Choice Award and The Wish Award, her most cherished regards come from readers around the world. She married her high-school sweetheart and raised four sons while simultaneously pursuing her dream of publication. She loves to laugh, read, take long walks and have long talks with friends, and write, write, write.

Mavericks

Mavericks: Tempting the Bachelor

SUSAN CARLISLE

SARAH M. ANDERSON

SANDRA STEFFEN

MILLS & BOON

First Published in Great Britain 2020
By Mills & Boon, an imprint of HarperCollins*Publishers*
1 London Bridge Street, London, SE1 9GF

MAVERICKS: TEMPTING THE BACHELOR
© 2020 Harlequin Books S.A.

Hot-Shot Doc Comes to Town © 2013 Susan Carlisle
Bringing Home the Bachelor © 2013 Sarah M. Anderson
A Bride Before Dawn © 2011 Sandra E. Steffen

ISBN: 978-0-263-28220-7

MIX
Paper from
responsible sources
FSC™ C007454

This book is produced from independently certified FSC™ paper to ensure responsible forest management.

For more information visit: www.harpercollins.co.uk/green

Printed and bound in Spain
by CPI, Barcelona

HOT-SHOT DOC COMES TO TOWN

SUSAN CARLISLE

To Mom
For all your love and support

CHAPTER ONE

THE flash of red in the parking space directly in front of the Benton Clinic door caught Dr. Shelby Wayne's attention. Great, this could only be the bad-boy doctor her uncle had told her to expect, and over six hours late.

Squinting, she looked through the dusty plate-glass window at the slick convertible sports car on the other side. As far as she knew, no one in that area of western Tennessee had a car nearly as fine as the one now almost blocking the door. This was big-truck not fancy-car country.

Babysitting her Uncle Gene's most recent personal project wasn't her idea of a good time. But needing help at the clinic so badly meant she couldn't send him back to Nashville. Still if she could get two weeks' worth of free medical help out of it, she'd bend over backwards to accommodate her uncle. Maybe if she played her cards right she could convince the doctor that his skills would be better utilized in Benton than where he was currently working.

If she wanted the clinic to remain open, she'd have to find some help soon.

She glanced at the clipboard for the name of her next patient then scanned the packed waiting room for Mrs. Stewart. It would be a waste of time to try to get the attention of the sweet little grandmotherly woman with a hearing problem over the din in the tiny room. As she walked towards Mrs.

Stewart the people waiting quieted, and all eyes turned to look out the window.

Shelby watched, along with everyone else, as the expensive-looking loafer touched the pavement. In one athletic movement a man slipped out of the low car. His gaze met hers through the window. Her breath caught in her throat. His piercing look made her wonder if he could see secrets she'd kept hidden. He gave her a slight nod of acknowledgement.

His gaze traveled back and forth along the line of stores in the mostly abandoned strip mall. If it hadn't been for the brief twist of contempt marring his looks he would've qualified for the term "dangerously attractive".

How dared he act as if Benton was beneath him? After her husband Jim had died, continuing to live and work here had been the best decision she'd ever made. Her parents had encouraged her to move back to her home town to practice but she'd decided Benton was where she belonged. It was where she and Jim had chosen to make their home. Benton had supported her a hundred and ten percent as she'd grieved. Each person had their own little quirks but they all had a big hearts. Here she felt secure.

The new doctor still held the room's attention as he stepped to the door and pulled. The front of his car rested so far over the sidewalk that it wouldn't allow the door to open far enough for him to enter.

Shelby couldn't stop the twitch of her lips as she checked a chuckle. He was making a notable first impression on the locals sitting in the waiting room. Everyone in town would be enjoying this story by bedtime. That was one of the great things about living in a small town, though it could also be the worst. Everyone knew everything. When you had a tragedy your friends and neighbors were there to support you, but when there was a good story to tell they spread it.

The man snarled and murmured a sharp word under his

breath. Turning, he took three quick strides back to the driver's door, opened it and slid behind the wheel with the same grace as when he'd alighted. Leaving one leg hanging outside the open door, he started the car. The windows of the clinic vibrated slightly as he backed the vehicle up until the entire sidewalk could be seen. As quickly as he'd started the car he shut off the engine, got out and slammed the door.

His long strides brought him towards the entrance of the clinic again. The only indication in his demeanor that he might still be annoyed was the jerk he gave the clinic door.

Shelby smiled but not too broadly so that he wouldn't think she'd been laughing at him. "You must be Dr. Stiles. I was expecting you hours ago."

"Are you Dr. Wayne?"

She offered him her hand. "I'm Dr. Shelby Wayne."

He shook her hand. "With the name Shelby I had expected a man. Taylor Stiles."

His clasp was firm. Warm and dry. Not the dead-fish handshake she'd anticipated from the fancy-dressed, showy-car-driving, big-city doctor.

"Sorry to disappoint you," Shelby said with a hint of sarcasm.

"If you two young people are through putting on a show..." Mrs. Stewart looked pointedly at Taylor Stiles "...and making nice, would one of you mind seeing about my sciatica?"

Taylor blinked in surprise. As if on cue, the room erupted in noise as though the curtain had closed and the play was over.

Shelby cleared her throat. She loved the outspoken and to-the-point woman. "Uh, yes, Mrs. Stewart. You're next." Shelby handed the clipboard to Dr. Stiles. "Call the next patient under Mrs. Stewart's name and put him or her in room two." She pointed down the short hallway. "I'll be in after I see Mrs. Stewart."

Dr. Stiles's dashing brow rose a fraction of an inch but he accepted the clipboard. Apparently he wasn't used to taking direction. His deep baritone voice called little Greg Hankins's name while she guided Mrs. Stewart to exam room one.

"Kind of snooty, that one, but still mighty handsome," Mrs. Stewart remarked as she took a seat in the chair in the room.

"Um, I guess," Shelby said as she flipped through the seventy-four-year-old's chart.

"I could tell by the look on your face you noticed it too. Doc Shelby, you have to start living again. It's been three years. Your Jim is dead, not you."

A stab of pain came with that frank statement about her husband. There had been nothing she could do when she'd reached the accident. Despite not being far behind Jim in her own car, his truck had already been wrapped around a tree when she arrived at the scene. Nothing she'd done had stopped his blood from pooling in the mangled metal. The sight, the smell… She'd retched. Three years later she could at least do everything in her power to honor his memory by keeping the clinic open any way she could. The people of Benton she loved so much needed the medical care and she needed the security of knowing she was needed.

"Now, Mrs. Stewart…" Shelby smiled "…I'm supposed to be taking care of you, not you seeing about me."

"Well, missy, I think you don't want to see about you, so I'm just going to have to."

Shelby took a deep breath and let it out slowly. "Why don't you let me examine you, then we can work on me?" Adjusting her bright pink stethoscope in her ears, she placed the disk on the woman's chest.

"All you think about is this clinic. Maybe with Dr. Kildare here you can have a little fun for a change," the old woman groused.

"Dr. Kildare?"

"Yeah, he was one of those handsome TV doctors before your time. That new doctor makes me think of him. All tall, dark and handsome."

Shelby laughed. "Mrs. Stewart, you're outrageous." Mrs. Stewart's youngest son had to be older than Dr. Stiles. "You don't even know him and I really don't either. Anyway, he's only going to be helping out for a couple of weeks."

"Yeah, but you could have a little fun for a while. You're not dead. So stop acting like it."

Shelby patted the woman's arm. "For you I will try, I promise."

Without a doubt he had messed up this time. There had been no talking the judge out of his decision. Community service in a rural area. His lawyer had cautioned against arguing with the judge but Taylor had tried anyway. If he didn't have such a lead foot, he'd still be in Nashville in his nice modern trauma department instead of in a town like Benton. He'd run from a town similar to this one years ago and had never returned.

Taylor lifted the large-for-his-age two-year-old boy up onto the metal exam table. *Where in the world did you go to find a piece of medical office equipment from the 1950s?*

Thump, thump the table responded in rebellion as the boy's heels hit its side.

It was a sturdy table, Taylor would give it that.

The thin, frail mother carefully placed a brown bag she'd been carrying on the floor. She reminded Taylor of how his mother had looked when he had been a child, work weary and sad.

"So what's wrong with Greg?" Taylor looked at the boy's mother while keeping a hand on the wiggling child.

At one time he'd been like this little boy, dirty and wearing hand-me-down clothes from the church thrift closet. The sharp bite of memory froze him for a second. He pushed it aside. He hadn't dwelled on his dysfunctional childhood in years and he refused to start again today.

"I think he has something in his nose. We'll wait and let Doc Wayne take it out."

The mother doesn't trust me. Taylor didn't like that. He was the one with the knowledge who worked in a well-respected hospital, who had managed to get out of a nowhere town like this one, and she questioned his abilities. Turning away as if to get something, he gathered his patience.

Taylor faced the mother again. "Well, why don't I just take a quick look, okay?" Taylor forced his best smile for the mother then sought the otoscope that should have been hanging on the wall. "Uh, excuse me I need to find a light."

"There's a flashlight in the drawer." The mother pointed to the metal stand beside him.

Taylor pulled the drawer open and found what he needed, including plastic gloves. He checked inside the boy's nose. "There it is. In his left nostril. A lima bean, I believe. Do you mind if I get it out? Dr. Wayne will be busy for a while."

"I guess it'll be all right," the mother said without much enthusiasm.

"Let me find—"

"The big tweezers thing is in the jar on top of the stand," the mother said in a dry tone.

"So how often has Greg been in with this type of problem?" Taylor asked as he reached for the instrument in the outdated clear sterile jar.

"This is the third time in two weeks."

"Really. That often?" Taylor nodded his head thoughtfully. "Greg, you just lean back and hold still. I'll have that old bean out in no time," he said sternly enough so the boy would do as instructed but not so harshly as to scare him.

The bean slipped out with a gentle tug and Taylor dropped it into the trash can, along with the gloves.

"Okay, young man, you're done here." Taylor picked up the boy and set him on his feet.

As if Taylor had pushed the button of a doorbell, the boy burst out crying then wailing. His slight mother hefted the child into her arms. "Shu, what's wrong, honey? Did the doctor hurt you?"

Great, now she's making the kid afraid of me.

"Sucker, I want a sucker," the child demanded between gasps.

Over the noise, Taylor asked, "Has Dr. Wayne been giving Greg a sucker each time she's taken something out of his nose?"

The woman nodded.

"Greg," Taylor said firmly, gaining the boy's attention and shutting off his tantrum. "If you don't put anything in your nose for one week then your mother will bring you by to get a sucker. Do you understand?"

The boy nodded his agreement and plopped his filthy thumb into his mouth.

"Good. See you next week."

As they exited the room the mother handed Taylor the brown sack she'd been carrying with extra care. "Your pay."

"Uh, thank you."

As the mother and child walked back down the hall toward the waiting area, Taylor unrolled the top of the bag. Nestled inside were six brown eggs. He crushed the top of the bag. He could remember his mother not being able to pay the doctor and bartering her house-cleaning services for medical care for him and his siblings. Of all the places the judge could have sent him, why did it have to be here?

"Where's my patient?" Dr. Wayne demanded as she looked around him into the room.

"He's gone."

"Gone where?"

"I examined him, and he's left."

Her shoulders went back, her chest came forward. He would've taken time to enjoy the sight if it hadn't been for her flashing gray eyes.

"That's not what I instructed you to do."

"I'm a doctor. I treated a patient. End of story."

She didn't say anything for a few moments. The blood rose in her face. More calmly than her appearance indicated she said, "We need to step into my office."

Turning, she walked to the end of the hallway. Apparently it wasn't until she reached the office door that she realized he hadn't moved. She glared at him.

Not appreciating being treated like a school child being called to the principal's office, Taylor resigned himself to putting up with her bossy ways for the time being. The judge had stated in no uncertain terms—clinic or jail.

"Coming, Dr. Wayne," he said, loud enough to be heard but with zero sincerity.

After he'd entered the office, she closed the flimsy door behind him. "Dr. Stiles, you will *not* come into my clinic six hours late and start doing as you please. If you'd been here on time I could've instructed you in the clinic protocol."

Straight chestnut hair that touched the ridge of her shoulders swayed as she spoke. Taylor would describe her as cute in a college co-ed sort of way. Her practical black slacks and white shirt did nothing to move her up on the looks scale.

"These are my people. I won't have you showing up for two short weeks and taking over. I cannot, will not, have you here for God knows what reason and let you destroy the trust I've built with my patients. I expect you to follow my instructions."

Who did this woman think she was, talking to him that

way? Taylor carefully set the bag of eggs down on the desk. Turning his back to it, he placed his hands on the edge of the desk and leaned back.

"Doctor," he said, with enough disdain to make the word sound like he questioned whether or not that was the correct term. He took pleasure in watching the thrust of her breasts indicating her indignation as his barb struck home. "I won't be relegated to being your nurse. I'm the chief trauma doctor of a major hospital in Nashville. I can assure you that there will be few, if any, problems you see in this small, backwards clinic that I'll need your handholding for.

"I don't like being here any more than you obviously like having me. But what I can tell you is that I'm a good doctor. By no choice of my own, your patients are also *my* patients for the time being. Now, I suggest that we get back to that room full of people you're so concerned about."

Her mouth opened and closed. A sense of satisfaction filled him at having so thoroughly shut her up. Based on the last few minutes the next couple of weeks wouldn't be dull.

The infuriating doctor was calling his next patient before Shelby gathered her wits enough to follow him out of the office and down the hall. She'd never before forgotten about having patients waiting. It was a source of pride that she'd always put them first. Not even here a day and this egotistical doctor her uncle had sent had scrambled her brain. How was she supposed to survive the days ahead while having the likes of him in her face?

Who did he think he was talking to? The Benton Medical Clinic was hers. Her and Jim's dream. She'd make it clear later this evening who was in charge. For now she had to admit the high-handed doctor was right, she had patients to see.

The afternoon wore on and the most contact she had with

Dr. Stiles was when they passed in the hall. It was narrow and their bodies brushed when they maneuvered by each other. For once she regretted not insisting that the landlord let her and Jim change the already existing partitions and make the hallway wider. Before they'd converted it to a medical clinic, the space had been an insurance company office without a large amount of traffic in the hallway.

The first time they passed each other her body went harp-string tight as a tingle rippled through her. She pushed it away, convincing herself it was a delayed reaction to being so irate with him. The next time he was too close was when he looked down at her with his dark steady gaze and said, "By the way, where's the nurse?"

"Don't have one. I have a teenager who's usually here but she's out sick today."

"Really," he said in astonishment. For a second she thought she saw admiration in his eyes. She wasn't sure why it mattered but she liked the thought that he might be impressed by something she did.

When he left her she felt like she'd just stepped out of a hot bath—all warm from head to toe. Thankfully she managed not to cross his path again.

Enough of those thoughts, Shelby scolded herself as she knelt to clean juice from the linoleum. The juice had spilt when a child had thrown a cup. Using a hand on her knee for balance, she pushed up and brushed her clothes off. Instead of her uniform of slacks and shirts she wished she could wear cute sundresses to work, but having to be the cleaning crew meant that wasn't practical.

She looked at the bright red car parked front and center of the door. Despite the fact the cost of it alone could finance the clinic for weeks, maybe months if she was thrifty, she'd love to climb into it and let her hair blow in the wind. Forget all her cares for a while. With a deep sigh she picked up the window cleaner. The trouble was, all her concerns would still be right here waiting. It was her responsibility to see that the clinic remained open.

Footfalls on the floor tiles drew her attention. Shelby moved out of the way so the last patient of the day could leave. "How're you, Mrs. Ferguson?" she asked the barrel-round woman with the white face.

"I would've been better if you hadn't been too busy to see me," she grumbled.

"How's that? Did Dr. Stiles not take good care of you?" The man was going to be out of here tonight if he'd upset Mrs. Ferguson.

"I don't like strange doctors looking me over," she groused.

Relieved there was nothing more to her concern than that, Shelby watched Taylor approach. As Mrs. Stewart had remarked, he was good looking but Shelby was more interested in his abilities, and those she couldn't question. He'd held up his end of the workload, she'd have to give him that. Most of the patients had been unsure about seeing him but had cautiously agreed when they'd been told how long they'd have to wait to see her. Most had given in and decided to let Taylor examine them. But there was a little part of Shelby that liked knowing she was their first choice.

"Dr. Stiles will only be helping out until the end of the month."

"Good," Mrs. Ferguson said, as she shifted her oversized bag on her ample hip. "Then things will get back to normal around here."

"So, are you two ladies talking about me?" Dr. Stiles came to stand beside them and flashed Mrs. Ferguson a grin.

Was there no end to the man's ego? "No." The word came out harsher than Shelby had intended, making her look guilty of doing exactly what he'd accused them of.

The twinkle in Taylor's eyes told her he knew it too. "Mrs. Ferguson, why don't I walk you out?"

She gave him a startled look. "Uh, I guess that would be all right." The woman clutched her purse in her sausage-sized fingers and shuffled towards the door.

Shelby made a swipe with the glass cleaner as she observed Taylor helping Mrs. Ferguson into her car. A summer breeze lifted the deep waves of his brown hair as he strolled back toward the clinic. Would it be soft and silky to the touch?

Shaking her head at thoughts like that, Shelby rubbed extra hard at a spot on the glass. It had been an easier day having Dr. Stile's help but she couldn't afford to get used to it. He wouldn't be there very long. Regardless of what good help he'd turned out to be, he made her angrier than anyone she'd ever known. She'd have a talk with him tonight and set the ground rules. This was her and Jim's clinic. She was in charge.

Shelby had stepped outside to wash the other side of the window by the time he'd reached the door. She glanced at him.

"Crusty old bird and a heart attack waiting to happen," he said, running a hand across his chin dark with stubble.

Suddenly she noticed the shadowy circles under his eyes. He looked tired. "I know. I've talked to her until I'm blue in the face. But she just can't bring herself to give up the carbs."

Shelby sprayed the window and began making circles with the rag. From the reflection in the glass she could tell the sun was turning pink in the western sky above the rolling hills and lush foliage of summer. She had to hurry or she wouldn't finish before she could no longer see.

"I'm bushed. I understand you have a place where I can stay," Taylor said as he pulled the door open.

"Yeah, but I have to finish up here before we leave."

"Don't you have a cleaning service?"

"Sure I do. Sometimes Carly, my receptionist, if she doesn't have a date. Which she almost always has." She glanced at him. He stood with his hands in his pockets and his head slanted in disbelief.

"Surely you don't do all the cleaning after seeing patients all day."

"Dr. Stiles—"

"Taylor. After hours I believe we can call each other by our first names."

Somehow it seemed petty not to agree. "Taylor, this is a state-supported clinic. And that may not last. Funding's tight and I have to constantly prove need. I'd rather put every dollar available into patient care."

Taylor looked through the glass at the room with the water-stained ceiling and mismatched chairs crowded against the wall. Shelby's voice spoke with pride but all he saw was a sad, needy place that he couldn't leave soon enough. It represented all that he had gladly left behind. He couldn't get back to his sparkling state-of-the-art hospital too soon. With a resigned breath he said, "Where do you keep the cleaning supplies?" He might as well help if he planned to get some sleep any time soon.

"Why?"

"I thought I'd help."

"I've got it."

Really, she was such a control freak that she even had to do all the cleaning? "It'll go twice as fast if I help."

"You're right. Stuff's in the closet in my office."

Taylor walked down the hall to the office and pulled the bucket full of cleaning materials out of the closet. The plastic pail was the same type his mother had carried when she'd cleaned people's homes. She had worked six days a week and even that hadn't always kept him and his two brothers in clothes or put food on the table. His drunken father...

"If you'll give me that, I'll do the restroom. I don't want you to mess up those pretty shoes," Shelby said.

"Oh, that's already happened. Little Jack Purdy threw up on them hours ago."

She wrinkled her nose. "Sorry."

"All part of the job. I'll sweep. Then can we get out of here."

"Yeah, I'll come in early and set up the rooms."

Was there anything she didn't do?

Thirty minutes later Shelby locked the door behind them and pulled the strap of her satchel over her slim shoulder. "Follow me."

He backed out of the parking space and was waiting before she'd made it to the ancient black pick-up across the three-row parking lot. He watched as Shelby pulled herself up into the truck. She was a petite woman, but she had a strong backbone to make up for any weakness she might have in other areas. A pit bull had nothing on her.

The whine of Shelby's starter refusing to co-operate and her hand hitting the steering-wheel told him he needed to offer her a lift. Taylor pulled in front of the truck. "Need a ride?"

She leaned out the open window. "Yeah, much as I hate to admit it."

"Is that riding with me you hate or that the truck won't start?"

"Both." She gave him a dry smile and climbed out of the truck, hefted her bag over her shoulder and came around the car.

He'd had no idea what to expect when the judge had ordered him here. He would've never imagined in a million years he'd find someone so smart, stubborn and surprisingly fascinating hiding out in some tiny 'burb in the middle of nowhere. Why was she here?

Taylor leaned across and unlatched the passenger door. Stretching farther, he pushed the door open. "Give me that." He pointed to the bag. Shelby handed it to him. "What've you got in this?" He put it in the space behind them.

"Charts." She slid into the low seat.

"You're taking work home? You've already put in, what? A twelve-hour day and now you're going to do paperwork. Don't you have a life?"

"The clinic is my life."

He gave her a long look. "I can see that."

She narrowed her eyes and said, "By the way, tomorrow please park away from the door. Leave the closer spaces for my patients. Some, like Mrs. Ferguson, can't walk very far."

He put up a hand. "Okay. I've been adequately rebuked. Which way?"

"Out of the lot and then to the left on the main road. My house isn't far."

That figured. She wouldn't live too far from her precious clinic. The only thing he'd ever been single-mindedly focused on had been getting the heck out of a town just like the one he was in now. Medicine had been the vehicle he'd used to achieve that goal. His lips twisted. Ironically, it had also been the vehicle that had brought him back.

"Turn to the left just past the white two-story house. My house is the third one on the right."

He pulled into the tree-lined street with perfect houses and immaculate lawns. The neighbors were out in the coolness of the evening. Two couples stood talking to each other while kids played nearby. At another house a man mowed his grass.

"True suburbia," Taylor murmured.

"Yes, it is and that's why I bought on this street. I wanted to live where neighbors spoke to each other, helped each other. Where children could play and be safe."

His stomach clinched. The scene she described was everything he'd ever dreamed of as a kid. Slowly releasing a breath, he pulled his car into the paved drive Shelby indicated. The house was a red-brick ranch style with a two-story detached wooden garage and stairs running along the outside.

"You'll be staying there." Shelby pointed at the garage when he turned off the car engine.

"I'm staying here?" If working in the makeshift clinic wasn't bad enough, staying in this homey neighborhood might kill him. "With you?"

"You're not staying *with* me. I rent this out. It just happens I don't have a tenant right now."

Things had just got more interesting.

She glanced over her shoulder to the neighbors watching from across the street, then turned to him and grinned. "You've already started the neighbors talking. We don't often see cars like this in Benton."

"I guess you don't." Taylor felt his lips thin. He didn't like being talked about. He'd spent his youth being the topic of gossip, being made fun of. At least these people weren't talking about him in relationship to the town drunk.

Her smile had disappeared by the time his gaze met hers. "You know, if you don't want people to notice you then you might try not living so extravagantly." She opened the door and climbed out, picking up her satchel.

How had she read him so well? Were his feelings that obvious? He'd spent years learning to hide them. How had this woman he known mere hours been able to see through him?

Taylor stepped out of the car and slammed the door, facing her. "Extravagantly?" His voice rose. "I'll have you know I work hard for what I have. I can afford this car and I don't have to justify it to you or anyone else."

"Little touchy, aren't you?" she replied with a noticeable effort to keep her voice down.

"Everything okay, Shelby?" a deep voice called.

Taylor glared at the man who had crossed the street to stand at the end of her drive. Small towns never changed. People were always in your business.

She walked a few steps toward the man and waved. "Everything's fine, Mr. Marshall. I'm just showing Dr. Stiles where he'll be staying while he's in town."

Taylor went to the trunk of the car, popped it and grabbed his suitcase.

"Okay," Mr. Marshall said. "We'll see you at the block party, won't we?"

"Sure. Looking forward to it."

"Bring the new doctor along if you wish. We'd like to meet him."

Taylor certainly hoped that she wasn't planning on him attending any party. The Arctic would become a beach before he'd attend any social function around here. He'd made himself into an arts and opera guy. Benton didn't even have a movie theater, from what he could tell.

Shelby turned, her gray eyes flashing, her tone tight with control. "Don't you ever raise your voice to me again where my neighbors can hear. They worry about me."

She motioned towards the garage stairs and headed that way. "You'll not come here and upset them or create fodder for talk at their dinner tables. For some reason I don't understand, Uncle Gene thinks I'm a halfway house warden for bad-boy trauma doctors." The last few words were said more to herself than to him.

So, Shelby didn't like being the talk of the town any more than he did. Maybe they had more in common than he'd given her credit for.

CHAPTER TWO

SHELBY dropped her bag on the bottom step of the stairs that ran alongside the garage.

"Since you don't want to be a topic of gossip any more than I do," Taylor said calmly, "maybe you should just agree to disagree about my car."

With great effort Shelby pushed down the temptation to say something. Having a public argument would certainly give her neighbors and friends a good tale to tell.

"Just what did you do to get on Uncle Gene's bad side?"

"Uncle Gene?" he asked in a puzzled tone.

"Judge Gene Robbins. He's my uncle," she said as she started to climb the stairs.

"So that's why I'm here." The words were little more than a mumble, as if he was contemplating the meaning of life. After a moment he commented, "We've had a few legal dealings. Nothing special."

Shelby stopped and looked down at him. What did he mean? Was he an ax murderer? No, her uncle wouldn't send anyone to work with her who wasn't a decent person.

Taylor's look moved slowly up from where his focus had been, on her bottom. Heat filled her cheeks. It had been a long time since a man had noticed her and made his appreciation so obvious. She and Jim had been an item since childhood, leaving little room for another man to show interest. The men in Benton had never approached her in anything other than friendship since Jim had been gone. In truth, she'd not given them a chance. She couldn't take the chance of losing someone she loved again.

Shelby hurried up the stairs. Taylor was here to help in the clinic and that was all. On the landing she opened the door to the apartment.

"You don't lock up?"

Turning round, she found Taylor too close for comfort. Standing on the small landing that made her a step higher than he, Shelby was almost at eye level with him.

From there she could see the tiny laugh lines that radiated out from the corners of his eyes. Apparently he wasn't always the hypercritical person his body language indicated he was. His eyes were brown with small flakes of gold.

The twist of the corner of his mouth brought her attention to his firm, full lips. She blinked.

"Doesn't your husband tell you to lock the doors?" he asked.

"I'm a widow."

"I'm sorry." He sounded like he meant it.

"I am too." She turned away from the sincerity in his eyes. The sadness that usually accompanied thoughts of Jim was suddenly not as sharp.

Shelby hadn't missed the look of displeasure on Taylor's face when he had entered the clinic or when he'd seen the working conditions. She'd also not missed the expression of disgust when he'd realized she drove an old truck. His knuckles had turned white on his steering-wheel when he'd pulled onto her street, as if he didn't like her neighborhood. Did he think that living here was beneath him? Or was it that she rubbed him the wrong way?

"How does your family feel about you being away from home?" she asked.

"No family." He made it sound like he liked it that way.

Entering the one-room apartment, Shelby moved to one side to prevent any physical contact. He made her feel nervous and she was never nervous around men. After dropping his bag on the floor, he looked around the place.

Shelby's gaze followed his. A full bed with her grandmother's hand-quilted blanket dominated the room. There was a small refrigerator-stove combo in one corner. A two-seater table with chairs sat in front of the double window that looked out onto the back of her house. A braided rug, sofa and chair finished off the living area. A bathroom took up the other corner. She was rather pleased with her decorating efforts. It made a cute place for one person to stay.

"I think you will be comfortable here," she said with a smile full of pride.

He didn't agree or disagree. Instead he picked up his bag, carried it to the bed and began unzipping it.

"Not up to your usual standards, I'm sure," she mumbled.

Taylor pulled clothing out of his bag, his back to her. "You don't know me well enough to know my standards. Now, if you'll excuse me, I'm going to get a much-needed shower and go to bed. I've been up almost twenty-four hours."

"What? Why?"

"Because I had to handle an emergency last night. A boy had been hit by a car. I didn't get out of the hospital until ten this morning and then I had to drive straight here or *Uncle Gene* would've been unhappy."

So that's why he'd been late. Why hadn't she noticed he wasn't just tired, he was exhausted? As a physician trained to observe the human condition she should've known. Had she completely missed it because of her strange reaction to his nearness?

Now she felt small and petty. Why hadn't he said something? She could've given him directions here. The clinic had been running with just her for three years and she could've certainly made it through another afternoon. Instead, Taylor had gone to work, never giving the patients or her any indication he was drained. His perfect bedside manner had never faltered. For that, he'd earned her admiration.

Taylor began unbuttoning his dress shirt.

Shelby headed for the door but turned back when she reached it. "One more thing about the clinic..." Her gaze went to where his hands worked the buttons open.

"Yeah?"

His shirt parted, revealing a broad chest lightly covered with dark hair. Her gaze rose to meet his. One of his dark brows rose quizzically.

Heaven help her, she'd been caught staring. Shelby drew in a quick breath. "Uh, do you mind keeping your clothes on until I'm gone?"

"Actually, I do. Can't whatever you have to say wait?"

Was she losing her mind? She didn't stand around in half-naked strangers' rooms. Holding her ground, she gave him her best piercing look. "No. I need to make a few things clear before tomorrow."

"Go ahead. I guess I can't stop you," he said as he shrugged out of his shirt and let it drop to the floor.

"Although I appreciate your help today, it needs to be clear to the patients that I'm in charge. I make the decisions. I determine what the patients require. I will not have you changing routines I've worked hard to implement. Is that clear?"

"So, to make it short and sweet, you're the boss."

Put that way, he made her sound like a shrew. That didn't sit well. "It's just that—"

He put up a hand, halting her words. "I've got it. Now, if you'll excuse me, I'd like to get some shut-eye."

Departing, she carried the feeling she'd been the one reprimanded. "The clinic opens at eight sharp," she said over her shoulder.

"I'll be there."

Taylor woke to threads of early morning sunshine through the window. He'd slept well, whether from exhaustion or because this simple room had offered him a good mattress he didn't know.

Shelby had been right. He didn't think much of the apartment but on second look it did have a rather homey feel. It was a great deal nicer than what he'd had growing up. To even have a bed to himself would've been considered high living.

He glanced at the electric clock on the bedside table. It said seven twenty-eight. The woman would have his hide if he didn't turn up on time this morning. He couldn't take a chance that she'd inform her Uncle Gene about his tardiness. More time he couldn't do.

Ten minutes later, freshly shaven and dressed in khakis, a knit shirt and loafers, he opened the door and almost stepped in the tray sitting on the stoop. There he found a Thermos of coffee, toast and a boiled egg. He smiled. Maybe the caustic doctor was feeling a little guilty about how she'd treated him when he'd been late. Apparently she wasn't all vinegar.

He checked the time. If he didn't get a move on she might chew him out again. Grabbing the Thermos and egg, he closed the door behind him and hurried down the stairs. Knocking on the back door of her house, he received no response. She must've found a ride to work. If she wasn't at the clinic when he got there, he'd hunt for her.

As Taylor walked across the parking lot towards the clinic, Shelby came out. "Coming in under the wire, aren't you, Doctor?" Her voice was full of censure as she worked the key until the deadbolt was drawn into the door to open the office for the day.

"I said I'd be here, and I'm here. And good morning to you too, Doctor. What time did you show up?"

"I've been here an hour or so. It usually takes me that long to set up for the day."

"I knocked to see if you needed a ride."

"I walked. Bert said he'd have my truck fixed this afternoon."

Taylor held the door for her to enter ahead of him. "You walked? I would've brought you if you'd woken me."

"You were tired. Walking isn't a problem. I do it pretty regularly. I'm safe enough and it's good exercise."

A couple of people who'd been waiting around outside came in behind them.

"Thanks for the breakfast." He showed her the egg and Thermos.

"No problem. Those'll have to wait, though. We've patients to see."

Her no-nonsense statement went along with her functional attire of navy slacks and white V-neck T-shirt that showed a hint of cleavage. Despite her simple attire, it couldn't hide the shapely curves of her body. Her waist was small enough that a man's hands could easily slip around it.

She'd pulled her hair back but at the nape it was too short to capture. The only flash of color was a bright neon-pink stethoscope hanging around her neck. Taylor followed her to the desk, where a blonde teenage girl sat, drumming a pencil and chewing gum.

"Carly, this is Dr. Stiles. He'll be helping us for the next couple of weeks," Shelby said as she picked up the sign-in clipboard.

Taylor nodded to the girl.

She looked up. He watched her eyes widen. She shifted, then straightened in her chair. "Hey." She flipped her long blonde hair behind her shoulder. He'd never thought of himself as vain, far from it, but he did know when a female appreciated his looks.

"Carly, do you think you could find Ms. Cooper's file? And get rid of the gum." Shelby turned to him, "I'll see Ms. Cooper since this is a check-up."

Carly didn't move. He didn't know why but he wished Shelby would have the same reaction to him that Carly did. Other than that one unguarded moment when he'd been unbuttoning his shirt, she'd acted as if she had no idea he was male. It intrigued and disappointed him. Simple admiration from Shelby would be hard earned.

"I'll call Dr. Stiles's patient for him," Carly said as she dropped her gum into the trash can at her feet and gave him a toothy smile.

"Will I be using exam one?" he asked Shelby.

"That'll be fine."

Her words were said so tersely that he glanced at her. What was her problem now?

For the rest of the morning he had little time to ponder what might have upset Shelby. The waiting room stayed full no matter how efficiently he tended to the patients or how simple the cases were.

Where Carly's reaction to him had been an ego booster earlier in the day, it had become borderline comical by midday. He noticed that she saw to all his patients, showing them to their exam room, asking him if he had everything he needed or if she could get him something to drink. All of it was nice but it was in direct contrast to how Carly treated Shelby. Carly offered her no assistance.

When Taylor asked Carly about that she shrugged in a typical teenage dramatic fashion and said, "Oh, Dr. Wayne likes to do everything herself."

Of course she does.

By lunchtime Taylor couldn't help but admit that he'd put

in a pretty hard morning. The little clinic was plenty busy. The mundane work sucked him back to another time. Each patient reminded him too much of the people he'd known growing up.

There was the kid with the cough that never disappeared, like Mike Walker's. He'd been in Taylor's third-grade class one year but wasn't there the next. Or others, such as old man Parsons, who'd had no teeth and had chewed tobacco until his gums were diseased. Or Mrs. Roberts, who might've been pretty at fifty, but with too many children and a sorry husband had looked like she was seventy.

Taylor would do his time and get back to where he belonged, where memories weren't darts being thrown at him constantly.

Around noon the egg he'd eaten in bites between patients was gone. He was glad to see that the crowd in the waiting room had dwindled. Maybe they would let him and Shelby have some lunch before every seat was filled again.

"Where do you get a good burger in this town?" Taylor asked as Shelby approached the front desk.

"There's a burger place on Main," Carly offered.

"We can all go. I'll buy," he offered.

Shelby gave a negative shake of her head. "I have paperwork to do. And someone may come in." She slipped a chart into the file cabinet.

Really? The woman couldn't even stop long enough to go out for a quick bite of lunch?

"I want to go. Can we ride in that cool car of yours?"

Taylor wasn't sure he wanted to be seen riding around town with the very young girl beside him but there was no choice because he had no idea where the burger joint was and he was starving. "Can we bring you back something?" Taylor asked Shelby.

"No, I have a pack of crackers in my desk."

"Okay." He shrugged. "But I bet a burger would be a lot better." He looked at Carly. "Come on. Show me the way. I guess I should learn my way around town."

Shelby pulled out the drawer of her desk and reached for the package of crackers but didn't pick them up. She would've been satisfied with them if Taylor hadn't mentioned a burger.

She popped the top of her diet drink and stared off into space. The sounds of Carly's high-pitched giggle and Taylor's deep rumble came from the front. It grew louder as they walked in her direction.

Taylor stopped and let Carly enter Shelby's office before him. "We decided to go through the drive-in and pick up something. We brought you a burger. Before you argue, I owe you for breakfast and the place to stay."

Carly's eyes widened with surprise. "You're staying at Doc Wayne's?"

"Yeah." Taylor pulled one of the spare chairs closer to the desk with his foot.

Carly looked from Taylor to Shelby and back to Taylor.

No telling what the rumor would be if she didn't clear this up now. "He's staying in my garage apartment."

"Oh, I thought—"

"I know what you thought." Shelby said in a tight voice.

Already this man was disrupting her life. Carly would have that information spread far and wide by the end of the day.

Maybe Uncle Gene could have sent her someone else less... She couldn't think of the word. Intrusive? Disruptive? Attractive?

Taylor sat down in one of the two folding chairs that suddenly appeared child-size beneath his large body and started digging through the paper bag in his hand. He acted as if he took his meals in a tiny, shabby office every day. It didn't take long for Taylor to act like he belonged. Carly took the other chair and he handed her a burger wrapped in paper before his hand slipped into the bag again. Pulling out another burger, he offered it to Shelby.

When she hesitated he said, "Take it. Don't act like you don't want it."

Shelby wished that wasn't the truth. She reached for the offered package. By the time she'd eaten a couple of bites of hers Taylor had already finished his first burger and was searching the bag for another.

The tinkle of the bell hanging on the door sounded.

"Doc Wayne! Doc Wayne!"

The urgent cry made Shelby stand and head towards the door. Taylor had hurried out and was moving up the hall by the time she stepped from the office.

The metallic smell of blood reached her nose before she saw the bright red drops on the floor. It seeped through the rag wrapped around Mr. Hardy's arm. Shelby's stomach rolled like a boat on a stormy sea, making her wish she hadn't eaten.

She mentally braced herself. She could do this.

"Sir," Taylor said, "I'm Dr. Stiles. Come back to the exam room and we'll see what we've got here."

For once Shelby was glad to have Taylor take over. When the injured man, in his mid-fifties, gave her a questioning look she said, "He's a trauma doctor. You're in good hands."

Shelby believed those words. Was it because of the way Taylor led with confidence or because of the quality of care she'd seen him provide? Either way, it kept her from having to deal with the blood.

"Carly," she called, "get out a suture kit in exam one. Now." She turned to the pale-faced woman left standing in the waiting room. Shelby took her arm and led her to a chair.

"Wait here, Mrs. Hardy. We'll let you see him as soon as we can."

Shelby headed toward the exam room. "Carly, get Mrs. Hardy a drink and sit with her. She looks a little shaken," Shelby said as she passed the girl in the hall.

In the examination room, Taylor gingerly unwrapped the rag from around the man's arm. Stepping to the table, she asked, "Mr. Hardy, what did you do to yourself?"

"I was cutting a limb off a tree that'd been damaged during the storm last week. Darn chainsaw kicked back and got me."

Shelby took a fortifying breath as Taylor revealed the gnarled flesh on Mr. Hardy's forearm. She'd never been a fan of blood to start with but after seeing so much of Jim's pouring from his body, her aversion to it had become worse. Red liquid continued to slowly drip onto the white cloth covering the table. "Looks like it got you three times before it let go," Taylor remarked as he examined the man's arm. "I don't see any bone damage."

"Do you mind if I have a look?" Shelby asked, stepping forward. Cases like these were her least favorite but she'd learned to deal with them because she was usually the only doctor available. She wouldn't let this know-it-all doctor make her look weak in front of a patient who would be hers long after he'd gone home.

Taylor shifted to the right so she could have a better view. Shelby gently rotated the arm. "Does that hurt?" Her stomach chose that moment to make a Waikiki surfing wave. She hoped her face didn't give away to Mr. Hardy and Taylor how awful she felt.

"No," the middle-aged man said.

She gently eased the man's arm down on the table. Her hands trembled and she tightened her jaw, willing her throat not to spasm. If she focused on what she was doing, she could get through it. She had before and she would again. "Well, I don't see any damage past the skin, which is good news. We just need to get you stitched up."

Something made her look at Taylor. He was studying her too closely for her comfort. Seconds later a look of realization entered his dark expressive eyes then surprise.

"Dr. Wayne," he said, his tone all business, "do you mind if I do the suturing? It's my expertise and I don't see many chainsaw injuries where I'm from."

A sense of relief washed over her. She looked at Mr. Hardy questioningly.

"I don't mind. Just need to get it done. My wife's already mad 'cos I got blood all over her freshly mopped kitchen floor."

The bell on the door sounded and Carly spoke to someone. "If you have this," Shelby said to Taylor, "I'll go see this other patient."

Taylor glanced up at Mr. Hardy, "We're good here?"

The man nodded agreement. Shelby left as Taylor untaped the suture kit.

Over an hour later Shelby stood beside the front desk ready to call her next patient. She watched as Taylor saw Mr. and Mrs. Hardy out with instructions to return in a couple of days.

Taylor approached the desk and stepped close enough she could smell the soap on his skin that she'd placed in his bath. "We need to talk."

A shiver ran up her spine. "Is something wrong with Mr. Hardy?"

"Your office," he said in a low voice.

"You don't order me around."

"Do you really want to broadcast our discussion to the entire county?" He turned his back to the handful of people in the waiting room. "I don't think you want people to know their doctor's little secret."

Her stomach dropped. He wasn't going to let what he'd learned pass without comment. She entered the office ahead of him. He came in and closed the door.

"What've you got to say that can't wait until after our patients are gone?" she demanded.

Taylor leaned casually against the door, crossing his arms over his chest and one foot over the other, a slight grin on his lips. "Interesting, a doctor who can't stand the sight of blood," he stated in complete amazement.

"I'm a general practitioner. I don't have to deal with blood to do my job well," she huffed.

"I guess you don't. But you must've had a devil of a time getting through emergency rotation in med school."

She looked him directly in the eyes. "I worked through it."

"Yeah, I could see how well you're working through it in there with Mr. Hardy." He had to admire her fortitude. She looked as if she was determined to do what had to be done, even at a cost to herself.

"You won't tell, will you?"

He wished he could tease her and make her think that he would but her wide-eyed, pleading look softened his heart. "Your secret is safe with me."

"You know, I would've stitched up Mr. Hardy if you hadn't been here. Wouldn't have enjoyed it but I would've gotten it done. Patients with major injuries don't normally come to the clinic. His wife refusing to drive outside Benton is the only reason they stopped here. Otherwise they would've gone straight to Nashville or Jackson."

"Either one of those places is around a hundred miles away."

"I know. Mr. Hardy could've gone into shock before he got there."

Shelby gave him a grateful look that made him feel heroic. "I appreciate your help."

The frustration she felt over her weakness shone in her large gray eyes. The desire to take her in his arms and re-assure her that she wasn't failing her patients flooded him. Taylor resisted the urge. Shelby wouldn't appreciate him not-ing her flaw any more than he'd already had. He shrugged. "I'm glad I was here too. The old man required a number of stitches."

Taylor had actually found Mr. Hardy's case interesting. Chainsaw accidents weren't common inside a metropolitan area. To his surprise, he'd enjoyed talking to the tell-it-like-it-is man. Straightening, Taylor prepared to open the door. "I did some of my finest work. He'll have scars but nothing as extensive as they could've been."

"Well, I'm glad it worked out for you *and* Mr. Hardy," Shelby said in a mocking tone.

She made it sound as if Taylor had caused the accident so he could show off his skills. At least that sad expression had left her eyes. He ignored her remark and asked, "So what's the plan when I'm gone?"

"The plan is to go on as I have been and look for a doctor who's trained in emergency medicine. Someone willing to work here at least part time."

"Well, it won't be me. I'm going to do what's required. Then I'm gone. Don't be getting any ideas."

"I don't have any ideas about you one way or another. Uncle Gene said he was sending me some help for a cou-ple of weeks. The minute I met you I knew you wouldn't be staying long."

He didn't understand why that remark annoyed him. He didn't like her thinking she knew him that well. "Why?"

"Well, let's see," she said with a sassy bob to her head, "car, clothes, attitude. All are a dead giveaway."

He'd covered his past well. Had worked hard at it. Tay-lor stepped closer, stopping just outside her personal space.

Her eyes shifted with apprehension. He made her nervous and he liked it.

Leaning down to her eye level, he said, "You of all people should know that appearances aren't always how things are." He paused. "For example, a doctor who hates the sight of blood."

A knock on the door punctuated his statement.

"It's standing room only out here," Carly called.

"Maybe you'd better go do what you have to do," Shelby said in an ice-cold voice as she moved past him to hold open the door.

Taylor spent Wednesday morning seeing patients, only able to snatch a quick lunch before the afternoon influx of people into the waiting room. Despite working in a small-town clinic, he was still keeping large trauma center hours. It amazed him that Shelby had managed to hold it together without help for so long. She had to be mentally and physically exhausted. The clinic was definitely a two-person set-up, and three would be better.

Late that afternoon, Taylor trailed behind his latest patient as he left. Going to the front to call his next one, he was pleasantly surprised to find that there was no one else needing attention. Shelby was busy giving Carly directions and shifting through papers at the same time. The picture had become so commonplace it seemed like he'd been working at the Benton Clinic for ever. It amazed him that he didn't feel more like an outsider.

He and Shelby had only spoken a few words to each other the entire day. For some reason, he'd missed their sparring. If nothing else it brought a little spark to the backwater town, something to challenge his mind.

The bell on the door rang. The peace hadn't lasted long enough for him to even say something that would aggravate Shelby. A girl of around sixteen with large, gloomy eyes and long blonde hair entered looking as if she'd like to turn and run. She wore a simple dress covering too much of her body for the warm day. The girl hesitated as the door closed behind her.

Shelby must have realized that the three of them looking at the girl was intimidating because she stepped forward and offered her hand. "I'm Dr. Wayne. Can I help you?"

The girl nodded but didn't make eye contact.

"Come this way." Shelby led the teen down the hall.

Ten minutes later Taylor entered the small lab area to find Shelby facing the counter, gripping it so hard the veins on the top of her hands stood out. She kept her head down.

He closed the door. "What's wrong?" he asked, keeping his voice low and stepping closer. "What's happened?" He didn't try to keep his concern out of his voice.

Shelby's actions seemed out of character. Even when blood had been an issue she'd hung tough, but now…

"Nothing." Her tone said differently.

"Something's obviously wrong. Let me help."

She turned so quickly that she caught him off guard. Her eyes glistened and her face was drawn with misery. "Really? You think you can help," she muttered. "I have an unwed pregnant teen in there…" she gestured toward the door across the hall "…who's terrified to talk to her parents. When she does find the courage to tell her family about the baby she also has to explain to them that she has a venereal disease. So just how can you help with this?"

Her bold stare said he couldn't fix this no matter what he did. As much as he hated to admit it, she was right.

"I can't help her but I can help you." He gathered Shelby into his arms. What was he doing? Nurses, other female doctors had been upset in his presence and he'd never hugged them. Something about Shelby made him want to comfort her, help her with her problems. Be there for her. He winced.

That was something he couldn't do. How had he become so involved in her life so quickly?

She resisted, remaining rigid against him. "Please let me go."

It pricked his ego that she wouldn't consent to his comfort, but he schooled his face not to show a reaction. He did as she asked and stepped back, missing the contact immediately. "Would you like me to talk to the girl?"

Shelby shook her head. "No, that's my job. She's scared enough without me sending a man in to discuss this. She lives in the county above us and wanted to go where she wouldn't be recognized. Someone told her that there was a female doctor here."

"In this day and age she's hiding? Afraid to tell her parents? The teenage girls I know are proud to be unwed and pregnant."

"You have to remember that there're still strong moral standards in this area. Everyone knows everyone. Has an opinion about everything."

Taylor was well aware of how those concepts worked.

Shelby continued, "Her parents, she says, aren't going to be happy or accepting." She moved past him. "I'd better go give her the news."

He placed a hand on her shoulder and her gaze met his. "Shelby, I wish I could do more than say I'm sorry."

She gave him a weak smile. "I am too," she said, before squaring her shoulders and knocking on the door to the exam room across the hall.

Her heart was too big for her own good. For once, Taylor thought that Uncle Gene sentencing him to the clinic had been a good thing. It had allowed him to be there for Shelby today.

The girl left the clinic thirty minutes later with a gentle pat on the shoulder from Shelby and the reassurance that she'd be there if the girl needed her. Shelby said not a word as she passed him. She entered her office and effectively closed everyone out.

After preparing the clinic for the next day, Taylor knocked lightly on the office door. "You ready to close up?"

"You go on. I'll see you in the morning."

She needed space and wouldn't appreciate him insisting she leave. He really shouldn't care. All doctors ran into cases that got under their skin. The problem was that Shelby cared too deeply. For the girl. For her all her patients.

Who took care of her?

Hours later, Taylor rolled over in bed and looked at the bedside clock for the umpteenth time. It was well past midnight.

Where was she?

With a sense of relief that amazed him he saw Shelby's headlights flash across the wall of the apartment as she pulled into the drive.

She worked far too hard, felt too much. The clinic, for all he could see, was her life. She took no down time. In his opinion it wasn't healthy. She needed to slow down or she'd be the one needing a doctor. He knew of few doctors who worked harder than Shelby.

He didn't want to care. No matter what happened he refused to get involved but with every day he stayed in Benton it made it more difficult to keep his distance. First it had been Mrs. Ferguson, then Mr. Hardy and now he was stressing about a workaholic tyrant of a doctor who lived in a one-red-light town. Heck, he didn't really know how to care. He'd certainly not gotten an example of how that worked from his family. Could he have picked a more foreign emotion?

The way Shelby's big gray eyes looked stormy when she was mad and turned soft and sad when she worried over a patient pulled at him. Even her sharp tongue didn't squelch his anxiety for the turbocharged woman.

Reassured Shelby was safely home, Taylor rolled over and punched his pillow, knowing he could now find sleep. He'd no idea why it mattered to him what she did. Shelby had been fine before he'd arrived and she'd be fine after he left.

But who would be there for her when she needed a shoulder to lean on next time?

CHAPTER THREE

THURSDAY evening Shelby pulled into her drive well after dark. She'd stayed late at the clinic to finish some charting. Now her plan was to spend the next few hours working on grant applications. She had to find some long-term help for the clinic soon or the state would shut it down. Taylor had made it abundantly clear he wouldn't be the answer to her problem.

The old truck rattled to a stop when Shelby shut it off. She regarded the sports car in front of her. She'd always liked nice cars but her parents were supportive but practical people who didn't encourage that type of extravagance. Shelby couldn't really see herself ever owning such a fancy vehicle. She was the wrong type of doctor, in the wrong area of the world, to even drive one. Still, a girl could appreciate a nice ride.

A movement in the garage window caught her attention. Taylor stood silhouetted there. He wore no shirt and was talking on the phone. Shelby's attention was riveted to his wide shoulders that tapered to a trim waist. Sliding down in the seat, she hoped he wouldn't see her and think she'd already gone into the house. His pants rode low on his hips. He must work out. A lot. She'd say his efforts were worth it.

Frustration welled within her. She had no business even noticing him. There could never be anything real between them. She had to keep reminding herself of that. He wasn't staying and she refused to care then be hurt when he left. She'd barely lived through that pain before and she couldn't do it again.

Taylor put a hand above his head and stretched. Shelby sucked in a breath. Good heavens. Her heart went into overdrive. Ignoring him was going to be much more difficult than she imagined. The tingle of desire that had lay dormant since Jim's death had returned, heating her from the inside out, catching her by surprise. She needed to go into the house. Stand under the air-conditioning vent. Her reaction to this well-built man was way over the top.

How would she get inside without looking like she'd become a peeping Tomette? She grinned. At least she hadn't lost her sense of humor even though she'd lost her mind. With relief, and disappointment she didn't want to examine, Taylor moved away from the window.

Gathering her bag, she opened the truck door and slid out. Closing the door with less force than usual, she accused herself of being silly. This was her house, her drive, her neighborhood. Seeing Taylor Stiles's chest from a distance wasn't that big a deal. She'd even seen it up close. As a doctor she'd seen all kinds of half-naked men.

Yeah, but chests as fine as Taylor's were few and far between. Great. Now she was starting to think like Carly. Lifting her shoulders and standing taller, Shelby walked to the back door. Why hadn't she left the porch light on?

"I was wondering how long it would take you to get out of the truck."

Shelby jumped, dropping her bag. "What're you doing, sneaking up on me?"

"I wasn't sneaking. I came down the stairs like I always do. Your mind must've been on something else."

Thankful for the shadows, she didn't want to contemplate

what her mind had been on and she certainly didn't need him to see the guilt covering her face.

"I wanted to speak to you a minute," Taylor said.

Shelby retrieved her bag. "Could we make it quick? I'm really not up for some long discussion right now. All I want is a sandwich and to get to bed early."

"Why don't you get that sandwich while we talk?" He followed her up the steps. "I wouldn't mind having one too."

She reached inside and flipped on the light switches for the kitchen and the outside. Glancing around at him, she was relieved to find he'd pulled on a T-shirt before coming out to meet her. "Do you make it a habit of inviting yourself into people's homes? To meals? Anyway, I thought you finally agreed to go to Vinnie's with Carly and her boyfriend. I heard her begging you to go."

"That was hours ago. I've a pretty big appetite."

Suddenly hers was gone. Her mouth went dry. Her mind was going places it shouldn't. That she didn't want it to go.

"Shelby?"

"Huh?"

"Aren't you going inside?"

Shelby opened the screen door and entered the kitchen, dropping her bag in one of the kitchen chairs. Taylor followed her.

"Hey, I still didn't say you could come in."

"Awe, come on, Shelby. Have pity on a hungry man with nothing in his pantry. Share a sandwich."

With a sigh, she said, "Okay, one sandwich and tell me what you need, then you're out of here."

The large family kitchen shrank, taking on a more intimate feel with Taylor in it. To cover her unease, Shelby gathered the sandwich fixings. Having Taylor in her home made them seem like more than colleagues. Maybe friends? In just a few short days. Could a woman be just friends with someone who exuded all-male sex-appeal as Taylor did? No, she needed to protect herself. He'd never settle here and she'd never be someone's two-week stand.

Placing the bread, ham, cheese and condiments on the table, Shelby poured two glasses of iced tea. She set Taylor's glass before him, taking special care not to touch him. Taking the chair opposite him, she reached for the bread. Her hand circled the mustard bottle at the same time his did. His fingers brushed across hers. Their warmth against the coolness of hers made her shiver. She let the bottle go but Taylor's touch lingered.

"Ladies first," he quipped, going after the cheese instead.

A sense of disgust filled her. She was acting like a ninny and he wasn't even affected. After her meltdown the other day, he probably wasn't surprised by the way she acted.

Taking a sip of tea, she carefully set the glass down and finished making her sandwich. She'd never let him know that even his casual touch rattled her. She took a restorative breath and said, "So what do you want to talk about?"

"I was wondering if the clinic is open on the weekends. I have a date for the opera in Nashville and need to know if I should cancel it."

It shouldn't have surprised her that Taylor might have a love interest back home but until then she'd not given it any thought. He'd said there was no family but that didn't mean he didn't have someone special waiting for his return. One he obviously missed. A girlfriend. The prick of rejection caught her unawares. Why should she feel that way? There wasn't anything between them.

"The clinic's open on Saturday from eight to noon. After that the weekend is yours. I'll expect you there at eight on Monday morning sharp."

"Yes, ma'am. Do you know how often you use the word

'expect'?" he asked around a bite of ham sandwich. It wasn't said as a putdown but more as a conversational question.

"I don't use it a lot," she said with a huff.

"Yeah, you do," he said nonchalantly as he looked over her head. "Nice pictures."

A swell of pride filled her at his compliment. "They were some of my husband's favorites." She'd been able to capture the essence of her subjects in the photos, showing the truth of what life was like in this rural area.

"His favorite photographer?"

"You could say that. Me."

"Really? You took these?" Taylor stood, moving closer to study the two lines of framed photographs, six pictures in all. "You really caught what the subjects were feeling. I'm impressed."

"Thanks." A warm glow filled her at his compliment. "Those are really old. I don't have time to take pictures now." She picked up her sandwich.

"Why's that?" He took his chair again, propping his elbows on the table and giving her his full attention.

Her hand tightened on her sandwich. Having his intent look focused on her made her feel self-conscious. "Well, I have the clinic to run."

"So what's the deal with the clinic? I'd think you could have your choice of positions anywhere you'd like."

Shelby pushed away the plate holding her half-eaten sandwich. "I want to work here. The clinic was our dream."

His brows rose. "'Our'?"

"Mine, and my husband's." To her surprise the stab of pain she normally felt when she spoke of Jim wasn't as strong as it had once been.

Taylor prompted, "So you and your husband started the clinic?"

"We grew up together. Jim wanted to be a doctor and I

did too. So we decided to go to medical school together and work where we were needed the most, which was here. It might be a small town, but it needed medical help and we could provide that, *wanted* to provide that."

"Well, I'm glad there are doctors like you because I couldn't do this."

"Do what?"

"Live here."

Her chair made a scraping noise as she pushed away from the table. Indignation and the need to defend Benton welled up in her. She stood and picked up her plate. "I can appreciate that Benton might not be for everyone but I happen to love living here. I love the town square with our wonderful old courthouse. I love the shops and the fact that the store owners call me by name when I go in. I love that we have no traffic!" She looked pointedly at him. "What I don't appreciate is people coming here and insulting it."

"I'm not insulting your precious town," Taylor said, following her. His arm brushed hers as he placed his plate in the sink.

A ripple of awareness went up her arm and ran through her body. She stepped out of reach, not liking the out-of-control feeling she had when he was near.

"I'm just saying living here isn't for me," Taylor continued, as if nothing had happened.

For him, she guessed it hadn't. "You know, I think it's time for you to go. I'm going to call it a night."

Taylor stepped to the door. "I'll see you in the morning."

At the slap of the screen door closing, loneliness filled her. The large country kitchen suddenly seemed cold and empty. She had enjoyed sharing a meal with someone. It was nice not to go into the house by herself and to have someone with whom she could discuss her passion for photography.

She sucked in a breath. Being around Taylor made her feel

like a desirable, interesting woman. To everyone in town she was "Doc" first and foremost. Until Taylor had arrived, she'd had no idea she missed being thought of as a person. She had to stay alert, think sharply to keep up with him. It was invigorating on a number of levels to have Taylor around. Even if the man made her temper flare faster than anyone else could.

He'd hardly been there four days. She had no doubt that she would miss him when he left. And leave he would.

"Greg, what're you doing here again?" Shelby asked in bewilderment when she walked into the waiting room to call her next patient on Friday afternoon. "Surely he hasn't stuck something else up his nose?" she said, looking at the boy's mother for confirmation.

The mother shook her head slowly.

"His ear?" Shelby asked with a note of disbelief surrounding her words.

The mother gave a negative shake of her head. "The other doctor told us to come back."

"Dr. Stiles?"

"Yeah."

Shelby couldn't imagine why Taylor had asked Greg's mother to bring him in if there was no reason. Other than the propensity to always put things where they didn't belong, Greg was a healthy child, too healthy, in fact.

"I'll let Dr. Stiles know you're here." She didn't like the fact that patients were now coming in to see Taylor. They had always been her patients. He wasn't staying around long and she didn't want the community to start relying on him. She didn't want to start to count on him.

Shelby went to her office where she'd left Taylor minutes earlier completing some paperwork. They'd taken to rotating time behind the desk to get their charting completed. Taylor opened the office door as she prepared to enter and she walked right into him.

"Whoa." His hand circled her waist and pulled her against him to stop her from falling.

A larger-than-average guy, he seemed even more overpowering close up. With her nose pressed against him, she smelled like soap and a unique scent. It surrounded her, drawing her to him.

A low rumble filled his chest. "If you're not careful you're going to fall at my feet."

Putting her hands on his chest, she pushed away. His chuckle reminded her she was still in his arms. "If you'd let me go, I could stand."

He did, and she rocked back and gained her footing, unsure if she was off balance because he'd been holding her or because he'd let her go so quickly.

"Were you looking for me?" he asked, as if he thought she'd been on a personal quest.

"I was, but only because you have a patient. Greg, the boy whose nose you removed the bean from, is here. His mother said they were to see you. Did you tell them to come in for a follow-up exam?"

"I did ask them to stop by."

"Why?"

"Come with me and you'll see." He allowed her to walk ahead of him up the hall.

If she'd had patients waiting she would've argued that she didn't have time for show and tell but for once the waiting room was empty, something that happen more often now that Taylor was helping out.

Even the time she spent working at home had gotten shorter. Taylor had been in town less than a week and he was already having a big impact on her life. He was efficient and thorough, and some of the patients were starting to warm up to him. When they came into the waiting room, Greg popped down from his mother's lap and ran to Taylor. "I good. Sucker." Greg tugged on Taylor's well-pressed slacks.

Taylor pulled something out of his pocket before squatting down on one heel, which brought him close to eye level with the boy.

Holding out a sucker, Taylor said, "Greg, you were good. You didn't stick anything in your nose for a week. Now, if you want another one you have to be good for two weeks. I won't be here but I'm sure Doc Wayne will give you one." Taylor looked at her for confirmation.

Something about Taylor not being there when the boy came back caused a catch in her chest. Pushing the thought to a back drawer in her mind, Shelby nodded and said to Greg, "I'll have it waiting for you. But you can't put anything in your nose or ears."

The boy nodded, unwrapped the sucker and popped it into his mouth, his cheeks going chubby with his wide smile.

The mother nodded her thanks, took the boy's hand and headed for the door. With them gone, Shelby turned to Taylor. "How did you know?"

"As soon as I removed the bean he started begging for a sucker. I asked his mother if you gave him one every time you removed something. She said yes and I knew something was up.

"Greg was stuffing his nose full in order to come here and get a sucker. I made a deal with him that if he didn't do it again then I'd see that he got one. I know how bad they are for the teeth but one thing at a time. You can wean him off them."

"It was a nice call. I should've caught on."

"Don't beat yourself up. You can't do it all perfectly. You have a lot to see about here. Greg's fine and now you know.

Just keep weaning him off. Soon it won't be a problem. Let up on yourself."

"I still should have realized what he was doing. Thanks."

"You don't have to sound like you're in pain when you say that."

She gave him a wry smile. "It's a little excruciating to admit I missed something so simple."

"You'll get it next time," he said, going to the reception desk.

Later that evening at closing time, Taylor said, "Hey, Mr. Teems gave me coupons for a free ice cream down at the Cream Castle. Why don't we all go and get a banana split after we close?"

"I've got a date. Got to go," Carly said, picking up her purse.

He turned to Shelby.

"I don't think so."

"Oh, come on, Shelby. Do something a little spontaneous for a change. All that paperwork will be here when you get back. I'll even help you."

"I still don't think so. And I don't need your help with my paperwork."

"Look, have pity on a stranger in town. I'm not even sure how to get there. I told Mr. Teems I'd stop by."

"Still—"

"I know you missed lunch because I did. Let's make this our supper."

"Well, put like that…"

"Great. I'll drive."

Even though she'd been hard to convince, it didn't take her long to get her purse, lock up and climb into his car.

"Which way?" He backed out of what had become his usual parking space.

"The best way to go is out to the bypass. Turn left out of the parking lot." She leaned her head back and closed her eyes.

She had to be worn out. He was. "Bypass? This town isn't large enough to have a bypass."

"They built it when the talk started about building a lake."

"Lake?"

"Lake Benton. The hope is that it'll bring business to this area. It'll be another couple of years, though, before there's water."

"From what little I've seen of the area, it could use it." He glanced her way. Her hair blew around her face. She looked totally relaxed. Something he'd rarely seen.

"It can. Most of the young people are leaving because there're no jobs. Make a left at the next light," she said, just loud enough that he could hear her over the wind. For the first time she'd not growled when he'd said something negative about the town, a sure sign she was tired.

"The Cream Castle is a mile down on the right." She indicated after he'd driven another mile.

He pulled into the gravel parking lot. They got out and walked to the window of the white building with the bright red awning. "One vanilla ice cream cone and one banana split with the works," he told the teenager at the window. "I used to work in a place like this when I was in high school."

"Really? I would've thought from looking at you that you would've spent all your time on the football or baseball field, being a star."

"Couldn't stay out of trouble long enough," he said flatly.

His words held a bitterness that surprised Shelby. The skinny teen with the earring pushed Taylor's huge banana split toward him and handed her the cone, stopping further questions.

Taylor took a seat on the bench of the cement table next to the building. He must have seen her hesitate and look towards the car because he said in a voice that wouldn't consent to an argument, "No way are we carrying this in my car. You can take a few minutes to enjoy." He dug a spoon into the bowl of nuts and chocolate sauce. "Mmm. Good," he said as he pulled the plastic spoon from his mouth.

"So you've found something in this town you like," Shelby said as she sat down and gave her ice cream a long lick.

Taylor's gaze lifted to meet hers. "I've found a few things."

If she wasn't careful, the ice cream in her hand would melt all over her fingers from the heat surging through her. Just as quickly his concentration returned to his ice cream. Was she reading something into what he'd said? Imagining things? Nothing was going to happen between them. He was just flirting. "What's Mr. Lambert's story?"

Shelby blinked. His question out of the blue caught her by surprise. The eighty-year-old man had refused to see Taylor earlier in the day, insisting that Shelby was the only one he would allow to take care of him.

"Some of the people around here are very set in their ways. He's lived in the same hollow a few miles out of town his entire life. He's tough. Been a logger since he was a boy. You wouldn't believe the house he lives in. No indoor plumbing. Animals living inside in the winter." Shelby shuddered. "It took me almost a year before Mr. Lambert would let me see him. It wasn't until he hurt his hand and his daughter came to get me that I ever took care of him."

"You do house calls?"

"When I have to. You know, it may be hard for some of the patients to relate to you because your clothes and shoes cost enough to feed their entire family for a year."

"There's nothing wrong with liking nice things."

"No, there isn't. Don't get me wrong, you look great—"

"Why, thank you, Shelby."

"That's not what I meant. I just think some of the older

patients might find you less, uh, intimidating if you maybe wore jeans and tennis shoes."

"Would you find me less intimidating?" His look bored into hers.

Somehow this conversation had gotten off track. "You don't intimidate me," Shelby said with as much conviction as she could muster.

His spoon fell into the empty plastic tray with a clunk, and he leaned back as if in deep thought. "I'm not sure you're telling me the truth, but that's beside the point. I also think it might surprise you just how much I know about how people around here think."

"Really?"

"Yes, but we need to be getting back. I promised to help you out with that charting."

"That's okay, I can manage it."

"I know you can. But I'm going to help anyway."

Shelby rubbed her hand along the seat of Taylor's car as they rode down the road a few minutes later. "You know, this is a nice car."

"Now, that wasn't that hard to admit, was it?"

She laughed, "No I guess it wasn't. I do love riding with the top down."

The sound of a police siren pierced the air.

Taylor's sharp word made her wince. He slowly pulled off onto the shoulder of the road and turned off the engine. His jaw muscles jumped and his hand shook almost imperceptibly as he leaned across her to reach into the glove compartment. She wouldn't have noticed if he hadn't been so close. "I'll handle this," he said gruffly. "I know I wasn't speeding," he said, more to himself than to her.

The deputy hadn't even approached the car yet and Taylor was angry. It seemed over the top. "Maybe you just have a taillight out?" Shelby suggested.

He glared at her. His look prevented her from offering further comments. "No hick deputy's going to give me a ticket for doing nothing," he mumbled as he pulled his wallet from his hip pocket and dug for his license.

"Hey, Shelby, I thought that was you," the deputy said from where he stood beside Taylor's door.

"Hi, Sam." Shelby smiled up at the man.

Taylor gave her an odd look before switching his attention to the deputy. Holding out his license and insurance information, Taylor looked even more exasperated when the deputy didn't immediately take them.

"I don't need those. I just wanted to see if Shelby's planning to bring her famous carrot cake to the block party."

A look of confusion then disbelief washed over Taylor's face. Shelby had to work to keep a straight face. "I hadn't planned to but since you asked I'll be sure to bake one. By the way, this is Dr. Stiles. He's working with me for a couple of weeks."

Sam looked down at Taylor. "Nice to meet you, Doc." His attention didn't linger but returned to Shelby. "I do love your carrot cake."

"Sam, that's so sweet."

Taylor's facial expression turned to complete disgust. Her grin grew. *And he thought he understood small towns.*

"We have to go. Sam. See you Saturday."

The palm of Sam's hand double-thumped the top of the car door. "I look forward to it."

Taylor started the car and pulled out onto the road. She had the impression he wished he could spin gravel and roar off, but instead he moved into traffic as if he was learning to drive.

"Just what was that all about?" he asked, his voice full of wonder and irritation.

"You heard. Cake and the block party."

"Do the cops around here regularly pull people over to discuss a party?" He gave her an incredulous look.

Shelby shrugged. "I guess when they want to. What's the big deal?" He shook his head as if trying to make sense of an abstract painting. She leaned forward enough to see his face. "You really were afraid that you were being stopped for speeding." She made no effort to hide her amazement.

His eyes remained on the road and he didn't answer.

She continued to watch his face. Her eyes narrowed. "What aren't you telling me?"

He glanced at her. "I've had a few speeding tickets."

"How many is a few?"

"Enough that your uncle sent me here instead of to jail."

She gave a low whistle and grinned. "So-o-o, that's what Uncle Gene meant when he said, and I quote, 'He needs to slow down for a while.'" She giggled.

"It's not funny, Shelby."

She giggled again. "Oh, yes, it is. So this fancy car is a police magnet."

"Sometimes I was on the way to an emergency," he said indignantly.

"Really?" She drew the word out.

"There might've been a few times when I exaggerated a bit. Someone checked, and dear sweet Uncle Gene decided to throw the book at me." His top lip curled as he said the last few words.

Shelby slapped her leg and howled with laughter. "So your lead foot got you sent to me." She gave his shoulder a friendly shove. "Uncle Gene has always been creative in his rulings."

"He outdid himself this time," Taylor grumbled.

For some reason, Taylor's obvious agitation tickled Shelby's funny bone. "What're you? Sixteen?"

Taylor pulled the car into his parking space next to her truck. "Now you're really making fun of me."

She laughed. "I'm sorry." Tears filled her eyes.

"Doesn't sound like it."

Shelby couldn't stop the merriment that continued to roll up from deep within her belly. She'd not laughed like this in years.

"It's not that funny," Taylor said, turning to look at her.

"I'm trying to stop but I can't help thinking about your face when you found out you'd been stopped because of a cake." Her laughter bubbled over again.

"Okay, that is kind of funny." His chuckle intertwined with her giggles. "Now I think you've had enough fun at my expense. If you don't stop…"

"What're you going to do?" She pointed at him. "You should have seen your face."

Another peal of mirth escaped her.

"Okay, that did it." Before she realized his intent, he'd grabbed her by the top of her arms and pulled her towards him. His mouth came down to cover hers.

Her laughter caught in her throat. His lips were firm, warm and confident. A red-hot flow of desire went through her. She didn't move. His mouth shifted to the side, finding a more secure place, sealing her mouth completely with his. For moments of pure bliss her world was nothing but Taylor's kiss. He pulled away and her eyelids fluttered open seconds after his hands no longer held her.

"I told you to stop."

She stared at his lips. "You did." Even to her own ears she sounded wistful. "I'll try to remember not to laugh at you again."

"That would be a good idea, unless you want more of the same."

"I don't." With effort she made the words sound sharp in the hope that it covered her true reaction. She couldn't make more of the kiss than it was. He was just trying to stop her from laughing at him, that was all.

"We'll see about that, but for now I think we should go in and get started on that paperwork." He stepped out of the car and Shelby followed more slowly.

She loved her husband. Missed him, but she'd never felt the fire with him that she'd experienced during Taylor's kiss. A shiver skated through her. If she had that kind of reaction to one playful kiss from Taylor, what would it be like to be on the receiving end of one of his seductive ones?

It was Saturday afternoon and Taylor's foot lay heavily on the gas pedal of the car. He was driving too fast but he couldn't get past the thought of what he had done yesterday evening.

God, he'd kissed Shelby and he desperately wanted to do it again. What had he been thinking? That was the problem, he hadn't been thinking. He'd reacted. The kiss had been far too short, far too cautious. He wanted to experience Shelby meeting him kiss for kiss, explore her wonderfully sensual mouth. He'd been hurt as a kid by laughter and ridicule but hers had made him want to join her. When he'd been a middle-school student, laughter at his expense had been an everyday occurrence. With her, he found he could appreciate the humor also.

But to kiss her. It only complicated things.

That he didn't need or want. He didn't even know how to give what Shelby would surely demand. He'd never been on the inside of a functional relationship. His parents' marriage certainly hadn't been a sterling example.

Shaking his head and lifting his foot a little, he slowed the car. As always Shelby had been efficient and business-like at the clinic that morning but there had been a change towards him. He should've been glad she wanted to remain at arm's length but he didn't like the idea one bit and he wasn't sure why.

It'd been a relief to say, "I'm out of here. See you Monday morning."

Shelby had nodded her understanding without looking up from the chart she was studying. Her giving him the cold shoulder irritated him.

What she thought of him or, for that matter, what the other hick people in this nothing town thought didn't matter. He had one more week to serve and he'd be out of there, never to think of any of them again. Right now he was getting some time away from Benton and Shelby and he planned to make the most of it.

The outskirts of Nashville were coming up quickly when his cellphone rang. It was his date for the evening, telling him she wasn't going to make the opera after all.

Taylor continued his conversation as he watched a state patrolman turn around and get behind him. The speedometer on the sports car let him know that he wasn't over the limit. At the next exit Taylor pulled off the interstate. With relief, he watched the patrol car go on down the road. All he needed was to be caught in town speeding. That would really make "Uncle Gene" irate. With no one expecting him now, he decided to play it safe and head back to Benton. He didn't need to take a chance on being sentenced to more time at the clinic.

Would it really be that bad to be stuck in Benton longer? With Shelby?

CHAPTER FOUR

SHELBY loved the quarterly block parties. She had little time to socialize and she made a point of joining these. They were an opportunity to connect with neighbors and one of the best parts of living in a small town.

She adored living in Benton and didn't understand Taylor's aversion to the town. Carly thought he was the best thing to come along since texting. To her surprise, she herself had nothing to complain about where his professional skills were concerned but she shouldn't learn to rely on him as he wasn't going to stay. It was a shame because the next doctor might not relate to her patients as well as Taylor did.

Some of the people had been slow to warm up to him but that was changing. If she did have an issue, it was that she had this unexplained attraction to him that made her feel uneasy. But the feeling of comfort and contentment at being surrounded by people who cared about you and watched after you washed over her, easing away her troubles.

Shelby swished her hips more than necessary as she carried her plate loaded with food to the folding chair she'd brought from home. The occasion not only let her leave the clinic problems for a while but gave her a chance to wear one of the sundresses she had hanging in her closet. The lightweight fabric with the tiny rosebuds brushed against her skin, making her feel very feminine. Something she hadn't experienced in a long time. At least, not until Taylor had come rolling into town.

He'd managed to make her feel warm, soft and womanly more than once, but she shook her head. She had no business thinking that way about him or his kiss. He was off with another woman. Taylor had no real interest in *her*. She was just the doctor he had to put up with until he'd done his time and could go home.

She sat with her neighbors in a lawn chair under a large oak tree to eat her meal and listened to their chatter. The saying "lonely in a crowd" flitted through her mind. Nibbling at her food, she placed the half-eaten meal on the ground. Leaning her head back against the top of the chair, she closed her eyes and enjoyed the warmth of the sun on her face. And drifted off.

A rustling noise nearby woke her. She lifted her eyelids, rolled her head in the direction of the sound and straightened in the chair. "What're you doing here? I thought you were in Nashville."

Taylor grinned. "And hello to you too." He took a seat in the empty chair next to her.

He looked completely at home in khaki shorts, knit shirt and leather sandals but his demeanor still screamed cosmopolitan man. Among her neighbors Taylor stood out but she had no doubt he would in any crowd. He was the type of man who drew attention and admiration.

A tingle flitted through her. She was happy to see him. Maybe too happy. "Why're you here, Taylor?"

"Mmm. Plans changed." He took a bite out of a fried chicken leg.

She lowered her voice. "I didn't think this was your idea of a good time. Too small town."

"It's not. I was pulling into the drive and Mr. Carter flagged me down. Said you were down here. He insisted

I come too. I gave in." His shoulders rose and fell. "Heck, I've got nothing better to do." He bit into the chicken again.

"Please don't hurt their feelings."

"Are you implying I don't know how to behave?" His skin drew taut across his strong jaw. Had she made him angry?

"You've made it clear on more than one occasion that you think you're too good for Benton," she whispered.

"I might not want to stay here for ever, but I do know how to be sociable and gracious when I have the right incentive."

"Incentive?"

His eyes bored into hers and then dropped to her lips. A flash of heat sped through her. Warmth pooled low in her belly. She wrapped her arms around her waist. Was he trying to coerce her into another kiss? Or more?

"Yeah, I wanted to see if the cake that the cop with the crush on you likes so much is that good." At the whoosh of her breath, he grinned. "Did you have something else in mind?"

"I did not. The cake's inside. Help yourself." She pointed in the direction of the door into the house from the carport.

Taylor stood and offered his hand to her. "Why don't you show me?"

Mrs. Nettleboom, the elderly lady who lived across the street, walked up. "Well, Dr. Stiles, I see you found her."

"Yes, I did. Thank you for pointing me in the correct direction. I was just telling Shelby how much I'd enjoy having some of that cake I've been hearing about." The woman nearly preened under the grin Taylor gave her. "The deputy over there..." he nodded in the direction of a group of men "...thought it was good enough to pull us over to ask about."

"That sounds like little Sam. He loves Shelby's carrot cake," Mrs. Nettleboom cooed. "He always requests that she bring it. Always makes sure he cuts an extra piece to take to the station the next day."

Taylor looked at Shelby and smirked. "He does, does he?"

"Honey," the woman said to Shelby, "go on and take this nice young man in and get him a slice."

Shelby feared she was well on her way to having a sugar stroke from listening to their conversation. The only way to put an end to it was to do as Mrs. Nettleboom instructed.

Ignoring his offer to help, she picked up her plate and stood. He trailed close behind her as she walked up the drive. She dropped her plate into the garbage beside the door and entered the house. "The desserts are in the kitchen."

The counter space was covered with cakes, pies and sweets of all kinds. Shelby waved her hand. "Help yourself. The plates and plastic forks are on the table," Shelby said.

The cozy kitchen suddenly didn't feel large enough for both of them. Taylor's presence filled the area, pressing against her. She needed to leave.

His hand gently circled her forearm, making her start. "Which one is yours?" he asked, much too close.

Shelby paused. His fingers slipped along her skin and away. "It's the cake on the blue plate over there." The touch had been casual but there was nothing ordinary about her body's reaction.

"You're not going to have any?"

"Not right now. Maybe later." She circled past the kitchen counter and headed out the door, grateful for the breeze that blew outside.

Had the kiss made her skittish? Taylor couldn't imagine strong, willful Shelby being intimidated by him or anyone else. She apparently didn't even trust him long enough to stay in the same room with him. He didn't like that at all. Taking the kiss back wasn't possible, even if he wanted to and he didn't. Instead he could only think of kissing her again but this time like she deserved to be kissed. Long, sweet and deep.

He ran his fingers through his hair. The last few days they'd worked together had been nice. The cases had been interesting and he found he liked working beside someone who so obviously cared about her patients and their feelings. Something he'd not always experienced in a large hospital.

He'd messed up with that kiss and he didn't know how to fix it.

Taylor cut a large slice of Shelby's cake, put it on a plate and carried it outside. Shelby wasn't visible anywhere. As he headed toward his chair the old insecure feeling of not being accepted made his stomach clench. He gained control by reminding himself that he was no longer the kid of the town drunk. No one here knew his secret. Instead he was a doctor and a well-respected one.

Still, he was surprised when Mr. Carter called, "Hey, Doc, come have a seat with us." Squaring his shoulders, he said, "Sure," with more enthusiasm than he felt and took the open place at the table.

Taylor filled his fork with cake and put it in his mouth. Taking a moment to savor the sweetness, he said, "You're right. It's great." He lifted his utensil in the direction of Shelby's boyfriend cop, who was seated across from him.

"Yeah, Shelby has many talents," the deputy said, grinning at Taylor.

"Don't mind him," Mr. Carter said, nudging the younger man in the ribs. "He's had a crush on her for ages, but she won't even look his way."

Lightness replaced the twinge of possessiveness in Taylor's heart. That baffled him. He and Shelby didn't have that kind of relationship. Their relationship didn't warrant jealousy. Yet, as illogical as it was, the pang had still been there.

Mr. Roster, a thin, white-headed man, said, "We're glad you're here to help out our Shelby. She works too hard. I know she has appreciated having you around."

Taylor wasn't so sure about that. "I'm only going to be at the clinic for another week then I'm headed home."

"You're not staying?" a man from the other end of the table asked. "We thought you might decide to make it permanent."

"No, this was only a temporary assignment." Taylor slid the last bit of cake off his fork, wishing he had more. Shelby certainly had other abilities besides caring for people and photography.

The conversation changed to the construction of the new dam that would create a recreational lake and what the town might expect from the influx of people. As for whether or not there would be a big change, the jury seemed to be out. Taylor listened, offering little input. The lake wasn't his worry. He'd be long gone.

When there was a lull in the conversation he looked around and asked, "Where did Shelby go?"

"I saw her heading around the side of the house. She had her camera," Mr. Roster said, before returning to the conversation with the others.

Minutes later, Taylor excused himself and strolled in the direction Shelby had gone. Children's laughter and the soft tinkle of Shelby's amusement told him he'd headed in the correct direction. Going through the gate of the chain-link fence, he found Shelby snapping pictures of a young girl as she glided back and forth on a swing set. A group of middle-school boys played baseball nearby.

Taylor leaned against a tree and watched. Encouraging the girl to continue swinging, Shelby moved around, taking pictures from different angles. Her dress blew around her legs in the light breeze, accenting her shapely behind. Occasionally, Shelby gave the thin strap of her dress an impatient push up her slim shoulder from where it had slipped. Taylor smiled. He liked seeing her relaxed, the worry lines on her face gone. She deserved an easier life but he wasn't the one to give her that.

The entire scene looked like a Norman Rockwell painting. Taylor had never really identified with images of Rockwell's homespun family life, because his own childhood had never been anything near resembling the pictures. Shelby brought that hometown feeling to life right in front of his eyes. He bet her photos would turn out to be wonderful. Unfortunately, she became so uptight around him he doubted he'd ever be invited to see them.

"You're dumb."

"Yeah, nobody likes you."

The ugly words took a moment to work their way through Shelby's concentration on the picture's subject.

"Everyone hates you."

Taking the viewfinder away from her eye, she turned to where the boys crowded around the smallest boy.

Before she could intervene, Taylor stalked past her. She'd been so absorbed in finding the right shot she'd not realized he stood nearby. He went to stand behind the child the others faced and placed his hand on the boy's shoulder.

"Now, what's going on here?" Taylor's gaze fell on each individual long enough so that they each looked at their feet instead of at Taylor. "Well?" he demanded in an even voice but giving the word a sharp edge.

A boy's head rose. "He always messes up. He doesn't know how to play."

"I see. And you do everything you try right all the time?"

The boy rubbed his bare foot back and forth in the dirt. "No, but—"

"Exactly. So why don't you let me and…?" He looked down at the boy in front of him.

"Charlie," the boy murmured.

"So why don't you let Charlie and I be a team and play against you guys?"

"That wouldn't be fair," a heavyset boy in the group complained. "You're big."

"No more than it's fair when three people gang up on one. How do you think you would feel? So why don't you guys try to play something that Charlie might be good at?"

Taylor looked at Charlie again.

"I'm pretty good at basketball," he said in a stronger voice than he'd used earlier.

"Great," Taylor said. "I saw a hoop in the driveway next door. Why don't you guys head that way?"

"I don't really like basketball," the leader of the group said.

"Why's that?" Taylor asked.

"Because he ain't any good at it," a tall, thin boy offered.

Taylor said nothing but look pointedly at the leader.

"Come on, guys. Let's go find a ball," the boy finally offered.

Shelby watched in amazement as the group walked past her on their way out the gate.

"Lauren, honey," she told the girl she'd been taking pictures of, "I bet your mother's looking for you. It's getting late."

The girl ran behind the boys towards the front of the house.

Taylor stood rigid, staring off into the distance. His breaths were coming shallow and fast as if he fought a demon. What was going on?

"Taylor?"

She received no response.

"Taylor?"

As if coming out of a trance, he looked at her but without really seeing her.

"You okay?"

"Oh, yeah, sure." A look of recognition flickered in his eyes.

"What you did with those boys was impressive. Did you get a child psych degree along with that MD?"

Taylor visibly relaxed, regaining his causal manner. "Nothing to it."

He might say that but she knew better.

The green light of fireflies blinked around them as they walked back along the sidewalk toward her house.

"Was the block party as bad as you thought it would be?" Shelby asked.

Taylor gave her a sideways glance. "I never said it was going to be bad."

"You sure acted that way."

He stuffed his hands in the pockets of his shorts. "It wasn't exactly what I'd expected."

"How's that?"

"I didn't think your neighbors would be so accepting of me. It has been my experience that small towns are pretty close knit. Don't let people in who don't fit their idea of acceptable. Shall we say judgmental?"

"Really?" she remarked, enjoying the soft breeze and the ruffling of Taylor's shirt against his body. "I grew up in a small town and I thought we were a wonderfully supportive group of people."

"Apparently you lived on the right side of the tracks." The words had a raw-edged roughness to them.

She searched his face. "What's that supposed to mean?"

He glanced at her. "That not everyone has such great memories of living in a small town."

"Why don't you just come on out with it? Quit beating around the bush."

He looked around the street as if he was searching for

something. The words, the right way to say them or the answer? She wasn't sure which.

Her fingertips touched his forearm briefly. He was warm, firm and all male.

"We aren't that different in some ways." He stated his words slowly. "I grew up in a town much like this one but in Kentucky."

"Really? I never would have guessed."

"And I had no intention that you ever would. It isn't something I share."

"Why not?" She didn't try to keep her astonishment out of her voice.

"I've worked hard to put that time, that place behind me." He stopped short, turned and looked at her.

"What happened?" she asked quietly.

His eyes turned stone hard then he stalked ahead. Shelby jogged to catch up, her sandals making a slapping noise against the concrete and her camera bouncing against her side from where the strap hung over her shoulder. When she came alongside him he began talking but didn't slow his pace.

"If you must know, I'm the son of the town drunk and the kid who used his fists to prove his worth." He snapped the words like gunshots.

Shelby slowed, stopped and watched as Taylor stalked off. It didn't surprise her that Taylor hadn't noticed she was no longer panting beside him. He'd slipped into his past.

By the time she'd reached her back door, he'd entered the apartment and effectively shut the world and her out.

At mid-morning on Sunday Shelby sat at her kitchen table, paying her personal bills as well as the clinic's. A knock at the door interrupted her concentration. Before she could move, the door opened and Taylor's head appeared.

"Taylor!" Shelby let out a squeak and pulled her lightweight robe over her thin gown. "You can't just barge into my house uninvited. I'm not even dressed."

"I knocked." His look traveled to her bare toes and slowly upwards until his gaze met hers. There was a twinkle of appreciation in his coffee-colored eyes. "Nice outfit."

Heat zipped to her cheeks. He had a way of making her blush and she was entirely too old for such silliness. "What do you need? I'm trying to get some work done."

"You know, it would be nice for you to be happy to see me just once."

She was glad to see that his bad mood from the day before had disappeared. She huffed.

He grinned. "How about showing me around? Maybe take me out to where they're building the dam for the lake?"

"I don't know. I've tons of paperwork to do." She waved her hand toward the table where the bills were stacked. "There might be an emergency and I'll be needed."

"And there might not be. You work too hard. It's not healthy. You need some down time to be ready for your patients. Besides, you'll have your cellphone with you."

Why this sudden interest in Benton, and the lake? She'd been surprised to see his car still parked in the drive this morning after the way they'd parted the evening before. She'd expected him to spend his day off far away from Benton. But she didn't plan to ruin his cheerful mood by quizzing him about his past now. "Okay, I guess this can wait."

"Get dressed. I'll wait." Taylor pulled a chair out from under the table, sat and propped an ankle over his knee.

He looked at home in her house and that disturbed her. He'd only been there a week and already he seemed like he belonged. It had been too easy to get used to having him around. When he left, which he'd assured her he would, she'd be on her own again. If she let him into her life there would be heartache and that she wouldn't chance.

Given little choice and beginning to look forward to spending time away from her mundane responsibilities, she headed to her bedroom to change. It would be nice to spend a day having fun, something she didn't often do.

She returned dressed similarly to Taylor in cut-off jeans, a T-shirt and sandals. He looked less like the slick, fashion-plate doctor and more like a regular guy out looking for adventure. She liked this newer version. This one she understood better. He smiled at her and her hand trembled as she pushed a stray strand of hair behind her ear.

"Come on," Taylor said impatiently. "Don't forget your camera," he said over his shoulder as the door slapped into place.

"Stop telling me what to do," she called after him in a playful voice, even though she was grateful for the reminder. She hadn't thought of taking her camera. At one time it had been as attached to her as her skin, though life and the clinic had pushed photography way down on her priority list. With a sudden feeling of liberation she picked up her case and followed him outside.

He opened his car door.

"Hey," she called, "if you want to really see the area, we need to go in my truck. The bottom of that car might not survive the back roads."

He gave the small battered truck a dubious look but slammed his car door shut. "Is there enough room for my legs in that thing?"

"You'll be fine."

Shelby slipped behind the wheel and couldn't help but grin as she watched Taylor settle in beside her. He overwhelmed the small interior. And her too. For once, she wished she drove a larger vehicle.

As she shifted into reverse, the back of her hand slid across his bare knee. The gears made a grinding sound as she found the correct slot. She glanced at Taylor. His mouth lifted slightly at the corners. She took special care that her fingers remained on the top of the gearshift instead of gripping it with her hand in order to avoid touching Taylor's knee again. She put the truck into first gear.

Pulling out onto the highway, she said, "I'm surprised you're interested in sightseeing."

"Not so much interested as bored. There's not even a movie theater in this town."

"We have some culture." She refused to become defensive.

"How's that? The cultures at the clinic?"

"Funny. No, we have a museum."

"What kind?"

She grinned. "The Benton Historical Museum."

"Figures."

His low chuckle rippled through her like water over stones in a brook. She wanted to hear that sound again. He'd relaxed somewhat since he'd arrived in town. Even the lines around his eyes had become less noticeable.

Shelby slowed for the car in front of them to make a turn. She looked at him. "You know," she said causally but with meaning, "for someone who insisted I show them around, you're not being very nice."

He gave her a lopsided grin. "I'm sorry. I'll keep my snide remarks to myself. So why did you and your husband decide Benton was the place to start a clinic?"

"Because this county qualified for state assistance and we thought it would be a great place to raise children."

Shelby winced. After his admission yesterday, he wouldn't be impressed by that plan. Thankfully the road she'd been looking for came into sight. She made a left turn.

"Where're we headed?"

"I thought you wanted to see the lake. Also there's a spot along here where I'd like to get some pictures. The last time

I made it out this way the light wasn't right. Today it looks perfect. I won't be long."

"I've got nothing but time." He ran one tan arm along the back of the seat, his fingers falling inches above her shoulder.

When she changed gears, the tips of his fingers brushed the top of her shoulder. Super-sensitive to each touch, she was thankful when she found the place where she could ease off onto the grassy roadside. "There's an old house in the woods here. I'll snap a few pictures and be right back."

"I'll come with you."

"It's pretty rough walking."

"Please, don't insult my manhood," he said in disgust as he opened the door and climbed out. Shelby followed suit, finding the path that hunters or animals used and following it into the stand of pines.

"I had no intention of besmirching your manhood." She certainly couldn't find anything to complain about in that department.

"Besmirching?" he said with interest. "I couldn't tell you the last time I heard that word used."

She glanced back at him. "Just because I live in a small town doesn't mean I don't know how to use big words."

"I was besmirched my entire childhood. Somehow using that word doesn't make it sound so bad."

She gave him a look of understanding and walked on. Taylor stayed close behind. She glanced back and found him sure-footed and confident as he walked over the pine-needle-padded track. He'd obviously done this type of hiking before.

"This area used to have head-high gullies. We'd play in them as kids. We'd show up at my dad's truck red from head to toe, covered in dirt."

"What caused the gullies?"

"Erosion of the farmland during the thirties and forties. *Grapes of Wrath* type stuff. A forester who knew what he was doing bought up the land for almost nothing and planted pines. Now you can hardly tell there was ever a dip in the land."

"What's he doing with the land now?"

"When the trees mature they'll be harvested and turned into pulp for paper and the land replanted. You know the renewable resource—trees."

"Yeah, I remember that old slogan. Just never saw it in action before."

Taylor was much more interested in watching the sway of Shelby's hips than hearing an environmental report. However, the more she talked the longer he had to enjoy the enticing view.

They'd not gone far before entering an open area. In the middle of a knoll stood a tumbledown shack built from clapboard that had mellowed to a pale gray. The porch, which extended across the entire front, listed on the right corner. A large oak tree stood off to the side, its limbs offering shade to half the house. Wildflowers grew in the knee-high grass surrounding the area.

It looked much like the house where he'd grown up, sharing a cramped bedroom with his two brothers. He refused to revisit those morose memories. The day was too pretty and he had too lovely a woman with him to let ugly thoughts spoil it. Last night had been difficult enough. He wouldn't let his emotions show like that again.

Shelby moved around, leaning one way and another then squatting as she brought the camera to her eye. He had no idea why she was so interested in taking pictures of the sad reminder of what had been. He spent every minute of his life trying to forget a place like this one.

When Shelby stepped onto the porch he headed towards her. "I don't think that's a good idea." His overprotective reaction surprised him. He usually let people do as they pleased. Fear that Shelby might get hurt disturbed him on a level he didn't wish to explore.

"I'm just going to stand here." She brought the camera to her face again. "I do know what I'm doing."

"Never doubted it," Taylor said, and went to lean a hand against the one post of the porch that appeared stable.

Taylor found he enjoyed discovering each new facet of Shelby's personality. She continued to surprise him daily. That aspect of being forced to be in Benton had turned into an interesting pastime. He tested the porch post for sturdiness then leaned his shoulder against it as he continued to watch her.

Standing, she stepped back a few feet. He straightened and she said, "No, don't move. I need to get a contrast in these. Something living and breathing."

With her camera still up to her eye, she continued to step back. He settled against the post again.

"That's great."

Click, click.

Shelby was totally engaged. She treated taking pictures just as she did working at the clinic. With complete absorption and focus. What would it be like to be on the receiving end of that focus? Was she just as intent and conscious of detail when making love?

Ooh, that wasn't a thought he should be having. Their plans for their lives diverged, not converged. She was the perfect house, perfect yard, and perfect family kind of person. He had no concept of that kind of life. It was like a fairy tale to him. He shifted, looking in the direction of a noise coming from under the trees.

"Stop right there," she ordered.

"What's wrong?"

"Nothing. It looks great."

Minutes later she breathed a sigh of satisfaction, suggesting she'd gotten all she wanted. Again he was thinking of things he had no business contemplating.

"I'm ready if you are."

Mind out of the bedroom, Stiles!

They made their way back to the truck. Just as they were preparing to cross the ditch bordering the road a yelping sound came from the weeds.

Shelby moved toward the sound, bent down and straightened out her hand. A tiny, deathly thin dog with matted hair sniffed at her fingers. "I hate it when people just throw animals out. I can't imagine what kind of person does that."

My father.

Shelby picked up the dog.

"What do you plan to do with him?" Taylor asked.

She turned to him as if he was suggesting they commit murder. "We can't leave it here!"

"I wasn't suggesting that we do. I was just wondering what you were thinking. Keeping him?"

"I'll just take him home and clean him up. Then see if I can find a home for him."

"He looks like he might need to see a vet."

"I'll see about that tomorrow. There's an old blanket behind my seat in the truck—would you get it?"

Did she take home every stray animal she found? In many ways he was one, and she had taken him in. "Sure."

He returned with the blanket and handed it to her. She wrapped the panic-stricken animal in it, bringing the dog close to her chest. "It'll be all right, little one. I'll take care of you," she cooed. She said to Taylor, "We're almost at the lake. I'll show it to you and then we'll head home and take care of this cutie."

Cutie. There was nothing cute about the sad little animal. For a brief second Taylor was jealous of the puppy and the attention it was receiving.

"Would you mind?" She indicated that she'd like him to hold the dog.

Taylor reached out for the bundle. He looked down at the dog, and the mixed-breed mutt with one floppy ear and wiry hair looked at Taylor as if he was his savior.

"He seems to like you." Shelby smiled at Taylor.

He grunted a response. He'd always wanted a dog as a boy. His father had said no more than once and the last time had been with the back of his hand. Taylor hadn't asked again. When he'd been in college and later working he hadn't had time for a dog so he'd never considered getting one. He ran a finger along the head of the confused little animal. Maybe it wasn't too late for him to make a change in his life and have a dog?

CHAPTER FIVE

SHELBY steered the truck along the windy tree-lined road until it sloped sharply downwards. Ahead lay a wide open area. It was level and clear of trees, with two unmaintained roads intersecting at the bottom.

"What do you think about the lake?" she asked.

"Where's the water?"

She smiled at Taylor's incredulous tone. "The dam's down the road a couple of miles. It'll take a few years to fill."

Shelby shifted into reverse.

"Hey! What're you doing? Aren't we going to drive across?"

"I don't think so. We're really not supposed to be this far down the road."

"Come on, Shelby. Live a little. I don't think the only doctors for miles around are going to be sent to jail for driving across a dry lake bed."

Taylor had managed to make her sound silly. With a huff of resignation Shelby changed gears. She eased the truck into terrain that would soon be under water. They rocked and bumped over the uneven road where heavy equipment had crossed.

"You don't like driving through here, do you?" Taylor asked.

Had it been that obvious that it unnerved her? She needed

to work on schooling her emotions or he'd learn things she'd rather keep hidden. Like her fear of caring too much for him, or her dread of being hurt. "There's something spooky about knowing that I should be under eight feet of water. I know it isn't rational but it makes me nervous. Maybe it's from watching old earthquake movies or something."

Taylor chuckled. "Interesting. So you're afraid of blood and dry lake beds."

She glanced at him. "What're you doing? Keeping a record?"

"I just find your little quirks intriguing." He grinned at her.

"Quirks? I don't have quirks."

"Okay. Foibles."

"Foibles! That makes me sound like I'm eighty."

A guffaw of Taylor's laughter filled the cab of the truck. "You know, it's fun to tease you. You blush every time."

Taylor's smile only grew wider at her huff of dismissal. He enjoyed the pink color on her cheeks that wasn't disappearing. Had a woman ever been more desirable? Had he ever wanted to kiss one more? With great effort he kept his hands to himself. Slowly she eased the truck down into the lake bed. His smile grew.

They had reached an area where the narrow road intersected another. Shelby concentrated on downshifting, veering to the right faster than necessary but correcting before the truck went off the road. She was really spooked by being on the lake bed. The road sloped upwards as they traveled farther to what she thought of as dry land. Taylor delighted in the sight of Shelby's chest rising and falling with her sigh of relief.

"Glad to be back on shore?" he quipped.

She snarled, her upper lip in a mock look of displeasure. "Funny. Very funny."

Shelby was adorable. He couldn't remember spending a

more enjoyable afternoon or one when he'd felt more sexually frustrated. The dog whimpered in his lap.

"We need to get him home. Feed him," she said, as much to herself as to Taylor.

We. It surprised him that her use of the word didn't disturb him. He kind of liked the sound of it. He'd been on his own so long that it was nice to be included, even if it had to do with a stray dog. Her kind of *we* he'd like to be a part of. If he knew how.

They were back out on the highway and headed towards town when Shelby pulled off in front of a small country store.

"I don't have anything around the house to feed him. I'll be right back." She climbed out of the truck.

A couple of grizzly looking men sat against the wall of the building, their wooden chairs leaning back on the back legs. From their appearance they could've been the same two guys who had hung out in front of the general store in Taylor's hometown. Men like these, he was sure, spent their days talking and spitting, and knew all the gossip in the county. Unfortunately, his family had provided much of the gossip back then.

The only time Taylor had ever seen one of those men move off the porch had been when he'd been around ten years old. A group of boys had followed Taylor into the store. When he'd caught them stealing they'd cornered him in the candy aisle and threatened to say that he was the thief. He had been preparing to fight when Old Man Carr, one of the men sitting out front, had stepped into the aisle and said, "Hey, you boys break it up."

The boys disappeared in seconds, leaving Taylor to stare up at Mr. Carr. "Sometimes it looks like life is ganging up on you," the old man said in a gravelly voice. "I hear you do good in school. If you use them smarts, you'll never have to worry about fighting boys like them again."

Those words had stuck with Taylor and he'd taken them to heart. He'd decided that he could make something of himself because of that old man. His had been the few encouraging words that an angry, rebellious boy had needed to hear. The ones that had dared him to dream, made him think his life could be more than battles and disillusionment.

Shelby came out of the store with a skip in her step and a smile on her face. That look would be something Taylor would definitely miss when he left.

Opening the door of the truck, she handed Taylor a small paper bag and climbed in.

"That stop sure made you happy." Taylor shifted the dog in his lap and put the bag on the floor between his feet.

"Yeah. I used to walk to an old general store much like this one. It always makes me feel good here."

"Same with me."

"You did?"

"Yeah, we even had the same type of old men hanging around out front."

She chuckled. "I think they just come with places like this."

Taylor glanced back at the men as Shelby pulled the truck onto the highway. Maybe so, but he wasn't sure that they all came with a Mr. Carr. No matter how hard Taylor worked at it as they wound their way back home, he couldn't seem to leave that part of his life behind.

Shelby stopped the truck in her drive and turned the engine off. She reached over to take the puppy.

"He's sleeping. I'll hold him until you get his food ready." He cradled the dog in the crook of his arm as he opened the passenger door. "You get the food." He kicked the truck door closed with his heel.

In the kitchen, Shelby emptied the can of puppy food she'd

bought into a bowl. Taylor set the puppy down. He wandered around the floor on weak legs.

"Come here, sweetie," Shelby placed the bowl on the floor. The dog tentatively approached the food. "Good boy," she cooed.

"You know," Taylor whispered, "if you talked to me like that, I'd do whatever you asked."

Her head jerked up. She glared at him. "You're making fun of me again."

A few seconds went by with the only sound coming from the dog eating with gusto.

"Maybe a little bit. But I can't help myself. I love your reactions. Like now. If looks could kill…" He looked down at the dog. "You know, this ragamuffin isn't the only one who's hungry. Is the burger joint open on Sunday?"

"No."

"You got anything I could fix us a meal out of?"

"I think I have some hamburger meat in the fridge."

"Great." The look on her face said she'd not planned to have dinner with him. He ignored it. "I'll cook while you see about the dog."

"You asking or telling?"

"More like suggesting."

"Only because I'm hungry too will I accept your suggestion. The frying pan is under there." She pointed to a lower cabinet then picked up the little dog with the now rounded belly. "I shouldn't be long."

Shelby returned with a wiggling puppy in her hands as she dried him off with a towel. Taylor stood at the stove, flipping burgers. There was something nice about having a man cook for her.

"How'd the bath go?" He turned in her direction when she entered. "Looks like you might've had one too." Taylor gaze didn't meet hers. Instead it was focused further south.

His eyes had darkened, grown intent. She'd not had some-one look at her like that in a long time. Jim had loved her. She'd never doubted that, but he had never regarded her with the same intensity, the same longing that Taylor showed now.

A river of heat flowed swiftly and sweetly through her, making her heart do the two-step. She glanced down and found that a large wet spot covered her breasts. Spinning round, she covered her embarrassment as well as her reac-tion to his regard. With a couple of quick rubs, she set the puppy on the floor and returned to her bedroom.

"You don't have to change on my account," he called. "I was enjoying the view."

Closing the door to her bedroom with a firm click, she sat on the bed and put her hands over her hot cheeks. She'd blushed more since Taylor had ridden into town than she had in her whole life before that.

She re-entered the kitchen in a dry shirt, to find the table set and a platter of burgers and buns front and center. It was good to have the kitchen used to prepare a real meal. She didn't cook often, it wasn't for just one.

"Got any chips to go with these burgers?" he asked.

Obviously those few heated moments earlier hadn't af-fected Taylor but they'd set her well-ordered world spinning.

"In the refrigerator freezer."

"The freezer?" he asked incredulously.

"Keeps them fresh. I'm not around enough and the chips go stale."

She sat in her usual chair while Taylor found the chips.

"You work too hard." The bag rattled as he opened it and stuck his hand in.

"How so?" Her tone betrayed the small spike of irritation igniting in her stomach. It had been years since someone had commented on the way she lived her life. She didn't think he knew her well enough to be making such a statement.

"Early to the clinic, staying late, no time off, no longer doing your photography. Do I need to go on?"

Who did he think he was to be saying something like that to her? "I don't need you telling me how I should live."

"I'm just making an observation." He bit into a cool chip, making a loud crunching sound. "I don't think anyone could make you do anything you don't want to."

"It sounded like an accusation to me."

"I didn't mean for it to. I just think you need to take better care of yourself."

"Do you make it a habit of cooking for people and then telling them how they need to live their lives?"

He cocked his head, saying nothing for a moment as if in deep thought. "No-o-o." He drew the word out. "I don't think I've ever done it before." He sounded astounded that he had this time. "I guess you're just special that way."

The puppy chose that moment to nose around their feet. Taylor scooped up the small ball of fur in his large hand. With a long index finger he stroked the small head between the ears. The puppy snuggled into his lap. The contrast between the broad-shouldered man and tiny trusting animal captured her whole attention.

What would it be like to be on the receiving end of a tender touch from this man?

Taylor was running late the next morning. He hurried to the car. He stopped short in the humid air when he saw that Shelby's truck was still parked behind his car.

Something must be wrong. He'd been there a little over a week and Shelby had always been gone by the time he'd left for the clinic. He loped to the back door and up the outside steps. Shaking his head to think she didn't lock her doors, he pulled the screen door open and called, "Shelby?"

Listening, he heard a movement from the direction she'd

gone the night before to change her shirt. He'd almost lost control when she'd returned from bathing the dog all wet and flushed, an enormous smile of pleasure on her face. He'd felt like he'd been sucker-punched, she'd been so beautiful.

Only by sheer willpower had he managed to make light of the situation. As soon as their meal had ended, he'd left before he did something he'd regret.

Now he headed to the bedroom that he'd been so tempted to find last night.

"Shelby, where are you?" His heart picked up speed as his concern increased. Why wasn't she answering?

A low whimper came from the room at the end of the hall and he went in that direction. If the puppy was here, Shelby would be nearby. Slowly pushing the bedroom door open, he called, "Shelby, are you okay? Can I come in?"

Receiving no response, he stepped farther into the room. The dog tried to climb out of the box next to the bed. Taylor lifted him into his arms. "So what have you done with Shelby, boy?" He rubbed the dog behind his ears. The puppy licked at Taylor's fingers as he looked at the bed. The only thing that might be Shelby was a large lump under the light blanket.

"Shelby, are you under there?"

Slowly the ball in the center of the bed began to move.

Relief filled him. At least she was alive. "What's wrong? It's past time to be at the clinic."

A groan and then "Oh, no" came from beneath the covers. Shelby pushed the pastel pink blanket back enough so that he could see her face.

Her hair went every direction as if she had been tossing and turning most of the night. A pale face and bloodshot eyes told him she was sick.

Taylor sat on the edge of the bed, the dog in the crook of one arm. "Shelby, you look awful." Maybe that wasn't the best example of his bedside manner but her misery took him by surprise.

"Get out. I'll get dressed and see you at the clinic," she said in a weak voice.

"How long have you been ill?"

"Since around midnight."

Her glassy-eyed look tore at his heart. "Ah, honey, you should've called me."

If she hadn't looked so pitiful, he would've laughed at her expression of disbelief. It had never occurred to her to call him for help. That hurt. He wouldn't let himself examine why it was significant.

"It's just a stomach virus. All I need is a shower and I'll feel better."

Taylor didn't move from the bed.

"Please leave."

"Are you sure you can make it to the shower without help?"

"I can take care of myself."

"Okay. I'll take Buster to the kitchen and feed him."

"Buster?" She looked at him in question.

"Yeah. I can't keep calling him 'Dog.' You yell if you need help."

He was confident she wouldn't be doing that no matter how terrible she felt. Shelby wouldn't admit any feebleness, to him or anyone else.

Taylor pulled the door shut but remained in the hall until he heard the shower running. He'd see that Buster got his breakfast then come back to check on Shelby.

By the time he returned, the water was no longer running. He knocked on the bedroom door but received no reply. Pushing it open, he didn't see Shelby. "You okay?" Still nothing. Going to the door of the bath, he knocked lightly. He couldn't take a chance that in her weakened state she'd fallen.

An unintelligible murmur came from the other side of the

door. Concern overriding any other thought, Taylor didn't wait for an answer before going in.

Shelby sat on the edge of the tub wrapped in a towel, with her wet head against the aqua tile wall. She had taken a hot shower by all the steam floating near the ceiling. Her illness and shower combination had zapped what little energy she'd had left.

"Let me dry your hair and then I'll get you back into bed." Under any other circumstances that would have been a suggestive statement.

"I can do it. Just leave me alone."

"For crying out loud, Shelby, just this once accept some help. Now, you sit right there while I see about your hair." He pulled a towel off the holder.

"Give it to me. I'll do it."

Taylor looked at her meaningfully and briskly rubbed her hair with the towel. "Where's your hairdryer?"

After a long moment she pointed to the cabinet under the sink. *Stubborn woman.* Taylor quickly retrieved the appliance, plugged it in and sat down beside her. Being a novice hairdresser, this job was way outside his comfort zone but he'd do his best. He turned on the dryer and directed the air flow towards her head. His fingers gently ran though the wet strands, separating her hair into sections.

"Lean against me so I can get underneath." Giving her no opportunity to argue, he guided her head to his chest.

She rested against him but never completely relaxed. Didn't the woman ever think she could use someone's help? As her hair dried it became warm silk flowing through his hand. Could anything be sexier? He rubbed his cheek against the glossy cloud.

He turned off the dryer. She slowly sat up. Did she ever let go? Stop being obstinate? "Shelby, honey, you need to get dressed."

She looked at him weakly. He stood and put the hairdryer away. On the corner of the vanity he found a lacy gown that would have made his blood sizzle had circumstances been different. With it suspended on his index fingers by the tiny straps he asked, "You need help with this?"

"I can do it," she said, sounding stronger than she looked.

Relief filled him. And disappointment. It would've been difficult to treat her as a patient if her luscious body had been on display. Still, it would've been his chance to see what he'd been daydreaming about for days.

He stepped into the bedroom but didn't completely close the door between them. Fear that she might fall kept him close. When she opened the door he scooped her into his arms, cradling her close.

She made a weak movement of protest. "Put me down."

He tightened his arms. As if she had no more energy to fight, she accepted his care and settled against him. "I assure you I have no intention of taking advantage of a woman when she's sick. I like my women willing and able, and obviously you're neither. So quit being so uncooperative. The sooner I have you tucked into bed the sooner I can get to the clinic."

"I need to go to work." She resisted his hold again.

"Not today you don't."

"But—"

"There's no but. I'll take care of the clinic. You need to rest."

"You can't tell me what to do."

"I can and I am. Doctor's orders."

"I have patients to see."

"Really, Shelby. Be reasonable. You don't want to give your patients whatever you have."

The fight left her. No matter what, she thought of her patients first, even before herself.

Taylor placed her on the sheets. Her short gown left an

enticing amount of leg showing, forcing him to suppress a groan. He'd always remained a professional when taking care of a patient but seeing to Shelby was testing his restraint. For the first time he was having a difficult time keeping his actions and reactions strictly professional.

He pulled the floral sheet up, concealing the silken skin that his fingers itched to touch. He needed to leave before he did something she wouldn't appreciate and he'd regret.

Brushing her hair away from her face, he said, "I'll take Buster with me to the clinic. We'll be back to check on you at lunchtime."

Shelby feeling miserable made him feel the same. Taylor stopped at the door to the hall and looked back at her. Her breathing had already become steady and deepened.

Never before had Taylor resented his work but this time he wished he could spend the entire day sitting beside Shelby, nursing her back to health. The tiny dynamo had slipped into a corner of his life where he had never let another person go.

Shelby rolled over and looked at the clock on her bedside table. Eleven. She couldn't believe she'd slept the morning away, even though she'd been up most of the night. It had been a long time since she'd felt so wretched.

The clinic!

She flipped the covers back and sat up. Her head spun. Lying back, she flung an arm over her eyes. In the four years the clinic had been open, she'd not missed a day of work. As horrible as she felt physically, it killed her to know that she had patients needing to be seen.

No, Taylor was there. He was taking care of her patients. Doing her work. Seeing that the community had medical care. She'd not relied on anyone in years, and she had to depend on him, of all people. She fought the rising panic the thought brought to her. The person who swore he was leaving as soon as he could, and she had to trust him.

Removing her arm from her eyes, she slowly sat up. Her stomach rose and fell in protest. Maybe if she ate something she'd feel better. Placing a hand over her stomach, she made her way to the kitchen. She was standing on her toes taking the soda cracker box off the top cabinet shelf when the door opened. With a squeak she dropped the box. "Don't you know to knock?"

Taylor entered, carrying the dog. "I thought you'd still be in bed. From the look of things you should be."

"Thanks for making me feel better." She retrieved the box and placed it on the counter.

"I'll say I'm sorry if you'll promise to dress like that for me when you feel good."

Trying to overlook his statement, she said, "Hey, shouldn't you be at the clinic instead of here? What if someone comes? I'll get dressed."

"Relax, I left a note that I'd be back at one. You know you can train people to come to the clinic during the hours you set, don't you? You need a lunch hour. Your number is on the door if there's an emergency. Otherwise they can wait."

She couldn't ignore the heat of desire that became evident in Taylor eyes, which stopped further argument from her. His eyes had turned dark and daring. He put Buster down and stepped toward her. The dog's tail wagged as he found his food bowl.

Not expecting anyone to come into her house unannounced, she'd not put on a robe. Now she stood in front of Taylor in her thinnest, shortest gown. She was just short of naked. By the way he was looking at her she might as well have been. "A gentleman would turn his back and let me get something to cover up with," she said with as much authority as a queen as she headed toward her bedroom.

"A gentleman would but I've never been accused of being one," he called.

Shelby returned to the kitchen to find Taylor pouring something into a small boiler. Surprisingly, sparring with Taylor had made her forget about her stomach troubles. Now it complained more from hunger than a sour feeling. "What're you doing now?"

"I brought you lunch. Home-made chicken soup," he said as he stirred the soup.

"Home-made? When've you had time to make chicken soup? You did open the clinic, didn't you?" Her voice held a note of alarm.

"Yes, I've seen patients this morning. Mrs. Stewart came in to have her sciatica checked and asked where you were. To make a long story short, she said she'd make some chicken-noodle soup."

"With her leg problem, you asked her to make soup for me?"

He did have the decency to look contrite. "I didn't ask. She volunteered. I thought her soup would be better than something out of a can."

"That's sweet of her."

"Now sit down before you fall down while I get this heated."

Once again Taylor was busy preparing a meal for her. Jim had done little if any domestic work during their marriage. His total focus had been the clinic. Much like how it had now become her sole interest.

It hadn't taken Taylor the "I'm leaving town as soon as I can" man long to feel comfortable in her kitchen. He moved around the room with easy grace, finding the utensils and bowls with ease. Somehow it seemed natural, even reassuring to have him there. It was nice to have someone taking care of her. She'd almost forgotten how it felt.

Sitting in a chair, she picked up Buster and brought his face up to hers. "So what've you been doing all morning, little guy?"

"He spent most of the time in a box in your office. The rest of the time he spent eating. He can really put it away."

She settled Buster in her lap and he fell asleep. "That's what happens when you've been starving. You never seem to get enough." Kind of like she couldn't seem to get enough of Taylor's attention. Oh, that was heartbreak waiting to happen.

Taylor's gaze met hers. Did he think she was talking about something else?

When had she become so self-sufficient that she no longer needed a man in her life? She hadn't realized until recently that she'd been starving for a man's notice. Her days were spent giving others care but no one had taken the time to be concerned about her. Until today. Until Taylor. It was a heady feeling she'd miss when he left. The man was slipping in under her defenses.

Taylor placed two filled bowls on the table, and pulled the box of crackers out from under his arm. He went back and returned with two large glasses of iced tea.

"I don't know if my stomach can handle all this," she said, looking at the full bowl of soup.

"You need to eat something or you'll get dehydrated."

Dipping her spoon into the liquid, she put it in her mouth. "Mmm. It tastes wonderful."

"Kind of a hot meal for the middle of the summer but I thought it might make you feel better."

"Thanks for doing this. It's really nice of you."

He shrugged. "Not a problem. Least I can do for my landlord."

A prick of disappointment touched her. So he was just being nice because she'd given him a place to stay for a couple of weeks. Had she been hoping for more? Pushing that disconcerting thought away, she asked, "Who did you see this morning?"

"Mr. Rogers came in with a cough. Mrs. Smith had plantar fasciitis. Mark Myers has a bad cold. The usual stuff."

"Did you do an X-ray of Mr. Rogers's lungs? Rule out pneumonia. He's eighty-five."

"I took good care of him." Taylor put down his spoon, sat back in his chair and looked straight at her. "I thought by now you'd quit questioning my abilities. Have I given you any reason to doubt me?"

She reached over and placed her hand on his forearm. The heat of him seeped into her. "I'm sorry. You didn't deserve that. You've done excellent work while you've been here. And I don't know what I would have done without you today."

Taylor rubbed the pad of his index finger across her cheek. "I bet that was hard for you to admit. I'm glad I was here to help." An emotion similar to shock crossed his face, as if he was surprised to hear himself utter those words. She was certainly surprised by them. It was the first time he hadn't acted like he had his car headed out of town.

His attention centered on her fingers as they trailed off his arm. Suddenly the large kitchen had turned small and intimate. The air between them vibrated with awareness. She returned to eating with a great deal of effort and concentration. Taylor stood and went back to the stove to refill his bowl.

"I'm feeling better. I should get dressed and go back with you."

Taylor wheeled around from the stove. "For someone so intelligent, you have some of the most bizarre ideas."

"I don't have bizarre ideas!"

"Do you honestly believe that you have any business at the clinic this afternoon?"

"Yes, I do. It my clinic. My responsibility."

"You're human. You got sick. Maybe even, despite how

horrible the thought, you might one day like to take a day off."

"What I'm I suppose to do here? I'm feeling much better."

"How about something you enjoy? While I'm here, take advantage of me. After I'm gone it may be a while before you get more help." He returned to the table with his bowl in hand.

Shelby hated to admit it but he was right. She loved her work at the clinic but it had consumed her life. It had been wonderful to spend yesterday outside, taking pictures, she'd even liked Taylor's company. It had been the first real leisure day she'd taken since Jim had died. One that wouldn't have happened if it hadn't been for Taylor's insistence.

"I'd better get back," Taylor said, scooting his chair back having finished his meal. "Mrs. Ferguson is on the schedule for a blood-pressure check so I'd better be there to help her in."

Shelby smiled. The old woman wouldn't be happy to learn that Taylor would be caring for her again.

"What?" He stood and started stacking the used bowls.

"Just thinking you might be taking a liking to us."

"I just might be," he said, soft enough that she looked at him. "Some more than others."

His intense stare made her wonder if she was starting to run a fever.

"You're kind of growing on us too," she murmured.

He leaned toward her.

"Don't get too close. You might catch what I've got."

His mouth moved closer. "I'll take my chances."

She placed a hand on his chest, stopping him. "I don't think this is a good idea."

"You're probably right," he murmured as his arm came around her. His hand settled low on her back and he pulled her against him. "But I've wanted to do it for too long to stop now."

His lips were dry and firm as they met hers. At first he tested and teased. This kiss was nothing like the first one. It was different than any she'd ever experienced. So tender it could've been her very first kiss. She moved forward, resting against him, soaking up the heaven that was being in his arms.

The squeal of an animal in pain pierced the air. She jerked back. She'd stepped on Buster's foot. Taylor's hands dropped away. The warmth and security of being next to him disappeared.

Taylor picked up the dog. "I get a chance to kiss a beautiful girl and you get in my way."

Beautiful girl. Taylor thought she was beautiful.

"Are you feeling well enough to have Buster for company this afternoon?" he asked, placing the dog on the floor again. "He wasn't as well behaved this morning as I had hoped."

"I think so." She forced herself to sound normal after that earthquake of a kiss. "We could both use a nap, I'm sure."

"Wish I could stay and join you," he said in a suggestive voice, along with a long passionate look, before abruptly turning and stepping through the screen door and letting it slam behind him.

How had he managed to reduce her to having a schoolgirl crush in only seven short days?

CHAPTER SIX

SHELBY woke from her nap feeling much improved. Bathing again, she dressed and styled her hair. With a surprise she realized that it had been nice to get some rest without worrying about the clinic. For at least today the concerns of the clinic had been Taylor's and that was a freeing feeling. She could too easily get used to not carrying all the burdens in her life.

Now she sat at her desk, with Buster asleep on a towel beside her. She'd love to spend more afternoons this way. Pushing a button on her computer, she brought up the pictures she'd taken the day before. She clicked on each individual photo in the rows of small squares. With one tap a photograph of Taylor standing causally in front of the shack filled the screen.

Even his picture made her blood hum. He was a handsome man with high cheekbones and a strong jaw. That she was well aware of already. His well cared-for appearance contrasting against the dilapidated building made him the focal point of the photo. He captivated her by simply looking into the camera.

Thoughts of his kisses made her heart break the speed limit. She shouldn't let that happen again. It would be too easy to let him into her heart. But what then?

She clicked through each picture. It wasn't until the picture where he'd looked directly at her that the veneer slipped.

There his vulnerability became visible. No doubt he'd not meant for that particular part of his personality to show. Aware of his need, she longed to soothe him.

"Hey, what're you doing?" Taylor interrupted her thoughts.

Shelby squealed, her hand going to her chest. "For heaven's sake, Taylor, are you trying to scare me to death?"

"I thought for sure you would've heard the door slam."

Buster made a whimpering sound and Taylor picked him up.

"So, I see you're feeling better. What are you up to?"

"Just looking over the pictures I took yesterday."

"Mind if I see?"

He pulled a chair up before she could respond. "Scoot over."

Now he was entirely too close for her comfort. She went back and began clicking through the photos. The house and surrounding landscape had turned out perfectly. Taylor made noises of appreciation and interest in his throat. A soft, warm feeling washed over her at each of his responses.

She leaned back in the chair and put her hands in her lap.

"What about those?" he pointed to the last row of pictures.

"They're just more of the house."

"I'd like to see them also."

With a resigned sigh she put the cursor over the first picture. His face popped into focus.

He moved nearer and gently pushed her hand off the mouse and continued clicking. "Why didn't you want me to see these?"

"I don't know. I thought they might make you feel uncomfortable."

"Why? You're an excellent photographer. Didn't you think I would like them?"

She shifted in the chair because of both his earnest question and him being so near. "I wasn't sure." Did he not see what she did?

Taylor stopped on the one where he'd been watching her, really watching. He studied it for a long moment before he sat back and said, "You have a real talent. One you should be sharing with the world."

She huffed.

He smiled. "Okay, at least this part of the country. You should see about setting up a show." His eyes widened and he lightly slapped his leg. "You know, it would be a great way to raise awareness and money for the clinic. Bring reality to the need for clinics like Benton's."

"I don't think so. I'm not that good and I certainly don't have time to prepare for something like that. The clinic has to come first." She leaned back.

"That's the point." He leaned toward her, his eyes earnest. "You could help the clinic while you're also taking care of yourself. You need to get away from work some."

Rolling her chair away from the computer and Taylor, she stood and faced him. The stab of anger and something else she wouldn't name rose again in her stomach. "I don't need you telling me what to do. If you're so interested in helping, maybe you should commit to staying here and working at the clinic indefinitely, or at least until I find someone to replace you."

Taylor stood, looked at her from across the room. "I've made it clear that I can't do that. I'm only here because your uncle gave me no real choice. Stop trying to drag me into something I want no part of!"

"Is it can't or won't? What would be so awful about having to live here for a little while longer? You seem to be doing fine. And people are starting to like you."

"Enough pushing!" he snapped, and headed out the door.

* * *

Taylor normally didn't care when someone was aggravated with him. After years of living with his father's drunken tirades, he'd learned to tune out people's negative emotions. Regardless of that discipline, the tension between Shelby and himself was starting to get to him. For some reason, her happiness mattered.

Why it was important he couldn't comprehend. He never let anyone get close enough for their feelings to affect him one way or another. He wished he could give her what she wanted but he couldn't. Making his life in Benton wasn't possible. Was he even capable of having a positive relationship with someone?

He'd worked too hard to gain his self-respect, and the respect of others. Now if people were talking about him, it was because of his skill as a doctor, not because he was the brainy son of the town drunk. This tiny town brought back bad memories and he refused to live with them even for Shelby's sake. Still she pushed against that well-established barrier he'd built to protect his emotions. That wall was swaying. He was afraid that if she continued to shove, the partition would fall. Then he'd be vulnerable to a pain greater than any he'd ever known.

Carly knocked on the office door, drawing his attention away from his turmoil. The paperwork he'd been trying to catch up on during a lag in patients that afternoon might have to wait.

"Yes?"

"You have a patient. I put him in exam one," she said.

"Thanks. I'll be right there."

As he opened the door of the exam room, he glanced at the chart for a name. "So, uh, Bill, what seems to be wrong?"

He looked up to find a boy of around ten sitting on the exam table. He was battered and bruised about the face and one sleeve of his shirt had been torn. One knee was badly skinned and the other was openly bleeding. A small trail of blood went down his shinbone.

The boy had been in a fight. He'd not been the winner. Taylor knew the blank look in the boy's eyes. Had seen it in the mirror countless times. Torment gripped Taylor like a strap squeezing his chest.

"What happened?" Taylor had to work to keep his voice steady.

"Some boys at school beat him up," said the haggard-looking mother standing beside the exam table.

"Tell me what happened," Taylor said as he gathered supplies. He would do what his training had taught him to do for now. Later, he'd try to forget.

"It has been an ongoing problem. Some of the boys won't leave him alone. They tease him. He won't let me talk to the kids' parents. Doesn't want me to talk to the teachers. Then this happened." The woman looked at Taylor with tearful eyes.

Taylor knew the feeling well. He'd been hit a number of times before his mother had found out. He wasn't sure his dad ever had. "The school authorities know?"

"Yes, they sent us here." She thrust a paper at him. Taylor glanced at it and set it aside.

"If this continues I'll have no choice but to contact the police."

The boy's eyes widened. Fear filled the blank look that had been in his eyes. Taylor wouldn't be the one giving the report. He was only going to be there a few more days.

Taylor finished examining the boy, relieved there were no broken bones or internal bleeding, then applied bandages to his knee. "You'll need to keep ice on that eye. Twenty minutes on and twenty minutes off."

The mother nodded.

"Now I'd like to speak to Bill for a minute, if you don't

mind?" he addressed the mother, while forcing a smile to reassure the boy. Smiling was the last thing Taylor felt like doing. One little boy's troubles had transported him back to days in his life he'd like to forget.

The mother stepped outside the door and Taylor pulled the chair up in front of the boy. "Bill, I know how hard this is for you because I was once you. I fought at school too. But a man told me that if I did my best in school I could one day be better than all the boys who gave me a hard time. I did work hard in school and it gave me a chance to go to college. There I slowly became proud of myself, liked myself, and that made me stronger than those boys who had always been mean to me.

"So stay in school and make the best grades you can. One day you'll be stronger than those boys picking on you too. Knowledge is power. You never know, one day you might even be their boss and tell them what to do." Taylor pulled one of the leftover coupons out of his pocket. "Now, go get yourself an ice cream."

The slightest smile came to Bill's lips and the sadness disappeared briefly from his eyes.

Minutes after the boy and his mother left the clinic, Taylor stalked out to his car, climbed in, put the top down and headed out to nowhere in particular. He just had to get away. Find some way to ease that band of pain.

That kid's fearful, beaten and disillusioned look tore at his gut. Taylor had worked hard to put those same horrific emotions behind him. That was a sham. All it took was one boy in one small town to make them return with a vengeance. He was still an inmate in the prison of his past. A childhood wasn't something he could make vanish. Somehow he had to learn to live with it or he would never be free of it.

* * *

Shelby searched the driveway from the kitchen window to see if Taylor had come home. Where was he? Surely he wouldn't have left town without saying goodbye, even if they'd had a disagreement.

She hadn't seen him all afternoon and the clinic was slow but even then they should've crossed paths. Finally she asked Carly if she'd seen him.

"He walked out with the little boy who'd been beaten up and his mother. I saw him get in his car and leave."

Taylor hadn't returned to the clinic by the time she'd locked up and his car hadn't been in the drive when she'd arrived home. He'd made it clear he wasn't interested in socializing with people who lived around here, so she couldn't imagine that he'd stopped at the local bar or was at a church event. Those were the only two places open in town that evening.

Now it was going on midnight and he'd still not shown up. Worry made her stomach tense. What had happened to make him leave so abruptly? To stay away?

She turned the light off over the kitchen sink to see more clearly. A misty rain fell and the red car hadn't returned to the drive. Had Taylor been in an accident? Was he in a ditch somewhere? He had a track record of driving too fast. What if he had skidded off the road and no one had seen him do it? A flash of Jim's car wrapped around the tree burst into her mind, but she shook off the image. As perturbed as she'd been with him for leaving without telling anyone, she still wouldn't want anything bad to happen to him.

A double beam of light skimmed across the glass. Shelby's heart rose and fell. The light straightened and then was extinguished. Taylor was home. Relief flooded through her and she was left with a nervousness that could only be the aftermath of fear.

Now she could go to bed.

Picking up the bed she'd bought for Buster, she walked through the dark house to her bedroom. Placing the sleeping dog on the floor beside her nightstand, she took one last look out her back window at the garage.

Taylor stood at the window with the dim glow of a light behind him. His normally strong shoulders were hunched, his head down and hands shoved into his pockets. His body language was in complete contrast to the one she'd seen the last time he'd stood there. He looked like a man totally isolated from the world. Taylor was in pain. Everything about him screamed it.

His head rose and he looked in her direction. She held her breath. Did he know that she was watching him? He ran a hand through his hair and turned away.

Shelby slipped under the bed covers. She should be exhausted but sleep eluded her. What was going on with Taylor? She rolled over, hugging a pillow to her. Would he be there in the morning? She needed to know for the clinic's sake. If she was truthful, she needed to know for herself.

Unable to stand it any longer, she tossed the sheet off and stood. Pulling on shorts and a light sweatshirt over her shorty gown, she headed for the back door. When Buster whimpered, she scooped him up.

Light still burned in Taylor's window. The gentle rain turned heavier as she crossed the short distance to the steps. It began to pour as she climbed the stairs. She knocked on the door of the apartment, her head down against the deluge. She cradled Buster closer as her hand went up to knock again. Before knuckle met wood, the door swung open.

Taylor stood there in nothing but navy slacks. They hung on his hips and were zipped but not buttoned.

"Shelby, what are you doing here?"

Before she could respond, he took her by the upper arms and pulled her out of the rain. She stood inside the door while he stalked to the bathroom and returned with a towel. "Give him to me." He reached for Buster, swapping the towel for the dog. As she dried her head, Taylor placed the dog on another towel on the floor.

"I just wanted—" she started.

"This isn't a good time for a lecture about how I should be more considerate of the clinic," he snapped. His mouth drew into a tight line and he stood with his hands fisted at his side.

"I—"

"You need to leave, Shelby. Just leave me alone."

She couldn't. Shelby stepped toward him, her wet hair hanging in ropes about her head. The sweatshirt lay heavy with water across her shoulders.

"Let me tell you something, Taylor Stiles. My being here has nothing to do with the clinic." She stepped closer, poking her index finger into his chest. He remained immobile but his eyes narrowed. "I've been worried about you." Another poke. "Afraid you'd had an accident." Another poke. "I'm sorry I wasted my time."

At the next poke Taylor grabbed her hand and pulled her to him. She slammed against his chest. His mouth lowered, taking control of hers. Strong arms circled her waist, lifting her. His mouth eased, shifted and took possession more thoroughly. Heat flooded her, pooled low in her middle, making her tingle with longing.

Her hands skimmed across the warm skin of his chest over the strong column of his neck, before wrapping around it. Taylor felt strong, secure, steady. Something she'd missed for so long. She leaned into him.

His tongue teased the seam of her lips and she opened for him, inviting him in. He swept her, teased her, and parried, asking her to play. Tentative at first, she joined him eagerly.

Taylor took the kiss deeper. One of his hands moved to cup her bottom, bringing her closer. Gradually he eased the kiss and his hands moved to grip her waist. He let her slowly slide down him. The evidence of his desire stood hard and prominent between them. When her feet touched his floor, he pushed her gently away.

"You should go."

This strong, intelligent man was a suffering soul and she had a soft spot for suffering souls. She couldn't leave him when he needed someone.

"No." She stood on trembling legs.

He moved to stand at the window, staring out into the night. She came up beside him, lifted a hand to touch his back.

"Don't," he growled.

She pulled her hand away. "Taylor, you need to talk."

"I want to do something more than talk with you." His voice carried a gritty sound of need.

"I know," she said softly. "I'm here. Please tell me what's wrong. You're scaring me."

Taylor hung his head. No one had worried about him in so long. He'd never allowed himself to dream that Shelby might. Could he explain his feelings to her? Would she understand? Dared he think she really cared?

Her fingertips were like points of fire on his skin when she touched his back. Gently the palm of her hand came to rest flat on him and moved in a soothing pattern.

"Tell me what's wrong. I want to help." Shelby continued her tender caress. "What happened today? Why did you leave?"

As her hand moved across his skin he felt his muscles relaxing, his breathing slowing.

"The kid that came in today had been bullied at school." *Just say it and get it over with then she'll leave.* "That was me. I was the kid of the town drunk. Which gave them a lot of material. As a little kid it was a daily occurrence until I started defending myself. That led into fights and escalated into rebelling against everything and everyone. It became a big ugly circle of pain. One that I don't want the kid I saw today to live through."

The movement of her hand faltered for a second. Her calming movement started again with more pressure from her fingertips. Her arms encircled his waist, her face coming to rest against his back. Dampness touched his skin. Shelby was crying for him! When had anyone cried for him?

He turned and enveloped her in his arms. Her face rested against his chest. She snuggled into him as if she wanted to absorb his pain. "Sweetie, don't cry. That was a long time ago."

"I'm crying for that boy that had to live with so much heartache."

He pulled her more securely against him. Her arms around his waist squeezed him closer. He'd never felt more humbled. This woman who had experienced great loss and worked herself almost beyond what was humanly possible was crying for a little boy she hadn't even known. What had he done to deserve her concern? Some of the pain of being an outsider with no one who really cared about him slowly seeped from him.

"I've seen kids in the ER numerous times who'd been beaten but none got to me like this boy. I've kept my childhood issues closed off for years, pushed them away as I focused on first med school then my career. I didn't even bring them out to examine when I had no family at my graduations, or spent my holidays alone. It just was. I accepted that. Until today, when they just came boiling out. I had to leave, take some down time. I'm sorry if I left you in the lurch."

He sucked in a breath at the soft touch of her lips on his chest. Seconds later, the brush of her mouth against him made him forget the past and concentrate fully on the here and now. Shelby was in his arms.

Her hands began to travel over his back, stopping to knead before moving on to explore another spot.

"Shelby? Do you know what you're doing?" His breath spurted unevenly against her hair.

"Mmm… Comforting you?" She nipped at his skin and his manhood stiffened.

Hands on her shoulders, he pushed her far enough away to meet her gaze. "I'm not interested in your pity. Admit it, you want me."

His skin rippled across his back as she trailed her fingers down to his waist and up over his pecs to his neck.

Standing on tiptoe, she stretched upwards. "I thought I was making that clear."

"I want to hear you say it."

"I want you," she whispered over his lips before they met his.

Need, strong, bottomless and more frightening than he'd ever experienced, filled him.

What was she doing? Shelby had never been the aggressor in lovemaking. But Taylor needed her. That little boy in him who'd lived daily in misery and the grown man who'd overcome so much touched her heart. She grieved for the boy and hurt for the scarred man.

He met her tentative kiss with one of fire, consuming her. His tongue entered, demanded. She accepted and gave. Fanning her fingers though his hair, she pulled his head closer. Heavenly, hot, hungry moments later his lips left hers to skim along her cheek, leaving butterfly kisses behind. His mouth traveled down her neck. She shivered.

"We need to get this damp shirt off you," he murmured against her neck as his hands went to the hem of the garment.

She raised her hands above her head, allowing him to slip

the shirt off. He dropped it to the floor and pushed her shorts over her hips and down, leaving her standing in her gown.

His index finger followed the line of lace that covered her right breast to where it ended at her cleavage. Her nipples puckered in response. His finger moved to tease the nipple of her left breast. A quake of delight ran through her.

"As much as I like this little slip of clothing, I know I'll like what's under it so much more," he said in a low gravelly voice that made her tremble.

Before she could respond, she stood naked before him.

"Mercy, you're beautiful." He bent his head and took her nipple into his mouth. His tongue teased and tugged just as he had done with his kisses. Her center melted, ready for him. There was an excitement to being in Taylor's arms that she'd never known existed between a man and a woman, despite her years of happy marriage. He moved to her other breast, giving it the same undivided attention. She shifted toward him, sliding her hands over his shoulders to prevent herself falling.

He chuckled lightly. "Like that, do you?"

Putting her hands on each side of his head, she encouraged him to meet her look. "I do, but I think before we go any further you should turn off the light. We've probably already given the neighbors the show of a lifetime."

He reached over and clicked off the floor lamp, leaving only the light from the bathroom, which prevented them from being in total darkness. Taking her hand, he led her towards the bed.

"What about the bathroom light?"

"No, I want to see you. I don't care what the neighbors know."

She didn't either. What she cared about was him.

He pulled the bedcovers away and she sat on the bed, tugging his hand to encourage him to join her. Instead of coming with her, he resisted, letting go of her hand. She scooted back, watching in fascination and anticipation as he unzipped his slacks and let them drop to the floor.

Taylor was all proud male, his desire evident. For her. There was a potent power in knowing she had such an effect on him.

Placing a knee on the edge of the bed, he leaned over and kissed her. She reached for him. He came down but instead of covering her, as she wanted, he lay on his side, his head supported by a hand. What began as a protest turned to a sharp intake of breath when he trailed his free hand over her hip bone and followed the curvature of her waist upwards.

She quivered as he continued his exploration by tracing the arc of one breast before tugging gently at a straining nipple. He then focused his attention on her other breast that ached for his devotion. Her breath came roughly and raggedly. Heat filled her, making her squirm.

"I love the way you respond to me," he said with a voice full of wonder. He lifted and tested the weight of her breast before his hand moved lower across her stomach.

"Taylor, please," she said, rolling her hips towards him.

"Please. I like the sound of that word coming from you."

"Don't tease." She pushed his shoulders to the bed and straddled him.

"Imagine you wanting to be in charge." His chuckle rumbled low in his chest but held a note of excitement. "This time I think I'll enjoy it."

She came up on her knees then bent to give him a wet, hot kiss, letting her breasts graze his chest. The moan of a man teetering at the edge of his limit filled the air. She smiled against his lips and he took control of the kiss.

His tongue circled her mouth, asking and demanding and tempting. One of his hands fondled a breast while the index finger of the other hand found her center. His finger slowly entered her, retreated and went deeper the next time. She gasped, absorbed the pleasure and begged for more.

Shifting, Taylor rolled Shelby over onto her back and followed her. She boldly met his gaze and offered herself.

The woman in his arms was killing him. She kept such a tight rein on her world yet she was so sweetly, and without reservations, offering her beautiful body to him. What had he done to deserve his dreams coming true? He reached for his wallet on the bedside table, found the small packet and covered himself.

Returning his focus to Shelby, he watched her expressive dove-gray eyes go from yearning anticipation to contemplation to exhilaration as he sheathed himself within her heat. Her eyes slowly closed. She whispered his name and he smiled. He thrust deeper and she met him with a lift of her hips in acceptance. His world rocked, never to be the same again.

Kissing her tenderly while giving her the pleasure she craved, he found his own but at the same time lost his heart.

Later Taylor lay back, pulling the warm sleeping Shelby more snugly against him. He didn't regret making love with Shelby. How could he? It was the closest to heaven he'd ever been.

Yet what had he done? This wasn't a quick fling. This was the real thing. The thing he'd thought he'd never have, could never have. He still couldn't.

Shelby had said she and her husband had moved to Benton with the idea of having a family. Could he offer her the same? What kind of father would he be? He had no experience in that area. Worse, he'd had no example to follow. Was it possible for him to move beyond how he'd been raised? Surely he could do a better job of parenting than his father? Anyone could.

But what he was confident of was that Shelby would accept no half-measures. She desired a family—had told him that was her dream—and would settle for nothing less than a lifetime.

It wasn't yet light outside when Shelby woke to an arm heavy across her waist and a hand cupping a breast. A shock-wave of contentment ran through her. Taylor didn't even have to be awake for her body to react to him being near. It had been a long time for her, and Jim had been her only one, but Taylor had loved her with such tenderness and so thoroughly she'd never felt a moment of apprehension. Her pleasure had seemed to be his only concern. She shifted slightly and the hand pulled her tighter against the solid wall of maleness behind her.

"Don't," his husky voice whispered against her ear, before his mouth lightly tugged at her earlobe. "Too nice here."

She rolled over and kissed him. "I'm not going anywhere. Just getting more comfortable."

The reality of the hurt she'd opened herself up to washed over her. She may not be going anywhere, but he'd be leaving soon. And it might kill her when he did. He'd only been there a short while but he'd managed to ingratiate himself so undeniably into her life, her heart that she might not recover from the loss.

"What's wrong?" Taylor asked, propping his head on a hand and looking down at her.

Had she made a movement or sound betraying her distress or was he so cognizant of her emotions that he sensed what she was feeling? If the latter was the case, she'd have to work hard to keep her thoughts from being transparent. She had to distract him. Was there more to his story than he'd told her?

"I was just wondering…" she trailed her hand across his chest and kissed a spot over his heart "…if you'd tell me about yesterday. What happened?"

Taylor flopped backwards on the bed and looked up at

the ceiling. When she moved closer, he put an arm loosely around her. She sighed. He wasn't pushing her away.

"Do you really want to hear all the ugly details?"

She pulled the sheet up over them and then placed her head on his chest. His heartbeat was steady beneath her ear but the tension in his body said there was nothing calm about him.

"Where did you go?" she whispered.

"Just around."

"You drove around for eight hours."

"Yeah."

Shelby barely heard the word it was said so softly. She sat up, bringing a corner of the sheet up with her, covering herself. Her movement left much of Taylor exposed to her view. Heaven help her, he was gorgeous. As much as she enjoyed his body, she still needed to understand him. She wanted to help him through whatever was hurting him. At least she could give him that before he left.

"Please tell me why."

He took a deep breath. His body shuddered as he released it. "I've already told you more than I've ever told anyone else."

"We all have something negative in our past. Why is it a secret?"

"Not a secret, just not something I enjoy talking about."

"I would like to understand."

"It wasn't the best time in my life."

She placed a hand on his forearm in encouragement. The muscles under her hand jumped.

"I was the youngest of the town drunk's three sons. My mother worked herself into an early grave cleaning houses and whatever else she could find to do to keep clothes on our backs and food on the table. She died when I was sixteen."

"I'm so sorry, Taylor." As if he hadn't heard her, he continued. His eyes seemed to focus on the gloomy night outside.

As if lost in his memories, his voice became a monotone. "The kids at school were particularly cruel. The teachers tried to help. But there was nothing they could really do. I was too angry. If I'd been a jock it might have been better but I stayed in so much trouble I never qualified for any school team. The only thing I had going for me was that school was easy for me."

She reached out to him, began to say something.

He pushed her hand away. "No. I don't need your sympathy. I've moved on. I have a completely different life now."

It stung that he didn't want her comfort. What he didn't see was that he hadn't really moved on. His past still controlled him. He still saw himself as that ne'er-do-well child he'd been told he would be.

"Are your father and brothers still living?"

"I heard that my father died while I was in college. I've not talked to my brothers in years. When I left for college they were on their way to becoming my father. I got my chance to get out of town and I've not been back." Bitterness surrounded each of his words.

"So what gave you your chance to leave?"

Couldn't he see that it was cathartic for him to be letting go after years of holding the disappointment and hurt inside? Glad she could be there for him, she waited.

"An old man telling me to use my brains instead of my fists made the difference. I did. My high-school counselor noticed me, knew my background, saw my grades and helped me with scholarships to college."

He said the last statement with a finality that said she shouldn't ask any additional questions. Instead, she wrapped her arms around his waist, settled her head on his chest and hugged him close. She wanted to absorb his painful memories, make them fade.

Long seconds ticked by before Taylor returned her embrace. Gently he rolled her over and brought his lips down to hers, letting her warmth push the coldness of the past away.

CHAPTER SEVEN

TAYLOR lightly rubbed his cheek against Shelby's soft hair as she lay nestled against his shoulder. He watched as the pink of the new morning edged the top of the large oak tree in her neighbor's yard. Having Shelby in his arms and a beautiful sunrise was the perfect way to start any day.

He'd learned early to accept what life dished out. This time he recognized that making love with Shelby had been a mistake. A wondrous, soul-touching mistake. He couldn't return to a town like the one he'd grown up in. He'd worked too hard to get out. No matter how much he cared for Shelby or how much he was needed here as a doctor, neither were strong enough to entice him to call this place home. He wouldn't break his promise to himself.

Shelby deserved better than what he could give her. She needed someone beside her who shared the same hopes and dreams. Who knew how to be a husband. A father. He wasn't that person. In the long run he'd only make her unhappy. He didn't want to live his life always on guard. No, small-town life wasn't for him.

The woman of his dreams shifted against him and leaned her head back. His gaze met her misty gray one. She blinked twice.

"Hi," she whispered, with a sweet smile on her lips.

"Hey, there." Unable to resist those lips, he kissed her

lightly. The knowledge that this sexy, exciting and generous woman had given herself so totally to him made his heart swell with pleasure yet at the same time caused it to ache. He couldn't keep her.

"Shelby, we need to talk."

She tensed in his arms then pulled away, rolling to the side of the bed. The sheet dropped away, leaving an enticing view of her back and the curve of her well-rounded behind. The desire to run his hand along those smooth curves made his fingers flex against the sheet.

"I'm not interested in an uncomfortable morning-after discussion."

He grabbed her wrist, stopping her from standing. She didn't turn to him. "Shelby, I wish you'd look at me."

She half turned but didn't meet his eyes.

"You know nothing can come of this. I can't stay in Benton," he said quietly. "Just as I know you can't leave."

"That's a cop-out but I'm a big girl. I understand. I need to get ready to go to the clinic now." She stood and started dressing.

The tempting view of her naked body made him want to pull her back against him and kiss her until she forgot about the last few minutes. But her jerky movements as she pulled on her sweatshirt said she wouldn't tolerate being touched.

He'd hurt her. She had a right to be hurt. And it had been the last thing in the world he'd wanted to do.

When he'd needed someone, she'd been there. She'd given herself. Even cried for him. What had he done? Used her.

Slipping out of bed, he started gathering his clothes. The silence in the room hung as heavy as humidity in the hot southern summer. He wanted to go to her, reassure her, tell her all she wanted to hear, but he couldn't lie.

Disgust brought a sour taste in his mouth. He'd fulfilled

the prophecy of his youth. He'd amounted to nothing when it mattered to someone he cared about.

"I'll see you at the clinic," she said as she closed the door on her way out.

She sounded too calm. As if she'd already relegated him to something in the past with no intention of ever giving him another thought. The urge to punch something flared in him.

Buster whimpered at his feet. He picked the dog up and scratched his belly. He'd finish out his time at the clinic. That he had no choice about but he'd try to keep his relationship with Shelby strictly professional. For both their sakes.

The tricky part was he couldn't think of anything more difficult to accomplish.

Shelby had thought her days long and stressful without help at work but they'd been nothing compared to what this morning brought. The tension between her and Taylor made working together almost intolerable.

The situation must be bad if Carly, a teen totally focused on her own world, asked what was going on. Shelby shrugged. "Nothing." A totally ineffectual lie.

Carly's nose wrinkled in disbelief. "Right."

"We need to get back to work."

"It had started to be fun to work here. You smiled and laughed," Carly mumbled as she logged into the computer. "Now even Dr. Stiles is all about work. You two need to try some of that adult advice you're always handing out."

The door opened with a jingle of a bell.

"That's enough, Carly," Shelby said repressively.

Mrs. Ferguson waddled towards them.

"Hello, what can we do for you today?" Shelby asked as she mustered a smile she'd didn't feel.

"I'm just stopping by to see that Dr. Stiles. He insisted I come by to have my blood pressure checked again."

"Do you want me to do it or would you rather see Dr. Stiles."

"I guess I might as well see him, since he's the one that told me to come in," Mrs. Ferguson said gruffly.

It seemed Shelby wasn't the only one who was starting to take a liking to Taylor.

"Carly, please let Dr. Stiles know that Mrs. Ferguson is here," Shelby said.

The girl didn't try to hide her surprise. Shelby had instructed her after the first day when she'd fallen all over herself to help Taylor that her job was to stay behind the deck.

The phone rang and Carly hesitated, looking at Shelby questioningly. "You get the phone. I'll find Dr. Stiles."

In reality, Shelby didn't have to hunt for Taylor. She knew where he was. She'd been aware of his movements all day. Her body hummed with the thought of him. She'd never given herself so totally to a man.

He'd taken what she'd offered but he'd freely given in return.

She wasn't angry with him, disappointed if anything but even that wasn't rational. He'd done nothing to deserve either of those responses. Did she really think that one night of passion would make him change his mind? She'd been the one who'd gone to his apartment. If she was angry with someone it should be herself. She'd created her own heartache.

The door to what was now their shared office stood open. Taylor had managed to carve out an area on the desk for his own pens and personal items. It amazed her that she'd so easily permitted him space. This room was her sanctuary, the door she closed on the world. Not even Carly came into this room freely. Stepping into the doorway, she found Taylor sitting behind the desk, staring off into space. Was he thinking about their discussion this morning or their lovemaking during the night?

"Taylor, Mrs. Ferguson is here." It didn't even bother her that the older woman was now more his patient than hers.

His gaze met hers. "Shelby—"

"Mrs. Ferguson is waiting." She didn't trust herself to say more when all she wanted to do was to walk into his arms and beg him to change his mind.

Shelby stepped into the lab. A minute later her body sent out a signal that Taylor stood nearby. Her hands shook as she placed the slide under the microscope.

"You can dodge me all you want," he said so softly he had to be standing right behind her, "but we will talk."

Twenty minutes after he left, she was preparing to call her next patient as Mrs. Ferguson came up the hall escorted by Taylor. The older woman stopped beside Shelby and placed a hand on her arm. "Honey, my kids have decided to give me a birthday tea this Saturday afternoon. I'd like you two to come." Mrs. Ferguson looked first at her and then at him.

Shelby glanced at Taylor. "I don't know if Dr. Stiles can make it. His work will be done here but I'll be there."

The words sounded catty even to her ears. She regretted them the second they were out.

Taylor's eyes narrowed, his brow wrinkled.

"Oh, are you leaving so soon?" Mrs. Ferguson's focus shifted to Taylor, oblivious to the stiffness between him and Shelby. "I had so hoped that you might decide to stay with us. I know Dr. Wayne has appreciated your help at the clinic. You'll be missed."

A flicker of shock entered his brown eyes and turned to a sparkle of pleasure. His face eased. He smiled at Shelby but spoke to Mrs. Ferguson, "I think I can hang around long enough to enjoy your birthday party."

"Good. It's being held in the church fellowship hall. Dr. Wayne can show you where to go. Now I must be going."

"I'll see you out." Taylor said, cupping the woman's elbow.

"I do love the personal touch I receive from my doctor," Mrs. Ferguson twittered.

Me, too.

Taylor finished his last charting chore and pushed the chair back from the desk. He and Shelby had swapped roles. Instead of her being the one to stay late, it was him.

As soon as it had been time to close the door for the day, she'd announced she was leaving. He was glad she was finely taking some time for herself, yet he knew it was also to put some space between them. He'd asked her to see to Buster. At least that had put a slight smile on her face. Taylor had gone home during lunch to check on the dog, but he needed to be let out to play that evening.

Refusing to spend another day like the one he had today, he had to clear the air between him and Shelby. He'd spent far too much time thinking about her and not enough focusing on his patients. He was grateful there hadn't been an emergency.

Even if he managed to get the stubborn, willful woman to listen to reason, could he keep his hands off her? Right now his body craved her touch, her warmth.

There were no lights on in or around her house when Taylor turned into the drive. Shelby's beat-up truck parked in the drive told him she was probably home. Maybe she'd gone to bed early? Was she out on a date? That latter question made his stomach clench. He didn't want Shelby seeing anyone, but he had no right to demand she didn't.

He walked toward his apartment and paused when he saw the dark form of Shelby sitting a couple of steps up on the stairs.

"Hi," she said so softly he almost missed hearing it above the noise from the night creatures talking to each other. "I've been waiting for you."

His heart fluttered. How he wanted her, wanted things to be right between them again.

"I need to apologize," she said in a steady, firm tone.

This wasn't what he'd been hoping for. By her tone of voice she wouldn't be sharing his bed tonight. How like her to meet the problem head on, though he didn't appreciate being considered an issue she had to solve. Being her knight in shining armor was more to his liking.

When he sat on the step below hers, she shifted her feet to one side to give him room. The riser was so short that one of her knees rested against his shoulder.

Having her touch, even in the slightest of ways, gave him a feeling of belonging. Something he'd not realized he missed so profoundly until then. "You don't owe me an apology. We're two intelligent, consenting adults who spent the night together," he said. The untruth of the description screamed *You are so wrong* in his head seconds after he'd uttered it. It may have been the truth with other women in his life but not Shelby.

She wasn't just any woman. Shelby was *the* woman. The woman he could never make happy.

Her knee tensed against his shoulder. He'd hurt her—again.

"I understand. I'd just like to say I'm sorry for my very unprofessional remark in front of Mrs. Ferguson about you not staying for the party. It was uncalled for."

"Apology accepted."

She stood. "Well, I do appreciate all the help you've given me while you've been here."

"You're welcome." Their relationship had taken three giant steps backwards. Now they were talking to each other like they had when he'd first arrived. He didn't like this new stalemate. Could they ever recover the easiness they'd once known?

"Shelby—"

She walked down the stairs to the pavement, turned and looked back at him. "I'm tired and we both have a full day tomorrow. I've got Buster. Goodnight, Taylor."

He couldn't see her very well in the night shadows but the wistful tone in her voice came through loud and clear. A yearning to reach out and pull her back into his arms gnawed at him, but he couldn't let himself do it. He knew what hurt and rejection and wishing life to be different could do to a person. Adding to Shelby's pain wasn't something he was willing do.

Shelby made it just inside the kitchen door before tears slid down her cheeks. Until she'd said Taylor's name she'd believed she'd held herself together pretty well. The shake in the last syllable had given her away.

She'd tried to play the adult game of sex with no strings. She'd lost. She'd fallen and fallen hard for a man who refused to be a part of the town she'd made a pledge to. One she couldn't break. She and Jim had made a commitment to Benton to provide medical care. She'd promised Jim the night he'd died that she'd uphold their pledge, keep their dream alive. If she broke that vow, she'd be dishonoring Jim's memory and everything she had spent the last few years working towards. To have Taylor in her life, he had to embrace the town of Benton too, and all it meant to her. In that tug of war, she wouldn't win. Taylor's childhood fears were stronger than his desire for her.

Heaving a sigh, she found her way to her bedroom and undressed without turning on the light. The full moon that had risen over the trees shone brightly enough that she didn't need to switch on a lamp.

She couldn't resist the urge to look out the window at the apartment. There was no light on but she knew with all her being that Taylor stood there, looking down at her. A tingle ran though her, leaving a path of longing deep and sharp. If there was a silver lining in their whole mixed-up relationship it was the knowledge that he seemed as out of sorts as she.

With the faintest of movement the connection was severed. Taylor was going to bed without her.

Some time later, a banging at her door brought her out of her fitful sleep.

"Doc Wayne! Shelby!" a frantic voice yelled.

"I'm coming," she called.

Flipping on the lamp, she went to the closet and found her robe. Jerking it on and tying the belt, she made her way to the front door.

The beating and shouting continued. "I'm here. Hold on a minute," she called, turning on the porch light and opening the door.

"Sam, what's the problem? Why didn't you call me instead of waking the whole neighborhood?"

"The station tried but got no answer. They sent me."

She been so tied in knots after talking to Taylor that she'd left her phone on the kitchen table instead of taking it to the bedroom.

"What's going on here, Deputy?" Taylor asked from behind Shelby. She turned, her nose making contact with his bare chest. She glanced downwards to find him dressed in nothing but red plaid boxers. She groaned.

"We didn't mean to wake you. I can handle this," she hissed.

"I wasn't asleep." Taylor's deadpan tone said he was having as rough a night as she.

He must have seen the patrol car drive up, realized there was an emergency and come in through the back door. No matter why he was there, his appearance in her house to Sam and soon to the entire town it would look like they'd been sleeping together. She couldn't worry about that now.

Turning back to Sam, she saw the slight smirk on his face that confirmed her fears. "What's happened?" she asked the deputy in her most professional voice.

"There's been an accident on the Hartman farm. Something to do with a tractor. You're needed out there."

"I'll get dressed and get my bag. The ambulance service has been notified?"

"Yeah, but they're out on another run. They'll meet us there as soon as they can."

When she turned around Taylor was gone. She wasted no time wondering where he was off to. Instead she concentrated on the emergency ahead. She dressed in record speed in T-shirt, jeans, and tennis shoes, pulling a light jacket off a peg by the door. She also snatched up the emergency bag she kept stocked for these types of occasions. Reaching her truck, she found Taylor waiting with his own medical bag in hand. He took her larger bag and placed it in the back before then taking to the passenger seat.

As she climbed behind the wheel she said, "You don't have to come."

"Do you really think I'd let you go alone?" He sounded disappointed that she might think he would not do his duty. "We're a team," he said firmly.

What he'd left unsaid was "until the end of the week."

A little later Taylor stepped out of the truck onto the well-worn gravel of the drive circling in front of the farmhouse. The lights around the house blazed and a couple of large late-model trucks were parked off to the side. A police patrol car sat in front of the main door.

A middle-aged woman and a girl of about fourteen hurried down the steps trailed by a large dog. Sam, the deputy, followed them and came to stand beside Shelby.

"Dr. Wayne," the woman said, panic filling her voice, "I'm so glad to see you. Bob's leg is trapped."

"Trapped by what?" Taylor asked.

"Mrs. Hartman, this is Dr. Stiles. He's a trauma doctor from Nashville here helping me."

The woman nodded curtly and quickly turned her attention back to Shelby. "The tractor."

Shelby looked toward a large structure behind the house that had to be the barn. "Where is he?"

Mrs. Hartman pointed off into the distance. "Down in the bottoms near the river. He was trying to get in some last-minute bush hogging before the rain set in." Her words rushed together as she spoke. "He didn't come in at dark. I sent our son, John, to look for him. He found the tractor jackknifed. His dad is pinned in. John's down there with him right now. That private ambulance service is off on another run. It'll be awhile before they get here, and even then I'm not sure they can handle this. That's why I called you."

Sirens sounded in the distance. Shelby glanced at Sam. "Volunteer fire department," the deputy said. She dipped her chin in understanding.

"We need to prepare for shock, maybe puncture wounds, a break at the least," Taylor told her.

She nodded in agreement. "Mrs. Hartman, we're going to need blankets and towels. Is there someone who can show us where to go while you gather them?"

"My girl, Jenny, will take you."

"I'll wait for the fire department," Sam said.

The girl ran to a four-wheel flatbed vehicle with two seats. Taylor sprinted to the truck to retrieve the medical bags and met Shelby and the girl. "I'll sit on the back," he called. Shelby's look questioned his choice but for once she didn't argue. He climbed on and scooted on his bottom along the metal platform until his back was against the seats.

Jenny had the vehicle moving by the time he and Shelby were settled. They traveled through an open gate and into the darkness. As they left the yard behind the ride became bumpier. Due to the rough terrain, Taylor had a hard time telling where they were going or what the land looked like, with the beam of the headlights darting up and down. He had to hang onto the low metal bar to keep from sliding or falling off the flatbed.

"How far?" Shelby asked.

"Ten minutes," the girl said, before shifting into a higher gear and throwing them all sideways as one wheel hit a bump. Behind the two women, Taylor grabbed again for the metal bar. They traveled into the night as the all-terrain continued its slow, steady pace over the rough terrain.

With no real idea about what to expect, he could tell from Shelby's look earlier this wasn't going to be an easy case. The fact that they'd be working in the pitch dark wouldn't help.

Shelby glanced at him. Even in almost non-existent light, he could see her apprehension. He squeezed her shoulder gently. Was she worried she couldn't handle the situation? Or the blood?

Being a small-town kid, he had no experience with farms or farm equipment. His nerves were strained at the thought of what they might encounter.

They rode in silence for a while, following a track through the field and into a stand of trees. While fording a creek, they listed heavily to one side and then to the other as they rode over large rocks. He braced himself with both hands on either side of the vehicle to manage the sway. Using a leg, he was able to stop the med bags from sliding off.

"What kind of vehicle is this?" he asked the girl in a voice loud enough to be heard over the motor beneath him.

"An army mule."

"Mule?"

"It's some kind of World War Two thing."

Minutes later they came out of the woods and crossed a large field, approaching the scene of the accident. The only light present came from a four-wheeler's headlights pointed in the direction of the tractor.

From what he could tell, the tractor was an antique. It had a long body, with dual wheels close together in the front and large, head-high ones at the rear. Didn't these people own anything from the last decade?

One of the large wheels rested in a wide, three-foot ditch while the front wheels hung in the air. Behind it at a right angle was the bush hog pressed against the other back wheel. Sandwiched between the two pieces of dangerous equipment was Mr. Hartman.

"We're going to need to get more light down here," Taylor said.

"Neighbors are on their way with more four-wheelers." Even as Jenny said the words Taylor heard the whine of the vehicles. The girl pulled to a stop and he jumped off the mule, grabbing both bags. He paused long enough to see that Shelby had climbed down safely.

"Jenny, you go back and get those blankets and towels. Tell your mother to call the neighbors and to get a couple of tractors out here. Hurry back."

The girl hesitated.

"Your daddy's going to be fine," Shelby said, standing on tiptoe to reach over and touch the girl's shoulder across the passenger seat. "You can help him best by helping us."

How like Shelby to not only take care of the patient but the family as well. In the big emergency room where he worked, he often never saw the family. The social worker did all the consoling.

"Shouldn't this be the EMTs' job?" Taylor asked as he and Shelby made their way over to the accident.

"Yeah, it would be if we had EMTs. We have a volunteer fire department and a private ambulance service. Nothing more. I'm the EMT on the rare cases like this."

A boy of about eighteen stood and came towards them from where he'd been sitting next to the injured man.

"John, I'm Dr. Wayne and this is Dr. Stiles. We're here to help your dad. We're going to get your father taken care of." At her reassuring words, the boy's shoulders relaxed.

He led them to where Taylor could see the man half lying, half sitting on the top of the bush hog, his body twisted in an unnatural position. Shelby fell to her knees beside the farmer. Taylor set the bags down and sat on one heel. Quickly, Shelby found a flashlight in the emergency bag.

"Mr. Hartman, you've managed to get yourself into quite a pickle this time." Shelby's bright tone played down the desperate situation. The man could lose his leg, possibly his life. "This is Dr. Stiles," she continued.

"Glad to see you, Doc," the man said weakly.

"Sorry it's under these circumstances." Taylor moved in close to Shelby as she shone the flashlight indirectly over Mr. Hartman's face. The man was already deathly pale. Pain lines circled his mouth.

"We're going to get you out of here as soon as we can. More help is on the way. While Dr. Stiles and I have a good look and listen to you, why don't you tell us what happened? Start with how long you've been here."

Taking the cue, Taylor reached for his own small bag, pulled out his stethoscope and began to listen to the farmer's heartbeat. It sounded thin but steady. His breathing sounds were what really concerned Taylor. They were rapid and shallow. Had he broken some ribs as he'd gone down? While Taylor worked, Shelby pulled out a small penlight to check the man's eyes. She then took his blood pressure.

"Been here since sunset." He paused, taking a breath.

"Got too close to the ditch. Heard a noise. Sheer pin rattled loose. Tried to put spare in. Knew better. Stepped between the tractor and bush hog…" He paused, exhausted.

"Dad said that the ground below the right back tire gave away," John offered. "The tractor slid into the ditch, jack-knifing the bushhog. He tried to jump backwards but didn't get his leg out in time."

"Well, that's quite a story, Mr. Hartman. You'll have something to tell your grandchildren one day," Taylor said, looping his stethoscope around his neck. "Where do you hurt?"

"I can't feel my foot."

"Can you wiggle your toes?"

The man shook his head.

Shelby glanced at Taylor. His face mirrored her concern. Did they share the same worry that the blood supply might be cut off to the lower part of Mr. Hartman's leg or, just as troublesome, that there a possibility he could be bleeding to death?

"John, sit with your father. I'd like to talk to Dr. Wayne," Taylor called. The boy came closer. "We'll be right over here if you need us."

Taylor quietly pulled Shelby out of their hearing. "I'm anxious about him bleeding out without us realizing it because we won't be able to see it. I'm going to try to get a look at his leg." Taylor pulled his stethoscope off.

"How're you going to do that?" Shelby asked, her voice raised an octave.

"I'll lie on the ground and stick my hand under the bush-hog and feel for his leg. If I can't do that then I'll feel on the ground for blood."

"Okay. I'll check his leg from above."

Taylor stuffed his stethoscope into his bag. Going down on his belly, he reached beneath the bush hog, searching for the man's leg. His fingertips brushed cloth that was wet and sticky. Stretching out as far as he could, he felt up and down the leg. It was bleeding but not as much as Taylor had feared.

Scooting back, he got to his feet. Shelby came to stand close beside him. "He's bleeding but not badly, considering," he said for Shelby's ears only. "The trick is to get pressure applied as soon as we can move the bush hog to prevent hemorrhage. The secondary concern is that he may lose the leg from loss of blood flow to the feet. When the ambulance does arrive, it isn't going to make it back here. We're going to have to figure out how to take him out ourselves." He looked around. "Where's that help?"

"They should be here soon." As she said the words an army of headlights came out of the woods and headed across the field.

"Thank God," Taylor whispered under his breath.

As two tractors that were part of the fire department, along with Mrs. Hartman and Jenny on the mule and several neighbors on their four-wheelers, arrived, Shelby returned to monitoring Mr. Hartman's vitals.

Taylor morphed into trauma doctor mode and began giving orders. He asked Sam to oversee the positioning of three of the four-wheelers on the other side of the ditch so that their headlights focused on the tractor and bush hog. Noise from all the engines was almost deafening in such a small area but Taylor's voice could still be heard over the din.

"John, I need you to swing your four-wheeler around to the right." The boy went running to follow Taylor's order.

A natural leader, Taylor had no trouble getting the people to respond as if they'd known and trusted him for ever.

Jenny and Mrs. Hartman appeared inside the circle of light and brought Shelby the blankets and towels. While she worked to reassure Mrs. Hartman that her husband would be fine, Taylor continued directing four-wheelers. He told two of the newly arrived drivers that he wanted them on that side of the ditch so that light would be coming from as many different angles as possible.

Shelby felt a sense of pride as she listened to Taylor organize the operation. His abilities to manage people and keep a level head in a crisis were outstanding. The man had special skills that would fit well into the community. Too bad he wasn't interested.

Rolling up a towel, she placed it under Mr. Hartman's head then covered him with a couple of blankets, tucking them in securely to hold the warmth in and slow down shock. She hoped they weren't too late to prevent it. If they couldn't get him out soon, he might die of it. He needed to be on his way to a hospital.

As the men on the tractors wrapped chains around the wrecked vehicle and attached another chain to the bush hog, Taylor instructed them on how to pull in order to minimize the damage to Mr. Hartman's leg.

Discussion broke out about the best way to perform the maneuver and Taylor interrupted the conversation, making it clear what had to be done and how otherwise Mr. Hartman could be injured further. Once again, Shelby was grateful to Taylor. Would the tough farmers have given her as much respect as they were now giving Taylor? With everything set as Taylor had ordered, and the driver of each tractor understanding his duty, Taylor approached her.

"My plan is for us to move the tractor and bush hog enough for us to assess again before we pull Mr. Hartman out. Do you agree?"

"I agree. Before the pressure is completely released we need to know how to handle it and where the bleeding is coming from. My only concern is if anything shifts when we examine him again, we might do him more harm."

"I've thought of that but I don't think we have a choice."

Shelby nodded her agreement.

She went back to Mr. Hartman. "We're getting ready to pull you out. It shouldn't be too much longer now."

The injured man did little more than grunt.

"Okay, everybody, stand back." Taylor shouted to be heard over the roar of the tractors. Shelby moved away but not so far that she couldn't be back to the farmer's side lightning fast.

"Slowly," Taylor yelled. At tortoise speed, the tractors pulled in opposite directions. The wheel of the tractor pinning Mr. Hartman shifted. Shelby sucked in a quick breath, held it. Was Taylor's strategy going to cause more damage? Seconds later the bush hog moved slightly.

Mr. Hartman let out a moan of pain. Shelby rushed to him, going down on her knees. "Hold your positions, guys," Taylor shouted to the tractor drivers, then joined her.

"He's passed out," Shelby said.

"It'll be better for him this way. It's going to be painful when we lift him," Taylor said, and Shelby couldn't disagree.

"I'm going into the ditch and underneath to see what we've got before we pull him out."

"That's too dangerous." She grabbed his forearm. "Is it really necessary?"

"I think it is. I'll be fine. The tractors aren't going anywhere. Hand me the flashlight." She did as she was told. Taylor moved to leave and she grabbed his hand. "Please be careful. I don't need you hurt too."

He squeezed her hand, then went to the edge of the ditch and sat on his butt before sliding down on it and disappearing into the gully.

"Get out of the light!" Taylor demanded from below.

She looked across the ditch to see one of the teenagers walking over to another four-wheeler.

"Hey," she hollered. "You're in the light."

The boy quickly stepped out of the way.

"That's better." Taylor's voice was muffled, telling her that he was moving farther under the tractor.

Shelby held her breath. As her imagination took hold she pictured the chains breaking, the tractor falling, Taylor being pinned underneath.

With enormous relief she watched Taylor climb out of the ditch. He came to stand beside her and offer his hand. She took it and he helped her stand.

Mrs. Hartman rushed by them to take Shelby's place beside her husband.

"We need to talk a sec." He led her out of the ring of light, where the two of them could speak without being overheard. "He has a puncture wound high on the left thigh. A smaller one on the right. We're going to need to pull him out quickly and apply pressure immediately.

"I know how you feel about blood and I hate it that there's no other way, but you're going to need to see to the wounds and stop the bleeding."

"I'll do what has to be done."

He ran a fingertip lightly down her cheek. "That's my girl. I never doubted it."

CHAPTER EIGHT

SHELBY searched through the emergency bag until she found plastic gloves. Next she pulled out the containers of four-by-four gauze bandages and broke the paper seals. With them stacked firmly in her hand, she nodded to Taylor that she was ready. Taking a cleansing breath, she prepared herself, refusing to let him or her patient down.

Taylor reassured her with a smile then motioned the largest-looking guy over and said, "I'm going to need your help lifting Mr. Hartman. When the tractors release him, on my mark—pull. You understand?"

The man nodded and Taylor looked directly at her.

"I'm ready." Shelby stood as close to the machinery as she dared, out of Taylor's and the man's way, and waited.

Taylor put his hand in the air, waved and the tractors moved in unison and in opposite directions. He placed his hands under Mr. Hartman's armpit and low on his back, showing the large man how he wanted him to pull Mr. Hartman out. When the man matched Taylor's hands, he shouted "Pull!" Seconds later the farmer was out and Shelby was kneeling beside him, applying pressure to the bleeding wound. She ignored the roll of her stomach. She must do whatever it took to save Mr. Hartman's life. Her and Taylor's patient.

Taylor hollered, "Hold." The tractors halted as he and

his helper laid Mr. Hartman on the bush hog. They adjusted their position before moving the injured man to a blanket that Jenny and her mother had placed on the ground. Across from her, Taylor remained on one knee and applied a bandage to the smaller wound, securing it.

"You got that?" He waited until she looked up.

"I'm good." Until her patient was out of her care, she had to be.

"I'm going to check for other injuries then we'll pack the wound and then splint." With efficient movements he ran his hands down Mr. Hartman's legs and up again. "Mr. Hartman, can you hear me?"

The man's groan affirmed he'd regained consciousness.

"Can you feel your toes?"

The man gave them the smallest of nods. Relief rushed through her as she returned Taylor's smile. "Great. Let's get this leg splinted and get him to a hospital," Shelby said.

"Yes, ma'am," he said in a whoosh of released breath.

He grabbed her bag, located the splints and handed one to her. Carefully and quickly they wrapped the leg, making sure the four-by-fours were securely in place.

"Jenny," she called, "pull the mule up alongside your dad." To Taylor she said, "We need to get blankets laid out on the back of the mule. This is going to be a painful ride out for him."

Taylor followed her instruction unquestioningly. Just as she'd followed his earlier. They'd switched roles, each finding their niche. She'd never experienced this type of rapport with any other doctor, not even with her husband. She and Taylor seemed to know what the other was thinking. They worked together as a smooth and skilled team.

He directed Jenny to where she needed to be and then she and Taylor saw to the padding.

"We need to keep him as level as possible," Shelby said,

and turned to one of the volunteer firemen. "You brought a board, didn't you?" The lack of light made it difficult to see and she'd been too busy to search beforehand.

"Right here, Doc," one of the men called, pulling the wooden backboard towards her.

"Okay, guys, I need us to get on each side of Mr. Hartman and put our arms under him as far as you can. On three— lift."

As the men lifted, Shelby supported Mr. Hartman's head. She made a mental note to include a neck brace in her emergency bag. Once the injured man was on the mule, she and Taylor rolled towels and placed them along the man's legs and neck to stabilize them. Jenny gave them a couple of industrial straps and they used them to secure the backboard to the mule. Mrs. Hartman climbed into the passenger seat. "He's going to be fine, Mrs. Hartman."

"Okay, Jenny. Dr. Stiles and I are going to ride in back with your father. Go slowly and the fewer bumps the better." Before Shelby could finish the sentence, Taylor had lifted her up onto the mule. Their gazes met for a second. She found her seat then he went around to the other side and climbed on.

There was little space for them to sit and it wasn't going to be a comfortable ride, but it would be much worse for Mr. Hartman. As they bumped and rocked along, Taylor grabbed her arm when she threatened to fall off. A tingle went through her, then it was gone when he let go. After the third time he held her hand across the barely conscious man's chest. Mr. Hartman groaned as they went but never woke fully. She was grateful for Taylor's steadying support.

Taylor's hand was gritty and rough from the dirt caked to his fingers, but she didn't care. They were warm and reassuring around hers. His touch said he would take care of her. She liked that feeling.

The trip seemed never-ending. It was a relief to see the

house lights in the distance. When they finally made it to the drive, the ambulance was waiting. As soon as Jenny stopped the mule, Taylor hopped off and came around to her to assist her in getting down. She'd been in one position for so long her legs were stiff.

"Walk around a second to ease your legs and I'll see about getting Mr. Hartman unloaded."

Shelby followed his advice and was soon able to help with getting Mr. Hartman situated in the ambulance. Mrs. Hartman gushed her thanks then climbed into the passenger seat for the ride to Nashville.

Taylor had instructed the ambulance men to take Mr. Hartman to the hospital where he himself worked, saying he'd call ahead and let them know they were coming.

"I need a phone. I left mine at home. It probably wouldn't get any service out here anyway," he said to no one in particular.

"You can use ours in the house," Jenny offered.

As the sun was coming up after a long night, Shelby watched Taylor walk towards the house. Those wide shoulders of his were solid, sure, and strong enough to lean on.

Taylor had finished his call then cleaned up in the bathroom Jenny had indicated on the way to the phone. He was headed back outside when Shelby's laughter drew him down the hallway of the old, two-story house. He liked hearing that soft ripple of sound. She didn't make it enough. Those notes led him to a huge family-style kitchen.

Shelby stood amidst volunteer firemen, tractor drivers and the kids who had been on the four-wheelers. They were all laughing and talking loudly as they filled their plates with food.

A woman Taylor had seen only briefly earlier came up beside him. "I'm Bess, a friend of the Hartmans. Mrs. Hartman told us to take care of everyone. To give you her thanks for saving her husband's life. We've prepared breakfast, so help yourself."

The group stopped talking and waved him forward to envelop him inside. Taylor hesitated before stepping forward to stand beside Shelby.

A few patted him on the back while others told him how impressed they'd been with the job he'd done. Treating him as a hero, they insisted he go first. He filled his plate with eggs, bacon and the most delicious-smelling home-made biscuits. Being accepted into a community was an alien experience but wholly wonderful.

He took a seat down at the family-style table. Shelby smiled widely as she took a seat across from him. Her eyes sparkled as she chatted with those around her. He was glad to see no visible lasting effects from Mr. Hartman's trauma. The blood hadn't prevented her from doing what had to be done. Picking up his fork, he started on his meal. He was ravenous for nourishment and for Shelby.

Shelby watched from under half-raised lids as Mr. Abernathy, a particularly boisterous, middle-aged farmer, shook Taylor's hand vigorously and invited him to go hunting. She grinned. Taylor faltered a second, before replying, "Thank you, sir. I'd like that." Taylor looked at her as if perplexed by all the camaraderie.

Shelby chuckled. When the man walked away she said to Taylor, "I guess you'll be back to hunt in the fall." That little boy who had always stood on the outside had been accepted into the fold. She just hoped he realized it.

As they ate, Taylor was peppered by questions about himself from the men and teens sitting around the table. At first he showed little enthusiasm for answering their questions but with some encouragement he became part of the crowd, even entertaining them with anecdotes.

Taylor called the hospital after finishing his meal and reported to the group that Mr. Hartman was in surgery and doing as well as expected. Taylor received high fives all round, which he acknowledged with a grin on his face. He had a wonderful smile.

Her heart swelled with the goodness of life as she looked around the table. These people were neighbors and friends who cared about one another. They'd worked together the night before to help Mr. Hartman and now it was time to celebrate their success. Taylor was smiling broadly and he seemed much happier and more at ease with himself than he'd been when he'd first come to town. She enjoyed the opportunity to visit with everyone outside the clinic. It's a shame it took a tragedy for her to socialize more with her community. She was going to do better in the future.

Finally, knowing they'd stayed long enough, Shelby said to Taylor, "We need to go. We should've been at the clinic an hour ago."

Taylor gave her a dubious look but said his goodbyes. The others mumbled their own need to leave and followed them out. The sun had risen high enough that the area they'd traveled in the dark was clearly visible. Looking at it made her realize that she didn't want to repeat that adventure again any time soon.

When they reached the truck Taylor said he'd drive and she'd gladly agreed, climbing into the passenger seat. "You know the way?"

"I believe I can make it," he said, as he got behind the wheel.

"Isn't it a beautiful day? I love this country." She looked at the low mountains creating the farm valley and the green fields butting up against them.

"Yes, beautiful."

Taylor's low tone filled with wonderment made her glance at him. He was looking at her. Her gaze met his and held. *He thinks I'm beautiful.* A fuzzy, pleasurable sensation trickled through her. Taylor believing that made her believe it too.

He leaned toward her, itching to kiss her, then glanced out the window at the others mingling in the yard and sat up. "Come on, Dr. Wayne. You've done a good night's work and I need to get you home."

"The clinic—"

"First things first. We both should clean up."

She rested her head against the back of the seat and closed her eyes. "We had a pretty amazing night, didn't we?" she murmured. "I guess you're used to that type of thing but I don't see it often. Mr. Hartman was a trouper. I hope he recovers quickly. You were great, by the way."

Taylor smiled. Shelby had been on an adrenalin high and now she'd crashed. She snored softly beside him. When her head drooped, he reached over and guided it to his shoulder. A gentle sigh of acceptance blew warmly over his bare arm as she snuggled into him. Resentment for the gearshift filled him. It didn't allow him to put his arm around her. He'd never given much thought to the benefits of a bench seat in an automobile until he'd met Shelby. He wanted her soft, warm curves next to him as much as possible.

When he pulled into the drive, Shelby roused enough to know they were home. "How come I'm so out of it and you don't seem to be tired?" she asked in a sexy, sleepy voice that made him wish to hear it every morning.

"I keep these hours way more often than you do. My body's used to it."

"I need to get it together and get to the clinic." She shook her head lightly.

"You go on and get a bath. Have a good nap and I'll handle things at the clinic this morning."

"You know, Dr. Stiles, you're starting to make yourself

indispensable," Shelby said, climbing out of the truck and walking toward her back door.

He chuckled. "I'll take that as a compliment."

Taylor hustled to his apartment and changed clothes. He'd get a bath later. He arrived at the clinic to find Carly behind the desk, fending off patients unhappy because no one had been there to see them. He saw to the patients and told Carly to start calling to reschedule appointments already on the book for that afternoon. He also asked Carly to stay until after lunch in case anyone showed up and to ask them to come back the next day. After that she could post a sign on the door to call him in case of an emergency and take the afternoon off.

A few hours later, Taylor exhaled in pleasure as he stood under the hot flow of water from the showerhead. Done, he stepped out naked into the cool of the air-conditioned room and slid beneath the sheet on his bed. The wish that Shelby lay warm and compliant next to him followed him into welcome sleep.

The thud of the door being pushed too far and the stomping of bare feet across the wooden floor snatched him from his dream. Shelby, dressed in a long T-shirt, glaring at him from above brought him fully awake.

"Why didn't you wake me? I trusted you to see to the clinic. It's after two o'clock and no one is there!"

That was his Shelby. All fire and brimstone.

He reached for her, capturing her before she could step away. With a short whoosh she landed on top of him, squirming. The smell of sleep and wild flowers tickled his nose.

"Stop wiggling, Shelby."

"Then let me go!"

"No, because I want you to listen to me."

She struggled against him. His body reacted by going to full attention. Heaven help him, he had no control around her.

"I'll listen. Just let me go," she snarled, putting her hands on either side of his head and pushing upwards. She glowered down at him.

The arching of her back brought her pelvis into more intimate contact with his swelling masculinity. "I don't think you will. Anyway, I like you right where you are." He flexed his hips.

Her eyes widened as if they had registered what she did to him. She brought her chest down to his but remained stiff against him. The only indication of her desire was her fingers curling into his shoulders. He nuzzled her neck, his lips traveling upwards to find the sweet spot behind her ear. She exhaled and turned her head slightly, giving him better access. He smiled. He had her attention now. Slowly she melted against him, purring her pleasure. He wanted her desperately, and he would have her.

Taylor moved his mouth upwards to whisper in her ear, "Listen, my little she-cat, Carly and I changed the afternoon appointments only, and she stayed until noon. I told her to take the rest of the day off and put a sign on the door to call us if there's an emergency."

He flipped her quickly onto her back, bringing his hips against her with a purposely suggestive flex. "Can you tell how much I want you, my little she-cat?" His mouth found hers.

She met him kiss for searing, slick kiss. She held his lips to hers, opening for him. All the fight and fury of earlier had been turned into red-hot passion and promise. One of her hands came up to circle his neck.

Her other hand made bold strokes over his body, exploring every dip and crevice. When her small hand pushed the sheet away and brushed over his straining manhood, he almost shattered.

Taylor pulled her hand away and captured it below his

on his belly. "I'm thinking one of us has on far too many clothes."

"Mmm, and one of us has just the right amount." She placed a kiss on his shoulder and smiled as the low rumble of his chuckle vibrated beneath her.

"I believe in equality," he murmured, as his hand moved under her shirt, pushing it up and over her head. His hand found her breasts. He bestowed devotion on them that made her womb contract with escalating hunger. In short order, he saw to it that her underwear found the floor.

"Now this is fairer," he murmured as he rose over her.

Shelby waited with anticipation, acceptance and an aching desire to be his again. There was no clinic, no obligation to Benton, nothing but Taylor and how he made her feel. She pulled his lips to hers as he entered her. Once again she was his.

Later, Shelby woke to the sky turning dark blue in the east and her head supported on Taylor's firm, comfy chest. His hands were clasped possessively around her waist. She'd slept the afternoon away in Taylor's arms and she'd never felt more contented.

"Hey, there. I was starting to wonder if I needed to kiss sleeping beauty awake." Taylor's deep voice rumbled from just above her. "Not that I'd mind."

"I think that would be a rather nice way to be woken up." She lifted her face. He took her hint and his lips found hers.

A long pleasurable minute later he pulled his mouth from hers and said, "I'm hungry. How about we go out for a meal?"

"Like a date?"

He shifted onto his side and looked down at her. "Yeah, a date. The kind where I come to the front door."

She couldn't remember the last time she'd been on a date. Maybe she never had. She and her husband being childhood sweethearts had meant they had attended school and church functions together, gone to college and med school, but she couldn't remember Jim ever asking her out on a real date. They had just gone places together. She liked the idea of being thought special enough to be asked out by Taylor.

She wanted this date to be memorable. It would probably be their one and only. Despite the passionate hours they'd spent in bed, nothing had really changed. Their differences weren't about Benton. They went deeper than that. Taylor couldn't move beyond his uncertainties and memories and she couldn't leave her obligations, face her own fear of change. Taylor would go back to Nashville and she'd remain in Benton. She wanted to snatch as many happy moments she could before then. After Taylor left life would go on, but it would be sadder and lonelier.

"I don't know if the neighbors can stand you showing up at the front door again. The last time you were in your boxers."

He grinned. "This time I'll make sure to have all my clothes on."

"I rather like the red plaid number."

"Then I have to make sure to wear them again for you some time." He gave her a playful swat on the behind. "So, do you want to get a bite to eat with me or not?"

"Thank you, that sounds nice," she said primly and properly. He chuckled. Something he was doing more often these days. She'd become fond of hearing that nice, easy-rolling sound. He had a wonderful laugh, one he should use often. She'd commit it to memory and pull it out late at night. She put on a bright smile. "I'll go get ready."

He ran a hand over her bare hip. "We have a few more minutes before you need to do that."

"How did you know about this place?" Shelby asked Taylor as they were being seated at a restaurant table with a crisp white tablecloth.

"I called Mrs. Ferguson and asked her advice."

"I bet she wanted to know why you were asking."

He grinned. "She did. I told her I had a date and needed advice on somewhere special to go. She said that she thought you'd enjoy coming here."

"Once again there are no secrets in Benton." She picked up the menu.

"Did you think there would be?"

He sounded much more resigned to that idea than he'd been in the past. "I guess not. I've heard of this place but I've not had a chance to try it."

"That figures."

She pursed her lips and narrowed her eyes. Taylor reached across the table and took her hand. "I shouldn't have said that. I don't want us to fight. Let's just enjoy our meal."

After the waiter took their orders and quietly moved away, Shelby said, "I feel guilty about not going to the clinic today. That's two days in the same week. I've never done that before." She looked into his warm brown eyes. "I did enjoy my afternoon, though," she said quietly.

He gave her the smile of a man who knew he'd satisfied his woman. "Why, thank you, ma'am. I believe that's the third compliment you've ever given me. I'm honored." She longed for more afternoons like the one they'd just shared but knew there was little chance of that.

"I didn't realize a smooth-talking, fast-driving, handsome doctor from the big city needed to have his ego stroked regularly."

"I think that there's at least one more compliment in there somewhere. My, with four so close together, you really make me feel special."

"Like you don't have people telling you you're wonderful all the time. Mrs. Ferguson all but melts at your feet now."

His lids went to half-mast over his darkening eyes. "That's not the same as having you say it."

She shivered with the longing Taylor evoked in her, something only he could do. "Am I that bad?"

"Yeah, in some ways. It's been pretty hard to coerce a smile out of you at times."

She gave him a bright smile she didn't really feel. "Better?"

"Perfect." He leaned over and kissed her too slowly to be appropriate in a public place but she didn't push him away.

Their meal was outstanding and Taylor turned out to be a dream dinner companion. She wasn't surprised. Over the past couple of weeks she'd found fewer of his traits to criticize.

While they ate local catfish, she and Taylor discussed their likes and dislikes from movies to books to politics. Shelby was pleased to find that they often agreed even on their food.

The only divide between them was that he hated living in a small town, couldn't see beyond his childhood memories to appreciate the good qualities. And that gulf was Grand Canyon wide, because Benton was her haven—her place of safety and security after Jim's death. But Shelby shoved those thoughts aside. Just for this one night she wanted to enjoy being with him and not have to think of tomorrow.

They were leaving the restaurant as Roger and Mary Albright were coming in. Shelby stopped to say hello. Taylor's hand rested possessively on her waist. When she tried to step away, he pulled her more securely against him, making it clear that they were out for more than a friendly meal.

"Well, hi, Shelby," Mary simpered as her gaze fell on Taylor. "And you must be the Dr. Stiles that we've been hearing so much about."

"Taylor Stiles," he said as he nodded to Mary and shook Roger's hand. "Nice to meet you both."

"We've heard all about what happened last night from Mildred Miller. She says you were heaven sent." Mary's focus remained on Taylor.

"I don't know about that." Taylor's lips curved into a small smile. He glanced at Shelby.

More like Uncle Gene sent.

"Dr. Wayne did an excellent job also." Taylor gave her waist a squeeze.

"Well, I'm sure the Hartmans were glad you were both available," Mary said smiling in too syrupy a way for Shelby's taste.

Was Mary making a veiled reference to the fact that Taylor had turned up wearing nothing but his boxers at her front door? Shelby had no doubt that Sam had told that story more than once.

As if Taylor knew where the conversation was headed, he said, "It was a pleasure to meet you both." He nudged Shelby in the direction of the door.

"That woman's the biggest busybody in town," Shelby said when they were outside on the way to the car.

"I suspected as much," he said in a flat voice. "I'm familiar with her kind."

"I guess everyone has spent their day getting caught up on us." She resigned herself to the fact that she and Taylor would be the hot topic in the town until something new and equally titillating replaced them.

"No doubt."

She glanced at him. "You okay with that?"

"That's just how small towns are. I've accepted that the good goes with the bad. The Hartman neighbors were wonderful to us last night. When I leave I can be assured that people are looking after you. That's a good thing."

They'd reached the car and Taylor held the door open for her, so with her heart in her mouth Shelby asked him directly. "Have you learned enough to consider staying for a while longer?"

"We've already covered this subject more than once." Taylor closed the door.

They remained quiet on the ride home. Apparently her optimism that their teamwork as doctors, their compatibility in bed and the fact they'd enjoyed a nice evening together hadn't changed his mind.

He pulled into the drive and turned the car engine off, leaving them in darkness. She really should have changed the bulb in the porch when it blew yesterday.She pulled on the door latch, preparing to get out. Taylor reached across and took her hand. "Wait." The shadows falling across his face accented the serious lines.

"I had a nice time. Thank you. But I'm tired and would really just like to go in." Shelby pulled her hand away, reaching for the handle again.

"Shelby, come with me to Nashville." His voice sounded as if this was a sudden thought that he'd just blurted out. "There are plenty of practices looking for another GP as partner. You're a great doctor. You'll have no trouble finding a position."

"I can't do that."

"Yes, you can. I'll help you find someone to take over the clinic. I'll even agree to work a Saturday a month for a while."

"No. This is my home. My community depends on me. I can't just pull up and leave."

He took both of her hands in his, encouraging her to face him. "Shelby, I realize and I think you do too, that what's between us is special. I don't want it to end. If you won't come with me then we'll just have to meet when we can. You come to Nashville or we can meet somewhere between there and here. I want to see you."

With a heavy heart she gave a shake of her head. "It would

never work. Long-distance relationships are hard under the best of conditions. Our schedules alone work against us. The clinic has to be my priority."

"Above everything, and apparently everybody." His words dripped sarcasm.

"What do you mean by that?"

"The clinic is your entire life. You need to stop hanging onto that dream you had as a child. You use this town, your job as a shield against the world, being hurt. Me. It's as if you are afraid to live your life. You have to let go, for your own good. You've convinced yourself that Benton needs you when it's really you that needs Benton. You're so caught up in safeguarding yourself from any pain or loss that you can't think of anything else. Can't let go. Certainly not for me."

"Are you about through?" She pulled her hands from his.

"Not yet. You can't take care of everybody else and not take care of yourself. Before long you'll have nothing left to give to anyone. What was your dream at one time? Yours alone? I bet you can't even remember."

"You seem to have all the answers for me but what about yours? You're running from your past. You hide it behind that well-respected profession you picked. All those fine clothes and the fancy car but you still carry those little-boy scars of not being good enough."

He shook his head.

"You don't believe me? Tell me, when was the last time you spoke to anyone from your home town? When's the last time you spoke to one of your brothers? Visited them?"

"That has nothing to do with us."

"It has everything to do with us. You've come to Benton and found a place where you can belong and you don't know what to do about it. Now you're scared that you might really form lasting relationships, invest in others' lives. That terrifies you because it would mean letting go of that security blanket of bitterness you carry around.

"You even refuse to see that the people of Benton like and accept you just as you are. They haven't asked you to prove yourself. What you can't see is that you're the one not accepting them." She waved trembling hands.

"Look what you have accomplished," she continued, her voice no longer gentle. "You're a doctor. And a darned good one. You've come to town and made friends. People like you. Here you could make a real difference. Here you've found that acceptance you've searched so hard for but you push it away."

Angry words hung heavily between them before Taylor asked in a tight voice, "Are you done? I see that you didn't have the same trouble with the psych rotation that you did with emergency."

Despite being unable to see his face well, Shelby had no doubt that his jaw was clenched piano-string tight. She'd hurt his feelings. Something she'd not intended to do. Still, she'd said things he'd needed to hear. She reached for him. "Taylor—"

"Look, I think we should just call it a night," he said, sliding out of the car.

She was already out and closing the door by the time he'd made it around to help her. If she didn't hurry inside she'd break down in front of him. Something she fought against doing.

He didn't touch her on the way to her door and they didn't speak. Taylor waited at the bottom of the steps, making no move to stop her from going in. She closed the door with a finality that made her heart break. She watched out the win-

dow through watery eyes as Taylor slowly climbed the stairs
to the apartment.

How was she going to survive the next two days with him
so near and them miles apart at the same time?

CHAPTER NINE

SHELBY arrived at the clinic earlier than usual on Saturday morning. She might as well be there as in her bed, willing her mind and body to stop thinking about Taylor. Her plan was to get some work done but that wasn't happening. She understood loss, had experienced it acutely, but Taylor's departure today was a deeper pain than she'd ever known.

Pushing the folders on the desk away, she crossed her arms, laid her head on them and closed her eyes. The stiffness in her shoulders remained no matter how often she'd rolled them, searching for relief. Taking a deep breath, she released it gradually, hoping the oxygen would clear her mind. Nothing could ease the despair that the next few hours would bring.

She'd feared this would happen. This horrible suffering was the reason she'd worked to keep Taylor uninvolved in her life. But it hadn't worked. He'd found a stronghold in her heart. She should've protected herself better. She would from now on.

Taking another deep breath and releasing it, she said, "Keep the connection friendly. Don't start to care. Do whatever it takes to survive."

Yesterday she'd given serious consideration to calling her uncle and bragging about Taylor, encouraging the judge to give him a day and a half's amnesty. That would at least allow the pain to be quick and sharp instead of the lingering ache she now carried. She hadn't called but only because she hadn't been able to stand the thought of Taylor leaving any sooner than scheduled. That made no sense. She'd become irrational. Her emotions were all over the place.

She and Taylor had made it through the workday Friday with little interaction. Because the clinic had been closed the afternoon before, they'd had little time to eat lunch, much less talk. Still her desire for him had simmered, threatening to burst into flame if he'd given her even the slightest touch.

She'd stayed in her office doing paperwork until her normal departure time. Hidden out, if she admitted the truth, until Taylor had left. He'd said a polite goodnight as she'd locked the door for the day. When she'd left, she'd gone to the grocery store for some much-needed staples and dog food, not trusting herself not to run into Taylor at home. She had decided to keep Buster. With a living and breathing thing around when she came home, it wasn't nearly as lonely.

To cheer herself up, she decided a haircut was in order. Plus, it would keep her away from the house until bedtime. Taylor had managed to stop her from going to her own home. Her haven. She'd become fragile where he was concerned. Her greatest fear was that she'd climb the stairs to the apartment and ask him to take her into his arms.

Enough of those thoughts. Sitting up, she pushed her clinic office chair back and went to the restroom. She studied her face in the mirror. Her eyes were bloodshot from crying and no rest. She couldn't show up looking like this to Mrs. Ferguson's tea. Turning on the cold water, she let it run until it was ice cold before splashing it in her face.

As she patted her cheeks dry, footsteps approached in the hall. She'd know those anywhere. Taylor. Pushing her hair back into place, she took a deep breath.

Opening the door, she found him propped against the wall,

his head down, shoulders slumped. His head rose. He gave her a direct look, studying her. That warmth that smoldered within her any time he came near began to bubble. The disks of darkness under both his eyes testified to the fact he'd not been sleeping any better than she had.

Her fingers spasmed with the need to pull him to her and make all that misery disappear. If she allowed that one show of weakness, she wouldn't be able to stop herself from begging him to stay. That she couldn't do. He had to want to be here or they'd never find happiness. Above all, she wished for him to be happy. Even if it wasn't with her.

"Shelby," he said longingly, as he straightened and stepped toward her.

She put a hand out, stopping his advance while being careful not to make physical contact. "Please don't." The need to feel sheltered in his embrace warred with her need to protect her heart from further pain.

"I'm sorry for those things I said," he said gently.

"I'm sorry for what I said too. How you live isn't my business."

He flinched but recovered quickly. "Can't we just start over?" his chocolatey eyes pleaded. "At least be friends."

"We are friends." With a firm resolve that Shelby would've never guessed she possessed, she said, "I think that's all it can ever be between us." She couldn't keep the melancholy out of her voice.

Taylor stepped toward her. She moved away, meeting the wall behind her. He didn't touch her but he stood close enough that she smelled the citrus of his shaving cream and the scent she knew so well. She took a deep breath, committing that aroma to memory.

"I don't want to go with this…uh…" he searched for the right word "…thing between us," he finished.

"Look, we just want different things. I can't leave and you

can't stay. It's as simple as that." But saying the words made her realize that it was so much more.

"You make it sound so final."

"Taylor, you've never led me to believe anything but that you'd be gone after your time here was over. You've been nothing but honest, so you have nothing to feel guilty about."

He moved nearer but didn't touch her. Close enough that if she inhaled deeply her breasts would brush his chest. "Come on, Shelby," he whispered in a raspy voice. "Reconsider my offer. We're so good together."

"I can't."

"Why?"

"Because I want things you can't give me."

"Like?" His breath brushed across her cheek.

Her gaze met his piercing one. "I want to work here, live here, raise a family here."

"Does it have to be all or nothing?"

"For me it does."

His hand gently cupped her cheek. "I'm sorry you feel that way. We could be so good together." His fingers caressed her skin before they fell away.

Taylor's words rang in her ears as he walked toward the front of the building.

At noon, Taylor logged out of Shelby's computer for the last time and pushed the chair back from the desk. Massaging his neck with his hands, he prepared himself for the next few hours. He had to return to Shelby's apartment and pack then attend Mrs. Ferguson's birthday tea. After that, he'd put Benton in his rearview mirror for good.

He'd already checked in with the hospital and learned he was scheduled to work the next morning at seven. He was pleased with that information because he was ready to return to the busy emergency room. There he would just practice medicine, not get involved in people's lives.

"Uncle Gene" would expect him to appear in court in the next day or so. Taylor was sure the judge would be calling Shelby for a report on how he'd done during the last two weeks. Would she let on to Uncle Gene that they had become more than colleagues? He didn't think so. He was completely confident that what happened between him and Shelby on a personal level wouldn't help his cause with the judge.

Taylor checked his watch. There was just enough time to pick up his dress shirt from the cleaners, get back to the apartment, shower and change, and pack before party time. He'd asked Carly for directions to the church, planning to leave town directly from there. He didn't even try to ask Shelby if she'd like to ride to the party with him. He already knew what her answer would be.

An hour and a half later, he came down the stairs with his bag over his shoulder. Shelby's truck was sitting out on the street. She must be inside, getting ready to attend the tea. The temptation to knock on her back door was only prevented by his better judgment. Hadn't they already said everything they needed to say?

Taylor opened the trunk of his car and tossed his bag in with more force than necessary. He stayed seated behind the wheel of the car for a moment before starting it and backing out of the drive. He'd never be required to come back here again. Mr. Marshall, the neighbor across the street, smiled and waved from his mailbox. Taylor returned the greeting then glanced at Shelby's house. What was he hoping? That she'd be looking out the window for a glimpse of him? His heart said he was leaving more than an unmade bed on this tree-lined street.

Minutes later he pulled into the parking lot of a small white clapboard church with a red-brick addition on the back. There were few cars in the lot. He'd made a point of coming early so he could be on his way back to Nashville before it got too late. He followed what looked like a family walking in the direction of the annexe. One of them carried a beautifully wrapped present.

Heck, he'd forgotten all about a gift. He'd just have to send one later. Maybe flowers.

He bet Shelby liked flowers. Were daisies her favorite or roses? Those thoughts were taking him nowhere.

He adjusted his tie. The irony that he had come full circle didn't escape him. He'd not worn these clothes since he'd arrived in town. Each day he'd become more casual in his choice of clothing. That morning he'd dressed in a T-shirt and cargo shorts to work the few hours at the clinic. Now he was back in his city clothes. He pulled at his collar.

Entering the fellowship hall, he was greeted with smiles by a couple of patients he recognized. Mrs. Ferguson, sitting in a wing-back chair at the end of the rectangular room, holding court. Children surrounded her dressed in what had to be their Sunday finest. They must be her grandchildren.

A young woman wearing a bright blue dress with large pink flowers on it approached him. "You must be Dr. Stiles. By my mother's description, I'd know you anywhere. She has nothing but high praise for you. I'm so glad you came."

Taylor smiled. Mrs. Ferguson's daughter might not look a great deal like her but she certainly had the old woman's personality. "Yes, I'm Taylor Stiles. Thank you for inviting me."

"Do help yourself to some food and tea." She indicated a long table covered in a white cloth across the room.

"Thank you, I will. But I'd like to speak to your mother first."

"She'll be glad to see you. She's so disappointed you're leaving."

He nodded, grateful that a couple entering the room caught the woman's attention.

Mrs. Ferguson smiled brightly as he approached and made

an effort to stand. "Please don't get up," he said, taking longer strides to get there before she could rise. "It's your birthday and you have the right to act like a queen today."

The woman giggled, her heavy jowls swinging. "I'm so happy you came."

"I wouldn't have missed it." He took her hand and grinned down at her. He liked the old bird. He would miss her.

"I can't talk you into staying with us? I'm sure Dr. Wayne would love to have your help."

"Dr. Stiles has a job and a life in Nashville. We can't expect him to just give that up."

He turned but hadn't needed to in order to know Shelby stood there. He heard the voice in his dreams, remembering her cries of pleasure as she reached her peak.

She wore a dress tucked and darted in all the correct places to accent the curves of her slim figure. The pale peach color complemented her complexion perfectly. Her shapely legs were showcased to their best advantage by the knee-length hem and her small feet were adorned by a pair of silver sandals.

She'd pulled her hair away from her face on one side, giving her a sophisticated look. There was a hint of pink on her lips that made him want to kiss it away. Shelby took his breath. She was a shining jewel in a room of uncut stones.

"I guess we can't ask him to completely change his life," Mrs. Ferguson said in a voice that implied she wasn't convinced.

What? Taylor was so utterly captivated by Shelby that he'd forgotten what they'd been discussing. His gaze met Shelby's for a second before she looked at Mrs. Ferguson. Her eyes held a sad but resigned look.

"Happy birthday, Mrs. Ferguson." Shelby offered a present wrapped in bright red paper. "This is from Dr. Stiles and me."

Taylor had to work to keep his surprise from showing.

"Honey, you two shouldn't have, but I do love presents."

One of the little girls playing nearby got up and came over. The child started tugging the corners of the paper off the present. "This is my fifth grandbaby, Audrey," she said, glancing up at Taylor and Shelby. "Would you like to help me open it, sugar pie?" she asked the girl. She nodded and went at the present in earnest.

Minutes later Mrs. Ferguson lifted out a floral print scarf that she promptly wrapped about her neck. "I love it. Thank you both." She smiled her pleasure.

"You're very welcome," Taylor said. "It looks wonderful on you." The woman beamed. "Dr. Wayne has good taste."

"It's does look perfect on you," Shelby said.

When another guest drew near he said, "I think I'll take Dr. Wayne over for a bite to eat. Again, happy birthday."

He cupped Shelby's elbow, counting on her not making a scene.

"Happy birthday," Shelby said, before Taylor ushered her away.

"Thank you for including me in on the present. I'd not thought to get one and was going to send her some flowers tomorrow."

"You're welcome," Shelby said, without looking at him.

He let his hand drop when she moved far enough away that he could no longer cradle her elbow.

Shelby balanced her plate on her lap as she took a sip of tea. Taylor sank onto a chair next to hers. They ate silently, as if they were strangers. She missed that simple camaraderie they'd shared so many times, longed for it again. Grief filled her for what they'd so briefly shared and lost. She cared too much for Taylor for them not to at least part as friends.

"Taylor, I'm sorry about…uh…things."

"I am too. Will you walk me out to the car?"

She wasn't sure it would make a difference in the long run

but she couldn't say no. "I guess so. We just need to stay long enough not to be rude."

A few minutes later Taylor took her plate and cup. "It's time I headed out," he said. He stood, walked over to where the dirty dishes were being gathered and placed theirs with the rest.

Her gaze followed him as he moved away in his self-assured, loose-hipped stride. He was too handsome for words. Dressed in a light blue shirt and striped tie that was no doubt silk, he sported the air of a suave and confident male. His navy slacks fit his trim hips and molded to his behind perfectly. They were supported by a thin brown belt. She smiled as she remembered the day he'd arrived. Taylor had been wearing those same shoes.

Shelby committed everything about him to memory so she could bring them out in the blackest part of the night.

As Taylor walked back to her, he smiled. This one reached his eyes. Her heartbeat did a clip-clop. She couldn't help but return it.

"Ready?" he asked, offering his hand.

"Shouldn't we say goodbye to Mrs. Ferguson?"

He glanced over at her. A group of people surrounded her. "I don't think she'll miss us."

Shelby placed her hand in his. It felt right to touch him. She let Taylor help her stand. As soon as she did, she pulled her fingers from his. Letting herself hope would only make it hurt more. They'd reached the door when "Oh"s and "Help"s rang out. She turned. Mrs. Ferguson was slumped in her chair.

"Taylor…" She grabbed his forearm for a second before they hurried to Mrs. Ferguson.

"Someone call nine-one-one," Shelby called.

"Move back," Taylor snapped in an authoritative voice that made those surrounding the limp woman react. Even the children quit playing. There was no clink of utensils on plates or sounds of laughter. Everyone was focused on Mrs. Ferguson.

Reaching the woman, Taylor went down on a knee and brushed her hair away from her face. "Mrs. Ferguson, can you hear me?" Getting no response, he said, "Help me get her on the floor."

With the help of three other men Taylor maneuvered the large woman out of the chair, cradling her head so that it wouldn't hit the floor. Her eyes remained closed. She was deathly pale and her lips were a dusky blue.

Shelby went down on her knees and placed two fingers on Mrs. Ferguson's neck to check for a pulse in her carotid artery. Taylor came down beside her.

"No pulse. We'll have to start CPR."

She checked the airway for obstructions. "I'll handle the airway. You do compressions."

Taylor removed his tie with two quick jerks and threw it to the floor. He then located the correct spot on Mrs. Ferguson's breastbone to push. Stacking his hands one on top of the other, straightening his arms and locking his elbows, he began to push down on Mrs. Ferguson's chest.

The only sound in the room was Taylor's calm but firm voice counting, "Twenty-seven, twenty-eight, twenty-nine, breath." That was her cue to lean over and give Mrs. Ferguson two breaths. Taylor continued, "One, two, three…"

Sweat popped out on his brow but she couldn't take the time to wipe it away. For what felt like an age they worked in tandem to save Mrs. Ferguson's life.

The puff of breath from Mrs. Ferguson touched Shelby's face as she went down to breathe. She sat up. Mrs. Ferguson's eyelids fluttered. Taylor must have seen it too because he stopped compressions. The woman's eyes opened, closed and opened again.

"Mrs. Ferguson, nice to see you back." Taylor gave the

woman a weak smile but sounded much more composed than Shelby felt. "Don't move. An ambulance is on the way."

Standing, he dug into his pocket and brought out his keys. Tossing them to the man nearest him, he said, "Get my bag out of my car, front seat. Red sports car."

The man hustled away.

"Don't try to speak," Shelby instructed as she picked up Mrs. Ferguson's wrist and began checking her pulse.

The man returned with the medical bag. Taylor pulled out his stethoscope and listened to their patient's chest. Done, he stuffed the instrument back into the bag. "Heartbeat's strong but not as steady as I'd like," he told Shelby.

With great relief she saw the private ambulance personnel enter the building with a gurney in tow. Not for the first time she wished the area could afford EMTs to staff the transportation but that just wasn't possible.

Mrs. Ferguson opened her eyes and looked at Taylor. "Doctor?" Her voice quivered.

Taylor took her hand. "Don't talk. You're going to be just fine." His voice was low and sweet with concern, which told Shelby he'd come to care for the feisty woman. As the ambulance personnel worked to prepare her for transport, he continued to hold Mrs. Ferguson's hand.

Without releasing her, he'd managed to pull his phone out of his pants pocket. He punched one number and gave a succinct report and rapid-fire instructions that assured his directions would be followed. He'd arranged for a cardiologist to be standing by in Trauma when Mrs. Ferguson arrived at the hospital.

Shelby continued to monitor the woman's vital signs as the ambulance personnel worked with the help of Taylor and a number of men to lift Mrs. Ferguson onto the gurney and then into the ambulance.

"I'm riding with her," Taylor announced in a tone that

dared anyone to argue with him. He climbed into the vehicle without a backward look. The doors closed with a slam of finality before the ambulance roared off, siren blaring.

Shelby stood mountain still, staring at the back of the emergency vehicle as it pulled onto the highway. A lump of finality became thick in her middle. Her heart squeezed tight in anguish. Blinking twice, three times, she tried to prevent moisture from forming in her eyes. Everything in her wanted to scream *Come back* but that wouldn't happen. Taylor was gone.

As Taylor left Benton in the back of the ambulance headed for Nashville, he made the decision not to return. He'd convinced himself that it was best for Shelby if he sent someone for his car and belongings. The truth was that he was a coward. He couldn't look into her gray eyes that compelled him to stay and say goodbye.

Mrs. Ferguson made it to the hospital without further issues but had to have surgery for two blocked arteries. She came through the operation well and recovered nicely. The only glitch, as she put it, was the rigid diet and lifestyle changes she had to agree to. The feisty old girl would make it hard on her cardiologist but she'd do as she was instructed. This time she'd been lucky.

Taylor visited her daily and spoke to her cardiologist regularly. He'd been informed by the attending doctor that Shelby had called a number of times to check on the patient. Everything in Taylor wished he'd been the one to pick up the phone when she'd been on the line. He yearned to hear her voice. When the time came for Mrs. Ferguson to be released from the hospital, Taylor was there to wheel her out.

"You need to think about where you belong, young man," Mrs. Ferguson told him firmly as he helped her into her daughter's car.

On their ride to Nashville he would've argued that it was right here, being a trauma doctor. But now…

Taylor had been confident that he'd return to his position in the emergency department as if he'd never been gone. A couple of shifts later he'd recognized he was taking more time with his patients than he'd done before, listening more carefully to their needs. The nurses had looked at him oddly when he'd requested to speak to the family of one of his patients.

One of his colleagues had asked, "Taylor, what're you doing, talking to the family? You never did that before."

"The family deserves to hear how their loved one is doing straight from the doctor. Rules can sometimes be more in the interest of the hospital than the needs of the patient and their family."

A week after his return his superior pulled him aside. "I hear you're taking time to speak to the families. As commendable as that is, I understand that it's causing a backlog on your shift. Especially on the busy nights."

"Maybe so, but I think it's important."

"In this hospital that job falls to the social workers. You need to let them do their jobs."

Taylor nodded in understanding but not in agreement. If he had to pick a point where his disillusionment with working in a large hospital began, it was then. He was no longer satisfied with caring for patients and passing them off to another doctor. Taylor wanted to follow up his patients, see their progress, continue to care for them, build relationships with them. To his shock, he sought what he'd had in Benton.

His time outside away from the hospital didn't ease his discontent with his life choices either. He missed looking out the window and being able to see the stars at night. Living in the center of a large city, the glow of lights all night didn't allow for stargazing. Regularly enjoying the sun rising over the tops of trees was out of the question also.

He'd lived on the seventh floor of a high-rise apartment building for the last three years and he still didn't know his neighbors. In less than a week he'd met everyone on Shelby's street and could call them by name. He would've never imagined something like that would've mattered to him.

More than anything, he missed Shelby. Thoughts of her were as continuous as a movie replaying over and over. Her smile, her eyes, her laugh, her touch...

Often, when he cared for a patient, he'd wonder what Shelby would say about this. How would she handle this situation? Would she do this differently? At work, at home or at social gatherings thoughts of her intruded. More than that he missed their sparring, her intellect, her soft heart. With Shelby could he have a solid relationship? Did he love her enough to try?

He'd made an effort to continue where he'd left off with his social life but it seemed dull and uninteresting after being around Shelby. She and Benton had so infiltrated his life that nothing in his old existence satisfied him any more. He missed the belonging and acceptance that he'd searched for his entire life and found in Benton. Now he wanted it back. How had the small town and a petite firecracker of a woman managed to change him so quickly, so totally?

If he had any hope of Shelby accepting him as more than a partner in the clinic, as her partner for a lifetime, he had to face the demons in his past.

CHAPTER TEN

SHELBY opened the clinic at the same time she had every workday for years. The one exception was that she didn't have the same enthusiasm she ordinarily did at the thought of a new day. The sun had risen big and bright and all she could think about was how much she'd love to spend the day taking pictures. Maybe sit in the back-yard swing and sip lemonade.

She was going to start taking some time off.

Taylor had been gone for six weeks and the truth of what he'd said was ringing true. She should train the community to see her during the hours she was open. An emergency number would always be posted if she was needed. Wednesdays were usually slow. If she took those afternoons then she'd have most of the week covered.

She'd try it starting next week. That way the word could get out. With a plan in place she went about preparing for the day with a little more spring in her step.

Flipping the computer on, she quickly checked her emails. The name Dr. Mark Singer caught her attention. Tapping a key, she opened the email and scanned the text. Dr. Singer wrote that he was interested in interviewing for a position at the clinic. He'd like her to contact him as soon as possible. Shelby's fingers flew over the keyboard as she shot off a reply. She couldn't replace Taylor in her heart but maybe she could find someone to measure up in patient care. But even that was going to be difficult.

Taylor had been gone only a few weeks but she felt his loss at the clinic daily. She'd not realized how much her workload had consumed her life until he'd been there. Weeks later the patients were still asking about Taylor, wanting to know if she had heard from him.

There were reminders of him everywhere at the clinic, in the apartment, in her kitchen, and more painfully in her heart. Since he'd left with Mrs. Ferguson he'd not called. It hurt. Terribly.

She'd seen to it that his car had been driven to her house from the church. A couple of days later she had been both surprised and offended when a uniformed stranger had shown up at the clinic.

"I'm here to pick up…" the man had looked at a paper "…a Taylor Stiles's car. I was given this address." He'd looked around as if unsure he'd been in the correct place.

"May I see that?" Shelby's hand had shaken slightly as she'd taken the official-looking sheet. Taylor's bold signature had appeared on the line in the bottom right-hand corner. She knew it well. He hadn't even bothered to come and get his car. Was he done with anything that had to do with Benton, including her?

Shelby had instructed the man to follow her home. She'd stood in the drive and watched as he'd driven away in the car. It had been the final, indisputable statement that Taylor wasn't returning.

She phoned the hospital daily to get a report on Mrs. Ferguson's progress but never spoke to Taylor. She'd not really anticipated she would. The cardiology service was in charge of Mrs. Ferguson's care now. That knowledge still didn't stop her heart from beating faster as she waited for the doctor to answer the phone or prevent the disappointment she felt when the voice on the other end wasn't Taylor's deep, sexy one.

After Carly arrived at the clinic, they went to work seeing patients. By lunchtime Shelby was ready to get off her feet. She dropped into the chair behind her desk. Selecting the correct key on the computer keyboard, she brought up her emails. There was a reply from Dr. Singer. He and his wife were going to be in the Benton area that afternoon and wondered if they might stop in and see the clinic.

Overwhelmed at the possibility of finding someone to help her at long last, she quickly responded with her phone number and that she'd love to meet him and his wife. With the idea of impressing the doctor, Shelby hustled around and saw that everything was neat and tidy in the clinic before she left for lunch.

An hour later she sat at her kitchen table, having a sandwich with her phone nearby. She pulled towards her the pile of mail she'd gotten out of the mailbox when she'd arrived home. Releasing the rubber band, she found the photography periodical she subscribed to encircling the rest of her mail. She pushed the envelopes aside and straightened out the bent magazine. Six months' worth of the same reading material was stacked on the footstool in the living room. She'd not had time to open even one of them in a long time.

That was another change she was going to make. Taking a bite out of her sandwich, she explored the glossy pages of the magazine. A photo contest advertisement caught her attention. It called for pictures taken in the outdoors. All entries would receive a critique and the winner would have a showing of their work. The pictures that she'd taken at the old house certainly met the criteria. This would be a good opportunity to receive some easy feedback on her photography and a chance to move forward towards doing more with her hobby. The due date was soon. The pictures needed to be sent in right away. This would be her first step out into the world. She'd do it.

As she took her plate to the sink, the phone rang. Setting the plate down, she hurried back to answer the call. Dr. Singer was on the line and said that he was driving into town. Shelby gave him directions to the clinic, ended the conversation and snatched up her keys. Maybe the doctor would be the solution to at least one of her problems. Only time could heal how she felt about Taylor.

"So, Dr. Singer, do you think you might be interested in working with me?" Shelby asked an hour later.

"I think this just might be the right place for me," the silver-haired man said. "What do you think, Betty?" He looked at his smiling wife.

"For a supposedly retired doctor who won't give medicine up completely, I think it would be ideal. But no more than a couple of days a week. I'll need help with our dream home."

At Shelby's questioning look, Dr. Singer said, "We heard about the lake and thought it would be a nice place to build. We'll look for a place to rent until we can buy the right lot. Hopefully I can start work in about a week."

"That sounds absolutely wonderful," Shelby said, with her first true smile since Taylor had left.

Having Dr. Singer's help wouldn't entirely solve her staffing problem at the clinic but it was a step in the right direction. No matter how good a physician Dr. Singer was, he couldn't replace Taylor. Certainly not in her heart. No one could substitute for Taylor there. It was wonderful to have the requirements of the clinic being met but what about her needs? Only Taylor could give her that. The clinic's issues were resolving while hers had intensified to an unrelenting ache in her heart.

Taylor had been right. The clinic was more than a two-person operation but having another doctor would at least satisfy the state's concerns. She'd still need to look for additional help but there was a sense of relief and release knowing now she could occasionally get away from the clinic. She was already planning how to spend her extra time off.

Maybe she would go to Nashville. She recognized Taylor had been right when she'd gotten over being mad and thought about it. She had been using her job and Benton to protect her from further unhappiness. Staying in Benton was safe for her, familiar. It offered her a haven that meant she didn't have to risk herself, her heart. It was easy to stay there and not have any conflict. Keeping Taylor at arm's length had done the same thing but it wasn't living. She refused to let any time she could spend with Taylor disappear because she was too scared to grasp it.

Was it too late to contact Taylor? She'd wanted to call him hundreds of times. Pride had stopped her. But pride was a cold and lonely bed companion in the middle of the night. Would Taylor still want her? Had he moved on?

She'd never know unless she took the chance to find out. He'd asked her to meet him halfway and she'd refused. If she wanted Taylor, she was going to have to tell him. If they both desired a relationship badly enough, they could work something out. Snatching some time here and there was better than nothing. Better than thinking about him day and night, and carrying around heartache that seemed to never ease.

Decision made. Next Wednesday, she was going to Nashville to see if Taylor was still willing to find that compromise he'd pleaded with her to consider. She hoped with all her heart he still wanted her.

Taylor slowed his car as he entered the city limits of the town he'd grown up in. His stomach knotted but he kept going. He'd not crossed this particular line since he'd been eighteen years old and that had been on his way out of town. If he'd been a betting man, he wouldn't have put money on him ever returning. He huffed. He would've lost.

As with a number of things he'd done in the last couple of months, he would've sworn it would never happen. He'd amazed himself more than once.

He'd looked on the internet for his brothers' addresses. He wasn't even sure they were still living here. There were a number of Stileses living in the area. Both brothers had such common first names that the list of possibilities was great so he'd decided to drive there, then ask around. Before going to the police station for help, he wanted to see if anything had changed. If any of the bad memories had dimmed.

Circling the stately red-brick courthouse with the white dome that still commanded the square in the heart of town, Taylor found that much about it remained the same. The stores surrounding the county building were the same type that had been there years earlier with a few new ones here and there. People mingled on the sidewalks, talking or going in and out of businesses. Nothing seemed as horrifying or uncaring as he remembered. It could have been Benton's twin town.

Astonished that he felt no animosity but curiosity instead, he turned right out of town, driving past the high school. It appeared no different than he remembered from the outside. Was there a kid in there having to fight every day to survive?

Continuing on for another mile, he made a right beside the rustic general store where old man Carr had given him those words of encouragement. He smirked. Even now there were a couple of men sitting there, talking. Nothing had changed.

The road took him out of the populated area to where the houses were spaced farther apart. As he traveled, his stomach constricted. Hadn't he buried all those ugly feelings about his father long ago? All he had to do was ride down this road to have them resurface. He went round the bend in the road and slowed to a crawl. The house he was looking for stood on the right, or at least the one he thought he was looking for. This one was nothing like he remembered.

The tiny clapboard house was painted a pristine white. The porch had large ferns hanging along the front of the porch. There was now a white picket fence surrounding the yard and late-summer flowers were blooming in the beds on either side of the wide limestone stone steps leading to the door.

Taylor would've sworn that this wasn't the boyhood home where he'd spent eighteen miserable years. It was the same house, but then again it wasn't. Now it looked like a place where a happy family lived.

A man came out the door and walked towards a truck parked on the white rock drive. A jolt of disbelief rocked through Taylor.

Matt. He looked different than Taylor remembered him but still it was his older brother. Why was he here?

Taylor pulled off onto the shoulder of the road. Taking a deep breath, he climbed out of his car. The man looked at him questioningly. Then a surprised look came over his face.

"Taylor? Is that you?"

"Hello, Matt," Taylor said flatly.

Matt came toward him and Taylor moved to meet him. "I never expected to see you again."

"And I never expected to come here again."

Matt offered his hand. Accepting it, Taylor shook it then was pulled into Matt's hug. Taylor's body tensed for a second then he returned the hug. His animosity wasn't towards his brother. He'd endured living with his father just as he himself had.

"It's so good to see you," Matt said. "Please come in. My wife and children should be back soon. I'd love you to meet them."

Taylor looked at the house, and hesitated.

"Why don't we sit on the front porch for a while?" Matt suggested.

Taylor nodded his agreement.

As they walk toward the house his brother said, "I've kept up with you, you know."

The astonishment Taylor felt must have shown on his face.

His brother grinned. "The internet makes the world a small place. I tell everyone from the old days that you became a doctor. From what I read, a good one."

They each took one of the two rockers on the porch.

"So what brought you here?" Matt asked.

"Actually, I came to see if I could find you and Bud. But I didn't think it would be so easy."

"Bud isn't in town. He's in the state pen for armed robbery. He's not due out for another five years," Matt said matter-of-factly. "I tried to help him but he was too much like Dad to listen."

Taylor felt nothing one way or the other about his brother being incarcerated. Truthfully, he was surprised he wasn't dead. The life Bud had been living when Taylor had left town had led to nothing but destruction. He'd had to deal with men like his brother during almost every night shift he'd ever worked.

"How did you come to be living here?" Taylor asked, wonder filling his voice.

"I was on the same road as Dad and Bud." His brother spoke as if he was looking into the dark past and not liking what he saw. Taylor knew well how they had been. His older brothers had been coming in drunk and high by the time Taylor had been in middle school.

"I was in and out of trouble with the law and the same with jobs until my wife came into my life. If I wanted her, I had to make a change. A major change in my life. I did and I'm a better man for it. We now have two kids. A boy and a girl. Our family..." he pointed between himself and Taylor "...wasn't pretty, no place to see an example, and I still have to work daily to beat my addiction, but life is good. We all have a past and I just choose not to let mine control me."

That was what Taylor had let his do to him and still did. Shelby had pointed that out loud and clear. If it hadn't been for her, he wouldn't be here today.

Matt lived in the same town he'd grown up in and he had been able to put his past behind him. Taylor had run away and guilded it in fast cars, society women and an expensive lifestyle. Truthfully, his brother seemed to have done a better job of dealing with his past than he had.

They rocked in silence for a while. "Why live here?" Taylor blurted. "This house?"

"Because I thought I could replace so many of my ugly memories with happy ones if I raised my family here. I could try to make this house have what Mother wanted it to have. A family who loved each other. Do you have a wife? Any children?" Matt asked.

"No."

"A good woman can change your life."

That Taylor already knew. He should take a lesson from his brother. They'd taken different roads when they'd left home but each had needed to overcome their shared past. Matt seemed to have done so, now it was his own turn.

If he hadn't hurt Shelby so badly that she no longer wanted him.

Shelby agreed to take pictures at Mrs. Ferguson's postponed birthday tea turned welcome-home party. Word had gotten out about Shelby's skills at photography when the local weekly paper was contacted about her being a finalist in the photo contest she'd entered.

After Mrs. Ferguson returned home from the hospital, she

visited the clinic to let Shelby check her over. The woman begged Shelby to take pictures at the party despite her insisting she wasn't that type of photographer. Mrs. Ferguson wouldn't take no for an answer. Giving in, Shelby decided she might as well make the most of the opportunity to add to her portfolio.

The party was winding down now, and for that Shelby was grateful. On her feet most of the day, all she could think about was propping them up, watching a good movie on TV and having Buster sit on her lap. She loved the little dog dearly, though he was a bitter-sweet reminder of Taylor.

"Dr. Stiles," someone said.

Shelby went stock still. It couldn't be.

"Hello, Mrs. Ferguson, you look wonderful."

Shelby's heart went to her throat. *Taylor.* She'd recognize that voice anywhere, even in a crowd. With her back to the door, she'd not seen him enter.

She turned. Her eyes feasted on him. He was everything she remembered and more. Charming smile, dark hair, and too handsome for words. He wore a knit shirt, tan slacks and loafers. There was a relaxed appearance about him that hadn't been there the first time he'd come to town.

Her chest ached, reminding her to breath.

What was he doing here? Had he come to town just for this party? Was there some other reason he was here? Dared she hope?

Giving herself a mental shake, she brought her camera up to her face. She struggled to steady her hands as she clicked the shutter. After all, picture-taking was what she was here for, not to gape at the people who attended. Continuously snapping pictures, she rotated to get the last of the attendees.

"Hi, Shelby."

Act cool. Don't let him see that he rattles you. "Hello, Taylor. I'm surprised to see you here."

"I figured you might be."

"What brought you back? Were you caught speeding again?" She couldn't keep the bite out of the question.

He smiled. "I was. I threw myself on the mercy of the court and asked your Uncle Gene to sentence me to Benton again."

She lowered the camera. "You are kidding, aren't you?"

"Yeah, sort of."

"What does that mean?"

He looked around the almost empty room. "You done here? I'd rather not have my driving record discussed around town if I can help it."

Nothing was secret in this town.

"I'll have to let Mrs. Ferguson know I'm leaving."

She had no idea what was going on in Taylor's mind. What she did know was that until she knew what he was doing here she wasn't going to let him hurt her again. She'd only barely managed to stop thinking about him all day long. The nights were still out of her control. Taylor dropping in for a friendly visit would be enough to tip the balance.

He waited at the door and joined her as she stepped out into the evening breeze. When her lightweight flowing silk dress threatened to blow upwards she hurriedly pushed it down.

"You know, you're the most beautiful creature." The awe in his voice made her look at him. "I've missed you. The hardest thing I've ever done was to stay away."

"Please don't…" She couldn't listen to those kinds of words from him. She so desperately wanted them to be true. Another gust of wind caught her dress. Her camera case slipped off her shoulder as she reached down to hold her dress in place.

Taylor took the bag from her and looked around the parking lot. "Where's your truck?"

"Darn, I forgot. It's in the shop. Sam had to give me a ride."

"That Sam sure is a handy guy to have around." The sarcasm in his voice didn't escape her but she didn't take the time to analyze it. He placed a hand on her waist. "Come on, I'll give you a ride home. Kind of reminds me of old times." He grinned at her.

Shelby moved away from his hand. She saw a flicker of hurt in his beautiful eyes. "I guess I don't really have a choice. Where's your car?"

"I'm driving a truck now." He led her to a blue late-model mid-size vehicle. He helped her in and closed the door before going to the driver's side.

"What happened to your car?" she asked as Taylor pulled out into the road and headed towards her house.

"I decided to give it away."

"Away? Why?" She couldn't imagine someone willingly giving away a car that nice.

"I thought she might enjoy driving it more than I did."

Pain filled her. He'd given his car to a woman. If she'd harbored any hope that he'd come to see her or that there might be a chance for them, she didn't any more. He'd found someone else. She wouldn't let him see her cry. "That's one lucky woman," she said quietly.

"She's very special. There's no one else in the world like her." Shelby didn't have to look at him to tell that he cared a great deal about the woman.

"I'm glad for you."

"Are you really?" He glanced at her and Shelby turned away, preventing him from seeing the tears threatening to spill over. It sure hadn't taken him long to find someone else.

"Yes, I am. I want you to be happy."

"I hope she'll accept it and me along with it."

The fingers of Shelby's right hand clutched the doorhandle

as the one in her lap curled into a fist. Why didn't he drive faster? All she wanted to do was get home, close the door and crawl into bed. "Why wouldn't she? You're a great guy."

"I haven't always been. I hurt her and I'm not sure she'll have me now."

"Just tell her how you feel. I'm sure she'll forgive you." Her voice started to break. She didn't want to have this conversation. Giving advice to the lovelorn, especially where it concerned Taylor, wasn't something she was emotionally strong enough to handle.

"So all I have to do is say I love you?" he asked.

She turned to face him. "Why are you here, Taylor? Why're you telling me all this?" Thank goodness he'd turned into her street. She waited for his answer. "Why, Taylor?"

"Because I thought we were friends."

He had a twisted idea of what her friendship meant. She couldn't do this any more. "There's no need to turn into the drive. Just pull up in front of the house."

"I don't think so. A gentleman sees that a lady gets home safely."

She wanted to slap the grin off his face. Didn't he know this was killing her? How could he be so dense?

"Taylor for heaven's sake!"

"Okay, if that's what you want." He pulled to a stop at the end of her drive.

She gathered her camera bag and climbed out of the truck, not looking at him or even where she was going. She just needed to get away. To breathe again. All those hopes and dreams of going to him in Nashville had turned to ash.

Not looking back, Shelby hurried up the drive. She was halfway to the back door when she made out the color red through watery eyes. Rubbing the dampness away, she saw Taylor's car sitting there with a large silver bow on top. She slowly lowered her camera bag to the ground. Her body flushed. "What?"

"As large an apology as I owe you, I figured flowers might not cover it," Taylor said from right behind her. "I hoped the car might ease the way."

Shelby's heart had gone into warp drive and didn't seem to be slowing down. "I kind of like flowers," she mumbled, a grin forming on her face.

"That figures. My little she-cat never disappoints. I come to you with my heart in my hand and you're not satisfied." He chuckled dryly. "Shelby, aren't you going to look at me?" Taylor asked quietly.

"You said you loved the woman you gave the car to."

"I did, and I do. With all my being." He still hadn't touched her, as if he was afraid of her reaction. "I'll live in Benton if that's what it takes. I want you to be a part of my life, every day, always."

She still couldn't move. It was her dream coming true.

"Shelby, please turn around. You're scaring me."

She slowly rotated, looking at him. His dear face for the first time she could remember lacked confidence. Did he really believe she might turn him down?

"Taylor Stiles…" she punched him playfully in the shoulder "…why did you make me think you were talking about another woman?" She gave him a light swat on the shoulder this time before her arms slid up to circle his neck and pull his mouth down to hers. "I love you too," she said softly against his lips. Seconds later he crushed her to him and took control of the kiss.

Some time later Taylor pulled back but didn't let go of her. For that she was glad, she couldn't have stood on her own anyway.

"Nice to see you back, Taylor," Mr. Marshall called. "Planning to stay around, I hope."

"That I am," Taylor replied with such conviction she knew he meant it. "For ever," he whispered into her ear.

"Glad to hear it," the man responded.

Releasing her enough to pick up the camera bag, Taylor said, "Let's take this inside."

It could have been hours or days later for all Shelby knew she was so caught up in the fog of bliss that Taylor created by being in her bed. As she was lounging against him while they ate peanut butter and jelly sandwiches and drank iced tea, she couldn't remember being happier.

"You know, when the man from the service came to get your car, I was sure I'd never see you again."

"I thought it best at the time."

"Why?"

"Because I didn't want to hurt you any more than I already had. Now I know it was because I was afraid. I couldn't say no to you if you asked me to stay again."

"Was I that hard to resist?"

He kissed her shoulder. "Oh, yes, you were." Then he nipped at the same spot. "Still are. I've been running away. Now I'm running to what I want—you."

She smiled at him. "Uncle Gene said you needed to slow down some, take a look at yourself. I guess he knew what he was talking about."

"You should've seen the look on his face when I told him I planned to marry his niece." Taylor chuckled. A sound she loved.

"When he sent me here I'm not sure he meant for me to join the family."

"What made you change your mind about living here? You were so adamant."

"I found out when I got back to Nashville that I wasn't happy without you and by some measure without Benton. It was a physical hurt to be away from you. I wasn't satisfied with my work, my home or my life there any more. Here I felt good about myself." He paused a second. "I've never seen a healthy relationship up close. Heavens knows, my parents didn't have one. I'm not sure I know how one works. Please be patient with me."

She gave him a gentle reassuring kissed. "Not a problem."

Looking down at her softly he said, "I love you."

"And I love you."

Taylor shifted slightly. "I went back to my hometown. Saw one of my brothers."

She turned and placed a hand on his cheek. "I know that had to be hard for you. I'm sorry I wasn't there for you."

"That's okay. It was something I had to do on my own. I'd like to take you with me to meet my brother some time soon."

"I'd enjoy that."

Buster made a whimpering noise from the floor and Taylor reached down, picked him up and placed him on the bed. "Have you been taking good care of my lady for me, boy?" Taylor asked, scratching Buster behind his ears.

"Yeah, we took care of each other. He missed you almost as much as I did," Shelby said, petting the dog.

"I'm surprised you had time to miss me. I heard all about you being a finalist in the photo contest."

"Thanks to your encouragement and handsome face. How did you know?"

"Mrs. Ferguson," they said in unison.

"You were right about me hiding out here. The photo contest was my first step towards my new life. I was coming to see you on Wednesday."

"You were?"

"Yes. You just beat me to it by coming here today." She grinned up at him.

"Can I have my car back, then?"

She gave him a playful swat on the belly. "You cannot!"

His mirth was a low rumble in his throat. "What was that you said about my handsome face?"

"I sent in the pictures I took of you at the old house. The judges loved them."

He moaned.

"That's the price you pay for being so good looking."

"You're not hard on the eyes either." His hand slipped under the sheet to run along the ridge of her hip.

She grabbed his wrist, stopping it short of moving up the inside of her thigh. "Before you distract me, let me tell you my other news. I have a doctor who's going to help out at the clinic two days a week."

"So you liked Mark. I thought you would."

Shelby glared at him.

Looking unconcerned, Taylor's gaze focused on her bare breasts.

Pulling the sheet up to cover herself, she said, "You know Dr. Singer?"

He nodded and tugged on the sheet. It slipped to reveal the top curve of one breast.

"You sent him?"

"I did, but his agreeing to work at the clinic was all about your considerable charm. Do you think there's a place for me also?"

"You know there is."

He tugged on the sheet again but she held it securely. "I'd like to lease one of the larger spaces so that we could dedicate part of the clinic to trauma care. The people of Benton and the surrounding area need to have a place close to come in case of an emergency. What do you think?"

"That's a great idea. Thank you, Taylor. You do know that because of you Benton will get to keep its clinic."

His eyes darkened. "I think you should show your appreciation." He gave the sheet a harder tug but she didn't let go, giving him a teasing, come-hither smile. Her heart beat fast when his heated gaze met hers. With one swift movement of his hand the sheet was jerked away and he reached for her.

His lips met hers, replacing the past with the passion of the present and dreams of the future.

* * * * *

BRINGING HOME
THE BACHELOR

SARAH M. ANDERSON

To Mary, the most responsible oldest sibling I've ever met! You've been with me for every step of the way and I truly couldn't do it without you. We may not be sisters, but we're friends and for that I'm forever grateful.

One

In the middle of the argument—the same argument Jenny had with her teenage son every morning—she found herself lost in a daydream. Just once, she wanted someone to take care of her. Just once, she wanted to feel pampered. *Just once,* she thought with a sigh, she wanted to know what it was like to have the world at her feet, instead of having everyone walk all over her.

"Why can't I go with Tige after school?" her son, Seth, whined from the passenger seat. Not that a fourteen-year-old boy would cop to whining. "He got a new motorcycle, said I could ride it. Better than wasting time waiting on you to get done with your stupid meeting."

"No motorcycles," Jenny said in the tone she used for attempting to reason with her first and second graders when her patience was thin. Hopefully, she and Seth would make it to school before she lost her temper. Only a few miles to go. She drove faster.

"Why not? Josey rides hers all over the place, and you know she wouldn't do it if it wasn't safe."

"Josey is a grown woman," Jenny said through gritted teeth. This was the difference between fourteen-year-old

Seth and eight-year-old Seth. The boy had always been able to tell when he shouldn't press his luck. "Josey's husband taught her how to ride, she's never had an accident, and you know good and well that she hasn't been on a bike since she got pregnant." Seth shuddered in immature horror. "May I remind you that Tige is a seventeen-year-old boy who drives too fast, doesn't own a helmet and has already crashed his bike twice? *No. Motorcycles.*"

"Aw, Mom. You're not being fair."

"Life isn't fair. Get used to it." Seth rolled his eyes so hard she heard it in the dark.

"If my dad were still here, he'd let me ride."

Before she could come up with a coherent response to Seth's newest favorite guilt trip, she rounded the last curve before the Pine Ridge Charter School, where she taught two grades in one classroom. Trucks and cars were parked everywhere, with massive, stadium-style lights ripping through the soft dawn light.

Shoot, Jenny thought as Seth leaned forward to stare at the three-ring circus. The battle with Seth had made her forget that today was the first day of filming at the school.

The Pine Ridge Charter School was the only school for grades one through eight within a two-hour drive. The school had been funded and built by her cousin Josey White Plume and her aunt, Sandra White Plume. They'd finished it before the first day of school last fall, mostly thanks to the donations of Crazy Horse Choppers, which was run by Ben Bolton and his brothers, Billy and Bobby. The Bolton boys made money hand over fist with their high-end, *very* expensive motorcycles. Josey had wound up marrying Ben Bolton—and was now pregnant with their first baby.

If that were all there was to it, it would be weird enough. But the crazy didn't stop there. Oh, no. Bobby Bolton had been filming "webisodes"—which Jenny didn't even think was a real word—of Billy Bolton building motorcycles at the Crazy Horse shop and posting the videos on the internet. Apparently, they were getting hundreds of thousands of hits, mostly because Billy cussed like a drunken sailor and occasionally threw tools at people. Jenny didn't have an internet connection, so she hadn't seen the show herself. She didn't want to. It sounded like entertainment aimed at the lowest common denominator.

But now the whole production had moved to her school. Billy Bolton was supposed to build a bike on site, teach the students how to use the tools and then the Boltons were going to auction the bike off and give the proceeds to the school. Bobby was going to film the whole thing.

Jenny didn't know which part of this plan she liked the least. Ben wasn't so bad. He was focused, intense and looked good on a bike, but he was a little too elite for Jenny's taste. He made Josey happy, though, so that made Jenny happy.

Bobby, the youngest of the Bolton brothers, talked to her only when he wanted something. He was handsome and charming and fabulously rich and she supposed that was more than enough for most women, but she didn't trust him.

She trusted Billy, the oldest, even less. He was—well, she didn't know if he was an actual Hell's Angel, but she wouldn't have been the least bit surprised to know he was in some sort of semicriminal biker gang. He was a massive man who everyone seemed mildly-to-severely afraid of. When she'd been introduced to him at Josey's wedding, he'd given off a vibe that had been something between quiet, dangerous and sexy. The combination had been thrilling—or would have been if she'd let herself be thrilled. He'd been a sight to behold, with his brown hair pulled back into a ponytail, a neatly trimmed beard and a tuxedo that fit him like a glove.

Like the other two Bolton brothers, Billy was gorgeous in his rough way and richer than sin—but of the three of them, he had waved his wealth around the least. Ben wasn't showy, but everything he owned was the best. Bobby let everyone know how rich and popular he was. But Billy? It was almost as if the family money pissed him off. Jenny had been struck mute by the way he'd glared down at her. She'd barely been able to squeak out a "pleased to meet you."

And now that man was going to have the run of *her* school and interact with *her* students.

It was one thing for that man to make her nervous while she was wearing a frilly dress at a wedding that cost more than her house and car put together. It was a whole different thing if that man looked at one of her students with that glare. She would not tolerate a whiff of improper, indecent or dangerous behavior from any Bolton, no matter how muscled he was. One step out of line, and Billy Bolton would find out exactly what kind of woman she was.

She pulled into her regular parking spot, and Seth was already out the door, gawking as a small group of people scurried around. Jenny was usually the first person at the school. She liked easing into the morning before a bunch of six-, seven- and eight-year-olds descended on her classroom. She made some tea, made sure she had all of her supplies ready and got herself mentally prepared for the day. And since Seth usually hung out in the multipurpose room practicing guitar, it was as close to Zen as Jenny got.

But today? No Zen for her. Instead, a woman yelled, "We have a problem—car in the shot," into a walkie-talkie as she brushed past Jenny while a man adjusted the lights—and managed to blind her with the beam.

Before she could shade her eyes, a figure spoke from beside her. "Jennifer? Hi, Bobby Bolton. We met at the wedding. Great to see you again. So glad to be out here, doing something good for the school. You do good work out here, and we're thrilled to be a part of it, but we're going to need you to move your car."

Jennifer. The hackles went up on the back of Jenny's neck. Yes, he'd been trying to compliment her, but her name was not Jennifer. It never had been. She had the legal documents to prove it. She was Jenny Marie Wawasuck.

She swung around slowly—slow enough that she heard Seth make a noise that sounded like *snerk.* Even a teenaged boy knew better than to call her *Jennifer.*

"Excuse me?" was the most polite thing Jenny could come up with.

Bobby had on a headset, and despite looking like the kind of guy who rarely got up before noon, he was as good-looking as ever. "As I'm sure you know, Jennifer, we're doing the shoot this morning. We're going to need you to move your car."

It was awfully early to have her last nerve snap, but it did. "Why?"

Bobby gave her the kind of smile that made her want to punch him in the stomach. "We're setting up a shot of Billy riding in, and we need the space." Bobby's voice was less complimentary now, more a direct order. "Move your car."

Of all the arrogant…Jenny paused—a trick she'd learned long ago worked on children of all ages to command attention. She drew herself up to her full height of five foot five inches, but she was still a good eight inches shorter than Bobby. She hated craning her neck, but she didn't have a stepstool handy.

"No. This is my spot. I always park here." Part of her knew she was being a tad irrational—it's not like moving the car was a huge deal—but she didn't want Bobby Bolton to think he could steamroll her whenever he felt like it.

Too often, too many people thought they could flatten her. They thought she wouldn't put up a fight because she was a nice girl or because she taught little kids or because she had nothing—especially that. Nothing but a parking spot.

Bobby's smile disappeared and he suddenly looked tired. "I know this is your spot, but I'd think a grown woman could handle parking somewhere else for one day. Thanks so much. Vicky?" he said into his headset. "Can we get Jennifer some coffee? Thanks." He turned his gaze back to her, and his fake-happy smile was back. "I know it's early, but once you move your car and have your coffee, I'm sure you'll feel better, Jennifer."

Jenny bristled under his patronizing tone, but before she could tell him that she didn't drink coffee, much less restate her position about not moving her darned car, a shadow loomed behind her, blocking out the spotlight.

A shiver raced up her arms and across her neck as a deep, powerful voice said, "Her name isn't Jennifer." As if to emphasize this point, a massive fist swung out from the shadows and hit Bobby in the arm so hard that he had to take a few steps back to keep his balance. "It's Jenny. Stop being a jerk."

Jenny swallowed as Billy Bolton brushed past her and stood next to his brother. She was not afraid of this man, she reminded herself. So what if he was a foot taller than she was, wearing really expensive-looking leather chaps over a pair of jeans and a tight-fitting black T-shirt that didn't look like the kind that cost seven dollars at Walmart? So what if he had on sunglasses and the sun hadn't even broken through the horizon? So what if he looked like some sort of bad-biker-boy fantasy come true?

He was on her territory, by God. She would not cower, and that was *that*.

So she squared her shoulders, put on her don't-mess-with-me glare and stood her ground. Then she realized what Billy had said.

He knew her name.

Weird goose bumps spread from her neck down her back. She would have been willing to bet that he wouldn't have been able to pick her out of a lineup, but here he was, punching Bobby because he'd called her the wrong name.

My school, my rez, she repeated to herself as she cleared her throat. "Right. Well, have fun making your little movie, gentlemen." She turned to walk into the building at a slow, deliberate pace, but Bobby circled around.

"We haven't solved our problem."

"Problem?" Billy asked. Jenny felt his voice rumble through her. She remembered now that he'd invoked that same sort of physical response in her the other time they'd met, too.

"Jennif—Jenny's car is in the shot." Bobby quickly corrected himself before Billy took another swing at him. "We need to get you on the bike riding up to the school with the sunrise, and her car will be in the way. I've asked her to move it—for the day," he added, giving her another sexy smile, "but because it's early and she hasn't had her coffee, she hasn't yet seen the value of temporarily relocating her vehicle."

What a load of hooey dressed up in double-talk. Did he think he could confuse her with a bunch of fancy language and the kind of smile that probably melted the average woman?

"Just because Josey gave you permission to film at this school does not mean I'm going to let you and your 'crew' disrupt my students' educations," she said through a forced smile.

Then something strange happened. Billy looked at her, leaned forward, took a deep breath—and appeared to be savoring it. "She doesn't drink coffee," he said as the woman Jenny had seen earlier walked up with a steaming mug of the stuff.

Okay, Billy Bolton was officially freaking her out. Jenny had been more or less invisible to the male race for—well, how old was Seth? Fourteen? Yes, fourteen years. No one wanted to mess with a single mother, and a mostly broke Indian one at that.

But Billy? He was not just paying attention to her name, or what she smelled like. He was paying attention to *her*. She had no idea if she should be flattered or terrified.

"You're not going to move your car?" he asked.

"No."

She couldn't see his eyes behind his glasses, but she got the feeling he was giving her the once-over. Then, with a curt nod, he turned around, walked to the front bumper of her car and picked up the whole dang thing. With his bare hands. True, it was a crappy little compact car that was about twenty years old, but still—he picked it up as if it didn't weigh much more than a laundry basket. If she wasn't so mad right now, she'd be tempted to do something ridiculous, like swoon at the sight of all his muscles in action. He was like every bad-boy fantasy she'd ever had rolled into one body.

"Hey—*hey!*" Jenny yelled as he rolled her car about thirty feet away and dropped it in the grass with a thud. "What the heck do you think you're doing?"

"Solving a problem." Billy dusted his hands off on his chaps and turned to face her, as if he regularly moved vehicles with his bare hands. "You."

That absolutely, totally *did it*. It was bad enough she had to take a constant stream of attitude from her son. She'd tried being nice and polite—like the good girl she was—but what had that gotten her? Nothing but grief.

"You listen to me, you—you—*you*." Before she knew what she was doing, she'd reached out and shoved—actually shoved—Billy Bolton.

Not that he moved or anything. Pushing his chest was

like pushing against a solid wall of stone. And all those stupid goose bumps set off again. She ignored them.

"I am not here for you or your brother or his film crew to treat like garbage. I am a teacher. This is my school. Got that?"

She thought she saw Billy's mouth curve up into something that might have been a grin. Was he laughing at her?

She reached up to shove him again—not that it would hurt him, but she had this irrational thought that something physical might be the only thing a man like him understood.

This time, Billy captured her hand with his massive fingers and held it. In an instant, all those goose bumps were erased by a licking flame of heat that ran roughshod over her body.

With effort, she held on to her anger and wrenched her hand away from his. "You listen to me—I don't care how big or scary or rich or famous you are—you're at my school, on my rez, mister. You make one mistake—touch one student, say something inappropriate—I'll personally grind you up into hamburger and feed you to the coyotes. Do I make myself clear?"

Billy didn't say a thing. He looked at her from behind his dark shades. The only reaction she could see was the possible curve of his lips behind his beard, but she couldn't even be sure about that.

"*Mom,*" Seth said from behind her.

"We need to get filming, Jenny," Bobby added. He stepped between her and Billy and tried to herd her away.

She leaned around Bobby and leveled her meanest glare at Billy. "We aren't done here." Then she turned around and stomped off.

As she went, she swore she heard Billy say behind her, "No, I don't think we are."

Two

Billy stood there, thinking that his day had taken a turn for the better.

Had that pretty little cousin of Josey's really threatened to feed him to the coyotes? Man, no one threatened him anymore—except for his brothers. Everyone else either knew about his Wild Bill reputation—even though all that stuff had happened more than ten years ago—or they knew he had enough money to sue them back into the Dark Ages.

Hell, the pretty little woman named Jenny probably knew both of those facts—and she had threatened him anyway. He ran his fingers over the spot on his chest where she'd amusingly tried to shove him—right where he had a rose wrapped in thorns tattooed. He could still feel the warmth from her touch. How long had it been since a woman had touched him?

He'd always had terrible taste in women. He had the scars to prove it. He'd had other offers since the biker babes who used to hit on him—high-class women who were more interested in his newly made money than him. But Billy wasn't interested in having his heart ripped out again. And he usually threw off enough stay-away vibes to scare most women away.

In fact, if memory served, he had been sure that Jenny Wawasuck had been afraid of him when they'd met at Ben and Josey's wedding. He supposed he hadn't helped put her at ease.

Josey had asked him to wear a tux to her wedding in such a sweet way that he'd dug deep into his closet to find the one he'd had custom-made a few years ago when Bobby had insisted on dragging him to some sort of posh party in Hollywood. Even though it was his own suit, and fit well, the bow tie hadn't done anything to improve his mood. Seeing how happy his brother had looked getting married had been just another reminder of what Billy didn't have.

Jenny had been this cute little thing—nothing like the kind of woman he'd taken home back when he'd hit the bars as Wild Bill. And nothing like the vacuous, high-maintenance women he'd run into when Bobby forced him into those high-society parties. Her long hair had been curled but not teased, and her bare shoulders had been free of any kind of ink. She'd looked beautiful that day. She'd obviously been the kind of sweet, good-natured woman who avoided the likes of him. And the fact that he hadn't come up with a single decent thing to say to her?

Damn. The memory still made him burn.

Of course, she wasn't his type—and her type never went for guys like him. Easier to let it go at that.

Now, he turned to Bobby and let his brother shoo him onto his bike and instruct him to drive up and down the gravel road to school until the film crew told him to stop. Bobby had this irritating habit of wanting twenty takes for every ten seconds of footage. Normally, it drove Billy nuts, but today he was glad to have the chance to think.

He did his best thinking on his bikes. Usually, that meant solving the latest design problem or figuring out how to work around his dad or brothers. But today, riding up and down the same mile of territory that hardly qualified as a road, the problem he found himself thinking about was Jenny.

She'd smelled of baby powder, a soft scent that matched the woman he'd met at the wedding but seemed out of place on the woman who'd threatened him. Not a hint of coffee, and he knew Josey preferred tea when she was on the rez. The guess hadn't been a huge leap, but the way Jenny's eyes had widened when he'd been right? Worth it.

He still couldn't get over how she'd promised it wasn't over. Maybe he was getting soft in his thirties, but he found himself hoping she was right.

Finally, after an hour of rolling up and down the same mile, Bobby decided they had the footage he wanted. By that time, the school was overflowing. All the kids were there, and a fair number of their parents had come to watch, too.

Back when he'd earned his reputation the hard way, people had been in awe of him. Some had wanted to be on his good side, some had tried to prove they were bigger or badder. People's reactions had only gotten worse since this whole webisode thing started. People were watching him, expecting him to be funny or crude or what, he didn't know. All he knew was they were here for Wild Bill Bolton. And he hated it.

His brother Ben's wife, Josey, came up to him as he parked his bike next to the shop where they were going to be building the bike. "Morning, Billy," she said. "Everything go okay so far?"

Right. No doubt Jenny had had a little powwow with her cousin. "Bobby's still an ass—"

"Language! There are children present!"

It was going to be such a long day. "Twit. Bobby's still a twit."

Josey sighed. "Billy, remember the rules."

"Yeah, yeah, I know—language, attitude, no throwing things."

Josey patted him on the arm. "It's just three weeks."

Sure, it was only three weeks at the school, but he was stuck with Bobby running his life for the foreseeable future. He'd only agreed to do this show because Ben said this was a good way to justify the cost of new equipment for the shop, and Billy loved new equipment. Hell, testing out a new tool was half the fun of building a bike. Plus, he'd thought it was a good way to keep the peace in the family. Now he wasn't so sure.

Sure, Billy guessed it was nice that people recognized him now, and yeah, it was probably good for his ego that someone had started a Facebook page called The Wild Bill Bolton Fan Club. But most of him wanted "Real American Bikers," which was what Bobby called the webisodes, to fail and fail big. That way, he could go back to doing what he did best—building custom motorcycles. No more cameras, no more groupies, no more being famous.

Back to building his bikes in peace and quiet.

Although that didn't look like it was going to happen anytime soon. "Real American Bikers" was getting a healthy number of hits on YouTube, where Bobby was hosting a channel for it—whatever the hell that meant. Billy hadn't actually watched more than about two minutes of the show. It was too painful. Too much of a reminder that he could never really leave his Wild Bill reputation behind him.

"Oh, here comes Don Two Eagles," Josey was saying as she waved an older guy over. "Don, this is—"

"Billy Bolton. You look like your old man," Don said. Didn't sound like a compliment, and Billy sure as hell didn't take it as one.

Ben had told Billy all about Don. "You're the guy who broke Dad's jaw back at Sturgis in the eighties, right?"

"Damn straight," Don said.

"Language!" Josey snipped as she checked to see if any kids had been listening.

"I put your old man down, and I ain't afraid to do the same to you, so you best behave, hear?"

"Don," Josey said under her breath. Billy got the feeling that this was a conversation they'd had before. Then she turned on the charm. "Now, the kids are going to come out and line up. Bobby thinks it'll be a nice shot if we introduce some of the older students to you personally and you shake their hands, so we'll start filing them past you. Can you handle that?"

"Yes."

"I'll be watching you," Don said before being called away by the production crew.

"Heavens, can you believe Bobby actually wants to bring your father out here and let him and Don go at it?" Josey's voice dropped down to a whisper. "Sometimes I don't know about that brother of yours."

"Makes two of us."

This was why he liked Josey. She understood how the Bolton family worked and was committed to keeping it from imploding. Ben had picked well.

Then he heard himself ask, "Will Jenny be bringing her class out?"

Josey gave him an odd look. "No, the first and second graders aren't allowed in the shop."

"I wasn't trying to break her car," he added.

"I know. Just solving a problem. That's what you do best, Billy." She patted him on the arm again—she had that whole mothering thing down.

Billy was about to rub the dust off his tires when Vicky,

the production assistant, came up to him. "We need to get you miked, Billy."

Vicky definitely fell into the category of women who were afraid of him. Her production company, Villainy Productions, sounded far tougher than she was. Miking Billy usually involved taping a mike to Billy's chest, and she didn't seem to think his tattoos were impressive.

"Well," she said, surveying the fitted T-shirt Billy wore. "I guess…you're going to have to take the shirt off?"

Billy grabbed the hem of his T-shirt, but before he could peel it off, the doors to the school burst open and about fifty kids came pouring out. Almost immediately, Josey was next to him, a hand on his arm. "Can we do this somewhere else?"

Vicky swallowed. She worked real hard on not being alone with him. Which was funny—Bobby was the much bigger threat to the female race. Billy hadn't even been with a woman in…

Damn. That turned into a depressing train of thought. The fact was, it'd been a long time since he'd gotten tired of going home with the kind of woman who looked like she was auditioning for a heavy-metal music video and waking up alone. Years.

Since then, he'd thrown himself into building bikes. Which wasn't such a bad thing—it kept him out of trouble. He was good at it, which had made him a boatload of money—also not a bad thing. However, with the money had come a different kind of woman—older, richer, more mercenary, if that were possible. Billy had no interest in those women. None. The one time he'd dated a woman out of his league, he'd gotten his heart run over like roadkill. It was easier just to build more bikes.

But now building bikes was making him famous. Hell, half the time he was afraid to leave his house in the morning. A few groupies had showed up at the Crazy Horse shop and tried to treat him like a rock star, screaming and even throwing a pair of panties. Which Bobby had filmed—if he hadn't set the whole thing up in the first place. No way, no how was Billy falling into that trap. He'd rather be alone than be with a woman who was only interested in using him.

Which meant he was alone.

"Go around the side of the school. We can't have him stripping out here in front of the students," Josey said before hurrying over to help explain the rules to the kids.

Not that it was stripping, but yeah, even he saw the wrong in taking off his shirt in front of kids. He had tattoos—lots of them. The kind that scared small children and little old ladies.

So he trudged around to the side of the building with Vicky following at a safe distance and whipped off his shirt. Vicky clipped the battery pack to his jeans, ducked under his upraised arm, and handed him the mike while she ripped off a piece of medical tape. They'd learned after the first show that clipping the mike to the collar of Billy's shirt didn't work—too much static from the machines ruined the audio feed. Now they taped the mike to his chest and let the shirt filter out the extra noise.

Vicky handed him the tape, and he put the mike on above the rose and thorns—above where Jenny had touched him.

As the thought of the sassy little teacher crossed his mind again, his ears developed a weird burning sensation, as if someone were talking about him. He glanced around and saw that—much to his chagrin—an entire class of undersized tykes was crowded around the windows, staring at him.

And behind them stood a shocked Jenny Wawasuck.

Her eyes were as wide as hubcaps and her mouth had

dropped open as she looked at his exposed torso. Billy froze—he was pretty sure this violated someone's rule.

If he were Ben, he would probably figure out some calm, cool way to exit the situation and mitigate the damage. If he were Bobby, he would flex and pose for the pretty little teacher. He wasn't either of them. And as such, he had no idea what to do besides brazen it out. So he stood there and stared back at her, almost daring her to come out and turn him into coyote food.

She said something sharply to the kids, who all scrambled back from the windows as if she'd poked them with a cattle prod. Then she shot him the meanest look he'd ever seen a woman give him—which was saying something—then pulled the blinds.

The whole thing took less than a minute.

Damn. He was screwed. The only question was, how badly? Would she kick him off this rez? Would Don Two Eagles do the kicking?

He sighed. This was how things went. He wasn't trying to stir up trouble, but it always found him anyway. All he could do now—since he'd promised to watch his language and not throw things—was wait for Jenny to storm out of the building and tear him a new one.

It'd be easier if it were Don. Billy knew men like Don, knew how they thought, knew what to expect. But a woman like Jenny was something else, someone he didn't know and couldn't anticipate. A sweet little first-grade teacher—with one hell of an edge to her.

Given the way his thoughts kept turning back to when she'd touched him this morning, he was going to be spending a lot more time trying to anticipate her.

Resigned to his fate, Billy slid his shirt back on and went out to his assigned position. He'd never understood why he had to be the one on camera—other than the fact that he was the one who built the bikes. Ben didn't have to be on camera at all. Bobby was the one who had the Hollywood thing going on, from the way he wore a tie every day to the way he talked circles around everyone. Times like this, Billy wished he could be as smooth as Bobby. The man was good with people—well, people who weren't Jenny Wawasuck.

Billy stood there, keeping an eye on the door as the smaller kids were introduced to him in a group. Where was Jenny? Surely she wouldn't let such an offensive act as taking off his shirt in front of a bunch of first and second graders pass. Flashing a lifetime of ink at a bunch of little kids didn't seem like something Jenny Wawasuck would let stand.

As he started shaking the hands of the bigger kids, the ones who'd be "helping" him build the bike for charity, Billy realized two things. One, Jenny wasn't going to come out and pick another fight with him, and two—he was disappointed.

One of the kids shook his hand and said, "Hi again, Mr. Bolton." Billy's attention snapped back to the present.

The kid looked familiar. Billy didn't have a head for names and faces, but he knew he'd met him before. "I know you, right?"

"We met at Josey's wedding," the boy said with a stammer. "I was an usher."

"Yeah." Billy shook his hand again. Probably some sort of nephew or cousin or something. "See you in the shop."

The kid's face brightened up. He couldn't be much more than thirteen. Billy remembered being that age once—although he tried not to think about it too much.

He got to the end of the line and mercifully, Bobby didn't make them do the whole meet-and-greet thing all over again. Don and Josey began herding the kids into the shop to set up the next shot—Billy explaining how the kids were going to help him—when it happened.

The back door of the school swung open and out stepped Jenny. Billy's temperature spiked, which didn't make a damn bit of sense. Now that he could see her in the full light of the morning, he noticed she had her long hair pulled back into a boring bun-thing at the base of her neck. She wore a white-collared shirt under a pale blue cardigan, all of which was over an exceptionally plain khaki skirt. The whole effect was of someone trying not to be noticed.

Billy noticed her anyway, his heart rate picking up an extra few RPMs. She shouldn't look sexy to him—but she did. Underneath that schoolmarm appearance was a hot-blooded woman with a smart mouth who wasn't afraid of him. The combination was heady.

She stood on the steps, hands on hips that couldn't be hidden by her boring skirt, and glared at him. Normally, Billy would either stare her down—he did that all the time—or turn away and pretend he hadn't seen the disapproval in her eyes.

Instead—and this was insane—he gave her a mock salute, just to make her mad all over again. He couldn't help himself. What had she thought of all the tattoos? Did they scare her, or had she liked them for the art they were?

"We need you inside," Bobby said, once again stepping between Billy and Jenny. Over Bobby's shoulder, Billy saw Jenny make a motion with her hands that perfectly conveyed both her disgust and also her fury before she turned and went back inside.

No, this wasn't over. Not by a long shot.

Three

Billy needed a drink.

Not that he drank much anymore, but still. A day of having to watch his temper around kids who kept picking up his tools and putting them down in the wrong places. A whole day of Bobby making him say the same thing over and over in different positions. A long day of *not* building a bike.

Better be a stiff drink.

It was almost over. The kids had, by and large, gone home. Only that one kid, the one he'd met at Josey's wedding, was still in the shop. Billy had been allowed to take his mike off, and while Bobby and his production crew were still doing things, none of them required Billy to smile for a camera.

What was that kid's name? Billy thought hard, but he drew a blank. "You're still here."

"Yeah, my mom stays late to talk with the pregnant girls."

Suddenly, the feeling that Billy should remember this kid's name got a lot stronger. "Yeah?"

"Yeah." The boy looked at his feet and scuffed his toe

on the floor. "I'm sorry about the way she blew up at you this morning. She gets like that sometimes."

Wait—wait a damn minute. Was this kid saying that Jenny was his *mom?*

No way—not possible. This kid was a teenager. Jenny couldn't be that old.

Unless...unless she'd been young. The familiar guilt tried to kick open the heavy steel door Billy kept it trapped behind. This kid could only be Jenny's son if she'd been a teenager. And she'd kept him.

Damn. Fate had a freakin' funny sense of humor sometimes.

The next question had to be whether or not she was married, because there was no way in hell that Billy was going to keep entertaining thoughts of a married woman. Bolton men were loyal for life. Whatever problems they might have as a family—and Lord knew there were a lot of them—they respected the family, which meant they respected other families, too.

"So where's your dad?" That probably wasn't the best way to ask the question, but Billy had never been known for his tact.

The kid shrugged. "Dunno. Gone before I was born, I guess. Mom says we're better off without him, anyway."

Two thoughts crossed his mind quick. First, Jenny was available, so he could keep right on thinking about how she looked at him with that passion—okay, passionate fury—in her eyes. Second, though, was that a boy needed a man in his life. Especially a boy on the verge of becoming a man.

"You kids aren't really going to help me build the bike, you know."

As if to illustrate this point, Vicky called over, "Okay, wave at the camera, Billy."

Feeling stupid, Billy waved to the camera that had been installed overhead. He was going to work nights and weekends to build the bike himself, hours of which would be compressed into two- to four-minute segments on the show. The rest would be staged shots with kids.

The rest of the crew went out to the truck, probably to review the footage. Bobby liked to check the tapes. Although Billy would never admit this to the little twit, he thought Bobby was impressively focused on making the show as good as it could be.

"Yeah, I know." The boy sounded positively depressed. Then he perked up. "I can still help. Mom always stays late for her after-school program, so I'm here a lot."

Billy worked alone. Even in his shop, he did his own thing while his guys did the assembly stuff. But something about this boy—and his mother—kept his mouth shut.

Billy wasn't looking to be a father. That ship had sailed seventeen years ago, and it wasn't going to make a return voyage. But a shop teacher could still make a big difference. Billy's shop teacher in high school, Cal Horton, had saved Billy's life on at least three occasions and kept him out of prison twice, which was more than his own father, Bruce Bolton, had ever done.

Yeah, he didn't have to be this kid's father. But Cal would expect him to pay it forward.

"You want to help?" The kid nodded eagerly, his eyes bright. "I could use an assistant. Find a broom and sweep up this place. It's a wreck, and a good shop is a clean shop. Keeps dust and junk from getting into the parts."

He thought the kid was going to balk at manual labor. Billy didn't nag. He went back to organizing his tools and waited for the kid to make up his mind.

Less than forty seconds later, the boy was sweeping.

Billy smiled to himself. "You do a good job and keep at it, maybe we'll get you on a bike."

"Really?" The kid grinned. Then it faded. "My mom won't like that."

Yeah, he knew that, too. His own mother had never been a fan of some of the things Billy did. Most of them, actually.

"Aw, hell. What your mom doesn't know won't hurt her."

"You don't know my mom very well." The boy kept sweeping. A moment later, he added, "I got a friend who's got a bike, but she won't let me near it. Says she doesn't want me to get hurt." He made a noise that sounded like teenager-speak for "can you believe that?" "It's not as cool a bike as yours, though."

Maybe half of Billy's childhood had been spent on the back of a bike, often directly against his mother's stated wishes. His father had loved his mother dearly, but they rarely saw eye to eye on basic parenting questions, such as which activities were fun versus life-threatening. And Billy had survived just fine.

Well, mostly fine.

"I'll make a deal with you. You keep your grades up and help me out in the shop, I'll get you on a bike." He leveled a finger at the huge smile on the kid's face. "*But* you do what I say, when I say it, no questions asked. I don't need some pissant kid jerking around my shop. I'll throw your ass out of here the moment you screw up. Got it?"

The sudden gasp that came from the doorway told him that someone had screwed up, all right.

Him.

Jenny waved goodbye to the last of the girls from her Teen and Parents—TAPS—meeting and checked the multipurpose room for Seth. Seth hated the TAPS meetings and put as much distance as possible between him and the pregnant girls—most of whom he'd grown up playing with. Jenny supposed she should be thrilled that Seth hadn't hit the age where he thought of girls in a sexual way, but would it have killed the boy to have a bit of compassion? After all, Jenny had been one of those girls once.

Seth wasn't in the multipurpose room. The guitar was still in its case. Where was that boy?

Oh, no. The shop. Billy Bolton.

That man, Jenny thought as she ran down the hall. Yup, his bike was still parked in her spot. The door to the shop was open, and she heard voices inside. There was no missing Billy's deep rumble—she wasn't sure she could forget the way that voice hummed through her body. Even now, she got goose bumps. She also heard the softer voice of her son.

Oh, Lord, Seth was talking with Billy—and, from the tone of it, Billy was yelling at her boy. Running faster, the first words she caught were "…need some pissant kid jerking around my shop. I'll throw your ass out of here the moment you screw up. Got it?"

She gasped as she flew into the shop. "*What* did you say to my son?"

Seth jumped six inches off the floor, but Billy—sitting behind a table with a massive tool-thing in his hands—didn't even move. At least this time he wasn't wearing glasses. Jenny wasn't sure that helped, though, because now she could see the way his light brown eyes bore into her, like heat-seeking missiles.

No one else was in the building. She'd gotten here just in time. Billy stared at her, something that looked like contempt on his face. Seth looked six kinds of miserable all at once. God only knew what Billy had been saying to her baby boy to make him look like he was on the verge of crying.

She intended to find out, by God. She stalked over to the table and slammed her hands down on the top. The tools rattled and Seth warned, *"Mom,"* behind her, but she had had it with this man.

"I asked you a question, and don't you dare pull that silent crud on me. I heard you—I know you can talk. What do you think you're doing, speaking to my son using that kind of language?" When she didn't get an immediate response, she shouted back over her shoulder, "Seth, get your things."

"But, *Mom*," he whined again.

Then Billy stood up—all God-only-knew how many inches and pounds of him rose to his feet, slow and steady and not the least bit intimidated by her.

Jenny swallowed, refusing to allow herself to be intimidated by him, either. Even though he could pick her up and throw her over his shoulder like some big, gorgeous caveman, if he wanted to.

"Calm down."

Of all the nerve—was he actually going to try to talk his way out of this? "I will do no such thing. If I have my way, you won't be back on this reservation tomorrow. What is wrong with you? Stripping in front of a bunch of school children? Picking up my car? Threatening Seth? Are you insane?"

As she spoke, Billy walked around the table. He wasn't moving at tackling speeds, but his destination was unmistakable. She took one step backward, then another as Billy advanced on her.

"What are you doing?" she demanded.

Another step toward her. When he saw the effect he was having on her, one of his eyebrows notched up, which made him look almost amused. "Talking. To you." Another step. "You still sweeping?"

"What?"

It was only when Seth said, "Yes, sir," that she realized he hadn't been talking to her.

One more step.

"This is talking? You're trying to frighten me, but it

won't work," she said as he boxed her into a corner, an intense look on his face. She should be terrified—maybe she was—but that didn't explain the goose bumps that were all over her. Everything about her was tuned in to him—the way his muscles coiled and uncoiled with each step, the way he was…smiling? Was that possible?

Then, unexpectedly, Billy stopped while still a good four feet from her and looked over his shoulder. She was almost in a corner, but if she broke to the left fast enough, she could probably make it out the door. But if she did that, she'd leave Seth in here with this man, and she didn't want to do that.

This was a clear example of the devil you know versus the devil you don't. Except that in both cases, Billy Bolton was the devil.

When he faced her again, one corner of his mouth was unmistakably curved into a smile. "No, *this* is talking."

The sight of Billy Bolton grinning—at her—threw whatever Jenny had been planning to say right out the window.

Oh, my. Somewhere, underneath that beard and the dark glares was a *very* handsome man with surprisingly kind eyes. Her mind flashed back to the expanse of muscle she'd seen earlier that afternoon. Muscles and more muscles, covered in tattoos that should have scared the stuffing out of her, but all she'd thought of doing was tracing the lines on his skin and reading the story he'd written there.

Those vicious goose bumps ran rough all over her body, but this time, heat flashed behind them, leaving her skin quivering. Heck, her whole body quivered. Including parts of her that hadn't quivered in years.

"What are you going to do?" she asked, and was mortified to hear her voice come out somewhat lower and huskier than normal.

His eyes—a silky brown—darkened, and for a flash of

a second, his gaze darted down to her lips. Her body, acting of its own volition, responded by darting her tongue out and licking her lips.

It was like they were doing a dance, one with tiny, complex steps. The air sharpened between them, and she felt her head tip back. He responded by sucking in air, and she felt her body do the same thing. Two bodies moving in time together, creating a rhythm all their own.

It had been a long time since she'd danced. A long time since she'd *wanted* to dance.

And she wanted to dance with Billy Bolton, of all the wildly inappropriate people.

She had to get control of this situation before something terrible happened, like Billy pinning her to the wall, pressing all those muscles against her and kissing the heck out of her.

Yes. That would be terrible, indeed. Awful. Possibly the worst thing that could ever happen to her.

So why did she want so badly for him to do exactly that?

"Nothing you don't want me to."

And he stopped. No more steps toward her, no more hungry looks. No more dancing.

Jenny forced away all thoughts of her body moving in time with Billy's. They didn't go very far, just to the back of her mind, but far enough that she could think. "I will not have you threaten my son with such language." Her voice was still sultry. "Nor will I have you putting on such an indecent display in front of the children."

"Josey told me to go around the side of the school to get miked up so I wasn't in front of the other kids. I didn't know your classroom was there." Almost imperceptibly, he leaned in. The distance between them felt so sharp she thought it might cut her.

She could see Josey doing that. She'd assumed he'd been acting like his brother Bobby—showing off, making a scene—but she could see him trying to do the right thing. Maybe. "You were threatening Seth."

"With kicking him out of the shop if he doesn't pull his weight. Are you going to feed me to the coyotes for that?"

He tilted his head and looked her over again. Anytime she wanted to stop quivering would be great.

"You moved my car."

"You want me to move it back?" Then he flexed. It wasn't an exaggerated thing, but his chest and arms tightened under the shirt, then released.

Jenny's breath caught. Apparently, she'd lost her mind at some point in the past few minutes, because she wanted to tell him to do just that—but only if he took his shirt off.

"No."

"How old are you?"

Heat flooded her cheeks. "You can't ask me that."

Billy jerked his chin over his shoulder. "How old is he?"

Much more heat and she was going to start sweating. "That is none of your business!" And before she could stop herself, she asked, "How old are you?"

He didn't even hesitate. Men. "Thirty-four."

Five years older than she was.

"Mr. Bolton? I swept the floor."

The sound of Seth's voice snapped Jenny out of her man-induced insanity. "You what?"

"He swept up." Billy swung around and surveyed the shop. "Not bad, kid."

"He *what?*" Jenny looked at the now-clean shop floor. "Seth cleaned something? Because you threatened him?"

Billy looked back over his shoulder at her—only a quick glance, but Jenny felt the disapproval of his gaze. Then he walked around the shop, studying the floor. "Not bad at all," he said to Seth, and Jenny couldn't miss the way Seth's face lit up at the compliment.

What the heck? She and Seth fought over chores all the time, but Billy Bolton had him looking happy to clean?

When had she lost all control over the situation?

Oh, yeah—the moment she'd gotten out of her car this morning.

"So, did I do a good enough job? Can I help you in the morning?"

Jenny shook her head, trying to remember the last time she'd seen Seth look this excited about something.

"Depends on what your mother says."

That was the last thing she expected to come out of Billy's mouth.

"What?" That was how many *what*s in the past five minutes? She was starting to sound clueless—a feeling she hated.

Billy motioned toward the far corner of the shop. "You signed a release for him to appear on the show, but if he's going to be helping me out in the shop, he'll be filmed the whole time."

Jenny stepped forward and looked. She hadn't noticed the small camera with the red light before, but she saw it now. "What's that for?"

"They'll film me the whole time I'm building, then speed up the footage. If the kid helps, he'll be on film a lot more." He leaned to the side, and Jenny realized that they were less than two feet apart. "It's your call." Then Billy turned to Seth, "You've got to pull your weight. I hear that you're not helping your mom at home or your grades drop, you're out of here. I don't tolerate slackers."

Seth's gaze darted between her and Billy. Clearly, he was waiting for her to blow up like she had that morning. And she was still mad about the language Billy had used around her son.

The only thing was, she liked everything Billy had said. She couldn't believe that she was on the verge of agreeing to let Seth spend more time with Billy Bolton, but what could she do? Seth wasn't a little boy anymore, and something told her that he'd be safer with Billy than he would be if he were running around with Tige or any of his thuggish friends.

Billy turned and looked at her, one eyebrow raised in silent challenge.

"Can I, Mom? *Please?*"

This was a rock, and Billy Bolton was a hard place. The way his chest had *not* moved when she pushed it? A very hard place.

"We'll see how tomorrow goes."

"Was that a yes?" Seth hopped from foot to foot, a ball of nervous energy. "That was a yes, right? Yes!"

"Hey," Billy thundered. "Settle. Your mom told you to go get your things, so get moving."

Seth was gone before the broom hit the ground. She turned to Billy to lay down the law on the probationary day, but he beat her to the punch. "I won't make any promises about cussing—too set in my ways. I'd bet you dimes to dollars that he's heard it all, anyway. He's safer with me than he is with any of those hotshot troublemakers he calls friends."

Had Seth told him about Tige? Or was he that good at guessing?

He leaned in closer—less than a foot separated them now, and she thought he was going to kiss her. Different parts of her brain screamed out "No!" and "Yes!" at the same time, paralyzing her. She couldn't lean in, and she couldn't pull away.

But he didn't kiss her. Instead, he took another one of those savoring breaths. "Yeah, tea," he said in a low voice that set off another round of quivering she could only pray he didn't notice. "You should know something about me, Jenny. I keep my promises, or I don't make them."

The air stopped moving into or out of her lungs. Heck, everything stopped as he looked down into her eyes, so focused that she wasn't sure she'd ever move again.

"Mom? I got my stuff." Seth's head popped back into the room as Billy straightened up and put a respectable distance between the two of them. "I'll do my homework when I get home, okay? And you'll be here in the morning, right, Mr. Bolton? And I can help?" He sounded so excited that she wouldn't have been surprised to see him start spinning in circles like he used to do when he was four.

Seth eager to do his homework? A man flirting with her? Jenny looked around the shop, wondering if she'd woken up in an alternate dimension that morning.

Billy huffed as if he were insulted. "Mr. Bolton is my grandpa. My name is Billy."

"Yes, sir, Billy!" Then Seth spun and all-out ran for the car.

Billy turned back to her. She needed to say something fast—she couldn't let him dominate this interaction—or whatever it was. She was still in control of things, by God. But her brain was still muddled up, so the best thing she came up with was, "Are we done here?"

He smiled—a full-on, melt-in-her-mouth smile, the likes of which she had never seen before. "No," he said, moving toward his workbench. "We're not."

Four

Seth was up and dressed before Jenny's alarm clock went off. He rushed her through her oatmeal. They arrived at the school a good twenty minutes earlier than normal.

Billy was already there. Light shined through the shop's open door, despite the chill of the October morning. "Bye" was all she heard as Seth threw the door open. Then he was gone.

Jenny fought the urge to follow him. He wasn't a baby anymore, she kept reminding herself. And she had no desire to see Billy Bolton first thing in the morning.

Unfortunately, her mind took that image and threw some sheets and pillows into the mix, and suddenly, she had a *great* desire to see Billy first thing in the morning.

Just because Billy was treating her son well and paying attention to her didn't mean she should develop a crush on him. It didn't matter if he had a melt-in-her-mouth smile, more muscles than God and money to burn. He was still a hard-core biker with a foul mouth. Heaven only knew what he did for a good time, but Jenny was willing to bet that it was something she would not approve of.

So she went inside and reviewed her lesson plans. When

she was done, she still had half an hour before the students showed up.

She stood in front of her electric teakettle, at war with herself. Should she go out there and check on the shop? Or was that being too overbearing?

Oh, to heck with it. Just because Billy had said all those things about promises in that serious manner didn't mean he was honorable. Wanting to visit the shop had nothing to do with how he looked with or without his shirt on. Nothing at all.

She made two cups of tea and walked out to the shop. For some reason, her stomach was turning. What the heck did she have to be nervous about?

That question was answered the moment she set foot inside. Blinking through the bright lights, she saw that devastating smile on Billy's face.

Maybe she was dreaming, but if she didn't know any better, she'd say that smile was for her.

It wasn't possible. Men didn't look at her with interest—with need. Men looked at her shabby clothes and her rusty car and her smart-mouthed teenager and kept right on walking. If they looked at her at all.

Except for yesterday. And, as Billy rose from his stool and made his way over to her, possibly also today. Seth hadn't given her a lot of time to apply makeup this morning, which she barely wore anyway, but she was suddenly quite glad she'd managed to brush on a little blush and hit her lids with some eyeliner.

"That for me?" Billy asked, looking down at the mugs in her hands.

"Yes."

She offered a mug up to him. His hand was so large that there was no way to avoid touching him unless she threw the tea at him.

So she had to stand there and not react as his fingertips

skimmed over the backs of hers so lightly that she found herself shivering. The touch was much gentler than she would have given a man of his size credit for. Immediately, her mind took off in crazy directions, although she tried to slam the door on those thoughts. She was *not* lusting after, crushing on or, God forbid, even *liking* Billy Bolton.

Then the mug was in his hand and the contact was over. They stood there for a second, looking at each other. Had he felt the same shock she had? Of course not, she tried to tell herself. She was being as silly as the girls in her TAPS meetings, falling head over heels because of a grin and a touch. She had one job here, and that was to make sure Seth was doing okay. No attraction, no flirting. Just mothering.

"How's it going?"

Billy held her gaze for a beat longer. She could almost hear him reminding her they weren't done here, but instead he said, "Got him sorting out fasteners. They got all mixed up when we unloaded." He pointed with his chin to where Seth was sitting at a table, staring at a pile of nuts and bolts with a look of intense concentration on his face.

"I can't tell if this is a one-half or a nine-sixteenths." Jenny could hear the frustration in Seth's voice.

"Here, let me see—"

She had taken two steps when Billy grabbed her shoulder, holding her in place. He boomed, "Figure it out, kid. It ain't rocket science. You can't size a bolt, you can't build a bike."

She froze, waiting for the fit Seth would pitch. It didn't happen. Seth screwed up his face, scratched his head and then Jenny almost saw the lightbulb go on. He looked around, grabbed a wrench and started measuring.

"Good job," Billy said, and his hand squeezed Jenny's shoulder. Not tight, just a gentle pressure. It sent shock waves down her back that almost buckled her knees. He was so strong, but the sensation straddled the line between tender and erotic.

Then he let go, trailing his fingers down her arm. That—that was purely erotic. If she weren't so determined not to let this man have an impact on her, her knees would have given way.

"Thanks for the tea," he said, low and quiet as he walked past her.

She stood there, wondering what the heck she was supposed to do with *that*. Billy was flirting with her, she was sure of it. Pretty sure, anyway. She was so out of practice that even if she wanted to flirt back, she wouldn't know how. Maybe that was the problem.

Billy settled back onto his stool, his gaze on her. "See you later?"

Was she being dismissed? That didn't match with everything he'd just made her feel. Maybe she'd read him wrong.

"What?"

He shot her one of those intimidating glares, and for a second she *knew* she was being dismissed. But then he turned, pointedly looking over his shoulder—right at the small camera with the steady red light. Then he stared at her again, and she realized he'd asked her a question, not given her an order.

"I'll, uh, stop by after my meeting?"

"Yeah, okay, Mom," Seth said, clearly preoccupied. "Bye."

But Billy? He favored her with one of those half-hidden smiles that told her loud and clear that was the answer he was looking for.

He wanted to see her later.

Jenny all but floated back to her classroom.

Billy couldn't say how he knew that Jenny had walked into the shop. He sure as hell didn't see or hear her. He had

his welding mask on and was holding down one end of a
pipe as Seth tried his hand at cutting it with a miter saw.
Don Two Eagles stood on the other side. Billy was watching Seth's hands; Don was watching Billy. He couldn't hear
anything over the whine of metal against metal.

He knew Jenny had come in, all the same. And he didn't
like it.

The shop—*any* shop—had always been a place apart
from femininity. Josey didn't come to the shop very often,
and when she did, she wasn't there very long. Even Cass,
the receptionist at the Crazy Horse Choppers headquar-
ters—who was as tough as a woman could be—stayed off
the shop floor. Billy liked it that way. Nothing and no one
to distract him from the choppers.

Except it didn't work like that here.

Seth finished cutting the pipe without also cutting off a
finger or thumb. He even remembered to turn the blade off
before doing anything else. Then he peeled off the welder's
mask Billy had made him wear. "That was so awesome!"

Billy took his mask off, too. Damned if that woman
wasn't sitting on his stool at his table, two cups of tea in
front of her and a small smile on her face.

Double damned if he wasn't thrilled to see her there.

"How's it going?" Her gaze danced between the three
men and their protective gear.

"Billy's letting me cut a pipe!" Seth grabbed the pipe
and took it over to Jenny.

She regarded the rough, angular cut with suspicion.
"How…nice, sweetie."

"Mom," Seth whined as Billy choked back a laugh.

"It's part of the frame," he explained, wondering if the
tea was for him, the kid or Don.

Jenny's eyes got a little wide.

"What?" Billy asked, mentally slapping himself when
it came out as defensive.

"You really are building this from scratch?"

"Women," Don muttered under his breath as he stripped off his shop apron and checked his watch. "Gotta get home. You guys going to be okay here?" He directed the question to Jenny, but he kept a wary eye on Billy.

For some reason, Billy thought about decking the old man. Who was he to suggest that Jenny and her kid weren't safe with Billy? He had been nothing but a gentleman so far. Except for the part where he'd moved her car. Oh, yeah, and stripped off his shirt. But other than that, he'd been a paragon of virtue.

"I'm not my old man," he muttered.

Don didn't back down. "It ain't a matter of if the apple falls from the tree. It's a matter of how far it fell."

The two men stared at each other.

"Don, we'll be fine." Jenny's voice was calm and surprisingly unconcerned with the standoff going on in front of her.

Don shot Billy a hell of a mean look, but said, "See you all tomorrow," and left.

Billy turned back to Jenny and Seth. The kid was holding his length of pipe against the plans, trying to figure out how to put a puzzle together with only one piece. Jenny, however, was still sitting on his stool, her lips hidden behind her cup of tea. She looked as if she were waiting for something. What, he didn't know.

This was why he didn't like women in the shop. The only expectations he was comfortable with were design specs and delivery dates, *not* rules of civility.

"He doesn't like you."

Seth snorted in amusement as he studied the design. "Yeah, but Don doesn't like any *wasicu*."

Jenny's eyes flew open as she slammed her cup back on the table. Tea sloshed everywhere. "Seth!"

"A what?"

The kid went red. "White...man," Jenny replied without meeting his gaze.

Yeah, right. Billy had been called enough names in his lifetime to know an insult when he heard one. He leveled one of his meaner looks at the kid, who physically shrank right before him. "Yeah, well, I'm not like any *whatever* he's ever met. Now suit up. We've got more pipe to cut."

Billy had never seen a kid move as fast as Seth did. Billy walked over to Jenny and held out a pair of earplugs. "Don't look at the saw without goggles," he told her as she stared at the plugs.

"It wasn't that loud when I came in. Do I really need these?"

If Billy had let her son get anywhere near a power tool without all the proper precautions, she'd probably have thrown a fit. But when it came to her own well-being?

She was the kind of woman who put herself last, he realized. Even when she didn't have to.

So he didn't bother telling her that the saw was always loudest at the beginning of the cut. Instead, he leaned forward, smoothed the few strands of hair that had come loose from her schoolmarm bun and tucked the plugs into her ears for her.

Her skin, from her cheeks to the back of her neck, flushed a beautiful pink as he pressed the plugs into place. Then, because he doubted that she wouldn't watch him and the kid work the saw, he snagged a pair of goggles from the table. He stretched the elastic back so that it wouldn't tangle on her hair and settled the plastic on the bridge of her nose. It wasn't his fault that this required him to lean over her so that he could smell the scent of her—baby powder and tea and chalk.

He inhaled, his nose coming within inches of her forehead. *This* was the reason why he didn't want women in the shop. Too distracting, and being distracted led to injuries.

When he managed to step away from her, he saw that she'd tucked her lower lip under her teeth with enough pressure that the flesh was bleaching white. What had been, up to that moment, a mere irritating attraction shifted right over to desire. He wanted the pretty little schoolteacher in a way that had nothing to do with civility. He wanted to kiss the color back into her lip, to find out how hard she was capable of biting.

Then she looked up at him through thick lashes, and he saw his own desire mirrored in her eyes. She wasn't scared of him, nor was she mad at him. As difficult as it was to believe, she wanted him, too.

Either that, or the goggles were distorting her eyes. Just like that, Billy felt the way he had when he'd been introduced to her at Ben and Josey's wedding—tongue-tied, unsure of what to do next.

Uncertainty was not a feeling he was comfortable with, especially not when it was stomping on some good old-fashioned temptation. So he forced himself to turn away from her and do the one thing he was always comfortable doing.

He got back to work.

Five

Jenny hadn't slept much. Her ears still burned where Billy had touched her with the barest hint of pressure. She couldn't get past how gentle his touch had been—or how much it had affected her. She'd have expected a man like him to be all rough, very tumble. But soft, tender caresses? Coupled with the heated looks he kept giving her?

No amount of tossing and turning in her bed had let her sleep.

"Billy said that he's going to let me help weld the frame," Seth repeated for the fourth time that morning.

Yawning, she turned the final corner, looking for Billy's bike. It wasn't in the parking lot, which left her feeling vaguely disappointed, but then Seth said, "That's his truck!"

Maybe it was. And it was parked right next to her spot.

She rolled up and came to a stop before she looked in the cab. Well, tried to, anyway. The truck sat a good two feet above her. Black, of course. She expected nothing less from Billy Bolton.

"Morning," Billy said as he rounded his truck and opened her door for her.

The gentlemanly act threw her for another loop, but if he was insulted that she sat there staring at him in the dawning morning, he didn't show it.

"Hey, where's your bike?" Seth got out of the car.

"Had to bring pipe," Billy said as he closed Jenny's door behind her, turned and opened up the passenger door of his truck. "Brought you some tea."

"Really?" She caught herself. "I mean, thank you."

"You're welcome," he replied, handing her a cup from a fancy coffeehouse she couldn't afford.

This time, Jenny's fingers had to linger over his, not the other way around. This time, she was the one who was doing the touching. This time, she let herself feel the span of his fingers. They were thick, but long. Perfectly balanced for their size.

Just like Billy.

She needed to say something—anything—to extricate herself from this situation. "How much do I owe you?"

It was hard to make out his features in the early-morning light, but she thought he raised an eyebrow at her—the same look he'd given her when she'd caught him stripping off his shirt in front of her class. "You don't owe me anything, Jenny."

"What do you need pipe for? I thought we cut the pipe for the frame last night? Aren't we going to weld it?"

She pulled her hand—and the tea—away from Billy and walked away from the narrow space between their vehicles.

On the one hand, Jenny was thankful for Seth's interruption. He was keeping her from doing something completely stupid, like continually touching Billy Bolton. Because that would be bad. Somehow.

On the other, she wanted to strangle her boy. Things with Billy had such interesting potential—potential that was always interrupted by a teenager or a bike. Yes, she was pitifully out of practice at flirting, but even an old pro would find it challenging in this situation.

"Whoa. We *might* get to welding after school today—if your mother says it's okay." As he opened the gate on the truck, Billy looked at her for approval.

"As long as he's got all the safety gear," Jenny replied, taking a sip of her tea. Lightly sweetened black tea. Still warm enough to be hot. Perfect, she thought with a satisfied sigh.

"But everyone else gets a crack at cutting pipe, too. Bobby says it'll look good for the camera. So the rest of the kids get to cut junk pipe. And you," he added, pointing a finger at Seth, "get to carry it all to the shop. Get started."

"Me? Why?"

"This is the grunt work, kid. And you are the grunt."

Jenny managed not to laugh at this keen observation. Mumbling under his breath about how this *totally* wasn't fair, Seth hauled out a few lengths of pipe and began carrying them to the shop. He dropped one, then another. Juggling the remaining pipe, he tried to kick the pipes on the ground, but only succeeded in stubbing his toe.

"Let him handle it," Billy said, close to her ear as his massive hand settled on her shoulder and pulled her back— gently—toward the truck.

Too late, she realized she'd gasped, although she would have been hard-pressed to say if her response was out of concern for Seth or because of the sudden pressure of Billy's touch.

She wanted to squirm—this was different than the last time he'd held her back. Instead of the middle of the well-lit shop, with a camera recording their every move, she was alone with Billy in the dark.

She tensed. Would he press her against the truck's side, all of those tattooed muscles giving her no place to go?

Would he take a kiss from her—or something more? Would she let him?

Good girls didn't let bad boys take those kisses, and Jenny had spent the past fourteen years being a good girl. Through hard work and dedication, she'd become a respectable woman—*not* someone who chased rich bad boys.

So why did she want him to kiss her so much?

Darn it all, he didn't do any of that. Instead, he trailed his hand down her back—which still made her insides quiver, especially when his hand traced the curve of her hips, just above her bottom.

God, she needed to say something. Anything.

"I…" Then she looked up, her gaze meeting Billy's.

His face was only a few inches from hers, and the look in his eyes melted the part of her brain that was trying to engage in polite conversation.

Billy grinned. Not a full-on display of teeth, just the corners of his mouth moving up in unison, but he looked as if he'd discovered the cookie jar and was about to stick his hand into it.

"This is the part," he said, his voice rumbling out of his broad chest as he reached up and smoothed her hair away from her face, "where you threaten to feed me to the coyotes."

Ah. Yes, that was her line. But she was powerless to say that, much less anything else. All she could think was, *dance with me. Dance with me and make it worth it.*

Then the sound of metal clanging on metal and what was most likely an inappropriate curse word muttered by her son snapped her out of her stupor. Seth was still about, after all. It wouldn't do to have him see his mother and this man making googly eyes at each other.

She pulled away. It took more effort than she thought it would.

"How you doing?" Billy called out, looking none the worse for wear.

"This is stupid," came the completely Seth-like response.

"You don't have to haul metal," Billy responded, still looking completely unflustered. "You also don't have to help with the welding. Your call, kid."

Seth stomped up to the truck, gave Billy the dirty look that was all-too-familiar to Jenny, and grabbed another couple of pipes.

"I carried metal when I was your age," Billy called out after him. "Builds character."

"Whatever."

This time, Jenny did giggle. She should have been irritated that Seth was snotty to Billy, but honestly, it was a relief to know that he wasn't like that only with her. And to know there were limits to Billy's ability to charm the boy.

Even if there didn't appear to be limits on how much he could charm her.

"What?" he asked over the lip of his cup.

"You're better at this than I thought you would be."

This hung out there for a moment. Truthfully, he was better at a lot of things than she would have given him credit for. Working with the kids. Managing Seth. Humoring Don.

Making her feel special. That was the biggest surprise of all.

After a heavy pause, he shrugged. "Shop is good for kids."

"Oh?"

He nodded. "You may have trouble believing this, but I wasn't exactly a perfect student back when I was his age."

"No!" she gasped in mock surprise, which made him chuckle. "Actually, neither was I." After all, she'd already lost her virginity by Seth's age. That's how a girl wound up pregnant at fifteen.

But then the silence between them stretched, and she realized that he was staring at her. And she remembered that he'd asked her how old she was, how old Seth was.

"That was a long time ago," she hurried to add, feeling the kind of shameful embarrassment she hadn't had time to feel in years. Then, after the words were out, she realized they made her sound old.

Maybe she should drink her tea.

"Interesting," he muttered as Seth stomped up, grabbed more pipes and hauled them off. When he was out of earshot, Billy continued—by tucking her hair behind her ears again.

There was no way in heck her hair was that messy this early in the morning. But she couldn't pull away. The pads of his fingertips grazed her earlobe and moved down her jawline with a steady pressure.

"What is?"

"You. I even look at your boy funny, and you'll rip my liver out and leave it for the vultures. But I look at you?" He leaned in—so close that she could feel the warmth of his breath on the side of her face as his fingers lifted her chin. "I look at you, I ask about you, I *touch* you—you curl up in your shell, like one of those crabs."

"I'm not a crab," she managed to get out.

"Says the woman who promised to feed me to the coyotes." She could hear the laughter in his voice, even if he wasn't laughing. A man had no right sounding that sexy. Not when he was only inches from her, not when his fingertips had complete control over her. None.

He was going to kiss her. He was going to kiss her and Seth was going to walk up and see him kissing her and she didn't know why but she couldn't let Seth see her like that. She couldn't. She was a good mom. She did not lose her head over men. Not anymore. So she said the first thing her mind threw up in defense. "Maybe I'm just scared of you."

The moment the words left her mouth, he pulled back. The sun was up high enough now that she could see the way he shut down—his eyes went blank, almost mean-looking, as he crossed his arms. His whole attitude became one of sullen rebellion.

Seth trudged back up. "Last three," he said. "Now what?"

Billy looked at her from behind his mask of attitude for a pained moment before his body uncoiled. He grabbed the pipe out of Seth's hands and took off for the shop at a good clip. "We get to work."

Jenny watched them go, too stunned to say anything.

What the heck had just happened?

Billy had been wrong. That's all there was to it.

He'd misread Jenny. The huge, wide eyes? The lip biting? The pretty blushes? Not desire. Fear. His own wishful thinking had him thinking she wanted him, when in reality? He scared the crap out of her.

He'd thought she'd been different. Hell, he thought *he'd* been different—that he wasn't making the same mistakes judging women that he always made. He'd thought he was getting it right this time.

He'd been wrong. Again.

It wasn't like this was the first time he'd misjudged a woman. Hell, he'd thought Ashley loved him back when he was young and stupid. He'd loved her, at the very least—loved her and been willing to marry her, even though he'd only been seventeen, even though it had felt like his life would end if he got married and had a baby before he was old enough to vote, much less drink. Then Ashley had gone and had that abortion, had thrown it in his face when he'd been crushed and furious about her doing it without telling him. "I got rid of *it* because I didn't want *you*" is what she'd said during their fight, right before she walked out of his life for good.

Yeah, he'd misjudged women before. Maybe he'd never *not* misjudged one. Which was why he was thirty-four and still damned alone. Just him and his bikes.

In this foul mood, Billy found himself cutting pointless pipe all damn day long. He got into an argument with Don about whether or not the kids could take their lengths of pipe home as a souvenir. He snarled at Seth when the kid tried to adjust the saw like Billy had shown him the night before. And when Billy's kid brother Bobby shoved a camera in his face to get him cussing at little kids on film, Billy punched him in the gut.

None of that made him feel any better. If anything, he felt worse. He wanted to hit a bar and drink until he didn't feel anything at all. He used to do that all the time, back when he was still young. Back when he was trying to forget Ashley and the baby that wasn't and never would be. Back when he would throw down at the drop of a hat.

Back when the cops knew him on a first-name basis.

Those days were long gone, though. He was too damn busy to spend his time drunk and brawling—he had the business to prove it. A business that provided him with a purpose—and more money than he knew what to do with and the "opportunity" to have his whole life filmed.

Yeah, he was in one hell of a bad mood.

The bell rang back in the main building and kids bailed. Billy sat in the shop, brooding. If Seth knew what was good for him, he'd steer clear today.

Kids never did seem to know what was good for them.

"Um, Billy? Mr. Bolton?" Seth poked his head around the door. "Are we going to weld today? On the frame?"

"No. Go home."

How had he gotten it so wrong? Of course he scared

her. She was a soft, delicate little woman—sensitive and pretty—and he was, well, he was still a badass biker, covered in ink. Nothing would ever be able to change that basic fact—not the money he'd made or how unwillingly famous he'd become.

"I can still sweep up…"

"Go. Home."

What the hell was wrong with him? He didn't go for women like Jenny Wawasuck—women who were smart and cared about kids. Who put other people first. The women he normally went for were women who weren't surprised that Wild Bill Bolton was, in fact, a little wild.

"Look, if this is about this morning, I'm sorry. It won't happen again."

Billy's attention snapped back on Seth as the kid edged into the room. "What?"

Seth looked as if he was on the verge of throwing up. "I wasn't trying to make you mad. I don't mind carrying pipes. I won't complain next time."

If this were just a misunderstanding between him and Jenny, well, that would suck enough. But the additional layer of the kid mucked everything up. Billy had half a mind to toss the boy out on his rear, but the moment the thought occurred to him, guilt hit him upside the head. Would Cal Horton, his shop teacher in high school, have thrown Billy out because Cal had had a bad day teaching? No. No matter what was going on with Cal, he was there when Billy needed an adult to talk to. If it hadn't been for Cal, Billy would be rotting in prison. If he weren't dead.

It wasn't this kid's fault that Billy couldn't read a woman. Even if that woman was the boy's mother. Damn. "I don't want to hear a lot of lip."

Seth's face brightened. "Understood."

Billy regarded him for a moment longer. Shop had saved him, back in school—shop and Cal. When Billy had finally made good and done something with his life, he'd promised Cal that he'd pay it forward.

"Suit up, kid. Let's weld."

Six

She was just checking on her son. That was all. Not talking to Billy Bolton, not touching Billy Bolton, not even *looking* at Billy Bolton.

The only person she was concerned with was Seth. That's how it had been for the past fourteen years. She didn't have time in her life to have her head spun around by a dangerous man. She didn't have time to wonder why she said the things she did, why she *did* the things she did. Her number one priority was shepherding Seth through adolescence and making sure he stayed on the straight and narrow. That's what good moms did.

Her walking out to the shop after her TAPS meeting had nothing to do with the way Billy's face changed when he grinned at her or how her body begged her to dance with him every time he traced a finger over her skin. Heavens, it certainly had nothing to do with the way he focused on everything about her with such a laserlike intensity that he could tell she only drank tea by catching her scent.

No, she was not thinking about that. She was thinking about Seth.

The shop door was locked.

She jiggled the doorknob again, but it wasn't her imagination—the thing was locked tight. Then she noticed the sign on the door—Welding. Do Not Enter—written in a heavy scrawl and fixed to the door with duct tape.

"Seth? Billy? Open up!"

The door swung open. Seth stood there, a welding helmet on his head, the visor part swung up. "What?"

She was a little taken aback by his appearance. Wearing a heavy jacket and an apron so long it covered his feet, he looked like he was dressed for battle, not shop. He looked... almost grown up. "What are you two doing in here?"

He gave her that special teenager look—the one that said she was a complete idiot. "Welding, Mom. Duh. Didn't you see the sign?" But then he cracked a smile. "It's *so* cool!"

Okay, so even if she'd made Billy mad this morning—and she still wasn't sure what, exactly, had been the straw that broke that camel's back—it was a relief to know that Billy was still honoring his promise to Seth.

"I want to talk to Billy."

"We're busy." Seth started to close the door on her, but she jammed her foot into the gap and gave him her no-monkey-business look.

"Let me in, Seth."

"Can't. Don't have enough gear for you, and Billy says everyone has to have gear if they're going to be around welding."

"Where's Don?"

"Left after school. Mom, we're busy." He started to shut the door on her foot.

"You tell Mr. Bolton I want to talk to him. *Now.*"

Seth hesitated for a moment before he buckled. "Fine, but you gotta wait here. You don't have any gear." At least he left the door open a crack.

Jenny peeked into the shop. Billy was dressed much like Seth was, except Billy's gear fit him better. The moment he turned his shielded head in her direction, he fired up the blowtorch.

Even though she couldn't see his eyes behind the darkened glass of his mask, she could feel him staring at her. If he was trying to intimidate her, he was succeeding. When he wanted to, the man could be positively menacing. Nothing she saw before her was even vaguely reminiscent of the thoughtful man who'd brought her tea and whispered in her ear this morning. She swallowed down her nerves. Clearly, she'd angered him. Even more clearly, she wanted to avoid doing that again in the future.

She still wasn't sure what had set him off. All she'd said was that maybe she was afraid of him. Why would that have upset him so much? It'd only been one little conditional clause, for Pete's sake—*maybe.* Because she wasn't actually afraid of him—she'd just been desperate to keep from kissing him in front of Seth.

Seth clomped over to Billy—from the back, she could see he was wearing huge work boots—and spoke to him. The flame clicked off long enough for Billy to respond— or at least, that's what it looked like. Then the blowtorch was blowing again. Definitely not a man she had to worry about kissing at this exact moment.

Seth came back over, looking irritated with her. "He's busy."

Okay, so he was unhappy with her. But he was still interacting with her son, and she had a right to check in on them. "You tell him I want to talk to him when he's done being 'busy.' I'll be in my classroom." Then, rather than wait around for another menacing flash from the blowtorch, she turned and headed back to her room.

The *maybe* bothered her. He'd heard the *maybe,* right? He had to have known that she wasn't being serious, right?

Maybe. Maybe not.

They weren't done here. Not by a long shot.

* * *

For the first time in a long time, Billy pulled open the doors to a school and stepped inside.

He couldn't believe he was doing this—walking into her classroom, on *her* turf.

It was easy to figure out which room was hers. Only one door was open, only one light was on. Everyone else had left hours ago. She got here first, stayed last. All she did was teach.

Just like all he did was build bikes for insane amounts of money.

He knew that she heard him coming. He'd never been exactly light on his feet. The sound of his steel-toe boots echoed down the otherwise silent halls. There was no turning back. He was all in for this little dressing down or whatever she had in mind—he knew it wouldn't be pretty.

Taking a deep breath, he turned into her classroom. The first—the only—things he saw were her legs. She was standing on a chair, trying to tack up some sort of border over the blackboard. As she reached over her head and stood on her tiptoes, the length of her calves, below the hem of her skirt, weren't exactly at eye level, but they were on more prominent display than normal. His blood ran hot. Nice legs. *Great* legs, he thought before he caught himself. That was exactly the kind of thinking that had gotten him in trouble this morning.

"Oh, good, you're here," she said, without turning around. "Can you hold this up for me?" She gestured toward a sagging section of paper. "Please," she added, almost as an afterthought.

He stood there for a moment—not because he was uncertain of what was going on. That wasn't it. More like he was admiring her backside, all tight and cupped by her skirt.

"Won't take long, Billy," she said, and he didn't hear

"scared" in her voice. He heard gentle teasing. And maybe something else—the same thing he'd deluded himself into thinking he'd heard for the past few days. Attraction. Desire.

He felt ridiculous standing this close to her, paper border in hand. She arranged the border to her liking and stapled it up. Then she handed him the stapler. "If you don't mind, since you're down there." And she smiled at him. Because of the chair, she was practically looking him straight in the eyes.

He didn't have the first clue about what to do. If he were his brother Ben, he'd come up with something logical to say that would get him out of this. If he were his brother Bobby, he'd make a move on her.

But he wasn't either. So he did some stapling and forced himself to look anywhere but at her.

Billy was trying so hard not to look at her that when she put her hands on his shoulders, he jumped. With a little bit of force, she turned him to face her. "You don't, you know."

He swallowed. "I don't what?"

"You don't scare me." She ran her tongue over her lower lip. It made her look hungry.

"Sure I do. You said so yourself."

Her hands slid from his shoulders toward his neck with a slow, sure pressure. "Maybe. There was a *maybe* in that sentence. Which means there's a *maybe not*."

She was pulling him in closer, and he'd be damned if he was powerless to stop her. She looked like she was going to kiss him and it looked like he was going to let her.

"Then why did you say it?" Shoot, his voice wasn't tough or even scary. It was something low and deep, but quiet, a voice that he rarely heard himself use—unless he was trying to sweet-talk a woman. And if he was trying to sweet-talk this woman, even he had to admit he was doing a poor job of it.

"Because I didn't want to do *this* in front of Seth."

She pulled him into her and kissed him. Her lips crushed against his with enough force that he let out a low groan. Man, she smelled so good, felt even better.

She kissed with her eyes closed. Billy knew this because he was so stunned that he couldn't do anything but stare at her. Her cheeks were flushed a delicate pink, which made her look soft. Beautiful. Innocent.

Innocent women didn't kiss him.

Which meant this had to be either a mistake or the most dangerous game of chicken he'd ever played.

Was she trying to prove that she wasn't afraid of him? Fine. He'd had that happen to him before, back when he was wild and crazy. For a long time, he'd enjoyed the attention. It'd felt good to have women throw themselves at him, even if it led to a lot of bar brawls with angry boyfriends. Every time he started making out with some nameless woman on a Saturday night, he'd felt like shoving Ashley's face in it—see? Other women wanted him. Other women *fought* over him.

It had been an ego trip—for a while. Then the nameless, faceless kissing—often followed by some nameless, faceless sex? It left him hurting more than any hangover ever would. So he'd stopped doing it. Going to bars, picking up women, getting drunk every other night—all of it.

Maybe that was why he hadn't done any dating after making the business a success. True, the business *was* a success because he stayed out of the bars. But when high-society women hit on him at the functions Bobby or Ben made him attend, it reminded him of how hollow he'd felt back in the day.

Which meant he was out of practice. If he were in a bar now, more than a little drunk, he'd pick Jenny up and push her against a wall. Because what he wanted was to sink into the softness of her body and forget everything but the woman who had a hold of him.

But he wasn't in a bar. He was standing in a classroom. And he would not rise to her bait. Although his body wasn't exactly paying attention to that direct order.

At the very least, he wasn't going to sweep her off that chair and pull her into his chest. He wasn't going to do anything like that, because if he did, he knew damn good and well that he *would* scare the hell out of her. She had no idea what kind of fire she was playing with.

Then she traced his lips with the tip of her tongue, and Billy's resolve weakened. Hell, everything weakened. He was physically shaking from holding his arms at his sides, when all he wanted to do was wrap them around her.

She was beautiful kissing him—so beautiful he wanted to step out of himself and watch the whole thing. He might never get another chance at this kind of sweetness.

Finally, she pulled back. Her lips parted, she was breathing heavily with her eyes still closed. Then she licked her lips again. She was trying to taste him, he realized. That made him want to kiss her again. He'd never wanted to kiss a woman so much.

Then her eyelids fluttered open, and he saw that look in her eyes—want. Pure and simple. She wanted him.

This would be the perfect time to fish a compliment out of the depths of his brain.

He had nothing. Instead, he said, "No kissing in front of the kid. Good rule."

A smile tugged at her mouth. She looked as if she was going to say something else, but then a door slammed.

"Hey, Billy," Seth called out, his voice echoing down the hall. Jenny's eyes shot wide with alarm. "I got the shop all swept."

Right. This would be test number one of the new no-kissing rule. Moving as fast as he could without pulling

Jenny off the chair, Billy stepped back and put a desk between them. Seconds later, Seth came bounding—there was no other word for it—into the room. "Oh, hey." He eyed them suspiciously.

"That border looks straight." It was the first thing that popped into Billy's mouth.

Jenny blinked at him before turning around. "Oh, yes. Great. Thanks for your help."

"Are we gonna weld again in the morning? I've got some boots at home. I'll wear those." At least the awkward moment didn't faze the kid.

"You do that."

Jenny climbed down off her chair. She wasn't exactly staring at the floor, but she wasn't exactly looking at him, either. But she wasn't afraid of him. That much he felt sure about now. She hadn't kissed him to prove a point. She'd kissed him because she wanted to.

That simple fact was more than enough to muddle his thinking. So when she ushered him and Seth outside and locked up the school, he found himself staring at her.

She caught him and rewarded him with one of her sunny smiles. "We'll see you tomorrow, right?"

"Yeah."

He watched them get in the car. He'd see them tomorrow.

Man, he couldn't wait to come back to school.

Seven

Billy got to the school extra early the next morning. He'd worked in his garage all night, as if he could *build* an eloquent response to Jenny. He wondered if he'd get another chance to kiss her today. Wasn't going to be easy. No kissing in front of her kid—or any other kid, for that matter—and no way in hell he was making a move on her anywhere near a camera. Which limited their options.

The bad news was that Jenny wasn't at school when he rolled up. The worse news? Bobby's sports car was. Damn. Billy was rarely in the mood to talk with his baby brother. He loved the guy, he did, but ever since Bobby had put Billy on camera he'd had trouble thinking charitable thoughts about the guy. Today was no exception.

Bobby was sitting at the worktable, sipping what was probably a twelve-dollar cup of coffee. At least he looked tired.

Bobby was everything Billy wasn't—handsome, smooth, smart, good with women—hell, good with people. And he always got his way. He had Bruce Bolton, their father, in his back pocket. Seriously, how many other people could just decide to put the family on a reality internet show and make it happen? Only Bobby. Everything he touched turned to gold.

This particular morning, Billy couldn't remember ever being as jealous of his little brother as he was right now. Bobby would know how to handle the situation with Jenny. But Billy wasn't about to ask his little brother for advice. That was the road straight to hell. So he stuck to the obvious. "What are you doing here?"

"I need a reason to hang out with you?"

"Before seven in the morning? Yeah, you do." To distract himself, Billy picked up the frame he and Seth had welded last night and tested the joints. They held. The kid's work wasn't half-bad.

"I wanted to talk to you." The only thing more dangerous than Bobby as a smooth talker was Bobby as a serious businessman. And that was his serious-business voice.

"Now what? Going to put cameras in my bedroom? Film me in the shower?"

When Bobby didn't have a snappy comeback, Billy knew he was screwed. He turned to his brother, frame still in hand. A man could do a lot of damage with some welded pipe. A *lot* of damage.

Bobby sat there, sipping his coffee as if this were another regular early-morning call. Maybe he hadn't done a good enough job keeping Jenny off the camera. No doubt Bobby wanted to develop the feelings Billy was having for the schoolmarm into some sort of plotline for his show.

"No way in hell—over my dead body."

"You don't even know what I'm going to ask you." Bobby had the nerve to smile. Billy wanted to cave his teeth in.

"Okay, fine. Ask away. The answer is *no.*"

"The footage looks good. You're doing well with that boy—what's his name?"

"Seth." Billy didn't so much say it as growl it.

"Yes, yes. Seth. I think women are going to go wild for this new, softer side of you."

Billy snorted. He didn't want "women" to go wild for him. Just the one.

That thought took him by such surprise that he didn't have a snappy comeback for what Bobby said next. "I've been in talks with the owner of the FreeFall network—heard of them?"

"I don't watch TV."

"You might have to start." Bobby grinned like some sort of fool, which made Billy think that was supposed to have been a joke. He wasn't laughing. "The man's name is David Caine. He's interested in picking up the show as a midseason replacement. If we can make the magic number of hits for the webisodes."

Billy wished he had gotten some sleep, because as it was, he couldn't be sure that this wasn't a nightmare. "You're serious? Filming me and putting it on the web isn't enough?"

"This is huge, Billy."

"I don't want to be famous." Fame was making it extra hard to figure out how to court a nice, normal woman like Jenny. Fame was making him twitchy. Fame was ruining his life. "You're the one who wants to be famous. Why don't you film yourself?"

"I'm not as interesting as you are." Billy rolled his eyes at this, but Bobby continued. "You make these awesome bikes and you don't take crap from anyone." Was that a compliment? A sincere one? But then Bobby ruined it by adding, "Not even first-grade teachers with attitude problems."

"You watch your mouth." It came out so fast that Billy didn't have time to realize what he was saying.

Bobby's eyes widened. "You *like* her?"

He could see the wheels in Bobby's head turning. Bobby

would try to strong-arm Jenny into playing out their little flirtation—or whatever the hell it was—on camera.

"Well. That's…interesting." Boy, Billy hated that grin. "But that's not what I want to talk to you about."

"It isn't?" That wasn't like the twit, to have an advantage and not press it. The warning bells in Billy's head got a little louder.

"Josey said I have to get your approval for this."

"Approval for what?"

"You're building that bike to be auctioned off for the school, correct?" He gestured to the frame Billy had forgotten he was still holding.

"Yeah…" Any second now, it'd hit—the catch. There was always a catch.

"I've come up with a way to auction the bike that's going to maximize both our profit and our exposure level."

"What the hell does that mean?"

Bobby smiled again, but this time Billy could tell he was nervous. "It means that, when we auction off the chopper, I think we should also auction off some bachelors."

Before Billy could process that, Bobby stood and began pacing. "Hear me out. You're the reason we're getting the views we've been getting, but we need to hit it hard. What better way than to sell you to the highest bidder for a night? We'd have a packed house of who's who. Hell, we could invite some of our celebrity customers. You know how high-society people like to buy things for charity. Plus, we'd get our webisode hits—gruff biker in a tux!—and we'd raise a hell of a lot of money for the school." He paused and turned to face Billy, beaming like an idiot. "Everyone wins!"

After several moments, Billy became aware that he was standing with his jaw hanging about midchest. Out of all the ludicrous things he'd ever heard—including making him an internet star—this took the cake. "Are you on drugs?"

Bobby's smile cracked a little. "It won't be just you. Dad said we could auction him off, and me, of course." He puffed out his chest a little. "Ben's out, though. Josey was firm about that. But the guys in Ben's band already said yes. I have a few other leads on eligible, *willing* bachelors. All I need is you."

"*Josey* thinks this is a good idea?" Their sister-in-law was an all-around down-to-earth woman. But she was also a corporate fund-raiser.... He was possibly screwed in the worst sort of way.

"Absolutely. I did a little research, put together a spreadsheet for her showing the kind of returns these sorts of events bring in. She was impressed."

"Let me see it." Not that he loved spreadsheets, but it must have been a hell of a file to sway Josey.

Bobby looked dumbfounded. "I didn't bring it."

Billy wanted to pummel his brother. Ben—the *good* brother—went over the company financial statements with Billy every month and they discussed Billy's portfolio every three months. He knew exactly where the company stood and which investments his own money was tied up in. He may not know what to do with it all, but he knew where it was. "There's no way in hell you can auction me off to the highest bidder."

Bobby's smile turned scheming. "A bachelor auction has the potential to raise another fifty thousand bucks for the school, *William*. You know who'd like another fifty grand? A certain teacher would probably *love* some additional money to buy supplies. I imagine those kids go through a lot of crayons. You want me to tell her you said no to more school supplies for those tykes?"

So that's what this was—blackmail. "I'll buy her a box of crayons. I'm not going to be auctioned off."

Bobby was ready for him. "You know who else would love a bigger budget? Don. He was telling me how he wants an after-school program for the boys—part sports, part shop, part keeping them out of trouble. He doesn't have any money for it now. You could change that."

Billy glared at his little brother. Of course he'd use Billy's love of shop against him. If Billy had had a program like that, he probably wouldn't have gotten his high school girlfriend pregnant, and probably wouldn't have been such a screwup that she'd known what a terrible father he would have made. If only Billy had had something like that, his whole life might have turned out differently.

He had plenty of money. Maybe he could ask Ben to move some of it around. Hell, he'd rather just cut the school a check than be a part of a bachelor auction. Bobby was looking at him, expecting Billy to agree to being bought and sold for what was little more than a ratings stunt.

"Go to hell, creep."

"Come *on,* man! I'm talking about one night of your life. I hadn't realized how selfish you are."

Billy was selfish? After he agreed to make his life a matter of public record for the sake of the family business? After he agreed to foot the bill for a custom-built chopper to auction off for the school? Hell, *no.*

Billy had never played football. He'd been plenty tough, but he'd never had grades that were even close enough for the coaches to look the other way. Both his brothers had, though. Which is why Bobby should have seen the hit coming.

Billy dropped the frame and covered the distance— maybe ten feet—between him and Bobby before the metal clanged on the ground. With a satisfying "Oomf!" Billy hit his baby brother with enough force that they moved the worktable a good six feet before forward momentum stopped.

They'd always done this—fighting, Mom had called it. Dad insisted it was harmless tussling and never broke it up. Some days, Bobby came out on top—he was a fast sucker and had a solid left hook. But he couldn't match Billy for sheer strength.

"I'll build bikes for you and your little show, but that doesn't give you the right to sell me on the open market. You got that?"

Behind them, a door slammed and someone gasped. Crap. Billy had forgotten about Seth. He dropped Bobby and spun around to see Seth's eyeballs all but jumping out of his head. "Hey."

"You, uh, you guys okay? I can come back later…." Seth edged for the door.

Billy shot Bobby a warning glance. Had Bobby connected the kid to Jenny? He hoped not. Manslaughter was a serious crime.

"No, we're done here. Right, Bobby?"

Bobby cleared his throat, gave Billy's shoulder a half-hearted slug and straightened out what was left of his shirt. "We're all good. Just messing around, kiddo. Brothers are like that."

Seth gave Bobby a look. "Yeah, whatever, mister." Then he turned his attention back to Billy. "Are we still going to weld?" He held up his booted foot to display his preparation.

"I'll leave you two to it." Bobby headed for the door at a respectable clip.

"Hey!" Billy yelled after him. He'd long since learned that if he didn't get a hard promise out of Bobby, the guy took it as a victory.

Bobby stopped, hand on the door. Then he turned back. "Fine. You won't do it."

Billy doubted that was the final word, though.

Eight

"What are we going to do tonight?" Jenny asked the fourteen girls sitting in her classroom. They were between eight and eighteen. Nine of them were pregnant.

"No drinking, no drugs," they chanted in unison. All except Cyndy in the back.

"And?" she prompted, keeping an eye on Cyndy.

"Do our homework, go to school tomorrow."

"Good job, girls. Remember—call me if you need to. Otherwise, I'll see you tomorrow, right?" Everyone gathered their things, snagged the last of the cookies to go and headed out. Except Cyndy.

She hadn't said anything during the TAPS meeting, which was unusual. Her eyes and nose were red. Jenny hoped that she hadn't skipped school today and gotten high. She sat beside the girl, waiting. Cyndy was still here, so there was still hope.

"I can't do this, Jenny." Cyndy threw herself into Jenny's arms, the sobs ripping through her. "I just can't."

Jenny's throat caught. Cyndy was only a year older than Jenny had been when she'd gotten pregnant. "What happened, honey?"

"Tige broke up with me. He doesn't care about me or the baby."

Yeah, she'd been there, too. Some days were good days—a girl had a healthy baby, another girl didn't get pregnant.

But today? Today was not one of the good days. Today was going to break her heart.

"Oh, honey." Of course, she hadn't figured Tige would man up. But telling Cyndy that would be pouring salt in the wound, and that wasn't her job here. Her job was to keep Cyndy from doing something that she'd spend the rest of her life regretting.

"My mom says I have to give it up and my grandma says that if I give it up then it won't be a Lakota anymore," Cyndy wept. "But I don't want to have it. I can't."

Jenny was going to have a talk with Bertha Speaks Fast. "No matter where that baby is," she said, patting Cyndy's seven-month-pregnant stomach, "it'll always be Lakota."

"I can't" was all Cyndy could say.

"Did you get high today? Drink?" When the girl shook her head no, Jenny exhaled in relief. "I'm sorry, honey, it's too late for an abortion."

As a rule, Jenny didn't support abortion. But she'd seen too many babies born with Fetal Alcohol Syndrome or addicted to drugs, too many babies who were neglected and abused because their parents didn't know that they had to feed or change a crying infant. Reality dictated that she keep all options open.

Jenny's mother had made her keep her baby and had made darned sure Jenny didn't mess up everyone's life. Everything she'd learned about being a mother had come from Frances Wawasuck.

When Cyndy's sobs had finally subsided into hiccups, Jenny said, "Honey, you have to do what's right for you and for your baby. If you want to keep it, your family and the tribe will be here for you. If you decide to place the baby with a loving family, then I'll put you in touch with an adoption counselor. There's no right or wrong here."

This brought on more tears. Jenny rubbed her back. "Go home and get some sleep. Tomorrow, *after* you go to school, we'll make a plan."

"Okay," the girl sniffled.

"One day at a time." Jenny wrapped up the last cookie and sent Cyndy home.

Then she turned her attention to the envelope from the South Dakota Department of Social Services. *Please be a check,* she prayed as she opened it. When she'd started TAPS, she'd had enough funding to serve a hot meal to the girls every afternoon. It was the only dinner some of them got. She got a small stipend out of it, too, most of which had gone directly into Seth's college fund. The rest had gone to a new-car fund.

However, the state was behind on its bills. Months behind. She'd cut the meals back, but it hadn't taken long before she couldn't pay the cook to stay late. Now she was paying for milk and cookies out of her own pocket. Soon, she wouldn't even be able to do that.

She refused to give up hope. These girls—girls in a difficult spot like she'd been—needed an adult they could trust. Some of them had involved parents or grandparents, but most of them didn't. If Jenny hadn't had her mom, God only knew where she'd be now. Certainly not a college graduate with a good job, able to take care of herself and her son.

That's what she wanted all the girls to have, too. A chance to become the women they wanted to be. To that end, Jenny gave them unconditional support, a strict set of well-being rules and made darned sure they got the most education they could. After the babies came, the girls could keep coming to the meetings. This was a safe place for them, and Jenny was going to keep it that way, come hell or high water.

So she took a deep breath and opened the envelope. Her heart sank as she read the brief letter. Not only would the state be unable to pay its months-old debt, it wasn't even going to try. And there would be no more money.

Her program—her mission—was officially dead.

She couldn't stop, though. That would mean leaving girls like Cyndy twisting in the wind.

She gathered her things and turned off the light in her room. If she stopped buying cookies, she could stretch the money left in Seth's college fund to cover milk for several more months—at least through the New Year. Long enough to make sure Cyndy and a few of the other girls safely delivered their babies. And after that?

Lost in thought, Jenny straightened the room and peeked out the window. The production truck was gone, but the door to the shop was open and light spilled out. At least Billy was still here. Kissing him yesterday had been... well, it had been *something.* It had been years since she'd kissed a man. No, wait—scratch that. She'd never kissed a man. Only boys who thought they were men. Boys slept with girls and abandoned them. Men took responsibility for their actions.

Billy, she sensed, was a man.

She honestly couldn't tell if he'd liked the kiss or not and before she could figure it out, Seth had come in.

But...she'd put herself out there. *Way* out there. She'd liked the feel of Billy's lips against hers—heck, she hadn't even minded the way his beard scratched at her chin. There'd been something deliciously naughty about it— which had to be why it felt so out of character. Jenny Wawasuck didn't mess around. And yet...

True, a kiss was just that, but she'd managed to fluster

herself so badly that she hadn't even been able to bring herself to deliver a cup of tea out to Billy this morning.

But that's where she was headed now—the shop. Today she wasn't even trying to lie to herself that this was about Seth.

She'd had a long day. She wanted to see Billy, to have him give her one of those looks, those light touches, that set her heart racing. She wanted to forget about budget cuts and unborn babies and that constant feeling of treading water but never quite getting anywhere.

Seth was sweeping up already. Talking with Cyndy must have taken longer than she'd realized. Billy sat at his table, studying what she assumed were plans. In the middle of the floor sat a hunk of welded metal that, at the moment, looked nothing like a motorcycle.

"Hey," Seth said, sweeping his pile of dirt out of her way as she headed for the table. "I just started."

"No rush, sweetie."

"Mom..."

Right, right. Guys who built things probably didn't get called "sweetie" in the shop. Billy looked up at her and smiled. Sort of. It was one of those looks where the corners of his mouth crooked up almost imperceptibly. But she perceived it anyway.

She gestured toward the angular metal on the ground. "Looks good."

His lips moved even more. Oh, yes, he was smiling. Some of the tension of her day melted away. "You can tell that, huh?"

"Oh, sure. Very...metallic."

His gaze drifted down to her lips and back up, which sent a shot of heat through her.

Maybe yesterday, she'd taken him by surprise. Maybe today, *he'd* kiss *her*.

Except for Seth. So she redirected. "How was your day? I saw your brother was here early."

The warmth drained from Billy's face. "It was a day. You?"

When was the last time someone had asked her about her day—someone who wasn't her mother? "Long," she admitted with a shrug.

"Anything I can do to help?"

The way he said it—all serious, with an intent look on his face that made it clear that he would quite possibly do whatever she asked—left her feeling a little unsteady. In the best way possible.

"Not unless you've got a few extra thousand dollars lying around," she joked. "The funding for my after-school program got cut, and they aren't going to pay the overdue bills." But he didn't take it as a joke. Instead, his scowl deepened—like it had yesterday, when she'd carelessly lobbed out her "Maybe."

"What?"

"It always comes down to money, doesn't it?" He slammed his hand on the table, making all of the tools and things rattle about. "That's all anyone ever wants. Money."

He glared at her, but she refused to back down. "I'm not asking you to pay for TAPS, you know. I thought we were having a conversation."

"I'm already building this bike. I'm already giving my time to the school. I don't have anything else to give." It was more of a snarl than a statement, punctuated by another smack on the table.

"You're trying to scare me again, but it won't work," she said in a low voice so that Seth wouldn't hear her. She leaned in closer to Billy. "I'm not afraid of you."

Then the strangest thing happened. Billy Bolton, currently the meanest-looking man she knew, blushed. And not one of those delicate reddening of the cheeks—oh, no. He shot hot pink, the color turning his ears an un-usual shade of red. Heck, even his neck—the part she could see—turned red.

The next thing she knew, he was up and moving, head-ing for the door with his head down, like a bull ready to do some damage to a neighborhood china shop.

She followed him out into the dim evening light. He'd covered a good deal of ground before he came to a stop, head down and hands on his hips. Not that he had hips. But, from this angle, she could see that he had a heck of a backside. One that, no doubt, matched all the muscles she'd seen a few days ago.

He heard her coming. "You should be, you know," he said without raising his head. "You should be very afraid of me."

"Give me one good reason." She circled around him.

"I'm not a nice guy, Jenny. I'm not even a good one. I have the reputation and the arrest record to prove it. No amount of money will ever change that. If you knew what was good for you and that boy of yours, you'd run from me right now."

He said it not as if he were proud of it, but as though he was resigned to carrying that burden of toughness for the rest of his life. He sounded tired.

Arrest record? She swallowed. Surely Josey would have mentioned something about a rap sheet before she agreed to let Billy work with children? Jenny knew a smart woman would probably take his advice and bail. He'd given voice to her worst fears—or at least, the fears she'd had a few days ago. Funny how much could change in a week.

She stepped in closer and saw the tension ripple through his shoulders. Moving slowly, she put her hand on his chest. She'd pushed him—or tried to, anyway—in that same spot on the first day. That had been the first time he'd confused her, when instead of pushing her back, he'd held on to her.

Like he did now. His fingers covered hers, and he pressed her hand into his chest. It was not the touch of a violent, dangerous man, no matter what he tried to tell her.

With her other hand, she ran her fingertips down his cheek, over his beard, and under his chin before she pulled his face up. "I am *not* afraid of you," she repeated in a breathy whisper.

This time, his hands cradled her waist. This time, he was going to dance with her. "You should be," he replied, pulling her in closer. "You *should* be."

"I'm not."

Later, she would be hard-pressed to say if she kissed him or if he kissed her. Later, all she would be able to say for certain was that she'd been hard-pressed against all of those muscles. Against Billy.

If yesterday's kiss had been nice, this one was a revelation. Her knees buckled under the force of Billy's mouth, but it didn't matter. He not only held her, but he also lifted her up as if she weighed next to nothing. She could feel his desire coiled below the surface of his skin as if he were waiting to unleash it all on her.

There were no confusing looks or miscommunicated ideas. This was a statement. He wanted her—all of her. It didn't matter that she had a teenaged son or was a boring schoolteacher or that she was perpetually broke. He still wanted her. In his arms, she felt lighter than a feather, lighter than air, even.

Despite the fact that he could pretty much do whatever he wanted with her, including throwing her over his shoulder and hauling her off—his tongue traced her lips, asking for permission. When she opened herself for him, though, he kissed her so hard that he almost bent her over backward.

As much as she didn't want that moment to end, she felt as though she were losing her balance. She pushed back.

He let her, but he didn't let go. Instead, he hugged her even harder. A deep rumble came directly out of his chest—the sound of pure satisfaction.

Folded within his muscular arms, she could feel his heart pounding through the fancy black T-shirt he wore. He was warm and solid and so strong it didn't matter that her feet weren't, in fact, on the ground. It felt like some part of her that she'd long ago shoved aside was waking up in his arms—the sensual, feminine part. She hugged him back, her face buried in the crook of his neck. The tang of metal and leather filled her nose, plus a deep, earthy musk that was his and his alone.

It ended slowly. First, he set her down, then he let her go. Each movement took several seconds, almost as if he was afraid that he'd never get this contact again.

As far as she was concerned, that wasn't an option. She smiled at him, feeling almost silly. "Feels a little naughty, kissing this close to the school."

He brushed her hair away from her face and cupped her cheek in his hand. "Maybe we should try to do that someplace else."

"Are you asking me out on a date?" The concept seemed foreign. Even when she'd been young and far too into boys, a formal request for a date had never happened. Other things had happened—obviously—but no one had ever asked her out before.

There it was again—that tired look. He was such a mystery to her. "I'm always working," he muttered, looking guilty.

"And I'm always at school."

"Not always. What do you do after you leave here?"

That struck a more hopeful note in her. "I cook dinner, do the dishes, hound Seth about his homework, talk to any girls that call and…fall into bed. And I do it all again the next day." He notched an eyebrow at her. It was a good look on him. "I catch up on house stuff on the weekends. Some of that stuff could keep, though...."

He nodded in understanding, then leaned down and kissed her forehead. It wasn't a huge thing, but the tenderness of it had her blushing again. "I'm going to ask you out on a date, Jenny, I promise. I want to take you out— someplace special. A night like you deserve."

God, that sounded wonderful—a night of nothing but her and him. A night like she hadn't had in, well, ever. "When?"

His chest heaved with a massive sigh. "The thing is, I've got to deal with my brother Bobby first. I don't want you on camera. You and I don't exist when there's a camera around."

At first, she was hurt by his words. How could they not exist after a searing kiss like that? But then the rest of what he'd said sunk in. They didn't exist *on camera*. He was protecting her.

"You can try to tell me you're not a good guy, but I know the real you, William Bolton." She turned her head and kissed the palm of his hand. "Let me know when you get it figured out. I'll be here."

She got a full-on smile that time. He practically beamed at her. One kiss—okay, it had been two kisses—wasn't going to be enough. She'd like to say that she hadn't felt this way in years, but honestly? She wasn't sure she'd ever felt this kind of pull for a man before. The way he made her body quiver with a gentle touch—to say nothing of the less-than-gentle touches—was something she was going to need a lot more of. The sooner the better. And, by the look on his face, he felt the same way.

"Yeah," he said, tracing her lips with his thumb, "I know where to find you."

Nine

As hard as it was, Jenny managed to wait until after Seth had closed his bedroom door before she bit the bullet and called Josey. Jenny didn't have a cell phone with all those unlimited anytime everybody minutes, so she saved calling Josey on her landline for emergencies.

And kissing Billy Bolton *after* he'd mentioned an arrest record was an emergency if she'd ever heard of one.

Josey answered on the third ring. "Hello?"

"It's me."

"You want me to call you back?"

Jenny smiled. Thanks to a trust fund, Josey had never hurt for money—and now that she was married to Ben Bolton, she never would. Still, she understood how the little things added up. Josey had unlimited anytime everybody minutes. It was thoughtful of her not to make Jenny pay for the call. "Yeah."

They hung up and Jenny sat, waiting. When her phone rang, she answered it before the end of the first ring.

"What's up? Is everything okay?"

Now *there* was a question Jenny would love to have an answer to. She opened her mouth to ask about Billy, but at the last second, she blinked. "It's official. Not only am I not getting any more TAPS funding from the state, but they're not going to bother covering back payments."

"Oh, no." Josey paused. "How much longer can you keep it going?"

Jenny rubbed her eyes. This was not the conversation she wanted to have. She wanted to know more about Billy, to find out that her trust in him wasn't totally misplaced. She wanted to not think about her mission in life dying a small, whimpering death at the hands of budget cuts.

"I don't know. I'd put most of the stipend in savings for Seth to go to college. If I start digging into that...I could maybe make it through part of the summer." Summer was the most important time to be there for the TAPS girls. Summer—with no school, no schedule—was when most of the girls got pregnant. It's when she'd gotten pregnant.

There was a long pause. Jenny couldn't guess what Josey was thinking. She'd never asked Josey for money before. Yes, Josey's very wealthy and very white grandfather had left her a trust fund—but she'd used almost all of it to pay for the school's construction. True, she was married to a very rich man, but Ben had also basically paid for the shop and all the equipment in it. She wasn't comfortable asking them for more.

At least, she was not comfortable asking them to cut her a check. But she was open to other ideas. If anything, the numbers man of the Bolton family should have some good ideas on how to fill the money gaps. Ben and Josey were a financial power couple. Josey was a professional corporate fund-raiser and Ben was a Chief Financial Officer. If anyone could get her out of this mess, it would be the two of them.

True to form, Josey said, "We can make sure you get something when we auction off the bike Billy's building."

"Yeah...about him."

"What about him? Is everything okay?"

"It's fine. Sort of."

"Jenny…"

Josey was as close to a sister as Jenny would ever have, which meant that there were very few things Jenny could hide from her. "Why didn't you tell me that Billy had an arrest record?"

"Oh, *that*."

"Yes, that."

"I didn't tell you because it wasn't important." When Jenny scoffed at this, Josey went on, "I mean it. He was arrested three times for public drunkenness, brawling and assault, which goes with public drunkenness and brawling, I think. But the last time was about ten years ago. He got probation and community service. Once he started seriously building bikes, he cleaned up and turned his life around." Josey dropped her voice to a whisper. "I know you're worried about him—he can *seem* really dangerous, but…"

"I'm not worried. He doesn't scare me." That defense was out before she could think better of it, and the thundering silence that followed was way, way louder than anything else Josey could have said.

Dang it. She'd overplayed her hand.

"How did you find out about his arrests?" Josey's voice was carefully casual—too casual. She probably could have pulled that tone on a stranger, but Jenny knew better. Josey was suddenly very interested in what Jenny thought of Billy.

She wouldn't be able to come up with a cover story on the fly that would convince her cousin. "He told me."

"Really." It wasn't a question. Jenny knew what Josey was going to say next before she even said it. "He doesn't usually tell people about that. He only told me because I ran a background check on him before I let him near the school and he didn't want me to be shocked."

Jenny could see Billy trying to have *that* conversation. "Well, he told me."

She left it at that. Anything else she said at this point would just further highlight the whatever-it-was that was going on between her and Billy.

Another pause. "Is something going on between you two?"

"Of course not."

How on earth could she entertain the notion of having a relationship with a man who'd been sentenced for public drunkenness? She was a responsible woman. She couldn't let Seth hang around someone who was a bad influence. Heavens, *she* shouldn't be hanging around with such a bad influence. Even if she really wanted to.

"He's spending a lot of time with Seth. Building the bike after school. I'm just checking. That's all."

"Uh-huh." She wasn't fooling Josey. "Listen, I'll start beating the bushes for more funding and you let me know if you have any other *questions* about Billy."

Jenny could hear the smile in Josey's voice. Part of her wanted to tell Josey all about the two kisses, about the way he brought her tea and got Seth to do chores, even at home. Part of her wanted to pump Josey for any and all information.

But a bigger part of her didn't. To talk about something made it real, and the whole thing—especially that kiss tonight—still had a dreamy feel to it. If Jenny told Josey, Josey might tell Jenny's mom, and the news that she was "involved" with Billy would filter its way through the school and the rez.

Even though it had been fourteen years since she'd blindly followed a boy over the edge of reason, everyone would say, *There goes that boy-crazy Jenny Wawasuck again. Some people never change.*

No. She'd worked too hard to become a respectable woman to let a couple of revelatory kisses muck up the works. Her first job was taking care of Seth. Her second job was guiding the TAPS girls into adulthood. Her third job was teaching. That was all she had room for in her life.

"Don't worry," she said with certainty. "I won't."

Ben paused when Josey's phone rang, but after she answered it, he sank the eight ball to win the round. Billy grunted in disgust. Normally, he could whip his brother at pool, but his game was off today.

And he knew why.

Then Josey sprinted—as fast as a woman in her condition could sprint—over to her and Ben's bedroom. What if it was Jenny? Was she calling her cousin to check up on him?

He felt ridiculous. What kind of man told a woman he was going to ask her out—later? It was nothing short of lame. But Jenny had a way of getting under his skin and muddling up his thinking.

Which probably explained what he was doing at his brother's place, playing pool instead of working on a bike. But it had been either this or hit a bar and get stupid, and Billy was done being stupid.

He hoped.

Once Josey was safely out of earshot, Ben started on him. "What's on your mind, bro?"

"What?"

Ben grinned at him. He smiled a lot more now than he used to. In fact, since he'd met Josey, he'd seemed happy. "You look lost in thought. It's a bit different from your usual seething."

Nothing like being the punch line in your own life. "Bobby give you that joke?"

"Take it easy. I'm just asking. If not as your brother, then as your financial partner."

Billy racked the balls. "Speaking of financials..."

"All safely invested. Been a little rough in this economy, but you're still firmly in the black. Why?"

Part of him wondered if he could just cash in some chips and cut a check to the school, specifically for Jenny's program. "How hard would it be to cash some out? Fifteen or twenty grand?"

Ben gave him a stricken look. "The financial penalties would be steep, man. I could move some around but it'd take me a few months. It'd be best to wait until next year—for tax purposes."

Damn, that was a long way off. All that money just sitting in the bank where he couldn't touch it. When Ben had told him about his most recent investment opportunities, he'd explained that the cash would be locked up tight for a while. Billy just hadn't realized how tight that would be.

He changed the subject—again. Sooner or later, Ben would catch on. "How's the remodel going?"

Now that Josey was expecting, they were making some changes to the huge, open space that was their loft home. Off the bedroom, walls that went all the way up to the ceiling now boxed in a baby's room.

Ben stared at him for a second before answering the question. "Good. On time and under budget." That was the thing Billy liked about Ben. Ben would let him dodge a conversation bullet, whereas Bobby would reload and come up firing. "How are things going at the school?"

"Okay, I guess. I think I scare the kids a little."

Ben broke, sinking a stripe. "You scare the hell out of everybody, dude."

Billy used to believe that. "Not everyone."

Ben missed his shot. "What?"

Damn it, he should have kept his mouth shut. Too late now. Because he didn't know what to say, he lined up a shot.

Ben waited until after he'd sunk in the four ball before starting in on him. "Who is she?"

Was there any way around this? Probably not. If Jenny wasn't talking to Josey right now, she'd talk to her later—Josey was supposed to be at the school in a couple of days. And Billy doubted that Josey wouldn't tell her husband that her cousin was messing around with his brother.

He gave it his best shot. "Bobby wants to auction me off, man. A bachelor auction."

Ben nodded, seemingly willing to let the "who" question slide. "I heard. Could raise a lot of money for the school."

Money that Jenny needed for the pregnant girls. Money that Don needed to keep the boys from getting the girls pregnant in the first place. Money that neither of them had, which meant that more kids would wind up screwing up their lives like Billy had.

He hadn't lied to Jenny. He wasn't a nice guy. If it had been any other woman in the world telling him she needed money, he probably wouldn't have even bothered to respond. But it wasn't any other woman. It was Jenny. He couldn't believe he was even considering this crazy plan to save her little program.

"So what you're saying is, you've got your eye on someone and being auctioned off to the highest bidder might trash your grand plans?"

That was his brother Ben, direct and to the point.

"Screw up my whole *life*. Bobby was talking about getting a big cable show. I don't wanna be a reality star. I didn't want to be a web star. I don't want any of this."

Ben rolled his eyes. "Seriously—that's what he told you?" When Billy gave him a confused look, Ben began to laugh. "That little jerk. Yes, he's working on a cable version, but Dad's going to be the focus—crazy Bruce Bolton and his three crazy sons. You won't be the only one on camera—hell, you probably will only be filmed when you're arguing with Dad or Bobby." He shook his head. "He was trying to get a rise out of you, brother."

"Why would he do that? Besides, you know, being Bobby."

Ben shot him a look. "Was there a camera nearby?"

At first, he was going to say no, but then he remembered—the camera Bobby had bolted to the wall of the shop. "Damn. Why does he do that?"

Ben shook his head, as if he couldn't quite get a handle on it himself. "He's got something to prove—at least, that's what Josey says. I guess he's got to prove it to us. Or to himself."

Billy wasn't sure he could believe that, but Ben was the straight shooter in the family. Why did Bobby have to prove anything? Yeah, he drove Billy nuts, but they were still brothers. He always had his brothers' backs. *Always.*

"Are you serious?"

Ben was always serious. "He didn't mention the real estate deal?"

"Just that he wanted to sell me to the highest bidder."

"Shoot, man. He's got this whole thing planned out—and you're a small part of it. Did he at least tell you that Josey thought the bachelor auction was a good idea?"

Being *a small part of it* didn't make Billy feel any better. "Just that she said I could say no. Which I did. I don't want anyone to buy me."

Anyone except Jenny. But he and Jenny didn't exist on camera. If Bobby were going to auction him off for the publicity, how would she buy him without being on camera? Hell, given the conversation they'd almost had this afternoon, how would she afford him at all?

"Buy yourself."

Billy's head snapped up so fast he might have sprained a neck muscle. "What?"

"Rig it." Ben grinned. "I know a woman who'd be willing to act as your proxy."

Billy blinked at his brother.

Josey walked over and took her seat on a stool. Billy noticed that she seemed more…thoughtful than she had before the phone call. For some reason, that made his ears burn. "What'd I miss?"

Ben kissed her on the cheek. His hand snaked around her back and rubbed. Then he put his other hand on her increasing belly and patted. Billy would have had to have been blind not to see the way Josey's face softened as she leaned into Ben's touch. But he wasn't blind. Watching that happy little family hurt so much that he turned his attention back to the pool table. Anything not to be reminded of what he didn't have.

"You're going to buy Billy at the auction," Ben announced, looking smug.

"I am?"

"She is?"

"You are. She is. That is, if you're willing to cover the cost. Bobby thinks you're worth a couple thousand. All of which would be tax deductible, of course."

Right. Because that was the most important part of this. What the hell was wrong with him that he was even considering agreeing to this madness?

It got worse. Josey shot him a look. "I'd be happy to give my winning bid to anyone you choose."

Billy slammed his pool cue on the table. He knew that Josey didn't like foul language, so he managed to keep the string of curse words in his head. That *had* to have been Jenny on the phone, or else someone had to have seen him kiss the hell out of her. Either way, Josey knew.

A fact that was hammered home when she added, "You know, Ben and I were thinking of having Seth over for a weekend—give Jenny a little parenting break. I'm sure we could coordinate the timing."

"Jenny?" Ben's jaw dropped as he stared at Billy, then at Josey. "Your *cousin* Jenny?"

Yup. There was no way around this mess. Only through it. He'd lost control of his own life again. "I'm only agreeing to this on *one* condition. Whatever I cost goes directly to Jenny's program."

"Deal." The speed at which Josey agreed let Billy know she'd been planning on that the whole time.

He felt tricked, but that was tempered by a secondary emotion—excitement. What if this actually worked?

"Wait—I have another condition. Bobby and his film crew aren't allowed to tail me when the winner cashes in the date night. Because that's what it is, right? A date? One whole night?"

"Jenny?" Ben asked again, not keeping up with the negotiations for possibly the first time in his life. "Jenny Wawasuck? And *you?*"

Josey looked worried. "If your brother catches wind of it…"

Yeah. If Bobby thought he could increase the number of hits he'd get, he'd start following Jenny around. And if he upset Jenny, Billy might not get his date.

"So don't tell him. Don't tell anyone." Ben seemed to have recovered a little. "Make it a surprise. If no one knows except the three of us, then it won't get out. We'll make sure Bobby doesn't follow you. You do the rest."

"Not even Jenny?" He asked this question of Josey, who appeared to think on it.

"A thoughtful surprise might be really nice. Heaven only knows she hasn't had enough surprises in her life." She spoke slowly, as if she wasn't sure that was the right answer. "No one's ever whisked her away for a—" she blushed "—a romantic night."

Billy wasn't sure, either. But Ben said, "Knowing Jenny, I bet if you told her you were going to plunk down a couple of grand, she'd throw a fit—even if it were for a good cause. She won't even let us help her out—there's no way in hell she'll let you do this without some serious grief."

Billy thought about it. He remembered how she'd tried to pay him back for the tea—and that had cost, what, three bucks? Ben was right. She'd threaten to feed him to the coyotes.

"Besides," Ben added, "women like it when you go the extra mile for them." He grinned at his wife. "I still have a few tricks up my sleeve."

Thoughtful. Was this what the world was coming to— Wild Bill Bolton debating romantic, thoughtful surprises? This would kill his reputation if it got out—or got on film.

"Fine. No one knows but us." But he was feeling greedy. He didn't want to wait three more weeks to see Jenny. But he couldn't do anything that would tip off Bobby.

Then it hit him. They were making good progress with the bike, him and Seth. They'd have to paint it—but that had to happen at the Crazy Horse shop. The school didn't have the setup for painting. "What about before then?"

Ben shook his head. "Man, you are *gone.*"

"What do you mean?" Josey asked.

"If we get the bike done soon enough, I could have them come into town—have Seth help me paint it. Could we all hang out here?"

The sly smile on Josey's face was all he needed. "I think we can reach an agreement on that."

A bonus day, and one guaranteed night with no classrooms, no kids, no shops and no damn cameras. He'd get one night with Jenny and she'd get the money she needed.

He could still say no. The bachelor auction would be

crawling with the kind of entitled society women he'd been avoiding ever since he'd earned his first million. Bobby would film the whole thing and maybe get his reality show and make Billy that much more famous. He *hated* being famous.

Being auctioned off was an assault on his dignity—and that was saying something. He could go back to what he'd been doing for years—building bikes day and night, trying not to look at how freaking happy his brother and sister-in-law were going to be with their new baby.

He could say no and go back to being left alone.

To being lonely.

One night…wasn't much of a guarantee that he wouldn't be lonelier after he finished the charity bike and didn't have an excuse, good or bad, to be out on the rez at the butt crack of dawn every morning.

Then he thought of the way Jenny stood before him, her hand on the thorn-covered rose tattooed over his heart, without a hint of fear in her eyes. He didn't expect one date to mean that Jenny would fall into bed with him. But given that last kiss…

He might be lonelier when it ended, but he was pretty sure someone, somewhere had once said something about it being better to have loved and lost than to have never loved at all.

One night with a woman like Jenny, a woman who was too good, too respectable for the likes of him.

He was in.

"She isn't afraid of me," Billy simply said.

Then he cleared the pool table.

Ten

Billy was waiting for them at school on Monday morning, his huge truck parked next to her spot. Jenny could see the extra cup of tea in his hand as she parked.

Was it wrong to be so thrilled that he'd brought her tea? Boy, she hoped not.

"Morning, kid." Billy nodded to the back of the truck. "Got some boxes for you today."

Seth grumbled. But he did so quietly, loading up his arms and trudging to the shop.

Jenny wasn't sure what would happen next. The last time she'd seen Billy, he'd kissed her, hard. She'd be lying if she said she didn't want him to do it again, but she wasn't entirely comfortable with the whole sneaking-around vibe. The problem with sneaking around was that, sooner or later, you got caught. She'd only been caught once and had spent years proving she was a responsible person. She had no desire to repeat the experience.

"Need to talk to you," Billy said in a tone of voice that made it pretty clear that he wasn't about to ravish her in a school parking lot. The sky was pinking overhead, giving him a warm, almost cuddly look.

"Oh?" She took her tea, not bothering to keep her touch on his fingertips light. Instead, she stood on her tiptoes and kissed the part of his cheek that wasn't covered with facial hair. "Everything okay?"

He didn't say anything for a moment, which made her nervous. Then his gaze darted behind her, and she heard Seth's plodding footsteps. "Yeah. About that…event we were discussing."

Was this biker code for date? "Yes?"

His words rushed out of him. "My brother wants to have a high-priced bachelor auction when we sell the bike. The funds would go to the school. So our *event* would have to wait until after the auction." His mouth snapped shut, and she saw him pull back.

Jenny felt herself blinking as she tried to process what he'd said. Bachelor. Auction.

"Bobby wants to sell you?"

Of all the ridiculous things she'd ever heard…the only thing that topped it was Billy agreeing to do it.

"Wasn't my idea."

That was a cop-out defense and they both knew it. Her event—her date—was going to take a backseat to some other woman buying him? "But you're going along with it."

They were silent as Seth came and went with the last box.

"Josey wants some of the kids—and your girls—to be there. I want you to come."

"Josey knows about this? But I talked to her a couple of days ago."

This explained why that woman had been so vague about additional funding for the school. She'd been holding out. Jenny was going to have words with her cousin.

Billy leaned forward. "It wasn't her fault." His voice was pitched low, even though Seth wasn't near. "I wanted you to hear about it from me."

There was something sexy about the way he said that. When had she gotten to the point where a man taking responsibility had become a turn-on?

"When?" It was cruel to ask her to watch someone else get him before she did.

"Three weeks."

Three whole weeks felt like a very long time to her. By then, the bike would be finished and she wouldn't see Billy first thing in the morning and last thing before she went home. But those three weeks would be like now—trying to have a conversation around Seth, without anyone recording it. Stolen hints of a relationship.

On the other hand, what was three weeks but another drop in the bucket? She found herself doing some quick math. She hadn't had a relationship since Seth had been three, when he'd started calling the last guy Jenny had been with "Daddy." Which had, predictably, freaked out the poor guy and sent him running for the hills. That had been the point when Jenny had realized her attempt to remain a typical teenager with a normal social life was hurting her son. That had been the point where she'd stopped dating.

She'd been eighteen then. Eleven years was a long time without sex. Far too long. What was three more weeks?

Then, like a bolt out of the blue, an idea struck Jenny. He was asking her to come to the auction, after all. Why not make the most of it? She had a little money saved up from back when the state had been paying the bills. True, she'd been hoping to save that for Seth's college, but she'd already been considering dipping into that to fund TAPS for a few more months. If she used that money to buy Billy, that was practically the same thing, right? The money would still go toward the program. And she'd have a chance to get Billy all to herself before their date.

She could make this work. She owned one dress that could blend in with high society—her bridesmaid's dress from Josey's wedding. It was a slinky, sleeveless pewter-gray gown with a cluster of rhinestones in the middle of her cleavage and a slit up the back—far sexier and fancier than anything else she had ever owned. And what's more, it had looked *good* on her. It had taken three trips to a tailor but combined with the heels, she'd looked surprisingly long and lean and, well, glamorous. More glamorous than she ever had before.

And where else would she wear such a fabulous dress? Certainly not to school, and not to the grocery store. No. The only other place in the world—or at least in South Dakota—where she could possibly wear this dress was to a charity bachelor's auction. And if she was going to go, she darned well wasn't going to sit around and watch someone else take Billy home. She wasn't going down without a fight.

He must have taken her silence wrong. "I'm on the clock, Jenny. If I don't get this bike done before the auction, I'm in a world of hurt. But I'm working on a way to see you before the auction. If we get the bike done, I'll be able to take some time off and we can do something. Just… be patient with me."

"I can't wait forever."

He gaped at her in surprise, which made her feel even more powerful. Yes, she wanted him and yes, she wasn't exactly in high demand right now. But she wasn't going to throw herself at a man, no matter how good his kisses were.

When he leaned forward this time, she responded in kind. So he was richer, bigger and infinitely more dangerous. They were still equals in this dance. Because that's what it was—a slow, exquisite dance of promise and hope.

"I promise you this, Jenny." She could hear the amusement in his voice, as if he liked it when she challenged him. But then his tone deepened, and heated goose bumps ran roughshod down her back as the scruff on his cheek rubbed against hers. His breath was warm on her ear, almost as if he'd touched her with his hand.

"Yes?" Her voice wavered, but she wasn't done dancing with him. Not by a long shot.

A deep, rumbling noise sprang out of his chest. If he'd been a big cat, it would have been a purr. As it was, it was something else—something much more sensual. Something that told her he'd keep his promise.

"I'll make it worth the wait."

The weeks until the auction passed at what felt like a snail's pace to Jenny. Every time Billy touched her, time slowed down. Which happened every day.

She brought him tea on the mornings he rode his bike. When he drove his truck, he had tea waiting for her. Their hands touched under the pretense of caffeinated beverages. In the afternoon, she'd head out to the shop after her TAPS meeting. Billy held to his word—when Jenny was in the shop, the hottest thing that happened was a few smoldering looks.

It was driving her insane. True, light touches and hot looks were far more interaction with the opposite sex than she'd had in a long time, but each day added to a frustration that became more and more physically painful. She tried to ignore the pressure. She'd done so without much problem for years now, so she didn't understand why it was harder this time. The motorcycle they'd be auctioning off took shape. One afternoon, wheels appeared on the bike. The next, handlebars and a seat. Finally, eight days before the Saturday night auction, the bike was finished, except for the paint.

When Jenny walked into the shop that Friday afternoon, Billy was on the phone with Seth hovering near him. When the boy saw her, he jumped up. "So, I got an A on that history test," he began, brandishing the paper. "Ms. Dunne says I'm getting an A this quarter."

"That's great, honey." And it was. But this sudden volunteering of information had her on high alert. She looked at Billy, who met her gaze with—was that a wink?

"And I think I aced that math test today," Seth went on as Billy continued to talk into his cell phone. It was the first time she'd seen him use one. "And Ms. Dunne says I pulled my science grade up to a B."

"Did she, now? That's great." Those were, hands down, the best grades Seth had gotten in a long time. Jenny paused to look at the bike.

"How do you paint it?" she asked, circling the silver-and-black thing. It was beautiful, in a way that she found slightly scary. After all, Seth had helped build it. Was it road worthy?

"And I already finished that book report that's due for English next Wednesday."

Jenny focused on her son. "Is that so? Okay, spill it. What's up?"

But Seth didn't say anything. He looked at her as though she were sentencing him to certain death.

Dear Lord, what had he done now? How big of a mess would this be? "Seth…"

As soon as she said it, Seth pointedly looked back at Billy. "You paint it," he said, answering the wrong question, "by taking it apart. I have specialized equipment at the shop. We have to do it there."

The tension in the air was something special. "And?"

"And I thought it'd be fun for the kid here to come down to the shop and see how the painting works, since he worked so hard to help me get it done on time."

She looked at Seth, who had puppy-dog eyes. "Can I, Mom? Please?"

"What's the catch?"

"No catch. But it's a long drive, so I asked Josey if you two could crash at their place Saturday night." Heat danced in his eyes, and Jenny felt her cheeks getting warm.

Boy, she hated the feeling that she was supposed to know what was going on and didn't.

"Us two?"

"Sure. I'd like you to come down." The casual way he said this didn't match his eyes at all. She saw nothing but want and need and desire in his gaze. "You can see the shop."

"And the bikes." Seth was hopping up and down again. "Billy said we could go look at all his bikes."

"Josey wants you to call her. You're supposed to use my phone." He held it out to her as if this whole thing were no big deal.

And maybe it wasn't supposed to be. She'd stayed over at Josey and Ben's modified warehouse mansion before.

But Billy was asking her—them—to come to the shop, to see his bikes. Maybe it wasn't supposed to be a big deal, but it felt huge.

Then he said, "Why don't you have a phone?"

She swallowed. The honest answer was that phones were far too expensive. The only slightly less honest, but still truthful answer was that reception on the rez was terrible on the best of days. She decided to hedge her bets. "Never needed one."

She took the phone, but was at a loss on how to make an actual call. Heck, she wasn't even sure how to turn the darn thing on. She'd used Josey's cell a few times, but this was a different one—sleek, silver and *very* expensive-looking. Billy stood and, without removing it from her hand, tapped until Josey's number appeared. Josey answered on the first ring. "Well?"

"What's going on?"

Josey laughed. "What's going on is that Billy wants to show you what he does when he's not in the school's shop."

"And what is that?"

"I suppose you'll have to see to find out. Come down for the day," Josey said.

Seth and Billy were hanging on her every word. They weren't even pretending to do something else.

"Well?" Josey asked, now sounding worried. "What do you want to do?"

Worst case, Jenny got to sleep in a big, soft bed for the night and eat a meal that someone else cooked and have someone else clean up afterward. Worst case, she got to hang out with her cousin. Worst case, Seth would learn a little more about how to build a bike.

Best case, though, was that she'd get to see what Billy Bolton was like when he wasn't working. He'd get to see what she was like when she wasn't being a teacher. He might even get to see her when she wasn't being a parent, first and foremost. Seth loved Billy's brother Ben—and he especially loved Ben's expensive gaming system.

Seth was still silently begging. Jenny locked gazes with Billy. Something in his eyes made her break out in goose bumps again—challenging her. She raised an eyebrow at him.

"What time should we get there?"

Eleven

"Dude, stop. You're making me dizzy."

Billy stopped pacing and turned to face Jack Roy, his painter. Normally, he liked Jack. Jack was about ten years older than he was and had worked for Billy's dad when Billy had been in high school. He smoked, drank, chased skirts and painted anything and everything he could get his hands on. But today, Billy didn't much care for Jack. The man sat on his stool, his hair slicked back under a red bandanna. His painter's coveralls were loosely knotted at his waist. The only thing covering his chest was a nearly see-through white tank top and a hemp necklace. He must be good-looking to women, because he was going to be auctioned off along with Billy in one week.

Billy didn't like it. What if Jenny did? So he grunted at Jack.

Jack laughed. "Seriously? You said this was some kid coming to watch. Why are your panties in a twist?"

"Watch your mouth," Billy shot out.

Jack looked Billy over. Billy had showered and cleaned up the edges of his beard. Hell, he'd even put on a little aftershave. A fact which did not go unnoticed by Jack.

"Hey, this kid—he wouldn't happen to have a mother, would he?" Jack threw up his hands. "Man, I've seen you go 'round with your old man enough. I got it. Kid and mom are off-limits."

Billy glared at him. "See to it." Which only got another laugh out of Jack.

Then, Billy saw the front door of Crazy Horse Choppers open up through the glass partition that separated the showroom from the shop floor. Cass, the receptionist, worked Saturdays and had gotten to be a pretty good saleslady. But otherwise, the place was deserted. The shop shut down at four-thirty on Friday and most everyone hit the bars. Hell, given that it was ten-thirty Saturday morning, half of his crew was probably still at a bar. The other half was sleeping it off.

Except on days like today. Jack had come in as a personal favor. Billy probably shouldn't kill him. "Be right back."

Cass was smiling at Jenny when Billy opened the door. Seth was doing that bunny-hop thing he did when he was excited. Billy felt himself grin at the boy. He remembered being that excited, once. Felt like a lifetime ago. "Hey, you found it."

Jenny's eyes were wide. Billy couldn't tell if she was as excited as her son or just plain old nervous.

Man, she looked *good*—not like a schoolmarm, not even like a mom. Hair flowing down her back, a pretty top and jeans that he knew would make her butt look amazing. She looked like she was far too good for him, but he didn't care. She looked like a woman—the woman he wanted.

"You gave good directions."

Cass made a small noise that almost qualified as a snort. Billy shot her a warning look. Between her and Jack, the whole shop would have the lowdown by Monday morning. Next week was going to be hell. And that was all *before* the auction. He wanted to be furious with Bobby for taking over his life, but then Jenny favored him with one of those small, challenging smiles, and he decided Monday didn't matter so much. "Come on back."

He couldn't help it. They were nowhere near a school and Bobby didn't film him when he wasn't at the school. So he put his hand on the small of her back as she passed him and didn't pull it away once she was through the door.

"Jenny, Seth, this is Jack Roy, my painter." Jack bowed, the rat fink.

"Nice to meet you," Jenny said. Then she looked at Billy and he realized he was growling. At Jack.

"Isn't this cool, Mom? See? Billy took it apart and now we're going to paint it!"

"Easy, kid. First, suit up." Jack tossed some coveralls at Seth. Then he looked at Jenny, held up a set of coveralls and waited.

"I'll just watch," Jenny said, not getting any closer.

"You'll have to stay in the waiting room. Too many fumes."

"Fumes? What about Seth?" Then Jack held up the extra mask. "Oh, okay. Well, then…have fun."

Billy walked her back to the door. "This will take a few hours. Will you be okay?" Man, he liked that smile on her. Warm and soft and sweet, but with a hint of tart challenge behind it. He liked it even more that she smiled at him and *not* at Jack. Then she touched his cheek and he almost forgot all about painting.

"I'll be fine."

"I'm coming over for dinner at Ben's," he added. "After we're done here."

He knew he couldn't rush the paint job. He never rushed a bike, because that's when mistakes happened, and as his brother Ben constantly pointed out, mistakes cost both time and money. But for the first time in a long time, he wanted to get done with the bike as fast as he could. For the first time in a stupid long time, he had plans that didn't involve welding.

Her fingers traced over the edge of his beard. He knew they had an audience, but he was powerless to do a damn thing about it. He wanted to stand there and look down into her eyes and not give a damn about what anyone else thought. Just him and her and this moment.

Then Jack whistled, Cass laughed and Seth said, "Ready!"

"Tonight," he said, feeling the pressure of her fingertips against his skin before she pulled away.

"It's a date" was all she said.

Jenny watched the three white-clad figures through the glass wall. As far as she could tell, no actual painting was occurring, but they were wearing masks and doing things, so she chose to assume that all was going well.

"You going to the auction?" Cass asked. Jenny tensed.

"Yes. You?"

She didn't know what else to say. Cass was the kind of hard-looking woman who fit in at a chopper shop. Cass wore a tank top and a leather vest and jeans that Jenny swore were acid-washed, and she could probably hold her own in a brawl.

By comparison, in the better of her two pairs of blue jeans and the cutest shirt she owned, a half-sleeve lilac top with big flowers outlined in embroidery and beads, she didn't feel like she belonged. Josey had gotten the top for Jenny last year on her birthday. It was only the second time she'd worn it. And she'd never been in a brawl. Heavens, she'd never even punched a person. That was not the sort of thing she did.

"Got my eye on someone," Cass said, staring extra hard through the glass.

This statement sent a spike of fear through Jenny. Surely this woman wasn't looking at Billy?

Then Cass laughed. "Don't worry, honey. We ain't after the same Bolton." She half patted, half slugged Jenny on the shoulder. Jenny managed to keep her balance in her one pair of fancy shoes—the satin pumps that went with her dress.

Should she ask which Bolton Cass was after? No—a certain measure of ignorance was, in fact, bliss. So she said, "That's good," as the front door opened and Cass went to attend to the customers.

Jenny sat in one of the big leather armchairs and kept an eye on the three figures. She couldn't tell which one was Billy and which one was Jack—they were both big men— but every so often, one white-clad figure would pause and turn his masked face in her direction.

Billy was keeping an eye on her. All she had to do was make it until tonight.

Five hours later, Jenny and Seth were riding up the freight elevator at Ben and Josey's. Jenny felt a little queasy, although she didn't think that was from the jerky elevator. No, the way Billy had peeled out of the lot on his bike after a hurried "I got something to do at home. I'll meet you there," had her nerves on edge.

Earlier, he'd said he was coming over, but had made no mention of *something he had to do.* This was supposed to be an almost date, wasn't it? That was the whole point, right? Well, how the heck could it be an almost date if he wasn't here?

The elevator lurched to a stop and Seth opened the doors. They'd been here enough that he knew what to do. Then he was out, running down the long aisle that divided Ben's warehouse into separate living quarters. "Josey! Ben! I painted a bike today!"

Ben's head popped out of the room he was converting into a nursery for the baby. The room had mint-green
walls and doors. In Jenny's opinion, Ben hadn't been overly
emotional about the baby, due in four months. But he was
putting a lot of time into that room, getting it just right.

"Hey, come tell me what you think of this bookcase
here," he said.

Jenny shook her head as she followed him into the nursery. Men. *Boltons*. Not so good with emotions, better with
tools. Maybe Ben didn't gush. But he was here, working
on behalf of the baby and Josey.

Was it wrong to want someone to take care of her, too?

She pushed the selfish thought away. She took care of
herself. That had always been enough before. Before she'd
met Billy.

Ben was waiting. Jenny studied the bookshelf. "Looks
good." He nodded his approval and asked Seth to help him
with something.

Josey appeared. "How was the shop?"

"Okay. Met Jack, the painter."

Josey's eyes wrinkled up with a deep smile. "Where's
Billy?"

"He said he had something to do at home and he'd meet
us here." This pronouncement was met with a frown, but
Jenny didn't want to dwell on how this evening could go
wrong. So she patted Josey's growing belly. "Any kicks
yet?"

"Maybe." Josey beamed as she moved Jenny's hand
below her belly button. "You're the expert here. You tell
me."

Another pang of loss hit Jenny as she felt the tiniest
of flutters. Fifteen years ago, she hadn't even known she
was pregnant until those little flutters got stronger, to the
point that Seth was karate-chopping her and she was forced
to admit that it wasn't just gas and she wasn't just gain-

ing a little weight. What had come after that had been sheer panic at telling her mom, then hope that Ricky would marry her and they'd live happily ever after. When that didn't happen, well, her world had kind of fallen apart.

At no point had she ever been able to enjoy being pregnant, to take the time to marvel at the gift of life she was creating. Years had passed before she got over not only the loss of Ricky, but also the loss of her carefree teenaged years. All because she'd lost her head over a bad boy. Well, maybe Ricky hadn't been all bad, but he certainly hadn't been good. Not as good as she'd tried to be ever since, as if she could make up for her mistakes.

Jenny was thrilled for Josey, she really was. But moments like this—Ben building a nursery by hand, Josey feeling the butterfly flutters—these were the moments she'd never had and probably never would. She couldn't even pull off an almost date. How was she supposed to settle down and take another crack at happily ever after?

"Definitely kicking," she said with a grin to Josey, trying to put her worries aside. "Give Sweet Pea here a few months. Remember how Seth kicked me so hard he rolled me over in bed once?"

Josey's eyes widened. She'd always thought that was a funny story, but now, she looked mildly terrified. "Yeah…"

Then she heard the freight elevator clanking, and her back stiffened. It had to be Billy. Part of her wanted to rush out and greet him. This was an almost date, after all. Wouldn't it be lovely to act like it?

But something held her back, and that something was the way he'd roared off after they had finished at the shop. She tried to tell herself that she was playing it cool, but that lie didn't hide the fact that she was more than a little unsure of what was going to happen next.

Josey went out first and said, "Oh!" in the tone of voice

that made it clear that the man outside wasn't what she'd been expecting.

Jenny tried not to rush out to see him, but she did walk a little quicker than normal. The first thing she noticed was the way Billy was standing. His feet were spread shoulder-length apart and his head was down. He looked like he could plow his way through a bar full of the baddest of bikers without getting a scratch on him.

She'd seen that look before, at Josey's wedding. Then, she'd thought he was pissed off at the world, a dangerous man to be avoided. Now, however, she saw something else. He didn't like that everyone had noticed him, and he liked it less that Josey had commented in surprise.

Then Jenny looked again, and saw why. Billy was wearing a pair of dark-washed jeans that looked expensive, instead of merely old and broken in. He had on another T-shirt, but this one was sea-foam green, with a texture to the fabric and a V at the neck. These things weren't so far beyond his normal attire, but the close-cut blazer he'd thrown on top of it all? The high shine to the shoes— that were not biker boots? The way his hair had been combed—but not pulled back into a ponytail? He was hot. Movie-star *hot*.

The heat that flashed down Jenny's back when Billy looked up and their gazes met was so fierce that it left her with an agonizing case of goose bumps. He'd gone home to change for *her*. And she appreciated the effort. Boy, did she appreciate it.

Then she saw the two small boxes tucked under one of his arms—one was a plain brown, the other had a bow on it. He noticed her looking.

"I had to go pick these up for you guys." He handed the plain one to Seth and the one with the bow to her.

"Presents? Awesome!" Seth snatched his up and began prying it open.

Jenny took the box much the same way she took her tea from him. Her fingers skimmed over the top of his, shimmering heat filling the air around them. It felt different this time. Everyone was watching them—and everyone knew what was going on.

"You didn't have to get us presents."

"A phone!" Seth yelled, snapping her out of her trance. "You got us phones? Man, that is so cool!"

"You got us phones?" The first thing she thought was, *How much did this cost?* Because it was one of those slick phones, just like Billy had. It wasn't just a phone. It was a sign that he had the money to walk right out and buy not one, but two of them.

"You need one." Then he blushed. "To call Josey," he added.

Behind them, Seth and Ben were talking about phone this and app that, but Jenny ignored them. After Bobby stopped filming at the school at the end of this week, Billy wouldn't be out there every morning and every night. However small and stolen the time they'd had in the past few weeks had been, it was all going to come to a crashing halt in a matter of days.

And he'd bought her a phone. No matter what he said, she knew it wasn't to call Josey. It was to call him. He wanted to keep talking to her.

It was the most thoughtful thing a man had ever done for her.

If they were alone, she'd kiss him. She'd kiss him long and hard, then she'd kiss him some more, hoping and praying the kiss led to something more, something selfish, something good.

But they weren't alone and her reality was unavoidable.

"I can't pay you back right now." Not when she was hording her precious few dollars to buy him at auction.

"You aren't paying me back at all. The plan is good for

a year. The kid's going to need a phone when he goes off the rez to high school next year, anyway. He earned it."

She wanted to protest—he couldn't spend this much money on *her*. Then Seth hit him midchest, a full-body hug-slash-tackle. "Thank you, thank you, thank you! This is *so* awesome!"

Billy awkwardly patted Seth on the head. "You're welcome, kid. Anytime you want to come back to the shop, give me a call. Had the guy put all the numbers in there."

Seth disengaged and started hopping. "Really? Man, that is *so* cool!"

Ben grinned over Seth's head. "Easy, kiddo. Come pick out what you want to drink for dinner—root beer or orange soda?" He and Josey led Seth away.

An awkward silence settled between Jenny and Billy. She needed to say something, but she was at a loss. No one had ever bought her such an extravagant gift, for that's what it was—extravagant. She knew there were cheaper phones on the market. She'd priced them. She still couldn't afford them, but she'd priced them.

"You didn't have to get me a phone." She realized she hadn't even opened her box yet.

"You don't like it." His blush deepened.

She was in danger of insulting him—again. So, even though it went against her financial principles, she stepped into him. "That's not it," she said, dropping her voice. "It's the most thoughtful thing anyone's ever given me." She stood on her tiptoes, put the hand without the box in it on his chest to balance herself and placed a kiss on his cheek, right above his beard. "Thank you."

One arm snaked around her waist and pulled her in tight, while his other hand captured hers and held it against his chest, right over his heart. The long, hard planes of his chest pressed against her front—muscles so firm they were almost unforgiving. But the way his hands held her body with that much gentleness? Her knees went weak.

A low rumble rose out of him, and the vibrations she felt as much as heard had such a sexual undertone that she wanted to do a whole lot more than kiss him. Heat flooded her belly.

"You look really pretty today."

All that heat pooled lower and she felt her hips shift against him. The pupils of his eyes widened in a look of pure desire. He leaned forward, his gaze glued to her lips.

Kiss me and make it worth it, she thought.

Then her box rang. "Mom?" Seth called out from the other side of the warehouse. "Are you going to answer it? Mom?"

A look of resignation blocked out the desire on Billy's face. But the amazing thing was, he didn't get mad or grumble about stupid kids or act like Seth's presence was a deal-breaker. Instead, he gave her a tiny smile and a quick squeeze around the waist and said, "We aren't done here," as he let her go.

"Better not be" was all she could say.

Then she answered the phone.

Twelve

Dinner took forever. Two forevers, by the time they ate dessert. Billy had to settle for sitting across from Jenny. The food was good, so there was that, but still, by the time Jenny made Seth carry in his dishes and Ben suggested they all play a game of pool, Billy was on the verge of punching something.

But Jenny smiled and blushed and said, "That would be fun," while she looked at him with those big eyes.

"Sounds good," he offered.

So that's how he found himself playing pool with Jenny against Ben and Seth while Josey sat and watched.

And Jenny was terrible. The only saving grace was that Seth was even worse, so the game was mostly Billy and Ben playing against each other. Which was fine, except Billy could do that anytime he wanted. And it wasn't how he wanted to spend his time with Jenny.

Luckily, his little brother wasn't stupid. After Ben sank the eight ball, he said, "Seth, did I tell you we got the newest 'Call of Duty'?"

"No way! Mom, can we play?"

Jenny got that look on her face that made it pretty clear

that, normally, she wouldn't exactly endorse a little warfare gaming. But she said, "I guess. But only for a little bit—you still have to go to bed at a reasonable hour."

Not that Seth heard that last part. He was already sprinting toward the TV room, Ben trailing him.

Josey sat on her stool for a bit before she said, "Well, I'm tired." She rubbed her back for emphasis. "Think I'll put the dishes in the dishwasher and go to bed."

"Need some help?"

Billy couldn't believe his ears. Had Jenny just offered to bail? When they were this close to not having anyone around?

But Josey quickly said, "No, I've got it. You have fun."

The women shared one of those feminine looks, and then, *finally,* he and Jenny were alone.

"We don't have to play pool, if you don't want."

Her cheeks pinked up real pretty. "I'm not that good...."

"You're holding your stick wrong." Her eyes flashed, but before she could snap off a smart response, he was behind her. "Here. I'll show you."

He angled her body, not bothering to keep any distance between them. He'd been waiting all day—all week—for this moment. No school, no cameras and no family. At least, not within line of sight.

Her body tensed against him. He moved her hair out of the way, giving him full access to her neck and ear. "I won't do anything you don't want me to, Jenny." Because he felt he had to prove to at least one of them that he wasn't lying, he leaned past her and picked up her cue. "Don't know why you loop your index finger over the cue. You're supposed to let it rest on your hand like this."

She hadn't said anything, and she continued not saying anything as he bent her forward, lined the cue up on her hand and guided her through a shot.

His thinking was blurring. The feeling of her pressed

against him was diverting all the blood from his brain to other parts—parts that were now straining behind his belt, against her backside. If he were a respectable man, he'd compliment her on that shot, maybe offer another tip on how to improve her aim and, most important, step away from her.

Too bad he had never been respectable.

He slid one hand around her waist under the swell of her breasts and pulled her in even tighter.

"I don't think you're playing fair," she said, her voice low and sultry.

"Never said I would."

She leaned back and ran her hand through his hair. "Your brother is in the next room."

He couldn't help it. He slid his hand up a few inches and took her breast in his palm.

She exhaled, her warm breath pulling him in closer. One taste, he thought as he dipped his head.

When their lips met, her body arched into his. Her nipple went rock-hard under his touch and his body responded in kind. Had he ever wanted a woman this badly? Was there anything he wouldn't do for her? Right now, with her soft curves melting into him, her teeth skimming his lips—sweet, merciful heaven, she was going to bring him to his knees.

She spun in his arms, which made everything better and worse at the same time. He picked her up and set her on the pool table. Her legs fell open. So it wasn't his fault that he had to step between them, and it wasn't his fault that he had to snake his hand back below her bottom to keep her from losing her balance and sprawling across the pool table. But it was a little bit his fault that he cupped her bottom and pulled her warm center toward him, and it was a whole hell of a lot his fault that he leaned into her, his full-on erection rubbing against her through two layers of denim.

Her head fell back as he ground against her, a low moan humming on her lips. Man, he had her right where he wanted her, and by the way she was digging her nails into his back, it was the same place she wanted to be.

"Jenny," he groaned. "Tell me what you want."

Even through his muddled thinking, he knew he'd promised her that he wouldn't do anything she didn't want him to. And that was the sort of promise a man kept, no matter what.

"I—"

"Oh, man! No fair!"

At the sound of Seth's whine from the TV room they both shrank back. How hard up was he? So hard up that he'd almost done unspeakable things on his brother's pool table.

Eyes wide, Jenny was obviously coming to the same conclusion. She pushed him back. Not away, but back. "Is this a date?"

He felt the corner of his mouth curl up. "No." What he wouldn't give for a date.

"No?"

He leaned forward so he could feel the pressure of her hands on his chest. "If this were a date, we'd be alone and I'd lay you out on this pool table, strip those jeans off you and I wouldn't stop until you screamed my name." It sounded so good that he was having a little trouble remembering why he didn't go ahead and do it now.

"Again," Seth demanded in the distance.

"You're on, kid," Ben replied.

Oh, yeah. This wasn't a date because they weren't alone. It came down to that.

"When are we going to have a date, Billy?" She leaned

up, her voice low as she went from holding him back to rubbing his chest.

"After the bachelor auction." One week. One week that might break him.

A look of doubt flashed over her face. "I don't know if I can wait that long."

He folded her into his arms. "I'll make it worth it," he promised again. Man, he hoped he was doing the right thing, planning their first date as a surprise.

She pushed him back and, with the sounds of the video game echoing behind them, he had no choice but to step away.

"What do we do until then?"

Right. What did they do if they weren't having sex? "Uh…"

What did people do on dates? It had been such a long time since he'd had a date—a real date, not getting drunk in a bar. Actually, it had been a long time since he'd done even that.

Then he looked down and saw the concentration on her face. For the first time, he found himself wondering how long it had been for her.

He wanted to make this count.

She took a deep breath and appeared to get more control over herself than he was currently feeling. "We could watch a movie. Lots of people do that."

Yeah, he remembered that. He'd gone with Ashley to the movies in high school. He didn't remember watching any films…no, what he remembered was getting in a hell of a lot of trouble in the dark.

Yeah—no cameras hovering around, no kids barging in on them. He'd been waiting for this for weeks. He was going to make the most of this. Bring on the darkness.

Except…Jenny wasn't the kind of woman who normally let things get heavy the moment the lights dimmed. He'd be lucky if she didn't haul off and smack him, because keeping his hands off of her was going to be one hell of a challenge.

Damn. He was going to have to work harder on being good enough for her.

"Okay. A movie."

Her eyes lit up. She was killing him.

"I'll send Seth to bed."

Seth went to bed grumbling, but Jenny didn't care. It was ten o'clock. Ben had taken far less convincing. All he'd said was, "Josey go to bed already?" Then he'd winked and left them alone.

She sat on the couch as Billy flipped through the movies available through Josey's television. Jenny's stomach was nervous. At this point, she didn't care what they watched. Just so long as he picked something and turned off the lights.

After that kiss on the pool table, she didn't know what to expect. The two of them, alone in the dark…God, she wanted another kiss like that—but…*but*…

But a man like Billy, who was rough and tumble and had just threatened to strip her pants off of her and do horrible, terrible, *wonderful* things to her…what would stop him from doing that now? What would stop *her* from stopping *him?*

She was a respectable, *responsible* woman now, by God. She did not lose her head over bad boys anymore. Even if they were men like Billy.

He started a movie and settled beside her on the couch. He slid his arm around her shoulder and pulled her in. "Feel like I'm a teenager again," he whispered.

"I know what you mean."

There was something old-school about this. Not that she knew firsthand—she'd never had much trouble climbing out her bedroom window and running wild. But all this sneaking around was probably something normal teenagers did all the time.

She couldn't help but remember that sneaking always led to getting caught. She didn't want to get caught again. She didn't want to throw away everything she'd worked so hard to become. She wasn't the same girl who threw caution to the wind because of an irresistible bad boy.

Which was all well and good except for one small thing: she *wanted* Billy in a way that had nothing to do with sneaking around or immature fumbling.

God, this contradiction was going to drive her crazy.

Billy didn't say anything as the movie started up, but once they hit a stretch of dialogue, he leaned down and brushed his lips against her forehead. "I want to see you after I'm done with the build at the school."

"You had mentioned a date after the auction." She felt good under his arm. His chest—so broad—was warm and surprisingly comfortable. She nuzzled in deeper.

"More than that."

He tilted her head up so he could capture her lips again.

Even now, the heat that pooled between her legs made thinking difficult. As Billy's fingertips brushed over her breasts again, his movements steady and sure and—above all else—confident, the desire that gripped her went way beyond what she'd experienced as a teen. This wasn't wanting sex for the sake of having sex—this was more. She wanted Billy. She was starting to think she needed him.

His hand slipped lower, over the front of her jeans. Then his hand was against the part of her that hurt for him the most. "Do you want this?"

He pressed—with exquisite precision, he simply pressed against her.

Jenny's body bucked against his hand—his finger—his fingertip and the pressure he was using to control her. Because she wanted to give up control. She wanted to give up everything—everything she'd worked so hard for, everything she'd worked so hard to be. A good mother, a good teacher, a good daughter—a responsible adult who did the right thing. None of that mattered. The only thing that mattered was him touching her.

Billy shifted the pressure and she shook in his arms. He only held her tighter. "Tell me you want this, Jenny."

His voice was a direct order, one that threatened to swamp her.

"Yes."

She didn't know if she'd thought it or said it when he shifted against her again. The climax whipped her body against his, but he didn't lose his grip as she rode the wave.

"Woman," he said as he buried his face in her neck, his teeth skimming her skin.

She wanted more. One touch—one *single* touch didn't make up for the past eleven years. She needed more. She needed *him*.

"I'm not too good at this relationship thing." His voice was so low and deep that its vibrations sent another shock of pleasure through her.

She grinned, although he probably couldn't see it in the dark. "I'm out of practice, too."

"I want to try. With you."

She didn't say anything. She didn't have to.

She just kissed him.

One moment, Jenny was snuggling against a warm, hard body while she pleasantly drifted through a hazy sleep.

The next, her eyes snapped open in a panic. Seth was standing over her—her and Billy. Asleep. On the couch. Sweet merciful heaven, she was on top of Billy, one of her legs draped over Billy's thigh. Were they dressed? Yes. Thank God for small favors.

"Hey…guys."

Seth had a funny look on his face. She jolted and tried to sit up, but Billy's arms didn't fall away from her. If anything, he tightened his grip. That was when she realized his hand was in the space between her top and her waistband. Caressing her bare back.

In front of her son.

The panic that hit her was so strong she could taste it in the back of her mouth. "Seth! Um, we were, um, we were— How did you sleep? Do you want some breakfast?" She couldn't tell if her hardwired Mom instincts were a good thing or not.

Seth didn't say anything. He kept on staring. Behind him, the TV was a huge wall of blue screen. They must have fallen asleep before the movie ended, before things had gone too far.

"Kid," Billy said. Jenny's gaze snapped back on him. His eyes were still closed, and he hadn't let go of her yet, but he was at least a little awake. "Don't you know not to wake a man up before the coffee's ready?"

Then the weirdest thing happened. Seth looked sheepish and said, "Sorry."

"Go check." The order was anything but subtle, but then Billy added, "After I get going, I'll show you my bikes."

Seth stared at them with undisguised suspicion before he said, "Okay." At least the kitchen was four rooms away. It would take the boy some time to get there.

Jenny tried to sit up again, but Billy kept his hold on her. "Morning, beautiful," he said, his eyes still closed. He pushed her up to his lips and took a quick kiss. "I like waking up with you."

Part of her wanted to do nothing more than snuggle back down into his arms and maybe see where the morning went. But that part was overridden by panic.

And the worst part was, she wasn't sure why she was panicking so badly. So Seth had caught her and Billy together. They were both still fully dressed and hadn't even been kissing. If she and Billy were going to keep seeing each other—and that did seem like the plan—then sooner or later Seth would put one and one together.

But she wasn't ready for that first thing on a Sunday morning. Heck, she wasn't sure when she'd be ready. For too long, her life had been about her son. To do something as selfish as spend some time with a man—with Billy—felt foreign.

With a squeeze that bordered on crushing, Billy hugged her. "He'll be fine," he said as they sat up, almost as if he'd been reading her mind.

"But—"

She didn't get the chance to freak out, though. From the other side of the apartment, she heard Ben's voice, then Josey's. The rest of the house was up.

He took her hand, kissed her cheek and whispered, "Only six more days."

Six days until the bachelor auction. And after that? A real date.

How was she ever going to make it?

Thirteen

Six of the longest days of Jenny's life had finally come and gone. She'd seen Billy only for the first three. He and Seth had reassembled the bike on Monday at the school, then Bobby had spent the next two days finishing his filming.

In other words, even though she'd seen Billy for three days, she hadn't gotten to really talk to him. He'd kissed her on the cheek when he'd given her the ticket for the event—the ticket that said Admission: $100. When she'd protested, he'd cut her off with a look. "I want you there" was all he'd said. Who was she to argue with that? Besides, she couldn't have afforded to pay him back even if she'd wanted to. Not if she had a hope of buying him.

The two school days without Billy in the morning and Billy in the evening were even longer. However, the Saturday of the bachelor auction flew by so fast it left her dizzy. Before she knew it, her mom had curled her hair and she'd shimmied into her bridesmaid's dress and had loaded up Seth, several of his classmates and a half-dozen of her TAPS girls in the school van, along with Josey's mom, Sandra, and was barreling toward the reception center in Rapid City.

In the small purse that Jenny had clutched to her chest was $743 dollars—all of the money she had left from what the state of South Dakota had paid her to run TAPS. She had no idea what Billy would go for, but it was the best she could do. She had to hope it would be enough.

The kids were all excited, nervously chattering and messing around with the pretied bow ties and white shirts that Josey had delivered to the school. Josey wanted them to help with registration, so everyone would have the chance to meet the kids their money would be helping. And everyone was, well, everyone. Josey had run down a preliminary guest list with her. Half the city council was on that list. So were a few starlets that Bobby had sweet-talked into showing up, no doubt with promises of internet stardom. A lot of the names Jenny hadn't known, but Josey had. Wives and daughters of industry titans from South Dakota, Wyoming and parts of Montana. Heavens, there were even a few women ranchers attending. The whole thing was crazy.

Even Sandra seemed to crackle with a nervous energy. "A bachelor auction! Did you ever think we'd see the day?"

"No," Jenny had to admit.

Sandra gave her an odd look out of the corner of her eye. "Nervous, dear?"

Jenny forced herself to breathe in and out. "Hoping to make it through the evening without something going wrong." Which was true. That was a concern. Just not her primary one. She realized she was fluffing her hair again, which was probably not helping her beachy waves stay very beachy. She put her hands in her lap.

"I can handle the children." As if to illustrate this state-ment, Sandra looked in the rearview mirror and shouted, "Randy, where do your hands belong?"

"To myself" came the sheepish reply from the rear of the van.

"See?" Sandra actually reached over and patted Jenny on the arm. "You have fun tonight. I've got this covered." Jenny swore Sandra winked at her. "Got more than a few tricks up my sleeve."

Fun? Was fun an option tonight? Heck, she hadn't been this nervous at Josey's wedding, and she'd been so distraught there she'd almost thrown up before she'd walked down the aisle. That had been more about remembering to smile in front of a huge crowd while simultaneously trying not to step on the hem of her dress.

This was different. This was the very real possibility of seeing the man she wanted to take home going home with someone else. Billy had promised her a date. How would she watch him leave with another woman?

Well, she sort of knew the answer to that one. Not well. Not well at all.

Soon enough, the van was pulling up in front of the reception hall. Although the auction didn't start for another hour and a half, the place was already humming with activity. Jenny recognized the camera crew from the school, but they weren't the only ones with cameras running around. She counted four different local news vans, all setting up to do live feeds for the ten o'clock news. And because of the starlets, Bobby had even rolled out a red carpet. The highest of South Dakota's high society was strutting down the catwalk while photographers snapped shots. The whole thing was completely insane—and entirely out of her league.

Wearing a tux that fit him like a second skin, Bobby left his post on the red carpet, where he'd been glad-handing all the guests, and came to greet them. The kids crowded around and Bobby turned on the charm. "Okay, troops, come with me!"

Avoiding the cameras, he herded the whole crew inside. Within ten minutes he had them practicing greetings for the people who'd be keeping their school in the black for the foreseeable future. Then Bobby snagged Seth and had him helping backstage.

Jenny tried to relax, but it wasn't easy. Bobby was being his normal, irritating self—telling her she was in the way here—no, still in the way over there. Josey came by, but was too busy dealing with last-minute credit-card issues to talk Jenny down from the edge. Even Sandra disappeared. She was giving a short welcome speech and had to go practice.

Keeping an eye on the kids, Jenny looked for Billy. Bobby wasn't hard to miss, and she caught sight of Ben ushering various men backstage—including Don Two Eagles and Jack Roy.

But no Billy.

Bobby reappeared and hustled her over to a table set slightly off from the rest of the crowd. "Darned shame you can't be on camera," he said with that used-car-salesman smile of his. "You look amazing tonight."

Jenny waited for the demand that she do something, or a jerky plea for assistance—but nothing.

Well, that was…odd. If she didn't know any better, she'd say that Bobby Bolton had paid her a compliment. "Thank you. This is, um, impressive. You pulled this off!"

Bobby's smile deepened and for a moment, he looked more…real, somehow. "Thanks, Jenny. I hope we make a ton of money for the school tonight."

Then he looked over her shoulder and was gone, back to schmoozing someone more important than she was.

The room filled. Women in slinky black dresses, in dark business suits, in sequined numbers that were better suited to Miss America than anything else—suddenly, the room was *filled*. The cash bar in one corner was doing a booming business as an excited hum filled the air.

Jenny eyed her potential competition, her stomach sink-

ing. A lot of the women looked smooth and elegant and effortless, like this was just another Saturday night. Jenny had
taken a literature class when she'd gone back to school to
get her teaching degree, and a line from a play she thought
was Shakespeare came back to her. These women—they
had a lean and hungry look about them, like they were
going to pounce on the first hunk they saw and quite possibly rip him to shreds.

She didn't stand a chance.

Then Cass, the Crazy Horse receptionist, came and
sat by her. Jenny almost hadn't recognized her. Cass had
clearly been to a salon. Her hair was swooped up into an
elegant French twist, and she was wearing an honest-to-
goodness ball gown. "Cass! Wow!"

Cass winked, and underneath the professional makeup
application, Jenny saw the same sparkling smile. "Hope
you get your man, honey."

That made two of them. "You, too."

Cass grinned and filled the rest of their time with a running commentary on the various women she knew in the
crowd. The statuesque blonde had ordered a bike for her
husband three years ago, but they'd divorced since then.
That woman with the bright white hair and the too-tight
face? Her family owned a trust company.

The more Cass shared, the more worried Jenny got.
These women weren't just rich—they were *really* rich.
The lights dimmed and a spotlight lit up the stage. In front
of a red-velvet curtain sat the bike that Seth had helped
build. Bobby Bolton came out and the crowd applauded.
He made some opening remarks in that smooth tone of
voice about the men that would soon be for sale— "For
the night, ladies!" He then introduced Sandra, who spoke
for ten minutes about the school and the children and what
the proceeds of the auction would go toward.

Jenny was surprised at the emphasis Sandra put on after-school programs—hers and the one Don wanted to start for the boys. Although the crowd remained polite, Jenny could sense the women getting restless. The teacher in her wanted to shush them, but she forced herself to be still.

Then Sandra was done, Bobby was back on stage, and the auction began. Bobby introduced everyone, but he'd brought in a real auctioneer to do the actual selling.

Jenny didn't know any of the men who went first. After the gavel fell the first few times, the only thing she was certain about was that she didn't have enough money. A guy with a slicked-back ponytail, a tie and a leather jacket oh-so-casually thrown over his shoulder went for nine hundred dollars. Jack Roy went for more than one thousand. Heavens, Don Two Eagles went for a healthy six hundred.

Then Bobby said, "Ladies, a true diamond in the rough—Bruce Bolton!" and the crowd went wild. Jenny had only met the senior Bolton once, at the wedding where he'd mostly stayed by the bar with a group of equally crusty-looking bikers. Josey didn't like him much and Jenny had gotten the feeling that Ben didn't exactly get along with his father.

Bruce Bolton trotted out on stage, looking for all the world like Hulk Hogan in a tux, only with less hair. The man was eating up the catcalls from the audience. He posed and preened while Bobby and the auctioneer cracked jokes about Bruce's "staying power."

Luckily, the bidding started. Jenny was shocked when Cass bid the first fifty dollars, and more shocked as she kept right on bidding, blowing all other hopefuls out of the water. She finally got her man for a cool $1,850.

"You bought Bruce?" Jenny couldn't help but whisper even as Cass smacked the tabletop in victory.

"That man's been bossing me around for years." Cass's smile was nothing short of wicked. "'Bout time that particular shoe was on the other foot."

Jenny decided it was best not to ask what, exactly, Cass meant and was thankful when she left to claim her prize.

The rest of the evening passed in a blur of good-looking men, insane bids and suggestive innuendo. Some of the guys from the rez—guys Jenny knew—brought in a pretty penny.

She tried to be happy at the huge dollar amounts being raised—all of this money was going to the school, to the TAPS program. They had to be nearing thirty-five thousand, at least—and they hadn't even gotten to the bike. This was wonderful. This was great.

She was on the verge of tears.

Finally, the end was near. She knew this not because she was keeping count of the number of hot men who'd paraded across the stage, but because Bobby auctioned himself off. He winked, blew kisses and waggled his eyebrows like a true lothario as the numbers went up and up.

Then the gavel fell. Jenny craned her neck around and spotted the busty redhead who was celebrating her victory in a sloshed way as the gavel fell. Nearly five thousand dollars.

Holy cow. Before the hugeness of that number could truly register, though, Bobby took the microphone. "And now, ladies, the moment we've all been waiting for—the man of the hour, 'Wild' Billy Bolton!"

Except the man who walked out on stage wasn't Billy—not the Billy she knew, anyway. Oh, he was tall and broad, and his hair was the same golden brown, but that's where the resemblance ended. This man had neatly cropped hair that sported a hint of wave. This man wore no beard, which made his strong jaw that much stronger. True, he was in a close-cut gray suit and not a tux—he didn't have on a tie, just a white button-up shirt with the top two buttons undone. He walked out on stage, paused, pivoted—and looked directly at her. The glare—for that's what it was—was white-hot, but she wasn't scared of it, nor of him.

Jenny wasn't sure if she was breathing or not. Billy looked ferocious, but she could see underneath the fury that he was unsure about this whole thing. That meanness was the cover he hid behind. Everyone else probably saw a brutal man, but she saw someone else. The man she wanted.

Bobby, darn his hide, opened the bidding up at five hundred dollars. Jenny knew she didn't have a prayer, but she held up her paddle anyway. So did half the room.

The bidding quickly left her in the dust. A thousand, two thousand—the number grew faster than Seth's shoe size. The auctioneer had abandoned the fifty-dollar increments he'd used for everyone else and was going up by two hundred dollars a shot. Even so, the bidding hit five thousand within five minutes, and at least four women were still in the running.

How ridiculous was she? Ridiculous enough to think she and her meager little $743 had a shot in heck of winning this auction. She almost wished Cass had come back to the table so that her saucy attitude would distract Jenny from her misery.

Billy seemed almost as miserable. He'd been standing up there for a long time, looking uncomfortable. For his sake, Jenny wanted the bidding to end so he could get off the stage.

Six thousand dollars came and went. The only consolation Jenny had was that another woman dropped out. Although she knew it was pouring salt into the wound, Jenny tried to see who the remaining three bidders were.

One was a raven-haired stunner in one of those slinky black dresses; the other was petite and curvy, with big blond hair. Jenny couldn't spot the third woman, but the auctioneer kept mentioning three numbers as the bids went up and up and up.

She wouldn't have thought it possible, but her hopes sank even further. She knew that if she'd bought Billy, she would have finally, *finally* broken her decades-long drought. She wouldn't have had to wait for another date—wait for the cameras to stop and the stars to align and the world to be perfect, because it already would have been. She would have gotten into his bed and stayed until she'd screamed in pleasure. She would have gone to sleep in his arms and woken up there, without a teenager standing over them. It would have been selfish and naughty and very, very good.

She eyed the two women she could see. Instead, Billy might be doing those things with one of them. She tried to hold on to the idea that he wouldn't sleep around at the drop of a hat, not when he was already involved with her, but she couldn't compete with those women and, really, how involved were they? Was Billy strong enough to resist those feminine charms? Seven thousand dollars came. The raven-haired woman dropped out, sitting down with a look of disgust. But the petite woman was still bidding against the last, unseen bidder.

The whole room was holding its breath as the bidding slowed near the eight-thousand dollar mark. The petite woman was clearly at her breaking point, taking longer and longer to think about each increase. The unseen bidder didn't waver, though. She hit each call without skipping a beat. Jenny scanned the room again, but couldn't see who was pulling the trigger.

Then it was over. The petite bidder couldn't break nine grand. The gavel swung down, and someone else bought Billy. Maybe it was better she didn't know what the winner looked like. That way, it wouldn't haunt her dreams.

One last thing remained, and that was the bike. Ben wheeled it out. Jenny tried to pay attention, because Bobby brought all the kids up on stage, with Seth front and center.

Billy was still out there, looking a little more relieved that the bidding was over. He put his arm around Seth's shoulders as people took photos of them and the bike.

It was hard to look at it. It should have been perfect. Heck, it was perfect. Seth looked up to Billy; Billy had taken her son—a boy he didn't have to do a darned thing for—under his wing. Together they'd built a bike, a real, tangible thing that Seth was proud of. She still wouldn't go so far as to say that Billy was father-material—even cleaned up, he projected an air of danger that was unmistakable—but he'd exceeded her every expectation, and then some.

Yes, it was perfect. Except that someone else had her man.

After the photos, the kids were ushered off stage and the bidding began. Billy stood behind the bike, his hands on the handlebars. He tried to smile—clearly Bobby had told him to—but it looked more like a snarl than anything else. Jenny knew she should pay attention—Seth would want to know how much his bike went for. But all she could think was that she needed to leave before she saw who held Billy's winning bid. And after that? She had a phone now. Maybe she could wait a few days and then call Billy. Hopefully, by then, his evening with the winner would be over and she could try to pretend that it had never happened.

God, what a depressing thought.

The bike went for nearly thirty thousand dollars, which was a darned impressive price. The whole evening had probably raised close to seventy-five thousand dollars for the school. She could run TAPS and feed the kids an evening meal and even pay for prenatal care for years on that kind of money—everything she'd ever wanted and probably some things she hadn't even thought of yet. She should be thrilled. She *would* be thrilled, by God.

Starting tomorrow.

Tonight, she needed to suffer her defeat in peace and quiet. She stood to go get the kids when someone grabbed her arm. "Come with me," Cass said in the kind of voice that left little room for disagreement.

"The kids…"

"You're needed at the registration desk."

Cass didn't explain. Maybe there was a problem with one of the girls helping Josey?

Cass cut through the crowd, pulling Jenny along so fast that she struggled to keep her shoes on. Some of the crowd was departing, but many of the women were hanging around in tight clusters, refreshed drinks in their hands. For them, the night wasn't over.

Cass led her past the line of people waiting to pay, right up to the front. Josey was standing behind Livvy as the girl ran credit cards. "Oh, there you are." Josey grabbed a sheet with a receipt stapled to it. "Here." She shoved the paper into Jenny's hands. "And take this."

"What?" Jenny looked down. It was a receipt, all right—for $8,750. And a ponytail holder. She looked at Josey. "Wait, what?"

"Don't worry about Seth. Mom and I have the kids covered. Have fun!"

"What?" Jenny stared at the paper in her hand again. $8,750—that was how much Billy had sold for. What was going on?

Then a hush came over the crowd. Still swamped with confusion, Jenny looked up and saw Billy—the new and improved Billy—coming toward her. His head was lowered, making him look like a bull charging. Straight at her.

All eyes were on Billy and, by extension, on her.

"Ready?" he asked in an extra-gruff voice.

"What?" Even to her own ears, the refrain was getting tired, but she had no idea what was going on.

"You won me, didn't you? It's time for our date." The

corner of his mouth curved up in a victorious smile—so much easier to see without the beard covering it up.

So much hotter, too.

The crowd around them murmured in curiosity. No doubt about it, she and Billy were the center of attention. Out of the corner of her eye, she thought she saw the petite blond glare at her.

But she didn't care. All she could do was look up into Billy's eyes in wonder. "Now?"

"It's after the auction, isn't it?" His grin got a little more wicked as he took a step closer. She felt the power ripple off of him and surround her. Despite the jealous looks, she felt safer near him now than she ever had.

He'd meant that literally? She looked at Josey, who nodded and waved her away. "I've got the kids," she said again.

Stunned, Jenny looked back down at the receipt in her hand. "Paid in full" was stamped on the top, but she sure as heck hadn't fronted the money.

Realization slapped her across the face. "You?"

There could be no mistaking the look of intent on his face, not with that wolfish grin and certainly not with that covetous gleam in his eyes. "Me."

And he guided her toward the door.

Fourteen

Billy led her to his bike in the parking lot, his hand firmly around her waist. Wait—this wasn't his normal bike. The bike that Jenny had seen at the school only had one seat.

This bike? Same black-and-chrome colors, but the handlebars were so low that they looked almost normal. But that wasn't the biggest change. No, the biggest difference between the other bike and this one was the extra seat on the back, complete with a backrest.

"You planned this all along, didn't you?" she heard herself ask.

"I told you we'd have a date after the auction." He spun her around in a tight embrace. "This is after the auction."

"Why didn't you tell me?"

"It was a surprise." Was she imagining things, or did he blush at that? "And we didn't want Bobby to find out."

That she could see. She didn't want Bobby involved with this at all. "Well, I am surprised." The understatement of the year.

He reached up and brushed her hair away from her mostly bare shoulders. His fingers trailed down her arms, setting off a cascade of goose bumps. "You'll get cold," he said as he stepped back and slipped off his jacket.

Jenny felt her breath catch in her throat. She'd seen his chest bare once, and she'd seen him in T-shirts, with and without his leather riding vest, plenty of times. But the wide expanse of his chest barely contained by a crisp button-up shirt took all of her confusion and uncertainty and agony over the auction and blew it away like a bunch of leaves in a fall breeze. The only thing that was left was sheer, knee-shaking desire.

So she hadn't realized he was such a literalist. He'd gone to this much trouble to rig the auction for her—and plunked down almost nine grand to get a night with her? No schools and—she looked around—not a single camera in sight. She had no idea how that was working—it wasn't a far stretch to say there were a hundred cameras here. But she wasn't in front of one.

A small crowd of jealous-looking women were milling around the front door of the building, looking daggers at her. Seth was out there, too, along with Livvy and a few of the other kids. But they were all standing around Sandra and Josey, waving. Even Seth smiled.

"He'll be okay," Billy said, doing that thing where he read her mind. "He's going home with Ben and Josey. Video games all night."

"You thought of everything, then?"

He draped his jacket around her shoulders and she slipped her arms in. She swam in the huge thing, but it was warm and smelled like Billy—faintly of leather and the wind. Then he swept her hair back into a low tail and waited until she'd secured it with the band Josey had given her.

Billy handed her a small helmet. It fit, another sign of how much he'd planned ahead. She hadn't exactly ridden a lot of motorcycles, but now was not the time to chicken out. Taking a deep breath, she looked at the bike, looked at her dress, and did the only thing she could—hiked her dress almost up to her hips and slid one leg over the seat.

A noise that was far too sexy to be a purr but not aggressive enough to be a straight-up growl came from deep in Billy's chest. Without another word, he slid onto the bike in front of her.

"Hold on," he commanded.

She was only too happy to comply. She slid her arms around his chest, loving the way the warmth of his body surrounded her. Then he fired up the bike and rolled slowly out of the parking lot.

She didn't know where they were going. Well, she knew they were probably headed for his house, the one with the fabled pool table, but she had no idea how long she would be on the back of this bike. Billy gunned it and they flew, the wind biting at her bare legs. She pressed herself farther into Billy's body, trying to steal as much of his body heat as she could.

Billy brought the bike to a stop at a red light. He reached back and slid a hand up her bare leg, all the way up under her dress. The feel of his hand on her bare skin—skin already chilled by the night air—had her doing a lot more than just breaking out in goose bumps. She out and out shivered against him.

Then they were off again, going faster this time. The warmth of Billy's back warred with the cold of the wind, and all of it was topped by the building excitement. A whole night with him. A night where she could be selfish and wouldn't have to second-guess herself in the morning.

Oh, she needed this.

She couldn't tell if Billy lived a great distance from the auction site or if time was playing tricks on her. The bike hummed between her legs, driving stark desire up into her body with a relentless pace. They took a couple of corners a little too fast, so she had to grip Billy extra hard to keep her balance.

Eleven years. The number kept repeating itself. Eleven whole years since she'd done something this wild, this crazy. Eleven years since she'd done something for her and her alone. But she wasn't the same girl she'd been back then. She'd never had sex as an adult, with a man as confident, as *capable,* as Billy. It didn't matter how wild his reputation was—she was making a conscious choice to be with him.

She had no idea what she was doing. Really, her life since Billy had rolled into it had been uncharted territory. None of it—not the slow flirtation, not the tension and most certainly not the dance—was something she'd been sure about.

She turned her face into his back. Even with the wind pulling at them, she could still smell the leather that was him. Without letting go, she spread her fingers against his chest, copping a feel of his massive muscles. She couldn't wait to strip the shirt off of him and touch what she'd only seen. She could hold on for a few more minutes, couldn't she?

Those minutes felt long, but finally they slowed. Jenny could see house lights off at great distances, but none were close to the long drive where Billy was pulling up. Before them was a wall of garage doors—three of them—but that's all she could see of the house. The center door opened and they rolled in before the bike came to a stop. Behind them, the garage door shut with a clang.

When Billy kicked out the stand and the bike lurched to the left, Jenny felt herself clawing at his chest to keep her balance.

"I got you," he said, and she heard the amusement in his voice. "Can you stand?"

She nodded, which was silly. He couldn't see her head

bobbing behind him. She got the helmet off and handed it to him. He hung it off the handlebar and waited. Going slow, she swung her leg over. Her dress was at the breaking point, but as she stood, Billy's hand slid up the inside of her leg to above her knee.

Her legs didn't hold, but it wasn't all bad—he twisted and caught her, that wolfish grin on his face as clear as day. "You okay?"

"Better now."

The time of uncertainty was over. She knew exactly what she wanted to happen, and what was going to happen. All that was left was fervently hoping that those two things were the same.

He was still on the bike, but she stepped into him, straddling his left thigh. It wasn't any closer than they'd been snuggled together on the couch, but the tension between them was so tight it almost crackled.

"You shaved," she whispered, running her fingertips over his newly smooth jaw.

His arm around her waist tightened. "You like it?"

"Makes you look respectable."

Billy notched his eyebrow at her and then pushed his leg up. Jenny gasped at the pressure that hit her center. Her whole body still tingled with the vibrations of the bike, but this? This went way past tingling and straight over to a kind of pain that only had her wanting more.

She ground down on him, although she didn't consciously choose to do so. Her body, so desperate for the good old-fashioned release of an orgasm at someone else's hands, suddenly had a mind of its own.

"Only thing is," Billy said in a smug tone, "I'm not that respectable."

How was it possible they were still on the bike? That he was still sitting there, looking ungodly handsome? Because, as his hands skimmed over her very bare thighs and pulled her dress up even farther, she wasn't even sure of her own name anymore.

"Promises, promises," she managed to get out, clutching at his nice white shirt so hard that the wrinkles might never come out.

His hands hit the edge of her panties and paused, exploring. They were a perfectly respectable pair of panties—pale pink with little brown polka dots. The fanciest pair she owned. What if they weren't sexy enough?

He ran his fingers up under the edges—over her backside, up on her hips, then down between her legs. The only thing that stopped him was his own thigh. The one she was riding.

"I promised you one thing." He slid his hands back—back farther, back higher, until he was palming each of her posterior cheeks underneath her panties.

Her mind spun, trying to think through the fog of want and need and desire that was making thinking very, very difficult. What had he said? She needed to remember. Then it came to her.

It would be worth the wait.

"I'm still waiting."

A quick smile flashed across his face, but it was lost underneath a hot look of focus as he pushed her up on his leg, driving the one spot that needed so much more than a little mechanical vibrating.

She gasped again, feeling the pressure from the inside matching the pressure on the outside as he pushed her up, raised his leg and pushed her up again. The friction—oh, the friction that built between them, barely separated by the thin layer of her panties—even if Jenny had wanted to say something else, she couldn't. She didn't have the words. The movements were small, but the dance? The dance between them was worth it *all*.

The whole time, he watched her with that look of intense concentration on his face. "You're so beautiful," he growled at her as the pressure built and built.

His words hit something inside her that vibrated even more than the bike had. "Yeah?"

Then all coherence left her behind when he leaned down, touching his forehead to hers. "The first time I saw you at the wedding? Yeah. Oh, yeah. You were *beautiful*. Just like now."

How she needed to hear that, needed to believe that. And she did.

Something inside her let go and she surrendered to the way he moved her body for her. The orgasm hit her like a car crash in slow motion, leaving her feeling like she'd been knocked flat while at the same time she crumpled onto him, panting. She could feel his fingerprints on her bottom where he was still stroking her. She'd never been so naked while still clothed before.

"No screaming?" He didn't sound disappointed, though. In fact, he sounded downright cheerful. "Guess I'll have to try harder."

Everything that had gone weak with sexual relief tightened up again in anticipation. He wasn't done with her. And, now that she thought of it, she hadn't even gotten started with him.

Then he picked her up—lifted her straight off the ground as he slung his leg over the bike. Her legs wrapped around his waist, but it wasn't because she was in danger of being dropped. No, he held her up as if she weighed next to nothing, all without losing his balance.

She felt the weight of his erection through his trousers, pressing hard against her very center. That was *harder,* all right. And she was going to have to try it. All of it.

Without another word, he carried her into the house. Jenny supposed it was a nice house, but it was dark and she couldn't see much past Billy's face, Billy's lips, Billy's shirt. She kissed his neck, his jaw, his mouth all while trying to undo the buttons on his shirt. She wanted to do all her seeing and touching at the same time.

She got about halfway down his shirt, just enough to give her a peek at the muscles and the tattoos, when he kicked open a door. The next thing she knew, she was being set down on something that felt suspiciously like a bed. A bed with silk sheets. The kind of bed she'd barely allowed herself to dream of—and now she was here with Billy.

"No pool table?" she asked as he knelt before her and peeled his jacket from her shoulders.

He threw the jacket to the side, then worked the zipper at the back of her dress. It had been a long time since anyone had undressed her, and she lost herself in the sensation of his fingers slipping down her back. All she could do was lean her head against his shoulder. When he had the dress unzipped, he slid his hands underneath the fabric and caressed her bare skin. For once, the danged goose bumps were banished by the scorching heat of his touch. Suddenly, she was hotter than she could ever remember being.

"You deserve more than a pool table."

"Oh."

At this, he paused and kissed her hard. "We can always play pool later."

Oh.

He pulled the dress over her head and threw it behind him. The dress was probably beyond all hope by this time, but she didn't care.

When the dress was gone, he said, "Where were we, from last week?" as he ran his hands up and down her back.

She lifted her legs back around his waist and pulled him closer. The weight of his erection hit her center, and a whole lot more than a shiver ran through her. As nice as that little moment in the garage had been—and it had been quite nice—it wasn't enough. Already, she wanted more. A whole night's worth.

"Right about here."

"Been waiting for this all week," Billy said, his voice so low that Jenny felt it right in her chest. He tangled his fingers in her hair. "Longer."

"Yeah?" But that was all she got out before his mouth took hold of hers.

Jenny wasn't going to let him have all the fun. She wanted to lose herself in his touch, but part of losing herself was touching back. So she kept at the buttons on his shirt, then the belt and his pants.

Her fingers brushed against his erection, and he groaned into her mouth before he pulled back, tilted her head and grazed his teeth down her neck. "You have protection?"

"Yeah." He leaned over to a small nightstand and snagged a condom.

She went to undo her bra—anything to speed up this process was a good thing—but he grabbed her hands. "I want to do that."

He leaned into her, working the clasp. She was loving the lavish, careful attention he was paying her, but she was getting darned tired of waiting. She wanted him inside her *now,* and each moment that didn't happen felt like another year of celibacy.

So she did the only thing she could. She bit his shoulder. Not hard enough to break his skin, but right now she didn't want slow and gentle or even lavish. She wanted rough and hard and Billy. She wanted the man who'd brought her to a shaking orgasm without even getting off his bike. *Now.*

"Woman," he growled and suddenly she was on her back, covered by his massive body. His shirt was open, his pants were half-off, and his boxer-briefs were straining to the point of failure.

He pressed the length of his body against her as his

tongue tangled with hers. She tried to shove his shirt off, but arms and legs and the remaining clothing were all being helplessly tangled. She shifted her hips, bringing her center in line with his erection, but they still had on too much fabric. "I need you—all of you," she told him while trying to hook her foot into the waistband of his pants so she could kick them off.

He stood back, shucking his shirt and his pants in two blissfully quick moments. Then he removed his boxer-briefs, and she saw.

"Wow" was all she could say.

Back when she'd been young and crazy and sleeping around the rez, she'd been sleeping with boys. For the first time, she saw exactly what sleeping with a man looked like. The difference was measureable—in inches.

His grin held nothing but the promise of what was to come next. Then he pulled her panties off. The bra came next, and he rolled on the condom.

Thank goodness, she thought as he climbed back into bed. The weight between her legs was more than heavy—it positively ached. She spread herself as wide as she could for him, but then he did something unexpected. He turned on the light, rolled onto his back and pulled her on top of him.

"I want to watch you."

She swallowed, feeling self-conscious. "Um..."

But he kept running his fingers over her breasts, her hips, her thighs—all places that she worried about, all places that weren't perfect. His fingertips skimmed the low part of her belly that still sported faint stretch marks after all these years. The whole while, his hips were moving under hers. The huge length of him pressed against her, awakening her to all sorts of wonderful feelings— feelings that weren't necessarily new, but weren't familiar, either. Instead of the hard, pressing want that Billy had sparked outside in his garage, this was a slow, almost languid heat—wet and warm and hard.

"Just when I think you can't get any more beautiful," he said as he sighed.

Jenny felt herself relax. "It's been a long time...." A long time since she'd felt pretty—since someone had *thought* she was pretty. She settled, feeling the pressure of him on the outside of her body. It wasn't enough—this slow, sensual pace. She raised herself and felt him spring up. Then, slowly, she let herself fall onto him.

He filled her and more, but she was able to take him in. Once she'd completely settled, she paused, savoring the feeling. She needed this, needed him, but she didn't want the frenzied, jackrabbit sex she'd had so long ago. She was in bed with a man. She wanted to appreciate the differences.

Billy let her rest, adjusting to his girth while he cupped both of her breasts in his hands. "You feel *good*." His fingers tweaked her nipples, which earned him a small gasp. "You like that?"

She nodded, biting her lip. So he did it again. Harder.

This time, the jolt hit her so hard that she had to rise and fall. Suddenly, he sat up in bed and took her left nipple in his mouth. "Don't stop, woman," he groaned against her skin. Then he scraped his teeth over her flesh and rolled her nipple between his teeth and his tongue and tweaked the other nipple with his hand and she was riding him. Oh, how she was riding him.

She'd wanted him, wanted to dance with him, since that first afternoon in the shop—the first time she'd seen that there was something underneath the scowl and the leather, something deeper, something good.

Billy's hands slipped down her backside as he licked her other nipple. His hands traced where he'd held her against him earlier, then he was pushing her again—up, down, back, forth—pushing her higher and higher. Her breath caught, then he dragged his teeth against her again.

As the climax unleashed itself on her, she cried out, *"Billy!"*

Suddenly he thrust harder and harder, taking her almost to the breaking point before he let out a low roar and fell back onto the bed. His hands didn't leave her, though. Instead, they kept right on stroking her back, her legs, her waist—he traced every inch of her body as she pulled herself free and collapsed next to him.

"Like I told you," Billy said, sounding breathless. It gave her a good feeling—she'd made him just as breathless as he'd made her. "I'm not that respectable."

Jenny pushed herself up and looked him in the eye. "Respectability," she whispered, stretching out against his body and loving the way his arm automatically went around her waist, "is overrated."

Fifteen

Jenny went to get cleaned up and Billy took care of the condom. Man, he thought to himself over and over. He'd been afraid that, after the weeks-long buildup, sex with Jenny wouldn't live up to the expectation. He'd never been more wrong.

He straightened out the sheets and got the pillows lined up. As great as that had been, he'd only had her home for about forty-five minutes. He still had her for the whole night. And a long morning.

Almost nine grand. He had no idea who Josey had been bidding against—but it had been someone who'd been freaking serious about it. Bobby hadn't thought he'd go for much more than four or five, tops. But almost nine? Yeah—he was keeping Jenny here for as long as he wanted.

As long as *she* wanted, that was. Already, he was hardening thinking about the way her warm wetness had taken him in, the way she'd moaned and then cried out his name. The way she'd looked, her breasts bouncing up and down with each thrust.

He shook his head, checking to see if it was on straight. She'd said it herself—it'd been a long time. Even though she'd been able to handle him, she would probably need more than ten minutes of recovery time.

But the image of all her curves wouldn't be banished. Would twenty minutes be enough?

To distract himself, he hung up his jacket and tried to shake out her dress. The thing was a crumpled mess, though. Then the bathroom door opened and he spun to see her backlit with the bathroom light. The sight of her, nude, in his room had him hard all over again. Man, she was so much more than he'd hoped. For such a small woman, she packed a hell of a punch.

"I think your dress is ruined," he said, trying to think about anything but the way the light shined between her legs as she walked over to him, making the V of hair covering her sex glow like a sunset. Didn't work. "I'll buy you another one."

"Can't think of anywhere I'd wear it." Her voice had that low, teasing tone that made his brain misfire.

"I'll take you someplace fancy."

The dress fell to the ground, forgotten again. "You look amazing," he managed to get out. And she did. As sweet as she looked when she was being a teacher and as glamorous as she'd looked tonight, nothing beat her in all of her glorious, nude beauty.

At this, her playfulness took a more anxious turn and she tried to cross her arms in front of those amazing breasts, only to appear to change her mind and try to cover up her lower parts.

"No, don't." He closed the distance between them and took her wrists in his hands. "Don't hide from me."

She was such a little thing—barely came up to his chest. Which was where she was looking now, right at the rose over his heart. When she pulled her hand away, he let her. "If we're not hiding, is this the part where I get to see your tattoos?" Her fingers traced the outline of the rose.

Billy swallowed. Sure, people knew he had tattoos—hard not to. People knew he had this tattoo, in fact. But no one knew what this tattoo represented, what all of them meant. Men—including his brothers—didn't ask. They just said, "Nice tats, man!" and left it at that. A few women had asked over the years but Billy had never wanted to tell those women what his skin meant. So he'd made up crap—the rose was for his mom or whatever sounded good at the time.

This? This was different. He didn't want to lie to her.

So he sucked it up. "Yup."

It was worth it to watch the greedy light in her eyes, worth it when she turned him and pointed him to the bed. "Go."

That's where he wanted her, anyway. Maybe this wouldn't be so bad. Maybe they'd get through the tattoos and get back to more sex real quick.

"Yes, ma'am." And it was totally worth it when she smacked him on the butt.

He sat down on the bed, but she shook her head at him. With her hands on her hips, she looked exactly like she did during daylight hours—scolding and irritated but with that trace of playfulness underneath. "On your stomach, please."

Billy complied, sprawling out on his belly. He felt the bed give under her weight as she climbed over his legs, shivered as her hand skimmed over his butt. She grabbed a handful of cheek and squeezed. She was going to kill him.

Her laugh was light and airy—not afraid of him or his ink. He felt something inside him unclench.

She moved—and suddenly she was straddling him. "No tattoos here?" He could feel each one of her fingertips cutting a path over his butt.

His erection strained against the bed, but it hadn't been

twenty minutes yet, and she wasn't done looking. "I've got a few ideas, but nothing I'm going to drop trou for."

"I see." Then she was running her hands over the swath of black that made up his lower back before it exploded into a tornado of blackbirds that flew free up and over his shoulders. "This is truly impressive, Billy."

"One of a kind." She wasn't just touching him—that would have been torture enough. But she'd scooted up a little, and he could feel the warmth of her body where she was sitting on his backside. All he'd have to do would be to turn over and he could be inside her. The need to do that was so strong that it took him a moment to realize he'd still have to fish a condom out of the nightstand drawer. Damn it. Instead, he fisted the sheets and tried to breathe.

A soft fingertip touched each bird. "What does it mean?"

Billy turned his head so that he could see her out of the corner of his eye. "It's my life. There was a time when I was only this massive tornado of darkness and destruction—I hurt myself, hurt people who cared about me."

"Then you saw the light?" Her weight shifted and he felt her warm breath on his back.

"More like I broke free. Grew up, got smarter, got over it."

Well, gotten *more* over it. He didn't know if he'd ever be all the way over it.

"It's beautiful."

And the funny thing was, she didn't sound like she was jerking his chain. She leaned down far enough that he could feel the weight of those amazing breasts on his back. She kissed one of the birds.

In that moment, Billy not only saw but *felt* the difference between being horny and being something else, something he didn't quite have a name for. Did he want to sink himself into Jenny's sweet body again? Hell, yes. But it wasn't just getting off that pushed him. It was something more—being with Jenny.

It was amazing how much a difference that made.

She slid off of him, which left him colder than he wanted to admit. But she rolled him onto his back—and straddled him again. He couldn't help himself—his hands found her hips and he began to rock back and forth under her—not enough to qualify as sex, but more than enough that she got the message.

She gasped, her eyes widening with what he hoped was pleasure. The feeling of skin on skin—his skin on her skin—was enough to drive all rational thought from his mind. He pulled her down harder, feeling her wetness coat him.

She bit her lip, which probably was a gesture of indecision but happened to look damn sexy. Had it been twenty minutes? Could he get a condom?

"Not yet." She got the words out through gritted teeth as she peeled his hands from her hips.

He had to admire her control, damn it all.

But she didn't scoot off of his erection. She sat there in that narrow space between intimate and not, her chest heaving. Finally, she turned her attention back to his tats. The main one on his chest was a huge skull with black flames on top and a rattlesnake coming out of one eye. The snake went up and over his shoulder.

But next to it was the rose wrapped in thorns. It was the only tattoo he had that was in color. The red was on the edges of the petals, like a tea rose, his mom's favorite flower. It had been the only tattoo of his that she'd ever thought was pretty, even if it was wrapped in thorns.

Billy could see Jenny looking from the big, scary tat to the small, pretty one and he knew that she was smart enough to make more than a few connections.

"So," she began, covering his rose with her palm, "you have a, um, *graphic* tattoo to distract from this one?"

"Yeah." He wanted to cut her off, distract both of them by sliding into her welcoming body—but he couldn't. He had to be honest with her. With himself.

But he couldn't do it with her naked body on top of his. Not when he could look into her eyes. So he squeezed his shut, focusing on the warmth of her hand over his heart.

To his surprise, she slid forward, wrapping her arms around his chest—full-body contact. *Yeah,* he thought, folding her into his arms, *that's better.*

"When I was seventeen, I was dating this girl," he began, not knowing a better place to start. "She was everything I wasn't—smart and pretty with rich parents. I think I was her wild streak—her family hated me. *Hated* me. But she'd sneak out at night."

He felt her head nod against his chest. No doubt, she'd done some of that sneaking out, too. "So what happened?"

"I got her pregnant." Jenny stilled—he didn't think she was even breathing—so he kept going. Stopping and thinking about it sucked more than getting it over with. "And I freaked out. I broke my hand punching a wall, threw a fit—I even broke my bike. Kicked it over. I'd gotten drunk before then, but I went out and got ripping drunk. I…" God, he was so ashamed of what a jerk he'd been. "I couldn't deal with it. Tried to start a fight at this bar I shouldn't have been in, almost got myself killed."

"Is that when you got arrested?"

"Actually, the bartender knew my dad. Called him up. He came and got me, dragged me home and tore me a new one." This part—the part that wasn't his fault—was easier to think of. "He'd gotten my mom pregnant—with me— when they were both eighteen. When I told him what I'd done, he slapped me and told me to get myself together.

Told me I had to marry her—that's what he'd done. Told me that any Bolton baby had to stay a Bolton."

"Did you?"

Billy realized he was stroking her hair. And that she was still here—hadn't bolted because he'd been a huge jerk. Not yet, anyway.

"I slept on it for a few days. Then bought a cheap ring and went to her house to propose."

God, this was hard. He'd only said these things out loud one other time. Not even his brothers knew this. As much of a loudmouth as his father was about some things, Bruce Bolton had kept his mouth shut about this. Billy wasn't even sure if Dad had told Mom before she died. He hoped not, anyway. He wouldn't have wanted her to be so disappointed in him.

He didn't want to disappoint Jenny, either.

"What happened?" Her voice was small—but not scared, not judgmental. She'd been on the other side after all. Maybe she understood being freaked out better than most.

"She said…" His voice caught, and suddenly talking was almost impossible.

Jenny leaned up and kissed him on the cheek before she returned back to her chest-to-chest hug. Then she waited.

"She'd had an abortion. Said she didn't want *it* because she didn't want me—she'd never wanted me. Then she slammed the door in my face."

Jenny gasped in surprise. "She did *what?*"

"Yeah."

They lay there for a few moments. Billy was keenly aware of Jenny—not so much in the sexual sense, but that she was still here in this bed with him, still wrapped up in his arms. That she hadn't called him a filthy, no-good dirtbag who was too stupid to know when he wasn't wanted. All those things that Ashley had said to him.

"I almost got an abortion," Jenny said in her super-quiet voice. "After Ricky left, I wanted it to be over. But my mom wouldn't let me. She said I had to live with what I'd done, and one day I'd thank her for it."

"Did you?"

"Eventually. Like you said, I grew up, got smart and got over it." She traced her fingers over the rose petals. "So, this isn't for the girl."

"No. It's for the baby."

She slid a hand behind his back and caressed the inches of inky blackness that had once been his life. "Then you were lost."

"Yeah." Funny, he didn't feel lost at all right now. More than anything, he felt right—more right than he'd felt in a long time.

"So, what happened?"

He smiled in spite of feeling a little raw. After all that, she was still here, holding him. "I got more and more *gone.* Spent half my days drunk, the other half hungover. Picked fights—earned my nickname, Wild Bill, the hard way. Got arrested a bunch. Then my dad stopped bailing me out. Told me I could rot in jail until I got my head screwed back on. Told me I was killing my mom, the way I was."

He swallowed again. His mom had been so worried about him for so long, no wonder his dad had been furious with him. Mom and Dad might have had to get married, but they'd stuck by each other, through good and bad, until the day the cancer took Mom. After that, Billy hadn't been the only one who was a little lost.

"He left you there?"

"Yup."

"Wow…my mom *just* made me have a baby."

"I wasn't there for years or anything. A couple of months. Then, when my case came up, I had a plea deal. Community service." This was the only part of the story he liked to think about. Coming into the light. "My old shop teacher spoke on my behalf, said he had a plan for how I could talk to the kids in school, kids like me who were lost. He'd make me work it off."

"Your shop teacher stood up for you?"

"Cal Horton. He's the only other person, besides Dad, who knows about this. And you," he added quickly. "So I did work it off. I was twenty-four. I'd lost seven years of my life to drinking and fighting. Cal is pretty much the anti-Dad—wiry little guy, soft-spoken. He'd been the only teacher who didn't write me off in school. The only person who never wrote me off. So he dragged me back to school, made me talk to the kids, made me lead them in picking up an adopted stretch of the highway—and put tools back in my hand. Gave me something to do with my life. After I'd finished with the community service, I went to work for my dad and started building bikes."

Her hand slid up his back, finding the birds again. "Free."

He held her tighter than before. "Free," he agreed.

But lonely. He'd built a hell of a business with his brothers. For ten years, his life had been work. He'd worked on bikes twelve, fourteen hours a day. He'd made a boatload of money, but he hadn't stopped long enough to enjoy it—like enjoying his money took something away from the reason why he did the work. It kept him busy and out of trouble, but hadn't left time for anything else.

Until now. Any other Saturday night, he might be working on his drawings or testing out a new angle for the handlebars—thinking about a bike. Tonight? Tonight he was in bed with a sweet, beautiful woman. And that's damn well where he was going to stay for as long as he could.

"You didn't take the easy way out. You did the right thing, even though it was hard. I want to be good enough for you, Jenny. Because you're so much better than I am."

Her head shot up, nearly clipping him in the chin. She stared at him, her mouth open. He smoothed her hair back from her face before he closed her mouth for her with a kiss. It was true—all of it.

She kissed him back without hesitation, their tongues tangling along with their limbs. *This* was freedom—here, in her arms, being loved by a good woman.

Then she tried to roll him on top of her, but he pulled away. "I like you on top," he said, and put her there.

She frowned at him, even as her hips worked small circles on his aching erection. "Why?"

"Better this way," he got out through gritted teeth. Man, the way she was grinding against him—he leaned over and snagged a condom.

She wasn't having any of that, though. She grabbed the hand holding the condom and pinned it against the bed. "Maybe I want you on top."

"No, you don't." He flexed, knowing good and well that he could break her hold on his hand. But he didn't want to.

Her eyes narrowed. "And why is *that?*"

"Better view."

"Baloney."

Right now—except for the fact that she was naked—she looked exactly like the kind of woman who would threaten to feed him to the coyotes.

"A lot—" No, that wasn't right. He started again. "Other women have complained that I'm too heavy."

The look on her face said, "You can't tell me what to do."

"I'm not afraid of you or your massive, gorgeous chest, Billy." As if to emphasize her point, she rolled off—and pulled him with her.

This wasn't a good idea, but it was clear that she had a point to prove and he wasn't going to get lucky again if he didn't let her prove it. So he rolled into her, pausing only long enough to sit back on his heels and put the condom on. "You tell me if it doesn't work?"

"Absolutely." She reached out and stroked his length, and suddenly, he was ready to go again. "And I'll tell you if it does. Deal?"

"Deal." Then her legs were around his waist, pulling him forward until he hit her wet center.

Billy surrendered himself to the sensations of her body—the way she took him in, the way she surrounded him with her warmth, the way her arms clung to his neck, holding him tight. He stroked into her. It had been so long since he'd been on top that it was like having sex for the first time all over again. Everything about Jenny felt new and different. Any worries he had were blown away with the breathy whispers of how much she liked being with him. Soon, she couldn't even whisper—all she could do was moan his name.

Soon, he couldn't hold anything back. And when her body tightened on his with the force of her orgasm, he lost it all. The release was so intense that, for a moment, everything got a little hazy at the edges. All he could think was of birds flying into the sky, free. That's how he felt with her. Free as a bird.

He pulled away, but he didn't get far. He lay on his side and wrapped his arms around her. Suddenly, he was tired— not the usual stayed-up-all-night-working tired, but something that was infinitely more satisfying.

"Was that okay?" He hoped so, because that was the kind of sex a man could get used to having more of. A lot more of.

Jenny surprised him by giggling. "No." He froze, but she added, "It was *wonderful*."

He exhaled in relief, which became a yawn. "Good."

"Maybe in the morning, we can try a different position."

That was enough to get his eyes open again. "Yeah?"

She kissed him. "Yeah."
Hot damn.
Billy had finally gotten lucky.

Sixteen

Billy hadn't had a lot of spooning sex. But waking up with Jenny in his arms? Yeah, that was the kind of intimate he wanted, with the woman he wanted.

He explored her breasts, her nipples, the space between her legs. And he loved hearing her telling him exactly how good he made her feel, to hear her cry out in pleasure.

But soon enough, they were lying spent and panting, and the morning sun shone bright through the windows. All she had to wear was the crumpled gown, which looked even worse in the light of day. So Jenny walked around in one of his T-shirts while he showed her his place.

"And this is the kitchen, which goes out to the garage." He hoped she liked it—hoped she might want to spend a little more time here with him, but he couldn't tell by the look on her face.

Jenny did a slow circle. "It is always this…empty?"

Billy glanced around, trying to see his house as she did. Everything was in its place—he kept his house like he kept his shop. But he could see her point. He had five bedrooms—and only one bed. His. "Yeah, I guess."

"How long have you lived here?"

"About six years. It's far enough away from the neighbors that they don't complain about engine noise." He got out the eggs and bacon and put the kettle on. Then he set out the four boxes of tea he'd bought for her. "Pick one."

Jenny chose the English breakfast and slid onto the chrome-and-black-leather stool he had at the island counter. "It's a big place."

"You like it? You can come back whenever you want. Seth, too." A strange look crossed her face and she dropped her gaze to the packet of tea in her hands. Maybe she didn't like his big, empty house? "I can get a bed for Seth. He can pick out whatever he'd like."

"I…"

Billy couldn't tell what was worse—the way she wasn't meeting his gaze, or the way her words trailed off. Suddenly, he was on edge.

Last night—this morning—had been amazing for both of them. He'd thought. Had he gotten a woman wrong again—she'd had her one night and that was that? "What?"

"It's just— I don't know— See, I haven't done this for a long time. Eleven years." Her words spilled out of her in a guilty rush. "The last guy I tried to date bailed when Seth started calling him Daddy, and Seth was *crushed.* So I stopped dating. He doesn't remember it, thank goodness. He was only three. But…" As fast as she'd started, she stopped.

Man, eleven years? And his almost-three years had felt like a long time. Then it hit him like a load of bricks. This was like when they'd woken up on Ben's couch last week—practically the first thing out of her mouth was asking Seth what he wanted for breakfast. She was putting herself last, again.

Jenny, the woman, needed some mind-blowing sex and probably had for a long time. But Jenny, the mom, had buried those needs and wants down deep. No wonder she'd had so much energy to unleash on him last night. Eleven years was a hell of a backlog to work through.

She looked up at him, and he was surprised to see tears welling up in her eyes. "I don't know if we should do *that*. *This*. I have to put his interests first. I mean, you've been wonderful with him, but I don't expect you to suddenly be a father figure to him. And we're so different. I don't have anything and you—you can have everything you want."

"I want you."

She shook her head. "My life is on the rez and your life is in the shop, and I…I don't know how this would work."

He gaped at her for a second, his mind spinning furiously as it tried to come up with the right response. If he were his brother Ben, he'd probably have some logical plan of how, exactly, this would work. If he were Bobby, he'd have the right words to calm her down.

But he wasn't his brothers and never would be. So he did the only thing he could. He walked around the island, took her tear-stained cheeks in his hands, and kissed her. After a few moments, her arms went back around his neck and she held on to him as if she were afraid she might never get the chance to do so again.

"This isn't about the boy, Jenny. He'll be fine. This is about you and me," he told her as he hugged her to his chest.

He felt like a jerk for saying it—for telling her that her own son wasn't important. But he didn't care. He didn't want her sense of duty to pull her away from him.

"I've never known another woman like you—you push me, challenge me—you aren't afraid of me. You make me want to *be* better. I'm not going to let *this* go without a fight because you think your boy might not like it or you think I'm too rich for a woman like you. None of that matters a damn bit to me. I want to be with you, even if it isn't easy."

She looked up at him, her eyes rimmed with red. It hurt

him to see her upset like this, to know he was the reason why. "I have to put my son first."

"Who puts you first?" Maybe he was selfish. Maybe he just wanted to keep her in his bed. But he wasn't going to let guilt ruin this. No way in hell. "That's all I want to do—put you first."

"What will people say if it doesn't work?"

"To hell with them—I don't care." Was she really worried about—what, her reputation? Or was she worried about his? Didn't matter. "If it doesn't work, then it doesn't work. But I know this—I won't regret trying. I'll only regret *not* trying."

She closed her eyes and nodded before breaking out into a watery grin. "No regrets."

He kissed her again. He'd never cared what anyone thought about him.

Until her. She was a good, sweet, thoughtful woman. Maybe she was *too* good for him. Maybe she'd realize that, sooner or later.

He had to show her—he could be good for her. Bacon and eggs and tea—it could all keep. Right now, what he needed was the woman in his arms. He picked her up, pausing only long enough to turn off the kettle.

"None," he told her as he carried her back to bed.

There was no way he could regret this.

No way he could regret *her*.

At first, it wasn't easy. Billy wasn't the kind of guy who liked to talk on the phone, so their conversations were mostly about when they could see each other again.

But in person, he was a different man. From the moment Jenny saw him until the unavoidable moment they parted, Jenny felt like she was the center of his world. She hadn't agreed to spending another night at Billy's house with Seth in tow, but they'd had a few dates. She'd left Seth with her mom and driven into the city. He'd bought her a new dress—a luscious red number with a little shawl—and taken her to the theater to see *Annie Get Your Gun.* He'd worn his suit again and had even made reservations at a super-fancy restaurant.

He was spoiling her. She let him do it. No one had ever spoiled her before.

He'd also come out to the rez and met Jenny's mom. That time, he'd taken her on a wind-whipped ride. They'd had sex on a blanket out in the middle of nowhere. Jenny had been on top for that one. The memory still made her smile.

Bobby had gotten his television deal and, as a result, was no longer filming the webisodes while the show was in preproduction. Jenny didn't know much about it—only that Billy wasn't on camera all day long and that made him happy. And Billy happy was an extremely good thing.

As far as she could tell, Seth was okay with her seeing Billy. They hadn't really talked about it much, so when Seth asked, "Are you and Billy going to get married?" one morning on the drive into school, he totally took her by surprise.

"I don't know," she admitted. There was still a lot to work around.

The drive between her house and his was almost an hour and a half, but she wasn't going to give up her job at the school to move in with him. She couldn't leave her mom, who was getting older, her students or her TAPS girls. She couldn't push all of those people aside because being with Billy made her happier than she could ever remember being.

And that was the other problem. She was starting to think it wasn't just happiness. She was starting to think it might be love.

"Not anytime soon," she added. That, at least, was 100 percent true.

"Would he be my dad?"

Now how was she supposed to answer that? So she hedged. "Sweetie, we'll cross that bridge when we come to it."

It wasn't like Billy was replacing some dearly departed father. But he and Seth were, well, *bonding* in a way that even she couldn't turn a blind eye to. A couple of times, she and Seth had driven in to the Crazy Horse Choppers shop on the weekend, where Billy and Seth worked on designing a new bike together—one that would be for Seth when he turned sixteen. Then Seth would go hang out with Ben and Josey while Billy and Jenny had dinner or played pool or had hot—if quick—sex.

It worked, sort of. Seth got to hang out with Billy, who kept on him about his grades, then Jenny got Billy to herself for a while. He kept asking her to come home with him for the weekend—with Seth in tow. She hadn't said yes yet, but she was thinking about it more and more. He was good with Seth in the shop, but Seth around the house was another thing entirely. Part of her couldn't help but wonder what would happen when Seth left the bathroom trashed and the water running, or what would happen when she and Seth got into one of their usual fights about homework. Would Billy decide he'd had enough?

She wanted to think that wouldn't happen, but she knew there were limits to Seth's star behavior. Sooner or later, it might come down to Seth or Billy.

She was falling for Billy.

But her son had to come first.

She'd cross that bridge when she came to it.

Billy was excited. This was the first Saturday that Jenny had agreed to come spend the night with him—and she was bringing Seth. If things kept moving in this direction, it might not be that much longer before she wanted to stay with him all the time. Permanently.

Because he was thinking about something permanent. He wasn't getting any younger and after finding a new kind of freedom in Jenny's arms, he sure as hell didn't want to go back to being lonely.

Everything was better now. His old man didn't bug him as much. Now that Bobby had his big production deal, he was spending more time in New York and there were no cameras on Billy, so that was a huge victory. It made it a hell of a lot easier to have Jenny meet him at the shop after school and have a date. He discovered he liked dating—taking Jenny out and making her feel special. He had the money. He'd never felt comfortable spending it on himself, but spending it on Jenny? Seeing the way her face lit up when she'd unwrapped the red dress alone had been worth the price tag.

Even work was smoother. Ben had hired some new guys and a full-time salesman. The bikes were selling, but they were meeting their production schedule. Billy had to admit, Bobby's plan to make Crazy Horse Choppers a national brand was working.

He didn't know if Jenny was what made it all work, but she made it all worth it. Recently, Billy had found himself looking at property halfway between the shop and the school—a place where they could meet in the middle. He wasn't married to his house, after all.

But the problem was, he wasn't at the point where he wanted to buy a house for her—and her kid. Because a woman like Jenny wouldn't want to shack up with the likes of him, not without a ring. And he wasn't sure he was the marrying kind. Getting married was something responsible grown-ups did. Sure, he ran a successful company and, yeah, he paid his bills but...wasn't he still the same guy who'd hit bars and got thrown into the drunk tank until he sobered up?

Wasn't he?

Lost in this train of thought, the door to the shop opened and Lance, the new salesman, stuck his head in. "There's a woman here to see you, Mr. Bolton. I mean, Billy."

"She can come on back," he said without looking up from the schematics of Seth's bike. The kid wanted something low and sleek that wasn't a crotch rocket. And it had to be something that Jenny would actually let him ride. Needless to say, they were still in the designing phase.

The first thing he noticed was that the sound wasn't right. Instead of Seth and Jenny talking about school, all he heard was the clicking of heels on concrete. Jenny didn't wear heels if she could help it.

The scent was the second thing. Suddenly, the shop was filled with a heavy floral perfume that clung to his nose.

But the final tip-off was the voice. "You've done well for yourself, Billy," a throaty woman's voice cooed.

It was probably supposed to sound seductive, but Billy heard a distinctive hard edge underneath. The hair on the back of his neck bristled.

Not Jenny. But there was still a chance this was a customer, so he vowed to keep things polite. Moving slowly, Billy pivoted on his stool. Standing about six feet away was a petite woman with big blond hair and huge heels who looked vaguely familiar. "Thanks," he said, purposefully keeping it short. "Can I help you?"

The woman's eyes narrowed even as she smiled and shifted her weight on those heels. She looked as though she were waiting for him to say something. Well, she could keep on waiting. Finally, she said, "You don't remember me." The hard edge in her voice got more distinctive.

The way she stuck a hand on her hip and jutted out her chest… "You were at the bachelor auction, right?"

That was a hell of a vicious smile. "You never were terribly bright, but I thought you'd remember *me*."

Was this some sort of psycho-fan who'd seen all those

webisodes and thought she "knew" him? And what sort of woman walked into his business and accused him of being dumb?

Not a very smart one, that much he knew. "We don't give tours. If you want to buy a bike, Lance is the salesman on duty." He pointed through the door.

"You really don't remember me."

She sounded like a broken record, as if repeating the same thing over and over would help. "No clue, lady."

"And after all we went through in high school."

Everything stopped—breathing, thinking—*everything*. "Ashley?"

No, no, *no*. This was not happening. He prayed to God that he'd gone momentarily insane and was having the worst hallucination ever, because even insanity would be preferable to seeing this woman again.

When he said her name, Ashley's features softened. "You *do* remember."

Like he'd forget the woman who ripped his heart out of his still-beating chest.

"You look different." Which was true enough.

"Better, I hope. And you! You filled out. Quite the tank now, aren't you?"

Had he ever been in love with this woman? Because the woman standing in front of him barely matched up with the girl he remembered. Short, yes—and still curvy. But nothing else seemed right. Hair, face, clothes—all different.

But her dismissive attitude toward him—was that so far off from the girl who'd slammed the door in his face? No. Same person, damn it all.

"What do you want?"

"You're quite famous now, you know that? I've seen all the episodes of your little show. And now you're going to have your own cable TV show? Very impressive, Billy."

He didn't like the way she said his name, and he really

didn't like the tone of her voice. All it did was make one thing painfully clear—she wanted *something,* and it sure as hell wasn't him.

He needed to get her out of here, fast. If Jenny came in—and Ashley recognized her as the woman he'd taken home from the auction—things could get ugly.

"Why are you here?"

"We were good together once, remember?" She preened. Probably trying to look sexy, but he wasn't falling for that. "We had a lot of fun back in high school."

"I was young and stupid then. What do you want?"

That wasn't the right thing to say. Anything friendly or fake about her disappeared, and he found himself looking at a viper in a woman's body. "Do you know that every time I have to fill out all those doctor forms, I have to put down that I had an abortion? Every single time."

"I didn't want you to get the abortion. You did that without asking me. Without even *telling* me."

"You weren't the pregnant one," she snapped back, looking frustrated. "I was the one who was scared and hurting and I'm the one who had to live with it."

"It was my kid, too." Too late, he realized he'd put his hand over his rose tattoo. "You took that away from me."

"And be stuck with you for the rest of my life?" She looked mad enough to spit bullets, but then everything about her changed again and he supposed she was trying to look warm and inviting. It didn't work. "I never thought you'd make it this far, that's for damn sure. If I had, well..." She pivoted and took in the shop. "I'm impressed. Truly."

This was about money, he realized. She saw that he had some and felt entitled to a share, all because he'd gotten her pregnant a long time ago. "How much?"

She smirked. "Never were one to beat around the bush, were you? Although I do recall you punching some walls."

"How much? That's what you want, isn't it?" He'd figured her out. She wanted a payoff or she'd tell everyone what she'd done seventeen years ago—but she'd make it sound like his fault.

He didn't like that smile, not one bit—because it said that he'd hit the nail on the head. "I didn't want it to go like this. I tried to buy you at that auction, see if we could rekindle the spark."

"See if you could get on the show."

She wiped a manicured finger down the side of her mouth, as if she'd tasted something spoiled. "Look at you, catching on so quickly. Maybe I didn't give you enough credit."

"How much to never see you again?" Because right now, that's what he wanted more than anything else in the world.

"Fine. Have it your way. Fifty thousand dollars."

His mouth fell open. So this was what blackmail felt like. This was exactly why he was never comfortable with money in the first place—as soon as you had some, people came out of the woodwork, looking for ways to take their cut.

He never should have let Bobby put him in front of a camera.

She waved her hand around. "Come on—what's the problem? Some of your bikes go for more than thirty thousand. Just build a couple more and sell them."

"It doesn't work like that. All that money is tied up—locked up tight." Hell, if he were able to start cutting checks for fifty grand, he'd have just written one to Jenny's school.

Disappointment flashed over her face, but it was buried beneath a predatory glare. "I wanted to keep this between us, Billy. I tried to buy you with every last dollar I had. I didn't want it to come to this. But I need the money." For a quick moment, she looked scared—and tired. But then it was gone. "And if you won't give it to me, well, there are other people who'll pay for a good scoop."

He needed Bobby here to negotiate—because that's what this was, a negotiation. But he was on his own. "You wouldn't."

"I would. Oh, not right away—I'd let the show get started, let you get more exposure—then the online gossip sites of the world would be willing to fork over a pretty penny for the whole story. Think of the headline—Biker Reality Star Abandoned Pregnant Teen Girlfriend." She waved her hands in front of her face as if she were seeing the title in lights. "I've heard that the head of your new cable network is a real stickler for conservative values. It'd be a damn shame to get your new show canceled after only a few episodes."

A part of him was tempted to let her go right ahead and do that—get it over with. But he knew that, even if the show got canceled, it wouldn't be the end of it. Tabloid stories fed on other tabloid stories. The show would go away, but he'd never have a moment's peace.

Ashley said as much. "Just think—once they get their claws in you? How many women have you slept with, Billy? How many of them would share all the details to get their picture in a magazine? I'm doing you a favor here—offering you a clean break with none of the photographers hiding out in your bushes."

He knew she was right. He also knew that later, he was going to punch Bobby. If his brother hadn't put Billy on camera, none of this would have happened.

Ashley must have interpreted his silence as disagreement. "*You* got me pregnant, Billy." The hard edges melted and she looked ten—no, seventeen—years younger. "*You* freaked out, punched a wall and disappeared for *days*. What was I supposed to do? I was scared, and my parents...well, they never trusted me again. Mom sends me birthday cards, but we don't really talk." She cleared her throat, and Billy could tell she was on the verge of tears.

"So I ended it. I had to. And I couldn't stand to face you. I know I said some horrible things, but I was upset and in pain and I…I didn't want to be the reason my dad didn't love me anymore. That meant you had to be."

"You should have trusted me. I would have taken care of you."

She shook her head, blinking hard. "We were *so* young. Couldn't take care of ourselves, much less a baby. I don't want to ruin your life, Billy—not any more than mine's already been ruined. I just need the money, then you'll never have to see me again. I promise," she added, sounding like she meant it.

The guilt was so heavy that Billy felt his shoulders bowing under it. She was right, damn it all. He'd scared her, then left her all alone. If he'd only…well, no amount of what-ifs were going to change the past. He'd been a jerk. If this was how he had to atone for his sins, so be it. Then he could let go of her and the lost baby.

He needed to let go. And then the rest of his life could be for Jenny and the kid she'd kept.

"Okay."

"Really?"

He stood and motioned her back to the waiting room. He didn't have any checks, but Ben did, up in his office. He wanted to get one written and get Ashley out the door before Jenny got here.

Lance was sitting at the desk, looking nervous. "Stay here," Billy told Ashley. "And don't let her talk to anyone," he added. Especially not Jenny.

He took the stairs to Ben's office two at a time and fumbled his key into the lock. Ben had some computer program that generated checks for the guys. When he'd started using this system, he'd walked Billy through it in case Ben couldn't be there to make payroll.

That had been three years ago—and Ben always made it to work on payday.

Frantic, Billy struggled to get the computer on and find the program. The whole process felt like it was taking hours. Finally, he got the program open and typed out Ashley's information. He had to assume her last name was still the same.

Fifty thousand dollars. Ben was going to kill him for taking this out of the company funds. Hell, the whole family was going to take turns beating the hell out of him. He'd pay the company back, of course, but there wouldn't be any way to hide this from them. As long as it stayed in the family, though...

Billy grabbed the check off the printer and headed down the stairs, praying the whole time that he'd been fast enough.

He hadn't.

Seventeen

Ashley was standing where he'd left her. And there, on the other side of the room, were Jenny and Seth. Seth was sitting in a chair, his backpack at his feet. Jenny stood in front of him, her feet spread and arms crossed over that top that looked so good on her. The look on her face made it perfectly clear that she recognized Ashley for what she was—a threat. The two women were staring at each other with undisguised distrust.

"Here." Billy held the check out to Ashley. Before turning to take it, she raised an eyebrow at Jenny.

He could tell by the small smile on her face that whatever honesty he'd gotten out of her a few minutes ago was gone. All the hard edges were back. "I see your taste in women hasn't changed."

Then she stepped toward him and stood on her tiptoes, as if she was going to kiss him goodbye.

"Don't touch me," he demanded, stepping away from her. "You got what you came for. Now go. That's the deal."

"Indeed." She made a show of inspecting the check. "Goodbye, Billy."

He didn't answer her, and after an awkward second,

she forced a wide smile and walked out of the shop, head held high.

No one in the room moved. Jenny's glare followed Ashley all the way out, then swung around and settled on Billy. Seth's gaze darted between the two of them. Even Lance cowered.

Jenny broke the silence. "Get your bag," she said to Seth. "We're leaving."

The kid opened his mouth to say something, but apparently thought better of it. He grabbed his backpack and stood.

"Wait a minute." Billy must have shouted it, because everyone—everyone but Jenny—shrank back. "Lance, you and Seth—outside. Now."

"We're leaving," Jenny repeated with more force. She didn't back down.

"The hell you are." He wasn't playing this battle. He told Lance, "Get," over his shoulder as he advanced on Jenny.

He was ready for Jenny to do something—bolt, take a swing at him—but he wasn't ready for what happened next. Seth stepped in between them.

"Don't you hurt my mom," he growled, sounding impressively dangerous for a kid who probably weighed a hundred pounds sopping wet. He dropped his bag and balled his hands into fists. "I'm warning you, Billy."

Behind him, Lance squeaked.

"I just want to talk to you," Billy said to Jenny over Seth's head. Then he added, "If you think I'd hurt your mom, kid, then you don't know me very well, do you?"

Seth wavered. Billy could see him turning it over. Then he said, "Fine—but you watch yourself."

Hell, at the rate he was going, Billy half expected the boy to threaten to feed him to the coyotes.

Jenny made a noise of displeasure as Seth hefted his bag and headed out with Lance, who looked relieved to be off the hook. Jenny made a move to follow them, but Billy stood in her way. "Wait, babe."

"Don't you *babe* me."

"At least let me explain." Although he wasn't sure how explaining anything would actually help.

"Explain what? I recognized her—she was the one who didn't win you at the auction. Did she come back to make you a better offer?" At this last bit, her voice broke. But the vulnerability didn't last. The fierceness was back in a heartbeat.

There wasn't a good way to say this. Unfortunately, she took his silence all wrong and tried to shove him away from the door.

Of course, she didn't make a lot of headway. He grabbed her hands and put them over his heart. Over the rose. "No, dammit, listen. That was Ashley."

"Oh, she has a name. How nice. I'm very happy for you."

"She was my high school girlfriend."

Suddenly, Jenny got very still. Her fingers curled into the fabric of his shirt. "The one…"

"Yeah." He knew it was a risk—she could still deck him—but he reached out and caressed her cheek. "She walked into the shop—" he glanced over the desk "—half an hour ago."

"What did she want?" This was quieter. Less angry.

"Money."

"For what?"

"Don't know. Said she needed it, or she'd sell her story to the tabloids."

Jenny's eyes shut, but that didn't mask the look of sorrow on her face. "How much did you give her?"

He had the overwhelming urge to pull Jenny deep into his arms and kiss her hard enough that she forgot all about old girlfriends and lost babies and everything he couldn't change about who he was.

But it wasn't going to happen.

"How much?"

"Fifty thousand dollars."

It was a hard thing to watch. Jenny curled into her self. It was harder to feel the weight of her hand push against his rose tattoo as she backed away from him. But the hardest part? Watching the tears slip past her closed eyes and cut a trail down her pale cheeks.

"Every day," she said, her voice quiet and shaky, "I get up and face my mistakes, Billy. I sit across from them at the table and drive them to school and nag them about homework and laundry. And every single day, I make peace with who I am, the choices I've made, what I've done."

When she opened her eyes, Billy knew he was screwed. He felt it deep in his gut—he'd messed up. He wasn't sure what had her so upset—she didn't *want* him in the tabloids, did she? But even the ink on his skin ached.

"I know I've made mistakes. I *know* that," he said.

Her smile was weak—not a thing of happiness, but a thing of pain. It hurt like hell to see it.

"Knowing what your mistakes are and taking responsibility for them are two different things." Her voice caught. "I can't be with a man who won't face his mistakes, Billy. I can't be with someone who's ashamed of who he is, of what he's done. I can't be with someone who thinks he can throw money at a problem and it'll magically make everything all better, because it won't. It won't change who you are or what you've done." Then she leveled the final blow, the one that went straight through him. "And I won't let my son be around someone like that, either. He has to come first. It was a mistake—*my* mistake—to forget that."

That was it. No "Goodbye, Billy," no "call me when you grow up." She wiped the tears from her face, stepped around him and walked out the door.

Just like that, she was gone.

Without shouting, without a fight, he'd lost Jenny. He'd signed the check himself.

And just like that, he was lost.

Seth hadn't said anything other than the heartbreaking, "Did he hurt you, Mom?" when Jenny had walked out of Crazy Horse Choppers crying.

"No, sweetie," she'd said. Not physically, anyway.

She thought she'd been heartbroken when Ricky had abandoned her when she was seven months pregnant. But then, she thought she'd been in love with him, too. And what the heck had a fifteen-year-old girl known about love? Nothing.

Now, though, she knew.

She knew *exactly* what she was walking away from, *exactly* how big the hole in her heart was going to be.

She walked anyway.

How could she have let it get that far? How could she have thrown caution to the wind and followed another bad boy—another boy who wouldn't take responsibility—off the edge of sanity? God, she'd wanted Billy to be different. She'd wanted to believe that underneath his bad-boy exterior, he was a good, decent, *honorable* man. A man she could be with. A man who would be a good example for her son.

Not someone who paid off old girlfriends. Not someone who put his public image above everything else. Not someone who used money like a bandage. No matter how hard she'd fallen for him, she had to put her son first. And she would not teach him that it paid to treat people as commodities, their loyalties to be bought and sold.

In the days that followed, Jenny was possessed with an almost manic energy. She cleaned her classroom from top to bottom. She did her laundry, her mom's laundry and even some of her neighbors' laundry. She scrubbed the floors in her house. She even considered painting the living room.

When that wasn't enough to keep her mind off the way Billy had looked—hollow—she hit the road. She visited every single girl who'd ever come to a TAPS meeting and a few who hadn't. She had all this great funding now, after all. Time to rededicate herself to the group. Those girls needed her.

Josey called, but Jenny didn't feel like talking on the phone Billy had bought her, so she let it go to voice mail. Eventually, the battery died and Jenny stopped charging it. She put the phone in a drawer.

Seth would go to college in four years. Until that time, she needed to focus on being a parent—to him, to the TAPS girls, to her students. That's who she was. That's what she did.

Four years.

That's at least how long it would take her to get over Billy.

In the weeks since his life had spun out of control, Billy had done nothing *but* think about Jenny. Didn't matter what he was doing—explaining to his family why he'd cut a check that big to a woman no one else remembered, drinking in a bar or getting speeding tickets for driving nowhere way too fast—Jenny was with him. Her tear-streaked face haunted him, awake or asleep.

The fallout could have been worse, he guessed. His father had cussed him out and demanded he pay the company back. Because Ben had his money so locked up, Billy had been forced to ask Bobby to sell off a few bikes from his private collection to make up the difference. To the twerp's credit, he'd not only done it, but he'd done it without a camera crew present.

Worse, though, was that Ben had told Josey. Billy was

sure that Jenny had told her cousin that she and Billy were done, but he didn't know if Jenny had told Josey everything. Either way, Josey knew and wasn't exactly looking at Billy anymore. It was as if he didn't exist.

Billy couldn't go home. The whole place made him think of Jenny and how much he'd wanted her to be there with him. He couldn't go to Ben's and have Josey not look at him. Bobby was in New York taking meetings, and Billy wasn't about to go to Dad's place. And, as much as he wanted to get drunker than he'd ever been before, he didn't. That's not who he was anymore.

So he worked. Building bikes was the only thing that had saved him before. It was his only hope now. Fourteen-hour days became sixteen-hour days became eighteen-hour days. Cass brought him in food or someone ordered a pizza. He slept in his office, when he slept at all. He got a ton of work done, but he didn't feel any better. Maybe he never would.

Maybe that's what he deserved. Part of him thought that she was wrong—Ashley had deserved something after what he'd put her through. And he *needed* Ashley to keep quiet or it might affect business. But that part, however logical it was, was buried by the realization that Jenny was right. He'd tried to work around a problem by paying Ashley off when the only way to eliminate the problem was to face up to it. The only way to be a better man, the man he wanted to be, was to finally accept the mistakes he'd made. And so what if he'd gotten some bad press and lost a little business? He already had more money than he knew what to do with. It's not like he'd be penniless.

Damn it all.

The days ran together. He was sure weekends happened, but he didn't know when. Someone was always in the shop with him—Ben, Jack Roy, even Bobby rolled in his crotch rocket and tuned it up. Billy got the feeling they were babysitting him, but didn't care. He just needed to not think about her.

Which meant she was all he thought about.

He didn't know what day it was, didn't care. He'd screwed up the cut on a tailpipe and, instead of cussing like he used to, he realized he was staring at it, dumbfounded. *Maybe I should take a break,* he realized. But he didn't want to. It was entirely possible he was afraid to, except he wasn't afraid of anything.

Then someone tapped him on the shoulder. Actually, it was more of a punch. Billy turned, expecting to see Cass with food she was going to insist he eat. But it wasn't Cass.

Seth stood before him, looking as mad as he'd ever looked. "Take off your mask," he demanded so loudly that Billy heard him through the earplugs.

"Seth? What are you doing here? How did you get here?" Billy pulled out the plugs and took off his welding mask. "Tell me you didn't steal—"

But that was as far as he got. Seth reared back and punched him with everything he had. It wasn't enough to break Billy's jaw, but it hurt.

The shop came to a screeching halt. Half the guys made a move to grab the kid, but with one look, Billy called them off.

Ben came flying down the stairs. Cass must have called him when Seth rolled in. She now stood in the shop, looking more worried than he'd ever seen her. To make matters worse, his dad had come out of his office and was watching the whole thing from the top of the stairs.

"She said you didn't hurt her, but she lied," Seth spat out, his fists still balled up. "You made her happier than I'd ever seen her. I didn't even know she could be happy like that. Then you *hurt* her."

"Seth—" But he didn't get very far.

"And I thought you liked me. I thought I made you

proud." The kid's voice broke and his eyes started to water. But he didn't stop. "I thought you were so cool. I wanted to be just like you. I wanted you to be my *dad*."

"Seth—" he tried again, although he didn't know if he wanted the kid to stop talking so he wouldn't cry in the middle of the shop—or so that he'd stop making Billy feel like crap.

"No!" Seth yelled. He was crying now, but he kept going. And Billy had no choice but to let him. "I'm not done. I don't want to be anything like you. Mom was right. We were better off without my dad, and we're better off without you." He dug into his pocket and slammed two cell phones down onto the workbench. "If you ever hurt her again, you'll have to answer to me."

Now sobbing, he turned and ran out of the shop, pushing Cass aside.

The shop was silent. No men cursed, no tools whined. The kid hadn't hit him that hard, but Billy had never hurt more. The new guys shuffled their feet, unsure about what was happening. But the older guys, guys like Jack Roy? Billy could see the wary look in their eyes. They were judging him. It was nothing compared to the look of contempt his own father was leveling at him, though. Even at this distance, he could see the disappointment on Dad's face. The same look he'd had all those years ago when he left Billy to rot in a jail cell until he got his head back on straight.

Was this what Jenny had meant—facing his mistakes? She was right. She'd always been right.

And now was the time to start facing them.

Billy dropped his mask and ran after the boy. Sure enough, Seth was climbing back into Jenny's rust bucket of a car. When he saw Billy, he fired up the engine and tried to drive off.

Except he didn't get out of neutral. The engine revved, but the wheels didn't turn. Billy got the driver's side door opened before Seth got it in gear. "Get out of there," he yelled, grabbing Seth's arm and hauling him out.

"No. No! You stay away from us!" He tried to jerk out of Billy's hold, and when that didn't work, he started kicking. Billy took his lumps, but he wasn't about to let a hysterical kid go roaring down the highway. No one needed to die today. "You messed everything up! I hate you—*hate* you!"

Billy gritted his teeth as his shins took the worst of it. The kid pounded on his chest for good measure, repeating, "I hate you," over and over until finally he wore down into racking sobs.

Billy did the only thing he could think of—he hugged the boy. "I am proud of you, Seth," he said, his own voice choking up on him. "You're a good kid, and I wanted to be your dad, too." The funny thing was, it was the truth—even if he hadn't realized it until now.

Seth was so worked up he couldn't do anything but shake his head *no*. He didn't believe Billy.

"Does your mom know where you are?" Seth shook his head no again. That settled it. "I'm taking you home."

Eighteen

"What are we going to do tonight?" Jenny asked the girls. She was up to twenty girls now. Only six of them were pregnant. She took this as a victory. It was the only victory she had these days.

"No drinking, no drugs," they chanted in unison.

"And?" she prompted. There was comfort in the familiar, in the routine.

"Do our homework, go to school tomorrow."

Cyndy didn't say this part, but she smiled. She was still recovering from the delivery of a healthy baby girl that had gone home with a loving family only two hours away. Cyndy was due back at school next week.

"Good job, girls. Remember—call me if you need to. Otherwise—" The sound of boots clomping down the hallway stopped her midsentence. She knew the sound of those boots.

Her stomach plummeted. No—*no*. What on God's green earth was Billy Bolton doing here? He couldn't be here! He couldn't walk in here like he owned the place!

But that was as far as she got before Billy opened the

door to her classroom—and shoved Seth in. Her son's whole face was red and he had an ice pack taped to his hand.

"Seth! What—"

Billy cut her off with a wave of his hand. "Tell her," he said, putting his hand on Seth's shoulder.

Seth didn't say a thing.

"What's going on?" Jenny demanded.

"He's the one who screwed up. He's the one who's got to face the music," Billy said, meeting her gaze.

"Fine thing coming from you," she muttered so quietly that only Billy and Seth could hear her.

Billy grunted, but he kept his hand on Seth's shoulder. "Go on, kid."

"I, uh…" Seth sniffed. Billy gave him a little shove without letting him go. "I took your car and went to Billy's shop and punched him."

She gaped at Seth, looking from his iced hand to Billy's face. She could see where one side was redder than the other. "You did *what*? You told me you were going to be helping Don outside!"

Billy gave him that little shove again. "I told Don I'd be in here with you." Billy cleared his throat. "I'm sorry I lied."

The wash of emotions that swamped her was so strong it made her knees wobble. Her son—driving down the highway in her rust bucket of a car? Punching Billy in the face? "Are you all right? Are you hurt?"

Seth swiped at his dripping nose with his unbandaged hand, but he didn't answer. Jenny got the feeling he was too afraid of crying in front of the girls—all of whom were paying rapt attention to the little soap opera playing out in front of them.

"Cass said she didn't think it was broken," Billy said. "She's patched me and my dad up enough after fights—she knows what she's talking about."

Jenny's mouth opened and shut. "Um, good? I guess?"

"Doesn't hurt that much." Seth tried to sound tough, but she could tell how upset he was.

Now, anyway. How upset had he been about the whole thing to take her car and drive the forty-five minutes into Billy's shop to punch down the bigger man? She'd failed—again. She'd been so focused on distracting herself from Billy that she hadn't noticed how much Seth had been bothered by suddenly losing Billy as a mentor—and a friend.

Billy stood there, hand on her son's shoulder, giving her the look that probably scared every other person—including the girls in this room—but she recognized it as the mask he used to hide his nerves.

Aside from the slight swelling where Seth had hit him, he looked good. His beard had grown out a little and his hair was already getting long enough to brush the back of his shirt. But he was still wearing the heavy leathers he wore when he was working.

She didn't want him here, didn't want to face this particular mistake with such an audience.

"I'll deal with you when I get home," she told Seth, pulling him away from Billy's grasp. "Thank you for bringing him back."

Billy notched an eyebrow at her. "I'm not done," he said, sounding serious. "I messed up, too. And I've got to pay the price."

Then he did the weirdest thing. He pulled her chair around to the front of the desk and sat down, facing the TAPS girls.

"Hi, girls," he said, trying to sound friendly but still sounding scary.

She was rooted to her spot. All she could do was watch and listen.

"Jenny's a good teacher, isn't she?" The girls all giggled—they called her Ms. Wawasuck—but they nodded.

"I've learned a lot from her," Billy went on. "I learned I have to face my mistakes."

"Billy—" she said, but then stopped. She didn't know what else to say.

"I know some of you are in here because you made a mistake. And some of you don't want to make the same mistake." Some of the girls were blushing, some were looking at the floor—but no one said a thing. "I want to tell you that I understand—I made the same mistake. I was seventeen when I got a girl pregnant."

A low sound—like a gasp that everyone was trying to keep inside—went through the room. Even Seth tensed next to her. But Billy went on.

"I freaked out. Told the girl I didn't want the baby, didn't want to be a dad. I didn't stand by her when she needed me. I bet some of you have had that happen, too."

Cyndy, sitting in the back, nodded, tears dripping down her face. Jenny realized she was nodding, too.

"I went back and asked her to marry me, but she'd already had an abortion. I told myself that was her mistake—not mine. I blamed her for taking a part of me away—but I never took responsibility for what happened. I—" He paused, his voice breaking.

There was no denying what he was doing—everything she'd asked him to.

When he spoke again, he sounded more vulnerable than she'd ever heard him sound before. "I saw her again a few weeks ago, and she's never made peace with what she did. And the truth is I'd never really faced what I'd done, either." His voice softened. "The truth is we both made mistakes. It takes two people to get pregnant. You can try to put the blame on him, but you have to deal with your part of the situation, too." He looked over his shoulder at Jenny, his eyes shining. "That's what you did," he said to her. "You accepted your part in it and raised a damn fine boy who'd put it all on the line to protect you. But I didn't. And you were right—I've been ashamed of that ever since."

She wouldn't have thought it possible, but as she listened to him, Jenny's heart broke all over again. This wasn't him hiding from the past or trying to bury it under piles of money or guilt. This was him laying it all on the line.

He turned his attention back to the girls. "You may think that we're a bunch of dumb boys—and maybe we all are—but we're just as scared as you are. The only difference is that we can walk away. And some guys do. That's what they have to live with. Make the choices you can live with. That means not having sex, or using condoms. That also means keeping the baby, or giving it up, or whatever. But whatever it is, you have to be able to get up every day of your life and look in the mirror and know you did the best you could."

The silence was profound. No one moved until the younger girls began squirming.

Jenny took a deep breath, hoping she could keep it together. "Okay, that's enough for today. I'll see everyone tomorrow."

She didn't have to say it twice. The room cleared in a matter of moments.

"You, too, kid," Billy said. When Seth didn't start walking, he added, "I gave you my word, remember?"

"Okay." Still holding his iced hand, Seth followed everyone else out.

It was just the two of them. Moving slowly, Billy stood and rolled the chair back under her desk. Then he came up to her.

Jenny wanted to back away from him, tell him that she'd feed him to the coyotes if he touched her—but she couldn't. She couldn't even move as he reached out for her, pulled her into the arms she'd missed so much, and kissed her.

She forgot what she wanted and what she didn't want

and whatever mistake had led her away from this man, because all she could think—all she could feel—was how the world had righted itself. God, she'd missed him. No matter how hard she tried, she'd never stop missing him.

He pulled away, but he didn't go far. Instead, crushing her to his massive chest, he said, "I didn't do right by you, Jenny—that was *my* mistake, the one I have to face every day when I look in the mirror. So I tried not looking in the mirror." A sad smile tugged one corner of his lips up. "Didn't work."

"Oh?" She reached up and touched his lips.

"Tried to get lost again—in work, not in beer," he added. "That didn't work, either."

His arms felt so good around her. How had she thought she could live without this? Without *him?*

"Me, too." At this, his smile got a little less sad. "Even painted my living room."

His arms tightened around her. "So I've been thinking that there's only one way to get over you." He let go of her, but before disappointment could sink her, he was on his knees in front of her, both of her hands in his. "If you'll have me, I'll do better—*be* better. For you and your son."

"You—you mean it?"

He nodded. "I won't make any promises about cussing—too set in my ways. He's heard it all, anyway. But he's a good kid. If he wants me as a dad, I'd be proud to have him as a son." He swallowed, and she saw the fear in his eyes. "I'm not perfect. I work too much. I'm grumpy. My family's a pain in the butt. But if you'll have me as a husband, Jenny, I want you as my wife. I love you."

All she could do was gasp in surprise. He'd broken her heart—but he was putting it back together, one word at a time.

"What if it doesn't work?" she heard herself ask.

"I won't regret trying, Jenny. I won't ever regret not giving up on you."

God, how she'd wanted to hear those words, wanted to believe them. How she wanted to say yes. But something held her back—the reason she'd walked away in the first place. "What if that woman comes back and wants more money?"

The blood drained out of his face—except where her son had hit him. The whole situation was unreal. "She won't get anything else out of me. And if she talks to the press, then I'll deal with that. I won't hide anymore. I don't need to. You taught me that." He swallowed again. "Marry me. The family that I want is you and Seth. That's all I need."

"You promise?"

His smile sharpened, making him look hot and wicked and, more than anything, just like the man she loved. "You should know something about me, Jenny. I keep my promises, or I don't make them. And I promise you that I'll do better by you every day for the rest of our lives."

She let out a breath she hadn't known she'd been holding. "Yes," she told him, and was immediately crushed in a gigantic bear hug.

Then the door opened and Seth stuck his head in. "Are you guys done yet?"

Billy grinned down at her. She'd never seen him look happier than he did right then.

"No," he said, brushing his lips over hers. "We're just getting started."

* * * * *

A BRIDE BEFORE DAWN

SANDRA STEFFEN

For my seven wonders of the world:
Anora, Leah, Landen, Anna, Erin,
Dalton & Brynn

Chapter One

Noah Sullivan understood airplanes the way physicists understood atoms and bakers understood bread.

He pulled back on the yoke, pushed the throttle forward and sliced through the clouds. He dived, leveled off and climbed, listening intently to the engine all the while, the control held loosely in his hands. This old Piper Cherokee was soaring like a kite at eighteen hundred feet. She had a lot of years left in her.

The same couldn't be said for all the planes he flew. The first time he'd executed an emergency landing he'd used a closed freeway outside of Detroit. Last month he'd had to set a Cessna down on a godforsaken strip of dirt in the Texas hill country. He'd never lost a plane, though, and was considered one of the best independent test pilots in his field.

He wasn't fearless. He was relentless. He couldn't take all the credit for that, though. He never forgot that.

When he was finished putting the Piper through her paces, he headed down, out of the clouds. He followed the Chestnut River west, then banked south above the tallest church spire in Orchard Hill. Halfway between the city-limit sign and the country airstrip was Sully's Orchard. It was where Noah grew up, and where he collected his mail every month or so when he flew through.

He buzzed the orchard on his way by, as he always did when he came home, and tipped his wing when his oldest brother, Marsh, came running out the back door of the old cider house, his ball cap waving. Their mother used to say Marsh and Noah had been born looking up—Marsh to their apple trees and Noah to the sky above them. The second oldest, Reed, stepped out of the office, shading his eyes with his right hand. Tall, blond and shamelessly confident, he waved, too.

Those two deserved the credit for Noah's success, for they'd given up their futures after their parents died in an icy pileup when Noah was fifteen and their baby sister, Madeline, was twelve. Noah hadn't made it easy for them, either. Truancy when he was fifteen, speeding and curfew violations when he was sixteen, drinking long before it was legal. They never gave up on him, and helped him make his dream of flying come true. Maybe someday he would find a way to repay them.

He still enjoyed getting a rise out of them from time to time, but today he didn't subject them to any grandstanding or showing off. He simply flashed his landing lights hello and started toward the airstrip a few miles away. He'd barely gotten turned around when a movement on the ground caught his eye.

A woman was hurrying across the wide front lawn. She was wearing a jacket and had a cumbersome-looking bag slung over each shoulder. He tipped his wing hello, but instead of looking up, she ducked.

That was odd, Noah thought. Not the snub. That he took in stride. But it was the middle of June, and too warm for a jacket of any kind.

And not even company used the Sullivans' front door.

Thirty years ago Tom Bender looked out across his ramshackle rural airstrip five miles east of Orchard Hill, Michigan, and saw his future. Today the pasture that had once been a bumpy runway, where he'd landed his first airplane, was a diamond-in-the-rough airfield operation with tarmac runways and hangars for commuter planes, helicopters, charters and hobbyists.

With the stub of a cold cigar clamped between his teeth and all that was left of a sparse comb-over swirling in the June breeze, he was waiting when Noah rolled to a stop along the edge of the runway. "How'd she do?" Tom asked as soon as Noah climbed down.

Running his hand reverently along the underside of the Piper's right wing, Noah said, "She handled like the prima donna she was destined to become."

"I'm glad to hear it. The paperwork's on the clipboard where it always is," Tom said, his attention already turning to the biplane coming in for a landing on the other runway. "As soon as you fill it out, Em will cut you a check."

With that check, Noah would make the final payment on the loan for his Airfield Operations Specialist training, a loan he'd been whittling away at for nine years. Anticipating the satisfaction he would feel when he read *Paid in Full* on his tattered IOU, he headed toward the small block building that comprised the customer waiting area and Tom's office.

All eight chairs were empty and Tom's wife, Emma,

was verifying a reservation over the phone on the other side of the counter. She waved as Noah took the clipboard from the peg behind Tom's desk and lowered himself into a cracked leather chair beside it.

He'd barely started on the checklist when the airstrip's best mechanic moseyed inside. "You aren't going to believe what I heard today, Noah," Digger Brown said before the door even closed. As tall as Noah, Digger had a good start on a hardy paunch he was in the habit of patting. "You care to guess?"

Noah shook his head without looking up. "I'm in a hurry, Dig."

"Lacey's back in town."

Noah's ears perked up and the tip of his pen came off the page. Lacey was in Orchard Hill? For a few moments, he completely forgot what he'd been doing.

Digger was wearing a know-it-all grin when Noah looked up. "I figured that'd get your attention."

A few grades behind Noah, Lacey Bell used to walk to school with a camera around her neck and a chip on her shoulder. Back then she'd worn her dark hair short and her jeans tight. Noah had been doing his best to get kicked out of the eleventh grade, so other than the fact that the boys her age used to taunt her, he hadn't paid her a lot of attention. He'd heard a lot about her, though. Whether in bars, at air shows or loitering around watercoolers, men liked to talk. They'd said she was easy, bragging about their conquests the way they bragged about golf scores and fishing trips and cars. Noah's relationship with Lacey had taught him what liars men could be.

One night after he'd come home following his Airfield Operations Specialist training in Florida, he'd noticed her sitting on the steps that led to the apartment over the bar where she'd lived with her father. They'd talked, him at the bottom of those rickety stairs, her at the top. He'd been twenty and by the end of the night he'd been completely enamored by an eighteen-year-old girl with dark hair, a sharp mind, a smart mouth and a smile she didn't over-use. When he returned the next night, she moved down a few steps and he moved up. By the third night, they sat side by side.

She was the only girl he'd ever known who'd under-stood his affinity for the sky. She'd left Orchard Hill two-and-a-half years ago after the worst argument they'd ever had. Coming home hadn't been the same for Noah since.

"I wondered if you'd already heard, or if Lacey's return was news to you, too," Digger said.

"Where would I have heard that? Air-traffic control?" Noah asked, for he'd spent the past month crop dusting in Texas, and Digger knew it.

"There's no need to get huffy," Digger groused. "Maybe you ought to pay Lacey a visit. I'll bet she could put a smile on your face. Wait, I forgot. You're just a notch on her bedpost nowadays, aren't ya?"

Ten years ago, after saying something like that, Dig-ger would have been wearing the wrench he was carry-ing. Luckily for everybody, Noah had developed a little willpower over the years.

Eventually, Digger grew bored with being ignored and sauntered back outside where the guys on the grounds' crew were moving two airplanes around on the tarmac. Noah's mind wandered to the last time he'd seen Lacey, a year ago.

He'd been home to attend the air show in Battle Creek. That same weekend Lacey had been summoned from Chi-cago to her father's bedside after he'd suffered a massive heart attack. Noah had gone to the burial a few days later to pay his respects. Late that night, she'd answered his knock on her door and, like so many times before, they'd wound up in her bed. She'd been spitting mad in the morning, more angry with herself than at him, but mad was mad, and she'd told him the previous night had been a mistake she had no intention of repeating. She'd lit out of Orchard Hill again with little more than her camera the same day.

Now, if Digger was right, she was back in town.

Thoughts of her stayed with Noah as he finished the paperwork and pocketed the check Em Bender handed him. For a second or two he considered knocking on Lacey's door and inviting her out to celebrate with him. Then he remembered the way she'd stuck her hands on her hips and lifted her chin in defiance that morning after her father's funeral.

As tempting as seeing her again was, Noah had his pride. He didn't go where he wasn't wanted. So instead, he pointed his truck toward the family orchard that, to this day, felt like home.

The Great Lakes were said to be the breath of Michigan. As Noah crested the hill and saw row upon row of neatly pruned apple trees with their crooked branches, gnarled bark and sturdy trunks, he was reminded of all the generations of orchard growers who'd believed their trees were its soul.

He parked his dusty blue Chevy in his old spot between Marsh's shiny SUV and Reed's Mustang, and entered the large white house through the back door, the way he always did. Other than the take-out menus scattered across the countertops, the kitchen was tidy. He could hear the weather report droning from the den—Marsh's domain. Reed was most likely in his home office off the living room.

Since the den was closer, Noah stopped there first. Marsh glanced at him and held up a hand, in case Noah hadn't learned to keep quiet when the weather report was on.

Six-and-a-half years older than Noah, Marsh had been fresh out of college when their parents were killed so tragically. It couldn't have been easy taking on the family business and a little sister who desperately needed her mother, and two younger brothers, one of whom was hell-bent on ruining his own life. Despite everything Noah had put him through, Marsh looked closer to thirty than thirty-six.

When the weatherman finally broke for a commercial, Noah pushed away from the doorway where he'd been leaning and said, "What's a guy got to do to get a hello around here?"

Marsh made no apologies as he muted the TV and got to his feet. He was on his way across the room to clasp Noah in a bear hug when a strange noise stopped him in his tracks.

Noah heard it, too. What the hell was it?

He spun out of the den, Marsh right behind him, and almost collided with Reed. "Do you hear that?" Reed asked.

As tall as the other two, but blond, Reed was always the first to ask questions and the first to reach his own conclusions. He'd been at Notre Dame when their parents died. He'd come home to Orchard Hill, too, as soon as he'd finished college. Noah owed him as much as he owed Marsh.

"It sounds like it's coming from right outside the front door," Reed said.

Marsh cranked the lock and threw open the door. He barreled through first, the other two on his heels. All three stopped short and stared down at the baby screaming at the top of his lungs on the porch.

A baby. Was on their porch.

Dressed all in blue, he had wisps of dark hair and an angry red face. He was strapped into some sort of seat with a handle, and was wailing shrilly. He kicked his feet. On one he wore a tiny blue sock. The other foot was bare. The strangest thing about him, though, was that he was alone.

Marsh, Reed and Noah had been told they were three fine specimens of the male species. Two dark-haired and one fair, all were throwbacks to past generations of rugged Sullivan men. The infant continued to cry pitifully, obviously unimpressed.

Noah was a magician in the cockpit of an airplane. Marsh had an almost ethereal affinity for his apple trees. Reed was a wizard with business plans and checks and balances. Yet all three of them were struck dumb while the baby cried in earnest.

He was getting worked up, his little fisted hands flailing, his legs jerking, his mouth wide open. In his vehemence, he punched himself in the nose.

Just like that he quieted.

But not for long. Skewing his little face, he gave the twilight hell.

Reed was the first to recover enough to bend down and pick the baby up, seat and all. The crying abated with the jiggling motion. Suddenly, the June evening was eerily still. In the ensuing silence, all three brothers shared a look of absolute bewilderment.

"Where'd he come from?" Marsh asked quietly, as if afraid any loud noises or sudden moves might set off another round of crying.

Remembering the woman he'd seen from the air, Noah looked out across the big lawn, past the parking area that would be teeming with cars in the fall but was empty now. He peered at the stand of pine trees and a huge willow near the lane where the property dropped away. Nothing moved as far as the eye could see.

Every day about this time the orchard became more shadow than light. The apple trees were lush and green, the two-track path through the orchard neatly mowed. The shed where the parking signs were stored, along with the four-wheelers, wagons and tractors they used for hayrides every autumn, was closed up tight. Noah could see the padlock on the door from here. Everything looked exactly as it always had.

"I don't see anybody, do you?" Marsh asked quietly.

Reed and Noah shook their heads.

"Did either of you hear a car?" Reed asked.

Noah and Marsh hadn't, and neither had Reed.

"That baby sure didn't come by way of the stork," Marsh insisted.

A stray current of air stirred the grass and the new leaves in the nearby trees. The weather vane on the cider house creaked the way it always did when the wind came out of the east. Nothing looked out of place, Noah thought. The only thing out of the ordinary was the sight of the tiny baby held stiffly in Reed's big hands.

"We'd better get him inside," Noah said as he reached for two bags that hadn't been on the porch an hour ago. A sheet of paper fluttered to the floor. He picked it up and read the handwritten note.

Our precious son, Joseph Daniel Sullivan.
I call him Joey. He's my life. I beg you,
take good care of him until I can return for him.

He turned the paper over then showed it to his brothers.

"*Our* precious son?" Reed repeated after reading it for himself.

"*Whose* precious son?" Marsh implored, for the note wasn't signed.

The entire situation grew stranger with every passing second. What the hell was going on here? The last one to the door, Noah looked back again, slowly scanning the familiar landscape. Was someone watching? The hair on his arms stood up as if he were crop dusting dangerously close to power lines.

Who left a baby on a doorstep in this day and age? But someone had. If whoever had done it was still out there, he didn't know where.

He was looking right at her. She was almost sure of it.

Her lips quivered and her throat convulsed as she fought a rising panic. She couldn't panic. And he couldn't possibly see her. He was too far away and she was well hidden. She was wearing dark clothing, purposefully blending with the shadows beneath the trees.

A dusty pickup truck had rattled past her hiding place ten minutes ago. The driver hadn't even slowed down. He hadn't seen her and neither could the last Sullivan on the porch. Surely he wouldn't have let the others go inside if he had.

From here she couldn't even tell which brother was still outside. It was difficult to see anything in this light. A sob lodged sideways in her throat, but she pushed it down. She'd cried enough. Out of options and nearly out of time, she was doing the right thing.

She had to go, and yet she couldn't seem to move. On the verge of hyperventilating, she wished she'd have thought to bring a paper sack to breathe into so she wouldn't pass out. She couldn't pass out. She couldn't allow herself the luxury of oblivion. Instead, she waited, her muscles aching from the strain of holding so still. Her empty arms ached most of all.

When the last of the men who'd gathered on the porch finally went inside, she took several deep calming breaths. She'd done it. She'd waited as long as she could, and she'd done what she had to do.

Their baby was safe. Now she had to leave.

"Take care of him for me for now," she whispered into the vast void of deepening twilight.

Reminding herself that this arrangement wasn't permanent, and that she would return for her baby the moment she was able to, she crept out from beneath the weeping-willow tree near the road and started back toward the car parked behind a stand of pine trees half a mile away.

She'd only taken a few steps when Joey's high-pitched wails carried through the early-evening air. She paused, for she recognized that cry. It had been three hours since his last bottle. She'd tried to feed him an hour ago, but he'd been too sleepy to eat. Evidently, he was ready now. Surely it wouldn't take his father long to find his bottles and formula and feed him.

Rather than cause her to run to the house and snatch him back into her arms, Joey's cries filled her with conviction. He had a mind of his own and would put his father through the wringer tonight, but Joey would be all right. He was a survivor, her precious son.

And so was she.

In five minutes' time, life as Noah, Reed and Marsh Sullivan knew it went from orderly to pandemonium. Joey—the note said his name was Joey—was crying again. Noah and Marsh were trying to figure out how to get him out of the contraption he was buckled into. Reed, who was normally cool, calm and collected, pawed through the contents of the bags until he found feeding supplies.

When the baby was finally freed from the carrier, Noah picked him up—he couldn't believe how small he was, and hurriedly followed the others to the kitchen where Reed was already scanning the directions on a cardboard canister of powdered formula he'd found in one of the bags. Marsh unscrewed the top of a clear plastic baby bottle and turned on the faucet.

"It says to use warm water." Reed had to yell in order to be heard over the crying.

Marsh switched the faucet to hot and Reed pried the lid off the canister. "Make sure it's not too hot," Reed called when he saw steam rising from the faucet.

Marsh swore.

Noah seconded the sentiment.

The baby wasn't happy about the situation, either. He continued to wail pathetically, banging his little red face against Noah's chest.

Marsh adjusted the temperature of the water again. The instant it was warm but not hot, he filled the bottle halfway. Using the small plastic scoop that came with the canister, Reed added the powdered formula. When the top was on, Noah grabbed the bottle and stuck the nipple in Joey's mouth. The kid didn't seem to care that Noah didn't know what he was doing. He clamped on and sucked as if he hadn't eaten all day.

Ah. Blessed silence.

They moved en masse back to the living room. Lowering himself awkwardly to the couch, Noah held the baby stiffly in one arm. All three men stared at Joey, who was making sucking sounds on the bottle. Slowly, they looked at each other, shell-shocked.

Last year had been a stellar season for the orchard.

Sales had been good and the profit margin high enough to make up for the apple blight that had swept through their orchards the year before. Their sister had survived the tragic death of her childhood sweetheart and was now happily married to a man who would do anything to make her happy. The newlyweds were expecting their first child and were settling into their home near Traverse City. Noah had the money in his pocket to pay off his loan. Somewhere along the way he'd finally made peace with his anger over losing his parents when he was fifteen. All three of the Sullivan men were free for the first time in their adult lives.

Or so they'd thought.

"It says," Reed said, his laptop open on the coffee table, "that you're supposed to burp him after an ounce or two."

Burp him? Noah thought. What did that mean?

"Try sitting him up," Reed said.

Noah took the nipple out of the baby's mouth and awkwardly did as Reed suggested. A huge burp erupted. All three brothers grinned. After all, they were men and some things were just plain funny. Their good humor didn't last long, though. Dismay, disbelief and the sneaking suspicion that there was a hell of a lot more trouble ahead immediately returned.

Looking around for the baby's missing sock, Noah laid him back down in the crook of his arm and offered him more formula. As he started to drink again, Joey stared up at him as if to say, "Who in the world are you?"

Noah looked back at him the same way.

Could he really be a Sullivan? His eyes were blue-gray, like Reed's, but his hair was dark like Marsh's and Noah's.

"How old do you think he is?" Noah asked.

Reed made a few clicks on his computer. Eying the

baby again, he said, "I would estimate him to be right around three months."

Although none of them were in a relationship at the present time, they did some mental math, and all three of their throats convulsed on a swallow. If Joey was indeed a Sullivan, he could *conceivably* have been any one of theirs.

The baby fell asleep before the bottle was empty. Too agitated to sit still, Noah handed him to Marsh, who was sitting the closest to him. When the child stirred, they all held their breath until his little eyelashes fluttered down again.

"I don't see how I could be his father," Marsh said so quietly he might have been thinking out loud. "I always take precautions."

"Me, too," Noah said, almost as quietly.

"Same here."

The baby hummed in his sleep. His very presence made the case of the reliability of protection a moot point.

"We're going to need a DNA test," Reed declared.

"I have a better idea," Noah said, already moving across the room toward the kitchen and escape.

"Not so fast!" Reed admonished, stopping Noah before he'd reached the arched doorway.

It rankled, but Noah figured he had it coming for all the times he'd hightailed it out of Orchard Hill in the past. "Can you guys handle the baby on your own for a little while?" he asked.

Two grown, capable, decent men cringed. It was Marsh who finally said, "We can if we have to. Where are you going?"

Noah looked Marsh in the eye first, and then Reed. "I heard Lacey's in town."

"Do you think she left Joey here?" Marsh asked.

Noah couldn't imagine it, but he'd never imagined that he and his brothers would find themselves in a situation like this, either. "I saw somebody on the front lawn when I buzzed the orchard earlier," he said. "It was a woman with bags slung over her shoulders. She was hunched over, so I couldn't see her well, but now I think she was hiding Joey under an oversize sweatshirt or poncho."

Reed got to his feet. "Was it Lacey?" he asked.

"I don't know. She was wearing a scarf or a hood or something. I couldn't even tell what color her hair was."

"Why would Lacey leave her baby that way?"

"Why would anybody?" Noah said. "I guess we'll know soon enough if it was her. I'll be back as quickly as I can."

He strode through the house, where the television was still muted and where diapers and bottles and other baby items lay heaped on the table and countertops. Pointing his old pickup truck toward town seconds later, his mind was blank but for one thought.

If Joey was his, Lacey had some explaining to do.

Just once, Lacey Bell wanted to be on the receiving end of good luck, not bad. Was that too much to ask? Truly?

Looking around her at the clutter she was painstakingly sifting through and boxing up, she sighed. She was searching for a hidden treasure she wasn't sure existed. Her father had spoken of it on his deathbed, but he'd been delirious and, knowing her dad, he could have been referring to a fine bottle of scotch. She so wanted to believe he'd left her something of value. Once a dreamer, always a dreamer, she supposed.

She'd emptied the closet and was filling boxes from her father's dresser when the pounding outside began. She wasn't concerned. She'd spent her formative years in this apartment and had stopped being afraid of loud noises, shattering beer bottles and things that went bump in the night a long time ago. It had been the first in a long line of conscious decisions.

Ignoring the racket, she swiped her hands across her wet cheeks and went back to work. After he'd died a year ago, she'd given her father the nicest funeral she could afford. She'd paid the property taxes with what little money was left, but she hadn't been able to bear the thought of going through all his things, knowing he would never be back. A year later, it was no easier.

He'd lived hard, her dad, but he'd been a good father in his own way. She wished she could ask him what she should do.

She filled another carton and was placing it with the others along the kitchen wall when she realized the noise wasn't coming from the alley, as she'd thought. Somebody was pounding on her door.

Being careful not to make a sound, she tiptoed closer and looked through the peephole. Her hand flew to her mouth, her heart fluttering wildly.

It was Noah.

"Lacey, open up."

She reeled backward as if he'd seen her. Gathering her wits about her, she reminded herself that unless Noah had X-ray vision he couldn't possibly know she was inside.

She caught her reflection in the mirror across the room. Her jeans were faded and there was a smudge of dirt on her cheek. She wondered when the rubber band had slipped out of her hair. Orchard Hill was a small city, so it stood to reason that she would run into Noah. Did it have to be tonight when she wasn't even remotely ready?

"I'm not leaving until I've talked to you," Noah called through the door.

"I'm busy," she said with more conviction than she felt.

"This won't take long."

Silence.

"Please, Lace?"

A shudder passed through her, for Noah Sullivan was proud and self-reliant and defiant. Saying *please* had never come easy for him.

"I'll break the damn door down if I have to."

Knowing him, he would, too. Shaking her head at Fate, she turned the dead bolt and slowly opened the door.

Noah stood on her threshold, his brown eyes hooded and half his face in shadow. He was lean and rugged and so tall she had to look up slightly to meet his gaze. The mercury light behind him cast a blue halo around his head. It was an optical illusion, for Noah Sullivan was no angel.

Before her traitorous heart could flutter up to her throat, she swallowed audibly and said, "What do you want, Noah?"

His eyes narrowed and he said, "I want you to tell me what the hell is going on."

Chapter Two

Noah was as ruggedly handsome as ever in faded jeans and a black T-shirt. His dark hair was a little shaggy, his jaw darkened as if he hadn't had time to shave, but that wasn't what made it so difficult to face him tonight.

"Have you been crying?" he asked.

Lacey tried not to react to the concern in his voice. It was dangerous and conjured up emotions she wasn't ready to deal with. "I must have gotten something in my eye. I'm in the middle of something here. Now's not a good time." She moved as if to close the door.

He narrowed his eyes and looked at her so hard she almost believed he could have X-ray vision. "This won't take long."

"I mean it, Noah. You're going to have to come back tomorrow. Or the next day," she said, praying he didn't hear the little quaver in her voice. The backward step she took was pure self-preservation, for the man was a weakness for which she had no immunity. "I've had a lousy day and I'm not in the mood for company."

She was taking another backward step when he reached for her hand. Her senses short-circuited like a string of lights at the end of a power surge. His fingers were long, his grip slightly possessive. It brought out a familiar yearning born of loneliness, need and a great sadness.

"Aw, Lace, don't cry," he said, tugging lightly on her hand.

"I told you, I must have gotten something in my—" The next thing she knew, she was toppling into his arms.

Noah didn't think about what he was doing, because what he was doing felt as natural as flying. Wrapping his arms around Lacey, he tilted his chin to make room for her head and widened his stance to make room for her feet between his. For once, it wasn't the vibration of flight he sensed, but her trembling. At first she held herself stiffly, but slowly the tension drained out of her. He didn't know what she'd been through since he'd last seen her, and he didn't want to guess what was at the root of her tears. In that place where instincts lived and survival reigned, he knew only that she needed something as simple and basic as a human touch.

It had been a year since he'd inhaled the scent of her shampoo, since he'd felt her warm breath against his neck or held her soft curves against the hard length of his body. He heard the rush of blood in his ears and he knew the cause.

He needed to stop this. He'd come here for a reason, a damn good one.

She sighed and lifted her head from his shoulder. Splaying her fingers wide against his chest as if to push away, she opened her eyes and looked up at him. For a moment, neither of them moved, not even to breathe.

Her eyes were luminous and her lashes were damp. Noah's heart skipped a beat then raced in double-time. Without conscious thought, he swooped down and covered her mouth with his.

He didn't know what the hell he was doing. Okay, he knew. He'd been imagining this ever since Digger told him Lacey was back in town.

He kissed her. It was demanding and rousing, and once it started, it was too late to ask what she was doing back in Orchard Hill, too late to ask her anything, or to do anything but pull her even closer and tip her head up and plunge into the heat and hunger springing to life between them.

She opened her mouth beneath his, and clutched fistfuls of his shirt to keep from falling. He wasn't going to let her fall. Keeping one arm around her back, he moved his other hand to her waist, along her ribs, to the delicate edges of her shoulder blades. He massaged the knot at the back of her neck until she moaned. It was a low, primal sound that brought an answering one from deep inside him.

The kiss stopped and started a dozen times. Raw and savage, it tore through him until his heart was thundering and holding her wasn't enough. It was never enough.

His ears rang and his lungs burned and need coursed through his veins. He was guilty of slipping his hands beneath her shirt, guilty of succumbing to her beauty and his need. His right hand took a slow journey the way it had come, along her ribs, to the small of her back and lower. She locked herself in his embrace and buried her fingers in his hair, as guilty of wanting this as he was.

He covered her breast with his other hand, the thin fabric of her bra the only barrier between her skin and his. He massaged and kneaded until she moaned again, her head tipping back. His eyes half-open, he made a sound, too, his gaze going to the boxes lining the room.

"You're packing," he said, easing the strap of her tank top off her right shoulder. "Where are you going?"

"It's no concern of yours."

"You leave a kid on my doorstep, it's sure as hell my concern," he said against her skin.

The censure in Noah's voice brought Lacey to her senses. Stiffening, she opened her eyes. She drew her right shoulder away from his lips and yanked herself out of his arms. Unable to get very far away without running into boxes, she had to make do with six feet of space between them.

She pulled her shirt down and pushed her strap up. Her breathing was ragged and her thoughts jumbled. Trying to get both under control wasn't easy. What an understatement. The passion that had erupted had temporarily thrown her into her old habits, for she'd never been able to resist him.

Catching sight of her reflection in the mirror again, she pushed her hair behind her ears and took several calming breaths. From six feet away she could see Noah's vehemence returning.

"Why the hell didn't you tell me you were pregnant?" he asked.

Something crashed in Lacey's mind like a whiskey bottle hurled against the alley wall below. That was why Noah was here? Because for some unfathomable reason he believed she'd gotten pregnant? If she could have laughed, it would have been bitter.

"Are you going to answer my question or aren't you?" he demanded.

Again, she heard the censure in his voice. When other young girls were learning to say *please* and *thank you* and how to walk in heels and fit in with their peers, Lacey had been learning how to fend for herself. Eventually, she'd acquired those other skills from teachers and friends, books and television, but self-preservation was as deeply ingrained as her pride.

She may have been raised over a shabby bar, but she didn't have to accept his or anyone else's unwarranted reproach. "I want you to leave," she said. "Now."

His eyes narrowed. "What game are you playing, Lacey?"

She squared off opposite him. "I'm not playing with you anymore. I thought I made that clear a year ago."

Her statement would have carried more impact if her lips weren't still wet and swollen from his kiss, but she could tell by the way he drew his next breath that she'd scraped a nerve.

"Tell me this," he said, his hands going to his hips, too. "Did you leave Joey on our front porch tonight?"

She lifted her chin a notch, surprise momentarily rendering her speechless. Finally, she managed to say, "What do you think?"

"I *think* that if you did, it's a hell of a way to tell a man he's responsible for a kid."

It was her turn to feel stung. Obviously, he didn't know her at all. That was the problem, wasn't it? He told her what he wanted and needed and she pretended to want and need the same thing. Until two-and-a-half years ago, that is. That was when the truth had come out. It was the same night they'd broken up. It hadn't been pretty, but it had been necessary in order for her to move forward in her life, and all the other mumbo jumbo she read in self-help books.

She straightened her back and stiffened her upper lip. It rankled slightly that she had to remind herself that she'd done nothing wrong and, consequently, owed him nothing.

"If he's mine," he said, on a roll, "the least you could have done was sign the damn note so we wouldn't have to wonder which of us is his father."

She didn't know how to respond to that. Noah made her head spin. He always had.

She'd fallen in love with him when she was eighteen years old. By the time she'd realized that he'd needed his lofty dreams of freedom more than he'd needed her, it had been too late to guard her heart from getting broken every time he flew off into the wild blue yonder. Eventually, she'd found the courage to chase her own dream.

Now here she was, back where she'd started. No matter what Noah thought, she wasn't the same girl she'd been ten years ago, or five, or even one. Now she had to think about what she needed.

She walked to the door and held it open. "I asked you to leave."

"Are you going to answer my question?" he asked roughly, squaring off opposite her in the doorway.

Gathering her dignity about her, she said, "A baby. That would be the ultimate tether, wouldn't it? What would you do if I said yes? Would you marry me, Noah?"

A slap wouldn't have stunned him more.

"That's what I thought," she said, unable to close the door while his foot was in it.

Tires screeched and a horn honked out on the street. The fracas seemed to bring him to some sort of decision. Staring into her eyes as if he could see all the way to her soul, he said, "Dinner is at one at the homestead tomorrow. Be there."

The deep cadence of his voice hung in the air for a long

time after he left. Lacey closed the door, but she moved around the cluttered apartment as if in a trance.

Noah Sullivan had a lot of nerve. It was just like him to threaten to break her door down if she didn't let him in and then trounce off as if everything that had happened was her fault. He made her so mad.

She closed her eyes, because that wasn't all she felt for him. She'd gone an entire year without seeing him, without talking to him or touching him, and then, bam, she'd spent one minute in his presence and wound up in his arms. Why did her body always seem to betray her when it came to Noah?

She knew the answer, and it had as much to do with love as it did with passion. She stomped her foot at the futility of it all.

From what she could gather from the little he'd told her tonight, somebody had left a baby on the Sullivans' doorstep. It wasn't clear to her why Marsh, Reed and Noah were uncertain which of them was the father. The entire situation seemed ludicrous, but if Noah believed the child might have been a product of their night of passion last year, the baby must be an infant.

What kind of a mother left her child that way?

A desperate one, Lacey thought as she looked around the old apartment where she'd spent her formative years. She understood desperation.

Shortly after her father died last year, the company she'd worked for in Chicago had downsized and she'd found herself unemployed. Her meager savings had quickly run out. Part-time and temp jobs barely put food on the table. Before long she was behind on her rent. And then things got worse.

She placed a hand over the scar on her abdomen, then just as quickly took her hand away.

She didn't have time to feel sorry for herself. She couldn't change the past, and who knew what the future held?

Right now, what she needed was a viable means of support. What she had—all she had—was this narrow building that housed her father's boarded-up bar and this ramshackle apartment above it. Although she'd promised herself that she would never move back to Orchard Hill, the deed to this property gave her a handful of options she wouldn't have had otherwise. She could reopen the bar, or rent out the building and this apartment, or sell it all—lock, stock and barrel.

As she returned to her packing, she thought about Noah's invitation. Okay, it had sounded more like an order. Dinner was at one tomorrow, he'd said. He expected her to be there.

She wondered what he would do when she didn't show up. She spent far too much time imagining what would happen if she did.

There were two types of guys. Those who asked permission. And those who begged forgiveness. Why, Noah wondered, did he always land in the latter category?

He'd had every intention of knocking on Lacey's door and asking her one simple question. "Is Joey my son?"

But he'd seen her tears, and he'd reached for her hand, and one thing had led to another. Now here he was, pulling into his own driveway, the remnants of unspent desire congealing in his bloodstream while guilt fought for equal space. Since there wasn't much he could do about his failings right now, he pulled his keys from the ignition, turned off his headlights and got out.

The house was lit up like a church. Even the attic light was on. The windows were open, but other than the bullfrogs croaking from a distant pond and a car driving by, he didn't hear anything. He hoped that was a good sign.

He went inside quietly, and found Marsh and Reed in the living room again. They were standing in the center of the room, staring down into the old wooden cradle between them. There was a streak of dirt on Marsh's white T-shirt and Reed's hair was sticking up as if he'd raked his fingers through it. Repeatedly.

Noah waited until they looked at him to mouth, "How long has he been sleeping?"

After glancing at his watch, Marsh mouthed back, "Four minutes."

"Did you talk to Lacey?" Reed whispered.

Noah nodded and tried not to grimace.

As if by unspoken agreement, they moved the discussion to the kitchen. Keeping his voice down once they were all assembled there, Noah said, "Lacey didn't leave Joey on our doorstep."

"She told you that?" Reed asked.

"She didn't have to. If I hadn't been in shock, I would have realized it right away. If she'd been pregnant with my kid, she would have gotten in my face or served me with papers. She wouldn't have left the baby on my porch and then crept away without telling me."

"You're positive?" Reed asked.

"Covert moves aren't her style," he said. "If Joey is a Sullivan, he isn't mine."

Marsh, Reed and Noah had personalities very different from one another. But one thing they had in common was an innate aversion to asking permission to do what they thought was best. Consequently, Noah wasn't the only member of this family who sometimes wound up in the uncomfortable position of asking for forgiveness. Remembering all the times these two had been waiting for him when he'd broken curfew or worse, and all the times they must have wondered what the hell they were going to do with him, he felt an enormous welling of affection for his brothers.

"Obviously, you were both with somebody a year ago. Do either of you have an address or phone number?" he asked.

The first to shake his head, Reed was also the first to drag out a chair and sit down. "She was a waitress I met when I was in Dallas last summer. She spilled salsa in my lap and was so flustered she tried to clean it up. I stopped her before— Anyway, she blushed adorably and said her shift was almost over. She had a nice smile, big hair and—" His voice trailed away.

"What was her name?" Marsh asked after he'd taken a seat, too.

In a voice so quiet it wasn't easy to hear, Reed said, "Cookie."

Noah didn't mean to grin. Marsh probably didn't, either. It was just that the fastidious middle Sullivan brother normally went out with women named Katherine or Margaret or Elizabeth.

"What's her last name?" Noah asked.

"I've been trying to remember ever since we brought Joey inside."

Reed Sullivan had sandy-blond hair, but his whisker stubble was as dark as Noah's and Marsh's. Letting whisker stubble accumulate was a rare occurrence, so rare in fact that Noah had forgotten how dark it was. Scratching his uncommonly stubbly cheek, Reed looked beyond mortified. If he expected chastisement, he wasn't going to get it from either of his brothers.

"You said she was a waitress," Noah said, trying to

make a little sense of a very strange situation. "What was the name of the restaurant?"

Reed said, "It was a small Mexican place near the airport. Now I wish I'd used a credit card so there would be a paper trail."

Noah turned his attention to Marsh, who had grown unusually quiet. "What about you? Are you dealing with a one-night stand, too?"

Marsh shook his head. "Her name is Julia Monroe. At least that's what she told me." His voice got husky and took on a dreamy quality Noah had never heard before. "I met her on vacation last year on Roanoke Island. We slept under the stars and visited just about every coffee shop up and down the Outer Banks."

"Have you talked to her since the week was over?" Reed asked, obviously as curious as Noah.

"The number she gave me was out of service," Marsh answered.

That seemed odd to Noah, but there wasn't much about this dilemma that didn't seem odd. "What about the note?" he asked. "Does the handwriting look familiar to either of you?"

Marsh and Reed wore similar expressions of uncertainty. After a moment of quiet contemplation, Reed asked, "Why wouldn't she have signed the note? Or addressed it?"

It was just one more thing about this situation that didn't make sense. Leaning back in his chair, Noah thought about the note. It hinted at desperation, contained a written plea and a promise that Joey's mother would return for him. Maybe that was all she wanted them to know.

"Does the middle name *Daniel* mean anything to either of you?" Noah asked.

Again, Marsh and Reed shook their heads.

Reed said, "We're back to square one. We're going to need a DNA test. I checked online a little while ago. Kits are available at drugstores everywhere. The test looks pretty straightforward and simple to perform, but it can take up to six weeks to get the results."

"I don't want to wait six weeks," Marsh said firmly.

"Neither do I," Reed said with the same amount of force. "Our only alternative is to hire a private investigator."

Reed reached across the table for his laptop. Marsh went to the cupboard and dragged out an old phone book.

Before either of them went a step further, Noah stopped them. "You can't pluck some name off the internet or from the phone book for something this important."

"Do you have a better idea?" Reed asked.

As a matter of fact, Noah did. For once in their lives, having a hellion for a brother was going to come in handy. "A few years ago I tested an airplane for a guy calling in a favor. He's a P.I. over in Grand Rapids and flies a blue biplane called Viper. I don't have a business card but I know somebody who does. I'll make a few phone calls first thing in the morning."

"Is this investigator any good?" Marsh asked.

Noah said, "He's found runaways and exes and bail jumpers and just about everything in between."

His stomach growled audibly. Trying to remember how long it had been since he'd eaten, he went to the refrigerator and opened the door. He saw various cartons, bags and containers of leftover takeout, one of which was starting to resemble a science experiment. This was why he always cooked when he was home.

"When are you leaving?" Marsh asked.

"I'm not," Noah said, cautiously sniffing a carton before tossing it into the trash. The science experiment went in next.

"You don't have another flying engagement lined up?" Reed asked.

"It'll keep." Unlike the leftovers on the top shelf. "I'm not going anywhere until this is resolved. I figure we can use a couple of extra hands around here."

While Noah threw out everything except eggs, butter, condiments and cans of soda and beer, Marsh and Reed talked about what they might expect on Joey's first night here. According to the information Reed had gotten from the 83,000 Google hits, children this age generally required a feeding every two to six hours.

"You're saying we could be in for a long night," Noah said, closing the refrigerator.

Reed was fast at work on a preliminary schedule. Following a little discussion, Noah was assigned the third watch.

He ate a peanut-butter sandwich standing up. After chasing it down with a cold beer, he strode to the stairway on the other side of the room. "I'm going to get some sleep. Wake me up when you need me. I mean it. We're in this together."

"Noah?" Marsh said quietly.

With one hand on the doorknob, Noah looked back at his oldest brother.

"I'm glad you're here," Marsh said.

"*Glad* barely scrapes the surface," Reed said, closing his laptop.

Something constricted deep in Noah's chest. "I'm glad to be here." It was the honest-to-God truth.

He could have left it at that, but opportunities like this didn't come along every day, so of course he cocked his head slightly and said, "Sex on the beach, and big hair and big—" He cleared his throat. "Who knew you two had it in you?"

He dodged the roll of paper towels Marsh threw at him, and took the steps two at a time. In his room at the end of the hall, he emptied his pockets of his keys and change and put the check from Tom Bender on his dresser, then quickly stripped down. Heading for the only bathroom on the second floor, he thought about the apology he owed Lacey.

He turned on the shower. While he waited for the water to get hot, he considered possible ways he might say he was sorry. Red roses, he thought as he lathered a washcloth and scrubbed the day's grime from his arms, chest and shoulders. In his mind's eye he saw a dozen red roses upside down in Lacey's trash can. A box of chocolates would meet with the same fate.

By the time he dried off, he knew what he had to do. It wasn't going to be easy.

Begging forgiveness never was.

Chapter Three

Sure, the rusty thermometer on the light pole in the alley behind Bell's Tavern registered eighty-one degrees, but the bright afternoon sunshine wasn't the only reason Ralph Jacobs was sweating.

"You're getting a bargain," Lacey said patiently as her dad's former customer placed another bill in her outstretched hand.

"Six hundred's a little steep, doncha think?" he groused, mopping his forehead with a folded handkerchief. "That old Chevy is close to twenty years old, you know."

She glanced at the pickup truck now sitting on Ralph's flatbed trailer. She could have gotten more for her dad's pickup if she'd had time to advertise, and they both knew it.

Turning her attention back to the transaction, she watched as Ralph wet his finger and reluctantly added another hundred spot to the others in her hand. "Dad always took good care of that truck," she said. "It was ten years old when he bought it. Remember how proud he was that day? It still has low mileage and started just now the first time you turned the key. You and I agreed on $600."

"It has four flat tires," he insisted.

"I threw those in at no extra charge."

Ralph made a sound she would have been hard-pressed to replicate. When he finally parted with the sixth hundred-dollar bill, she handed him the signed title and tucked the money into the pocket of her faded cutoffs for safekeeping.

Just then Lacey's best friend came hurrying down the steps, her light brown curls bouncing and her white blouse nearly as bright as the sunshine. "It was good of you to offer to drop these boxes at Good Neighbors on your way home, Mr. Jacobs," April Avery called as she secured the last carton on the trailer with the others.

Ralph made that sound again, because it hadn't been his idea.

April was one of those savvy, quirky women nobody could say no to. She'd moved to Orchard Hill after she married into the large Avery brood seven years ago. She and Lacey had clicked the first time they met and had become the best of friends in almost no time.

Together they watched as the trailer carrying many of the things Harlan Bell could no longer use rattled away. The moment they were alone again, April pushed her curly hair behind her ears and exclaimed, "I thought he would never leave. Now, finish your story."

"Where was I?" Lacey asked. As if she didn't know.

"You were just getting to the good part," April said. "Noah threatened to break your door down if you didn't open it, and the instant you did, he took you in his arms and kissed you so thoroughly you swooned. That is so romantic."

There was never much activity in the alley at this time of the afternoon in the middle of the week. Two boys had taken a shortcut through here on their bikes a few minutes ago. A panel truck was making a delivery to the appliance store at the other end of the alley, but the deliverymen were too far away to hear Lacey say, "I did not swoon. And it wasn't romantic."

"Then your heart *didn't* race and your knees *didn't* weaken and butterflies *didn't* flutter their naughty little wings in unmentionable places?" April asked.

Lacey held up a hand in a halting gesture. Just thinking about Noah's kiss was stirring up those butterflies again.

"That's what I thought," April said, nudging her with one shoulder. "You're lucky. The only romance I've had since Jay's been deployed is via webcam. Trust me, it's not the same as real kissing."

Lacey stared at her friend. "You and Jay have webcam sex?"

"Never until after the twins are in bed, but we're talking about you."

Smiling at April's one-of-a-kind sense of humor, Lacey wandered to the metal trash can lying on its side under the stairway. She set the can upright and put the lid on with a loud clank. Next, she unlocked the tavern's back door and the two of them went inside.

April's in-laws owned the busiest realty company in Orchard Hill. She'd been working in the office and pursuing her real estate license since her husband, a guardsman, had been called to active duty eight months ago. She was here this afternoon as Lacey's friend but also to offer her professional opinion regarding a selling strategy for the tavern. It would be her first solo listing.

While April poked her head into the empty storage room that had once housed kegs of beer and crates of liquor, Lacey went to the front door and propped that open, too. Standing in the slight cross breeze, she tried to see the place through a Realtor's eyes.

When it came to bars in Orchard Hill, Bell's Tavern had been near the bottom of the food chain. Lacey had always gotten the impression that her dad had liked it that way. Originally, the building had been a mercantile exchange. It had passed hands several times before being converted into a tavern eighty years ago. The ceilings were low, the sidewalls were exposed brick and the hardwood floors desperately needed refinishing. The tavern's most redeeming features were the old speakeasy door from Prohibition days, now leaning against the wall in the storeroom, and the ornate hand-carved mahogany bar and matching shelves behind it. The mirror had been cracked when her dad bought the place, so she couldn't blame that for her run of bad luck this past year.

She thought about the itemized hospital bill tucked inside her suitcase upstairs. Before her phone had been shut off, bill collectors had called at all hours of the day and night. The wolves were at her door.

"Do you think Avery Realty will be able to find a buyer for this place?" she asked.

"Is that really what you want?" April countered.

Sliding her hands into the pockets of her cutoffs where all the money she had to her name crinkled reassuringly, she said, "I have to sell, April."

April gave one of the barstools a good spin. "Don't mind me. I've been having serious separation issues ever since Jay left for Afghanistan. It's selfish of me, but I want you to stay. Don't worry, we'll find a buyer for this place, although in this economy it could take a little while. In the meantime, I've been thinking about the hidden treasure your dad mentioned before he died."

"I've searched everywhere," Lacey insisted, putting one of the cameras from her mother's collection back on the high shelf where she'd found it. "There's nothing here. Even this old Brownie has more sentimental value than monetary worth."

"Maybe the hidden treasure isn't a tangible object," April said. "I think that's what your father was trying to tell you."

"What do you mean?" Lacey asked.

April stopped testing every barstool and looked back at her. "You're in Orchard Hill and Noah is in Orchard Hill. Maybe the hidden treasure is the lodestar that keeps bringing you two together. You know, Fate."

"Oh, man, I hope that wasn't what he was talking about," Lacey declared. "I'm not even on speaking terms with Fate anymore."

Lacey was relieved when April let the subject drop, because she couldn't have argued about the unreliability of Fate with someone whose husband was dodging land mines and shrapnel on the other side of the world. Leaving her friend to get the measurements she would use in the real-estate listing, Lacey took stock of her situation.

She'd taken a leap of faith when she'd moved to Chicago more than two years ago. It was never easy to start over in a new place, but she'd made a few friends there, and although her job as an administrative assistant had been mundane much of the time, it had paid the bills. She'd taken night classes and dared to believe that her future had potential.

Then her dad died and the company she'd worked for downsized and she was let go. A few months later she'd wound up in the emergency room, and what was supposed to have been a simple surgery sprouted complications. Not long after that, she'd received an eviction notice. Her last temp job had barely left her with enough money to cover the bus ticket back to Orchard Hill. She didn't know how she would ever repay the hospital unless she sold the tavern. So, no, she didn't care to place her faith in something as flighty as Fate.

When April had all the information and measurements she needed to pull some comparables and start working on a selling strategy, Lacey saw her to the front door. After promising to come by later to see April's three-year-old twin daughters, Lacey flipped the dead bolt. She was on her way to turn out the light in the storeroom when she noticed a cue stick lying on the pool table in the corner. She headed over to take care of it, the quiet slap of her flip-flops the only sound in the room.

There was a nagging in the back of her mind because she didn't recall seeing the cue stick lying out when she'd been down here yesterday. Wondering if she simply hadn't noticed, she went around to the other side of the pool table to put the stick away. She hadn't gotten far when she saw something on the floor beneath the pool table.

She bent down for a closer look and found a sleeping bag carefully tucked under the wood skirting of the pool table. Her breath caught and a shiver ran up her spine.

She might have overlooked the cue stick, but she'd swept these floors yesterday and was positive the bedroll hadn't been here then. That meant somebody had been here between last night and today.

How could anyone have gotten in? The doors and windows had been locked, the whole place battened down tight.

She searched her mind for a possible explanation. If Orchard Hill were a larger city, she might suspect that a homeless person was camping out in the empty tavern. She was more inclined to think a teenager or a college student might have done it. That didn't explain how someone could have gotten in. And since when did teenagers or college students fold things up neatly? It didn't make sense to leave the sleeping bag here.

Lacey went perfectly still. Maybe the intruder hadn't left.

Was someone here now?

Her heart raced and goose bumps scurried across her shoulders. Shattering beer bottles and loud voices didn't frighten her, but this eerie quiet had her imagination running wild.

There was a light on over the bar and another one over the pool table. The windows on the east wall faced the brick building next door, allowing very little natural light inside. Suddenly, every corner in the room seemed too dark and every doorway a potential hiding place for someone lurking menacingly in the shadows.

From behind her came a soft thud. Her hand flew to her mouth and her breath lodged in her throat.

The sound came again. It was a footstep—she was sure of it—followed by the creak of a floorboard. She spun around. And saw Noah pause just inside the back door.

"Oh! It's you," she said on a gasp.

Noah came closer, one thumb hitched in the front pocket of low-slung jeans. The fingers of his other hand were curled around the handle of an infant carrier.

His eyes were in shadow, but one corner of his mouth lifted in a humorless grin. "The door was open so I didn't knock. I didn't mean to startle you," he said. "I came here to tell you I'm sorry. I guess I should apologize for scaring the daylights out of you while I'm at it."

Prying the cue stick out of her clenched hands, she laid

it on the table where she'd found it. She carefully wound her way around small tables with mismatched chairs, and arrived at the bar shortly after him. She was glad when he started talking, because she would have had a hard time getting anything past the knot in her vocal cords.

"There's someone I'd like you to meet." He lifted the car seat a little higher so she could see the baby sleeping inside. "My nephew, Joseph Daniel Sullivan. He likes to be called Joey."

"Your *nephew?*" she managed to ask.

"You don't have to keep your voice down," Noah said. "He can sleep through anything, as long as it's his idea."

So the child already had a mind of his own. He sounded like a Sullivan, Lacey thought.

Gently, Noah placed the car seat on the bar and continued. "I had no right to accuse you of leaving Joey on our doorstep last night. It's no wonder you didn't join us for dinner today. That reminds me." He reached into a canvas bag he'd placed beside the baby, and brought out a clear, covered bowl of spaghetti. "I brought a peace offering."

The next thing she knew she was holding the bowl, still slightly warm, in her hands.

"Are you ever going to say anything, Lacey?"

She raised her chin and opened her mouth only to reverse the process. She didn't know what to say. What did a girl say when she was standing three feet away from her first love, a man who looked as if he hadn't slept, a man whose dark hair was a little too long to be considered civilized, but who continued to keep a steady hand on the car seat where an unbelievably small baby slept?

"Did you use your homemade spaghetti sauce?" she asked, only to groan aloud.

She could tell by the slight indentation in his left cheek

that his grin was no longer humorless. "Would you accept my apology if I said yes?" he asked.

Lacey wasn't ready to smile. She wasn't one to get angry and get over it. For her, forgiveness was a process. "So this is Joey," she said, moving to a safer topic. "Have you determined whose son he is?"

With a shake of his head, Noah said, "We won't know for sure until Marsh and Reed have a DNA test and get the results. Meanwhile, they're hoping they can locate Joey's mother as quickly as possible, not that it's going to be easy. They're meeting with the P.I. right now. I'm on baby duty. You can ask me anything you want, but first, I'd like to finish my apology."

Lacey placed the bowl of spaghetti on the bar with her camera. Settling onto one of the stools, she made a show of getting comfortable.

Noah eased onto the stool next to her. Looking at her in the mirror, he said, "Our breakup two-and-a-half years ago came as a shock to me. Hell, it blew me out of the sky. Looking back, I realize it shouldn't have."

She wanted to tell him to stop, because this was dangerous territory, more dangerous than he knew. She took a deep breath and willed herself to hear him out.

"I don't know how I could have missed the clues," he said. "But I did. If there was a little kid within a hundred feet, your eyes were on him. Just like now."

She dragged her gaze from Joey and stared at Noah's reflection. He had the tall, rangy build of a barroom brawler. One of these days he would probably get around to shaving, but it wouldn't change that moody set of his lips or the depth in his brown eyes. He rarely talked about himself. On the surface, he was all bluster and swagger. If a woman was patient and paid attention, every once in a while she caught a glimpse of the part of him he kept hidden most of the time.

One day after she'd been seeing him for about a year, he'd taken her flying. It was during that flight that she'd learned how he felt about becoming a father. He was wonderful with kids—she'd seen that for herself—but his feelings about parenthood had nothing to do with how children responded to him and vice versa. That May morning, two thousand feet above the ground, he told her about the day his parents died in an icy pileup on the interstate.

Every now and then someone in Orchard Hill recalled a memory of Neil and Mary Beth Sullivan. Noah's mother and father had been well liked and were sadly missed. It was common knowledge that Marsh had stepped directly out of college and into the role of head of the family after they'd died, and that Reed came home two years later to help. The youngest, Madeline, had been everyone's darling, and Noah was the hell-raiser everybody worried about.

Until that day, Lacey hadn't known he'd been in the car when it crashed. With his eyes on the vast blue sky outside the cockpit and the control held loosely in his able hands, he'd described the discordant screech of tires and the deafening crunch of metal. Trapped in the back, he hadn't been able to see his parents. But he'd heard the utter stillness. The silence. Fifteen-year-old Noah had walked away with a broken arm and minor cuts and bruises—an orphan. He didn't remember much about the days immediately following the accident. During the burial, the fog in his brain had lifted and he'd solemnly vowed that he was never going to put a kid of his through that. He wasn't going to have children. Period.

Over the years she'd tried to find the words to tell him that lightning didn't strike twice and that their children wouldn't be orphaned. But who was she to make that promise?

She'd loved him, and for a long time she'd told herself what they shared was enough. He was right, though. She never had been able to keep her eyes off little ones. After April and Jay had their twins three years ago, yearning to have a baby of her own became an ache she couldn't pretend didn't exist.

"Until you spelled it out for me," he said, drawing her back to the present, "I didn't know you even *wanted* kids. But you did. And I didn't. It was a classic breakup. End of story, right?"

Lacey remembered the day she'd ended things with Noah. They used to fight sometimes. When it happened, their arguments were messy and noisy. That final night neither had raised their voices. It made their breakup unforgettable on every level.

"Then we wound up in bed last year," Noah said. "And Joey is about the right age to have been a product of that night. That's no excuse for barging into your apartment last night and accusing you of deserting him. I hadn't seen you in a while, but I should have known. People don't change. You knew how it felt to lose your mother. *You* never would have left a baby on my doorstep. Slapping me with a lawsuit or siccing the cops on me—that I could see you doing."

Nothing else could have made her smile just then.

Their gazes met, and this time it wasn't in the mirror. Emotion swirled inside her, welling in her eyes. Her doctor in Chicago had told her that sudden tears were part of her healing process. She had a feeling it was too much to hope that Noah didn't notice.

She knew how she looked. Her fine dark hair skimmed her shoulders and turned wavy in the summer humidity.

Her shorts were threadbare, her T-shirt was thin and her breasts were sensitive. No doubt he noticed that, too.

She found herself looking into his eyes again. It was easy to get lost in that dark brown gaze. There was a time when she wouldn't have been able to drag her eyes away. Last night, for example, and a hundred other nights, too.

Today she flattened her hands on the worn surface of the bar and slid off the far side of her stool. "Okay. I forgive you for scaring the daylights out of me and for accusing me of leaving Joey on your doorstep."

He stood, too. Cocking his head slightly, he said, "Can I get that in writing?"

She rolled her eyes, but she couldn't help smiling, too. Feeling lighter—perhaps there was something to this forgiveness business—she spied her favorite 35 mm camera. The instant it was in her hands, she felt back in her element. She aimed it at Joey, adjusted the focus and snapped a picture.

The poor baby jerked. His little hands flew up and his eyes popped open. Surprisingly, he didn't cry. Instead, he found her with his unwavering gaze.

His eyes were blue and his cheeks were adorably chubby. Fleetingly, she wondered how his mother could stand to be away from him for even a day.

"I'm sorry," she murmured quietly. "I didn't mean to startle you. The next time I'll ask for permission before I take your picture. Deal?"

The change in his expression began in his eyes. Like the wick of an oil lamp at the first touch of a lighted match, delight spread across his little features, tugging the corners of his lips up until his entire face shone.

"May I take another one?" she asked him.

He smiled again, this time for the camera. He was a

Sullivan all right. Marsh and Reed didn't need a DNA test to determine that much.

"I can't believe it," Noah said.

She glanced up and snapped his picture, too. "What can't you believe?"

"It's the first time I've seen him smile. He obviously has good taste in women."

She wished she didn't feel so complimented.

"Would you like to hold him?" he asked.

She ached to. "Maybe some other time."

There was a moment of awkwardness between them. They weren't a couple anymore, and neither knew what to say. After a few more seconds of uncomfortable silence, Noah picked the baby carrier up by the handle, an effortless shifting of muscles and ease, and said, "I guess I should get this little guy home." He slipped the strap of the diaper bag over one shoulder then started toward the back door where he'd entered ten minutes earlier.

Lacey slid her hand inside her pocket. Reassured that her nest egg was still safe and sound, she glanced into the shadowy corners around the room. Goose bumps popped out up and down her arms all over again.

With her camera suspended from the strap around her neck, her key in one hand and the bowl of spaghetti in the other, she hurried after Noah, locking the door behind her as she left. While he wrestled to secure the car seat properly in the seat of his truck, she started up the stairs.

"Lacey?" he called when she was halfway to the top.

She glanced down at him. "Yes?"

He was looking up at her, his eyes hidden behind dark glasses. "I'm glad you're back. Orchard Hill hasn't been the same without you."

She didn't have a reply to that because she wasn't sure how she felt about being back. She climbed the remaining stairs and let herself into the apartment. After putting her camera and the spaghetti away, she stood for a moment catching her breath and willing her heart rate to settle into its rightful rhythm.

When Noah was gone, she went out again, locking that door, too. She cut through the alley and emerged onto Division Street.

Orchard Hill was a college town of nearly 25,000 residents. Three seasons of the year, the downtown was teeming with activity. Now that most of the students had gone home for the summer, Division Street had turned into a sleepy hometown main street. That didn't keep her from looking over her shoulder this afternoon.

Her first visit was to the electronics store three blocks away where she studied the wide assortment of cell phones before choosing one she could afford. Her first call an hour later on her prepaid, bare-bones cell phone was to the Orchard Hill Police Department. After all, it was one thing to be unafraid of things that went bump in the night and another thing to ignore evidence that somebody had gotten into a locked tavern and slipped out again with barely a trace.

Lacey knew how a shadow felt.

She'd waited an hour for the police cruiser to arrive. Now she wasn't letting the man in blue out of her sight.

She'd shown Officer Pratt the sleeping bag and cue stick, and explained the situation as best she could. She answered his questions then remained an unwavering six feet behind him as he checked the perimeter of the tavern inside and out.

A tall man with thinning gray hair, he didn't seem to mind having a shadow. He painstakingly rattled windows, inspected sashes, jiggled locks and shone his silver flashlight into corners, behind doors and inside both restrooms.

After examining the doors and dead bolts and finding that nothing seemed to have been disturbed, he returned to the pool table where the narrow sleeping bag now lay. "You've never seen this before today?" he asked.

Lacey shook her head.

"Are you sure you didn't give out any keys to anybody? An old boyfriend, maybe?"

He was only doing his job, so she answered his question. "I had new dead bolts installed after my father passed away. Nobody has a key except me. I know I locked the doors yesterday because I had to unlock them this afternoon before I could get in."

He turned the narrow sleeping bag upside down and gave it a little shake. A plastic bottle of water rolled out, across the floor. With a great creaking of his hips and knees, he squatted down to reach it. Hauling himself back to his feet, he unscrewed the top.

"Do you wear pink lipstick?" he asked, holding the bottle toward the light.

She shook her head and took a closer look, too. The clear plastic bottle was half-full. She recognized the brand of sparkling spring water as one sold locally, but the pale pink shade of the lip print around the top didn't look familiar to her at all.

"Frankly," Officer Pratt said, "I'm stumped. Nothing inside the tavern has been taken, broken, meddled with, defaced or damaged in any way. Judging from the size of the sleeping bag and the pink print on the bottle, it's safe to assume we're dealing with a female. I don't know how she got in and out, or why. The windows are all intact and the locks appear secure. It looks to me as if we have a Houdini on our hands. I'd call it breaking and entering, except nothing's been broken. Other than the sleeping bag and water bottle, there's not even any evidence that an actual trespassing has occurred. It feels more like a mystery than a crime, doesn't it?"

He capped his pen and closed his book, obviously finished here. She followed him to the door, where she said, "Then you're not going to do anything?"

"There's nothing more I can do," he said. "I'll make a note of your call and the subsequent findings for my report, and I'll have a patrol car drive by periodically if it'll make you feel better. Call the department if you notice anything else or if she comes back, but I don't think she will."

She thanked the policeman for coming. After he was gone, she put the cap back on the bottle and started to gather the sleeping bag into a heap for the trash. Something made her stop short of the trash can.

She hadn't heard any news reports about recent serial killers wearing pink lip gloss and sleeping under pool tables. Officer Pratt said it himself. The entire situation felt more like a mystery than a crime.

Crimes were frightening, but mysteries were, well, mysterious. The goose bumps that had been popping up all over her body dissolved. Rather than throw the items away, she shook out the bedroll and refolded it, then put it back where she'd found it under the pool table, the bottle of water with its cap screwed on tight beside it.

After cataloging everything in her mind, she turned out the lights and locked the tavern's back door. As she climbed the stairs to her apartment, she wondered if Officer Pratt was right, and whoever had visited the tavern was long gone, never to return.

Upstairs, she wandered through the little kitchen and the living room with its ancient sofa and her father's old chair. She wasn't surprised when she found herself in the tiny storage room her dad had converted into a darkroom for her when she was fourteen.

She hadn't used anything here since she'd left town two-and-a-half years ago. The amber safe light still worked and the four flat trays were stacked neatly on the counter. The enlarger, developer, chemical thermometer and the rubber-ended tongs were on the shelf where she'd left them. Maybe later she would develop the pictures she'd taken today.

The coming night no longer seemed bleak. Miraculously, neither did the immediate future.

She had a roof over her head, enough money to live on for a little while, although she was going to have to find a job soon. She had a dear, quirky friend to talk to, a mystery to ponder and a heartfelt apology from Noah to savor. Maybe there *was* a reason she was in Orchard Hill and Noah was in Orchard Hill. In her mind she pictured him as he'd looked this afternoon, a sleeping baby in one hand, his hair a little too long and his eyes hinting of intimacies they'd shared.

"People don't change," he'd said.

Perhaps not, she thought as she took the spaghetti from the refrigerator and sampled her first bite, but sometimes circumstances did. Noah had told her he was glad she was back. It was beginning to feel good to be back. And that was the last thing she'd expected.

Chapter Four

A phone was ringing. And ringing.

Lacey was leaving the restaurant on Division Street when it dawned on her that the ringing was coming from her purse. This was her first incoming call, and since only one person had her number, she said hello to April as soon as she answered.

"Any luck with your job hunt?" April asked.

"Not yet." She stepped out of the way of two customers heading for the busy restaurant. "Everyone I've talked to so far is cutting back. Rosy promised she'd call me if one of her waitresses quits. Oh, and Henry Brewbaker proposed while I was there."

Henry Brewbaker walked with a cane and tottered to The Hill for a late breakfast every morning where he had a standing order of two eggs over easy, crisp bacon and blackened toast. Not even Henry could remember exactly how old he was.

"I hate to break this to you, but Henry Brewbaker proposes to somebody at least once a day." April's laugh was cut short by a soft moan.

"Is something wrong?" Lacey asked.

"I called to tell you that your paperwork will be ready for your signature later this afternoon. Remind me to have my head examined if I ever so much as think about trying to drink you under the table again."

Lacey smiled into the phone. After she'd eaten her fill of leftover spaghetti last night, she'd walked over to April's house on Baldwin Street. April's three-year-old twins had fallen asleep in the middle of the bedtime story Lacey had been reading to them. Once the little ones had been tucked in, April had uncorked a bottle of strawberry wine and she and Lacey had talked about everything under the sun. By the second glass, April was giggling.

"No offense," Lacey said as she smoothed a crease from her navy slacks, "but you couldn't drink a teetotaler under the table."

"I know. It comes from being a preacher's daughter. You really haven't had any luck at your job hunt this morning?"

"Other than one maybe and that marriage proposal, no." Lacey had left her apartment two hours ago. So far she'd spoken with every shop owner and office manager in every business on the first five blocks of Division Street. Most were friendly and talkative, but nobody was hiring. She still had two lawyers' offices, a title company, two dress stores and a CPA firm to try.

"I'm surprised you haven't found something," April said.

"Why?"

"Because I had a dream about you last night."

Lacey was intrigued because April's dreams ranged

from prophetic to unsettling to just plain weird. "You dreamed about me? What was I doing?"

"For a long time you were in the distance, lost in your reveries, walking, walking, walking. When you finally got closer, Johnny Appleseed stepped in front of you, blocking your path."

"Johnny Appleseed?" Lacey asked.

"You know, the sculpture on the town square. He came to life and handed you a sign. On one side it said Welcome Home. On the other side it said Now Hiring. That's why I was sure you'd find a job today. What else could it mean?"

"I think it means no more strawberry wine for you," Lacey said, smiling. She didn't get any arguments from April. After promising to stop by the real-estate office later to go over the listing contract, Lacey stood for a moment in front of the first dress shop she came to. She didn't know why she didn't go inside.

She started walking, walking, walking. A car backfired and easy-listening music played over the speaker on the corner. Lost in her reveries, she barely heard the sounds around her, her eyes on the bronze sculpture at the head of the town square.

Orchard Hill historians couldn't agree how long the sculpture had been standing in its place of prominence in front of the courthouse. To the residents of Orchard Hill, he was iconic. Children tried to climb him, every year the varsity football team was photographed in front of him and couples became engaged beneath him. He was often cited in directions. "When you come to the sculpture, turn right." Or "If you can see Johnny Appleseed, you've gone too far."

A whimsical fellow, the statue stood eight feet tall in patched dungarees and a tattered shirt. On his head he wore a kettle for a hat. Lacey didn't see any Welcome

Home or Now Hiring signs in his outstretched hand this morning. However, she did see Noah and his brothers standing nearby.

She knew better than to stare, for staring at any of the Sullivan men was like staring at the sun. It caused her eyes to water and her head to spin far more than strawberry wine. Even after she managed to close her eyes against the onslaught of all that testosterone-laden brawn, the imprint was burned on her retinas, scratched into her brain. Nothing could have prevented her from looking again, though. This time, her gaze rested on Noah alone.

She found herself crossing the street as if she was gliding on a current of air. She didn't stop until she was three feet away.

This was a bad idea.

Noah had known it since the moment Marsh and Reed had mentioned it after they'd returned from their meeting with the P.I. in Grand Rapids yesterday. He wasn't surprised they were impressed by Sam Lafferty's probing questions, straightforward approach and expertise. It was the P.I.'s advice that they contact someone in the court system that Noah questioned. According to Sam, the youth protection agency, a branch of State Services, had the authority to swoop in and move Joey to foster care unless Marsh and Reed went through the proper channels.

"Believe me," Sam had said, "you don't want that to happen."

Reed had called their great-uncle, Judge Ivan Sullivan, and Marsh was backing the decision. Joey wasn't happy about it, and frankly, Noah didn't blame him.

The baby had started crying as soon as they'd parked in the lot fifteen minutes ago. The meeting with the judge was scheduled to begin in five minutes, and the elder

Sullivan didn't take kindly to being kept waiting, great-nephews notwithstanding. They had five minutes to quiet Joey. Unfortunately, he showed no signs of relenting. His little face was red and his mouth quivered with every waaa-waaa-waaa. They'd tried feeding him, walking him, jiggling him and singing to him. He wanted nothing to do with being appeased. Noah hated to imagine what the judge was going to say about their ability to care for an infant if they couldn't find a way to comfort him by the time the meeting began.

This was a bad idea. Presenting a crying baby to the judge had as much potential for disaster as the proverbial apple cart careening downhill.

"Is something wrong with Joey?"

Noah turned at the sound of Lacey's voice. For the span of one heartbeat, everything else disappeared. There was no noise, no confusion. There was only Lacey. He was either having an embolism or a revelation.

"He won't stop crying." Reed had to raise his voice in order to be heard over the baby, who was screaming in his ear.

Noah blinked as if returning from a great distance. When he first met Lacey, she'd worn her dark hair short. It was long and slightly wavy today. The breeze fluttered the delicate collar of her blouse, the fabric nearly the same shade of blue as her eyes.

"What have you tried?" she asked.

"Everything." This time Marsh answered. "Do you know anything about babies?"

"I know a little."

"Do you have any suggestions?" Reed asked.

Lacey held out her hands to Joey and carefully lifted him from Reed. Cradling him in her arms, she swayed to and fro and crooned unintelligible words to him, gently holding his flailing hands to his sides.

Before everyone's eyes, Joey stilled. He took one ragged breath, then another. His lips trembled, and tears matted his eyelashes, but he stopped crying. He looked up at Lacey so forlornly that Noah didn't know what to say. Marsh and Reed were in awe, too.

All around them, normal life resumed. The bell in the nearby church tower chimed hosanna as it did every day at half-past eleven. The sun peeked through holes in the clouds like grace in old Sunday-school posters. The breeze carried the scent of the Thursday lunch special from the restaurant a block away. A panel truck rattled through the intersection. Two lawyers conversed on their way from the courthouse. Flowers bloomed along the sidewalk, and tinny music played over speakers nearby.

In the midst of it all, Noah felt the stirring of something he couldn't name. It was part desire—there was always desire when it came to Lacey—but there was something else, too, something akin to enchantment. She'd always been a looker, with her full, pouty lips and centerfold body. There was more to her than beauty, though. Sassy and witty, she could spar with the best of them. She wore sandals with cork heels and slim navy slacks that made her legs look a mile long. He'd felt those legs wrap around him many a night. There wasn't much he wouldn't give to experience that again.

"He's falling asleep," Marsh declared quietly.

"How did you do that?" Reed asked at the same time.

Noah watched Lacey as she looked down at the baby in her arms and then at Marsh, Reed and finally at him. She'd undoubtedly noticed that he hadn't spoken a word. He ran his hand along his clean-shaven jaw, and saw her taking everything in, from Marsh's black polo shirt, to Reed's tie, to Noah's white broadcloth shirt, the cuffs rolled up to his forearms.

"I learned that tactic from April," she said quietly. "Babies this small like to be wrapped up tightly. It's called swaddling. I don't have a blanket so I'm using my arms to simulate that feeling of security. Why are you three dressed up?"

"Joey has an appointment to see the judge in a few minutes."

"What did he do?" she asked.

Noah laughed out loud. The only one who reacted to her dry wit, he found himself looking into her eyes the way he gazed at the horizon, as if he could see all the way to infinity. He felt the stirring of something otherworldly again, and he didn't want it to stop.

Beside him, Marsh, who obviously had no sense of humor whatsoever today, said, "We called the judge because we have to go through the proper channels or risk the child-protection agency getting involved and taking control of Joey's care."

"We're going to be late," Reed said. "Here, Lacey. I'll take the baby."

"Wait," Noah said.

Marsh and Reed looked at him, and so did Lacey.

"You're dressed up, too," Noah said. "Do you have someplace you have to be?" The moment Lacey shook her head, he asked, "Would you do us a huge favor?"

"That's a great idea, Noah," Marsh exclaimed.

She turned her round blue eyes to each of them in silent question.

"Joey's sleeping now," Reed said quietly. "If you could hold him in the outer office while we meet with the judge in his private chambers, it would be an enormous help."

"You want me to go up to the judge's private chamber with you?" she asked.

Three tall, broad-shouldered grown men nodded in earnest. "He's squeezing our appointment in between cases," Noah explained.

It didn't take her long to make up her mind. In a matter of seconds, the entire entourage was hurrying along the curved walkway, up the courthouse steps, through the metal detectors and into the waiting elevator.

They emerged onto the third floor and arrived at the judge's office at twenty-five minutes before twelve on the nose. They were right on time.

Reed left the bag that held a spare bottle and diaper with Lacey in the outer waiting area. Marsh knocked on the raised panel door.

While they waited for the gruff summons, Noah quietly said, "Don't stare him down. Don't fidget. And whatever you do, don't act like teenagers caught with toilet paper on a Friday night."

Reed smoothed his tie. Marsh took a deep breath.

From the other side of the door, the judge said, "Don't just stand there. Come in."

Marsh went first, and then Reed followed. After casting a look at Lacey over his shoulder, Noah went in last, closing the door behind him. In the adjoining room they fell into rank, feet apart, shoulders back, arms at their sides.

Ivan Sullivan was one of those men few people liked but nearly everyone respected. He'd earned the nickname Ivan the Terrible his first year on the bench. During his forty-year career, he'd also earned the reputation as one of the toughest, shrewdest and fairest judges in Acorn County. Everyone, including his great-nephews, called him Judge.

In his late seventies now, his fingers were gnarled from gripping a gavel. Although his brown eyes had faded to amber, his stare was no less haughty as he gestured impatiently for each of them to sit down in one of the chairs arranged in front of his desk.

The moment they were all seated, he leveled his gaze at Noah. "I thought I told you I didn't want to see you here again."

"Yes, sir."

"How long has it been?"

"Ten years." As if the old codger didn't know exactly how long it had been since Noah had stood in his courtroom, hoping his fear didn't show.

Older now, Noah admitted that he'd been on a road to self-destruction back then. The last infraction had been for fighting. Technically, he'd been defending some young woman's honor by hitting a jerk who thought he had certain rights when it came to women who'd had a little too much to drink.

Noah hadn't known the girl, but he'd seen her struggling in the alley behind Bell's Tavern, and, hell, what choice did he have? A fight had broken out and some do-gooder called the police. It turned out the jerk had been the woman's boyfriend, and she'd refused to press charges. When the judge had pointed his gavel at Noah and asked him if he had any plans to break any more noses, he couldn't lie. He assumed he'd get slapped with a fine and maybe be sentenced to a weekend in the county jail.

Judge Sullivan had something else in mind. He gave Noah a choice: a year behind bars or a year pursuing a higher education. Noah had been stunned. The very thought of being locked up, unable to see the sky for a week, let alone for a year, had rendered him speechless, his Adam's apple wobbling and his hands shaking. At the time, the thought of being confined to a classroom had seemed nearly as confining and limiting as jail. And the judge knew it. On rare occasions, the old man had given other misunderstood and misguided hellions options that had the potential to change their lives for the better. Noah had chosen a higher education, in this case, an Airfield Operations Specialist training program open to new enrollment down in Florida. What he'd wanted to do was wipe the condescending smirk off the judge's lined face.

Ten years later, that smirk hadn't changed. Noah was smarter now and knew better than to try to stare the other man down.

Marsh began, explaining why they'd requested this meeting. Reed drew the handwritten note from Joey's mother from his pocket and slid it across the large wooden desk. Just as they'd rehearsed, they stuck to the facts about their surprising discovery of the baby on their doorstep. They described the woman Noah had seen crossing the lawn when he'd flown over, and they outlined the steps they were taking to locate Joey's mother.

The judge read the letter and turned it over much the way each of them had. "Who is she?"

This was the part that was most difficult to explain. "We're not certain," Reed said.

"What do you mean you're not certain?"

"She's either a woman from my past," Reed said quietly.

"Or a woman from mine," Marsh added.

The judge's eyes narrowed. "You're telling me you don't know which one of you is the father?"

Marsh and Reed both remained silent, the equivalent of taking the Fifth. Their discomfiture wasn't easy to witness.

"Where is the baby now?" the judge asked.

"He's in your outer office."

Noah didn't like the way the judge's lips formed a thin line. He'd seen that expression before. It meant his mind was already made up. Marsh, Reed and Noah flicked a glance at one another. Noah wasn't the only one growing more uncomfortable by the second.

"Don't just sit there," the judge said. "I want to see him."

With little choice, Marsh went to the door and opened it. "Lacey, would you bring Joey in?"

Noah and Reed rose as Lacey entered the small room. As far as Noah knew, she'd never faced a judge. Not one to let that stop her, she raised that fighter's chin of hers and strode into his chamber as if she'd done this a thousand times.

She kept her arms firmly around Joey and planted her feet well away from the judge's desk. If he wanted a closer look, he was either going to have to bid her to come closer or go to her. Noah's chest expanded again, this time with burgeoning admiration.

Judge Sullivan pushed his large leather chair back and stood, his cold, assessing, rheumy eyes on the baby in Lacey's arms. The clock ticked on the shelf beside musty old law tomes and the judge's framed law degree. For what felt like forever nobody moved.

The judge broke the silence when he said, "Take him down to State Services. I'll let them know you're coming."

Marsh backed up until he stood directly between Lacey and the judge. "All due respect, sir, no one's taking my son."

"Or mine," Reed said, going to stand beside Marsh.

"Or my nephew," Noah said, completing the wall of shoulders and determination. They remained that way, three abreast, a united front of protection for the baby they had every intention of caring for themselves.

The judge's expression didn't change, but everyone in the room felt his agitation and determination. Noah waited for the explosion.

"A baby this young needs his mother," the old man said indignantly. "At the very least, he needs to be in a woman's care, and by God—"

Before Marsh could remind their great-uncle that he didn't have children and, therefore, was hardly an expert, and before Reed could call the judge a chauvinist and Noah could call him a lot worse, Lacey spoke up behind them. "Excuse me, Your Honor, but I am a woman."

The judge gestured impatiently with his hands. Noah took a step to the right, making room for Lacey to fall into formation between him and Marsh, Joey still fast asleep in her arms.

After looking her up and down, the judge said, "You're Harlan Bell's daughter, aren't you?"

"I'm Lacey Bell, yes." After a barely perceptible hesitation, she added, "I'm little Joseph's nanny."

The judge looked as surprised as Marsh and Reed. Noah felt a grin coming on.

"Is this true?" the judge demanded.

Since Reed and Marsh were honest to a fault, and therefore couldn't be trusted not to mess this up, Noah said, "You said it yourself, Your Honor. Babies this young need to be in a woman's care."

"Lacey is extremely good with him," Reed said, recovering.

"Have you ever heard of swaddling?" Marsh asked their uncle. "Until Lacey demonstrated and explained the technique, I never had, either. We should be getting Joey home. He'll want to eat again soon."

"Not so fast."

Noah, Marsh and Reed didn't move. Lacey broke away from the others and came to stand directly in front of the judge's desk. "Would you like to hold your great-great-nephew, Your Honor?"

The judge took his wire-rimmed glasses off, cleaned them and put them back on. Even Noah was having a hard time refraining from fidgeting.

After what felt like a very long time, Judge Sullivan said, "No, I would not. He does look like a Sullivan, I'll give him that."

For a moment, Noah almost thought the judge was going to say something complimentary or perhaps bestow some memory of their childhoods, or his. Instead, he said, "I expect a weekly progress report and a phone call the moment you locate his mother."

"Yes, sir." Marsh opened the door.

"Thank you, sir," Reed said, gesturing for Lacey to precede him from the room.

Lacey carried the baby out, Reed right behind her, followed by Marsh. The last one through the door, Noah couldn't be sure whether the judge was hiding a smug smile or indigestion.

Noah wasn't prone to smiles, either, but he couldn't keep a grin off his face as he followed the others back the way they'd come, through the judge's outer office, down the long corridor, into the elevator, out through the lobby, down the courthouse steps and out into the valiant unfolding of a mild but far-from-ordinary summer day.

He'd never put a lot of faith in Fate. In his experience, life randomly knocked people on their ass. Those who could hauled themselves back to their feet and those who couldn't either crawled to a safe corner or gave up.

Lacey was a fighter. They were alike that way. He'd

said it yesterday. It was good to have her back in town. Orchard Hill hadn't been the same without her. And neither had he.

As he followed Lacey and his brothers to the bronze Johnny Appleseed sculpture, he realized that he wanted another chance with her. He wasn't sure how to go about it. They couldn't just pick up where they'd left off. Their differences were still between them. Where exactly did that leave them?

Lacey could feel three sets of eyes on her back. She was accustomed to that. She turned around and faced Noah and his brothers. "This is where I came in," she said. "Who wants to take the baby?"

Marsh and Reed both held out their hands for Joey. It occurred to her that one of them was going to be terribly disappointed before this situation was resolved.

"Why don't you give him to me?" Noah said.

The transfer was handled a little awkwardly but safely. Joey woke up, but he didn't cry. He looked around, unbelievably tiny, but perfect in every way. Her heart gave a little thump, because babies were miracles. Joey was extremely alert. It seemed to Lacey that he was already starting to recognize all three of the Sullivan men. It was almost as if he realized he was one of them, a throwback to past generations of rugged, smart Sullivans.

"I don't know how to thank you," Marsh said.

"You were amazing, Lacey," Reed added.

"I, for one, am not surprised," Noah said, his voice huskier than the others'.

She could hold her own with nearly anybody, but even she got a little breathless when these three turned on the charm at the same time. Flexing the kink out of her arm now that she was no longer holding Joey, she said, "You can have me canonized, throw quarters, whatever, but, for the record, you're welcome. I just hope I don't go to jail for lying to a judge."

"It doesn't have to be a lie," Reed said.

She tilted her head ever so much and backed up a step. "I have to find a job. That's what I was doing when you shanghaied me."

"That's what I mean," he said. "It pains me to admit it, but the judge was right. We're in over our heads. Joey needs a nanny. We need a nanny for him. We'll pay you."

She caught a movement out of the corner of her eye. Marsh and Noah flashed each other a quick glance.

"Reed," Noah said.

"Reed's right," Marsh insisted.

"Guys," Noah said, more firmly this time.

"But I haven't had any official training as a nanny," she stammered.

"He likes you," Reed stated. "That's all that matters."

"But…"

"Before you arrived this morning, none of us could do a thing to calm him," Reed said. "He responds to you, Lacey. Maybe it's your scent or the sound of your voice or your gentle touch."

Lacey couldn't hide her surprise. Her—Joey's nanny? It was ludicrous.

If Marsh was the rule breaker and Noah the risk taker, Reed, the golden-haired son, was the smooth talker. There was an unmistakable earnestness on his face as he added, "You said it yourself. You're looking for a job. Come to work for us as Joey's nanny."

"Even if you would just agree to a temporary position," Marsh said, as earnest as Reed. "We'll make it worth your while."

Noah was noticeably silent.

After a brief discussion with Reed, Marsh named a dollar amount that widened her eyes. It was far more than she would earn waitressing or working at the clothing store or as an administrative assistant, provided somebody actually hired her.

"Define *temporary*," she said in spite of herself.

Again, Marsh and Reed spoke among themselves for a moment. Evidently, having reached a consensus, Reed said, "Whatever you can give us, we'll appreciate. A day, a week, indefinitely or just until I've had a chance to place an ad and we hire a permanent nanny."

"What hours are you thinking?" she asked.

At the same time, Marsh and Reed both smiled.

"What hours do you want?" Marsh asked.

"How soon can you start?" Reed added.

"Tomorrow morning?" she asked.

Marsh tipped his face to the sun and laughed for the first time in days. Out of the blue, he swooped down, wrapped his arms around her waist and spun her off her feet. She'd no sooner touched the ground before Reed spun her, too. Dizzy, she noticed Noah standing to one side, the baby in his arms, a pensive expression on his face.

"We'll see you tomorrow," Marsh declared. The next thing she knew, all three of the Sullivans were turning around and heading toward the parking lot west of the courthouse.

Slightly dazed, she started in the opposite direction. She happened to glance up at the bronze sculpture as she passed. At that exact moment, a single ray of sunshine poked between two clouds and slanted toward the sculpture like a staircase to heaven. Johnny Appleseed winked.

She stopped and stared. Then blinked. "An optical illusion. A trick of the sun. Just my imagination," she murmured under her breath.

As she meandered back the way she'd come, she had to

pinch herself. Sculptures didn't wink and sunbeams were not staircases to heaven. She couldn't discount one coincidence, though. One minute she'd been looking for a job, and seemingly the next she'd agreed to become little Joey Sullivan's temporary nanny. Strangely, April's dream had come true.

She recalled how quiet Noah had grown when Reed had made the suggestion. Something was on his mind. Was he thinking about the night they broke up? Was he remembering that kiss the night before last? Or was he wondering, as she was, if they dared try again? She had no idea what that would entail, or if it was even possible. And, yet, she was thinking about it.

Chicago was a bustling, vibrant city, but nobody she knew had discovered a baby on a doorstep there. Sculptures there didn't wink and mysterious escape artists didn't sleep under pool tables. She'd lived there for over two years, but during that time she'd never experienced this giddy sense of anticipation, as if anything was possible.

Chapter Five

For nearly two years, Noah had been painstakingly restoring an old Piper Cherokee in one of Tom Bender's spare hangars. A lifelong dream, it required an aptitude for aerodynamics, an innate knowledge of the mechanics of moving parts and unfailing patience. So the fact that he'd spent the past hour assembling baby furniture wasn't the reason he felt like biting through his cheek.

He'd had an errand to run after the meeting with the judge, and had gotten home twenty minutes behind the others. A delivery truck had been pulling out of the driveway as he was driving in. Now the entire first floor looked like Christmas morning in a war zone. That didn't bother him, either.

Last night Reed had ordered nearly every imaginable baby item they could possibly need from a local store. There were boxes of disposable diapers, baby clothes, toys, a wireless baby monitor, two more car seats, a baby swing, a mobile, discarded cardboard, cellophane and packing foam, and baby furniture in various stages of assembly.

On baby duty this afternoon, Reed had Joey with him in his home office off the living room at the front of the house. Marsh and Noah were on the floor in the den, a room they were converting into a daytime nursery. At night Joey would sleep upstairs in the heirloom cradle Marsh had found in the attic on the baby's first night here.

The changing table and dresser were assembled. Noah was working on the baby swing. Next to him, Marsh was rereading the directions for the crib.

"Hand me those pliers," Noah said.

Marsh was studying the directions and didn't hear him. What else was new? It rankled, but then, Noah had been stewing ever since they'd left Lacey in the courthouse square.

"If you have something to say, say it," Marsh said without looking up.

So he *had* noticed.

"It's a little late to ask for my input now, isn't it?"

"What's your problem?" Marsh turned the directions over noisily. "Tell me you're not jealous because I hugged your girlfriend."

"Jealous of you?" Noah decided not to even address the fact that she wasn't his girlfriend. He was still eyeing the pliers that were lying on the other side of Marsh's knee. Beside him Marsh wadded the directions into a ball. He supposed he should have taken that as a hint that Marsh's patience was wearing thin. But Noah wasn't in the mood to take hints.

He admitted that he *could* have been more careful when he reached for the pliers. Maybe the way he *accidentally* bumped Marsh with his shoulder could have been construed as a *slight* shove. Marsh *probably* meant to give him only a little push in return. But Noah was on his haunches and the return jostle caused him to lose his balance. He automatically grabbed Marsh's arm. Unfortunately, Marsh was on the balls of his feet, too.

The two of them toppled backward, landing with a crash on discarded cardboard and packaging foam. Marsh went up on one elbow. Noah sat up and brushed himself off, prepared to get back to work.

"Not so fast, flyboy." Marsh threw his arm around Noah's chest and pulled him backward.

Noah's surprise lasted just long enough to glimpse the confidence on his brother's face. As the oldest, Marsh apparently assumed he had the upper hand, the way he had when they were kids. Noah wasn't smaller anymore, but he was still six years younger, an asset now if there ever was one. He was more agile, too, not to mention more experienced in fighting. He was going to enjoy pinning Marsh until he cried uncle.

Marsh had something else in mind. He drove that fact home when Noah landed with a loud thump on his back on the floor. Letting loose a war cry, Noah got serious. Marsh didn't stay on top for long. They rolled around on the floor, grunting when an elbow was jabbed into an opponent's midsection and knees collided and heads knocked. The wrestling match got rowdier and the banging and thumping and slamming of bodies into furniture louder.

"What's going on?" It seemed that Reed had come to investigate the racket.

"Noah started it."

"The hell I did."

Reed planted his Cole Haans and folded his arms. He was the only person Noah knew who could look down his nose at somebody with his nose still in the air.

"If you're going to behave like children," he said, "take it outside."

"Where's Joey?" Marsh asked.

"He's asleep in my office."

Marsh and Noah looked each other. At the same time, they lunged toward Reed.

He toppled like a stack of building blocks. "Are you both out of your minds? Ooof. Get off me."

"What's the matter? Afraid to get your chinos wrinkled?" Marsh asked.

"Or are you just afraid to lose?" Noah added.

Those were fighting words. The years fell away, along with Reed's air of polish and sophistication. He dived into the foray with all the gusto of a street fighter.

The exercise caused an adrenaline rush that invigorated all three of them. A one-on-one skirmish was a fair match. This was every man for himself. Whoever was on top of the heap was winning. That changed too often to track. Arms and legs got tangled, expletives exchanged and retaliation promised. If the momentum hadn't sent them careening into the end table, which in turn sent a lamp crashing to the floor, there was no telling who would have come out ahead.

The explosion of ceramic and shattering glass had the effect of a bell at a boxing match. It officially ended the round. Noah had Reed in a headlock, Reed had Marsh's left leg bent like a pretzel and Marsh had an arm around Noah's chest. It took a little doing to get untangled.

Free at last, Reed sat up. "What in the world is going on with you two?" he asked as he examined his shirt and chinos for damage.

"Noah has something to say to us," Marsh said as if the scuffle hadn't interrupted the conversation.

Reed looked sideways at Noah. "Let's hear it."

Still on his back on the floor, Noah tested his legs to see if they would straighten out. "I just made the last payment on the loan for my Airfield Operations Specialist training."

"A fight broke out over that?" With a slight groan, Reed rolled up on all fours. "You should be celebrating."

"Lacey was the first person I wanted to tell." When Noah had found the training program open to new enrollment down in Florida ten years ago, Marsh and Reed had wanted to help him find a way to pay for the expensive course, but Noah had already owed them for giving up their futures for him, and even if he could have let them do more, Noah had needed to prove to them and to himself that he could do it his own way, to try to succeed on his own. He'd found another lender, and had been diligently paying it off for nine years.

Reed was right; it was cause for celebration. "So tell her," he said.

"I can't, thanks to the two of you. She would think it had more to do with gratitude because she agreed to be Joey's temporary nanny." Noah wanted something a hell of a lot more substantial than gratitude. "We dodged a bullet with the judge because of her."

"She saved our asses," Marsh agreed.

"And Joey," Reed said reverently.

"You should have asked me before you coerced her into accepting the position as Joey's nanny."

Marsh stared at Noah from his feet, Reed from his knees. "You're angry because we didn't consult you first?" Reed asked.

"I'd probably have a heart attack if you ever did that." He could tell he'd struck a nerve. "Expecting Lacey to be Joey's nanny was unfair to her, especially considering the reason we broke up."

Marsh stopped tucking his shirt in long enough to share a look with Reed. "Why *did* you two break up?"

Noah was sorry he'd brought it up. Until now he'd kept the reason vague, saying they'd wanted different things. Taking a deep breath, he blurted, "Because she wanted kids."

Marsh looked at Noah as if something was finally starting to make sense. "You mean you don't?" he asked kindly.

Noah didn't reply.

"Have you always felt this way?" Marsh continued in the same patient tone of voice.

"Don't psychoanalyze me, okay?"

On his feet now, too, Reed said, "Noah? Have you?"

When they were kids, it seemed that one or another of them was always getting caught someplace they shouldn't have been, doing something they shouldn't have been doing. Rather than lie when questioned by an adult, they'd developed a little gesture that entailed shrugging just one shoulder. It meant *I'd rather not say.* Noah demonstrated it now.

Marsh's sigh came from a place deep inside him. "I always worried that the chances you took with your life and your future had to do with being in the car with Mom and Dad that day."

Reed was watching Noah as intently as Marsh was. "It wasn't your fault, buddy," Reed said. "You couldn't have prevented what happened."

Their dad used to call Noah *buddy.* Hearing it again caught him below his breastbone. "I know that."

"I would have bet money on the fact that you were disappointed when you found out Joey wasn't yours," Marsh said.

"Yeah," he said, sitting up. "Nobody was more surprised about that than me."

Marsh and Reed each held out a hand and practically launched Noah to his feet. "Are you saying you've changed your mind?" Marsh asked now that they were all looking eye to eye.

"I made a vow the day we buried Mom and Dad."

"It sounds to me as if you made a *decision,*" Reed countered. "A decision based on witnessing a tragedy no fifteen-year-old should ever witness."

Other than the time he'd told Lacey, Noah never talked about the day his parents died. He didn't talk about the funeral, either, or how utterly empty and silent the house and the orchard had been after their parents were suddenly just gone. Everything had changed, and that, in turn, changed the three of them and their younger sister, Madeline. That wasn't what was at the front of his mind today. "It's been two-and-a-half years since Lacey left," he said. "I don't even know how she feels about me anymore."

"How do you feel about her?" Reed asked.

"Are you in love with her?" Marsh said, more to the point.

"She's in my blood. Either of you ever have that happen?"

Marsh said nothing.

Reed shrugged one shoulder much as Noah had a moment ago. "Maybe you should ask her if she feels the same way about you," he said.

This from a man who hadn't thought to get the last name of the woman he'd slept with and possibly fathered a child with. All his life Noah had been the wiry kid brother everybody worried about, while rugged, man-of-the-earth Marsh had the patience of a saint and brainy, brawny Reed was shamelessly self-confident. Joey's unexpected arrival was leveling the playing field.

"Maybe we *should* have consulted you before asking

Lacey to accept the job as Joey's nanny," Marsh said. "But she doesn't strike me as the type of woman who would do something she doesn't want to do."

Noah was reminded of the other night when she'd opened her door, tears in her eyes. He'd reached for her hand, put his arms around her and kissed her. She *had* reacted, turning warm and pliant and oh-so-willing. Passion had flamed between them straight to inferno level.

"You might want to grab some ice for that cracked lip before you pay her another visit," Reed said as if he'd read Noah's mind.

Gingerly touching his sore lip with one finger, Noah looked around the room. A sense of calm was settling over him. He recalled the silent promise he'd made the day he'd watched his parents' caskets being lowered into the ground. Joey's arrival was causing him to question his stand. It scared the spit out of him, but it wasn't enough to keep him from wanting to knock on Lacey's door all over again.

"We got lucky today," he said. "Let's get this nursery finished for Joey before the judge decides to send somebody out here for a surprise home visit."

Marsh and Reed both shuddered.

Hunkering down in front of the baby swing he'd been assembling when that little fight broke out, Noah recalled how Lacey's voice had sounded today after the judge had proclaimed that babies needed a woman's care. "Your Honor," she'd said, "I am a woman."

She was a woman, all right—an amazing one—but he couldn't just race over to her place and haul her off to bed. As tempting as that notion was, he couldn't burn this passion off as if sex was enough.

She *was* in his blood. Two-and-a-half years apart hadn't diminished that. If she was going to give him another chance she was going to need a good reason. He couldn't fly by the seat of his pants this time. Winning her back would require careful thought and a well-devised plan.

She would be here in the morning. That didn't leave him much time.

He set the baby swing upright and viewed his handiwork. Marsh fished the wadded-up directions from the other debris. Reed returned with a broom and dustpan and started cleaning up the broken lamp. Noah noticed that Reed was favoring his right elbow and Marsh was limping. Had it not been for his cracked lip, Noah would have smiled.

They would all be sore tomorrow. They weren't kids anymore. Despite an occasional sojourn back to adolescence, like the one they'd taken a few minutes ago, they were grown-ups. He didn't know when that had happened. Even more astonishing, when had he started thinking like one?

Lacey waved goodbye to Miss Fergusson, the administrator of the Orchard Hill Public Library, and with her stack of library books tucked under one arm, started toward home.

The evening was balmy and the sun still bright in the western sky. Lacey loved this time of year in Michigan when it stayed light until nearly ten o'clock. It was eight now. The library was closing. Many of the other businesses were rolling up their sidewalks, too. In a little while, April and her sister-in-law were stopping over with the for-sale signs for the tavern's windows.

Since she'd been back, Lacey had noticed that the women in Jay's family fussed over April like mother hens. After her mom's death, Lacey had received her mothering from more unexpected sources. She'd been introduced to the "It takes a village to raise a child" philosophy shortly after she and her dad moved to Orchard Hill when she was twelve. Miss Fergusson had noticed her sneaking a book off a library shelf and followed her to the bathroom. Blushing to the roots of her steel-gray hair, the stern, no-nonsense librarian had assured Lacey that she wasn't dying. The bleeding was *normal*.

Lacey had been unabashedly relieved, until Miss Fergusson explained about Mother Nature's monthly gift. "Every month?" Lacey had quipped. "Are you frickin' kidding me?"

"You're becoming a woman," Miss Fergusson had declared with a smile that had grown brighter before Lacey's eyes. "And that's a marvelous, beautiful creature, indeed."

Six months ago, two emergency surgeries days apart had left Lacey feeling the opposite of beautiful. The angry red scars on her belly were slowly fading, just as her doctor had promised. Although there had been internal scarring, too, and she couldn't forget the impact the scarring had on her future, every day she felt a little more like her old self.

The evening stretched languidly before her. She still hadn't developed those photographs of Joey, and now she had books to read, too. Trying to decide whether she should begin with the *Hands-On Guide to Infant Child Care* or delve into the two hardcovers about Houdini and modern-day escape artists, she darted across First Street. She hadn't gone far when she heard a horn honk behind her.

She glanced over her shoulder as a dusty-blue pickup truck pulled to a stop at the curb beside her. She knew that Chevy well.

The grin Noah slanted her made him appear relaxed and sinuous, like an alley cat taking a break from his tomcatting to stretch languidly in a warm patch of sunshine. "Need a lift?" he called through the open passenger window.

"Thanks, but I'm only two blocks from home."

He continued to stare at her. In the ensuing silence, she backed up a few steps. When he still made no move to leave, she said, "Is something wrong?"

"Not really."

Homing in on his mouth, she said, "What happened to your lip?"

"I ran into something." He tilted his head self-mockingly. "I've narrowed it down to either Marsh's elbow or Reed's knee."

Obviously, it had been a guy thing, but she had to ask, "Did you win?"

"It was a three-way tie."

"What were you fighting about?" she asked.

"We were just burning off steam. You know how guys are, although, if you must know, they aren't making it easy for me to gallop in on my great white steed and rescue you from a future of celibacy and regret."

She glanced over her shoulder as a group of teenage boys too young to drive ambled by on their way to wherever teenage boys went on balmy Thursday nights these days. Rather than continue this conversation where anyone could hear, she strolled to Noah's open passenger-side window. "Excuse me, did you say celibacy and regret?"

He gave her a crooked smile that went straight to her head. "Today I made the final payment on the loan for my Airfield Operations Specialist training," he said.

She knew Noah well enough to understand that he was a man of few words. And while that didn't always make his conversation easy to follow, what he said eventually fit together like pieces of a beautiful puzzle.

"You're free, Noah. It's what you've always wanted."

"I'd like to talk to you about that."

His gaze was as soft as a caress and almost as possessive. He wanted her. Being wanted by him sent those butterflies fluttering their naughty little wings again.

"Digger found a used propeller for the old airplane we're restoring," he said, his voice deepening as if he felt those butterflies, too. "He picked it up over in Rockford today. I was on my way to the airstrip to take a look at it. Care to ride along?"

"I ca—"

"If you'd rather just grab a beer, or something to eat, I'll call Dig and reschedule."

She was shaking her head before he'd completed the invitation. She thought about those scars and hospital bills. Noah might be free, but she wasn't. "I can't just forget everything that's happened, Noah."

"That's just it," he said. "I can't forget, either. Any of it. Not how good we were together, not how much I've missed you, not how damn good it is to see you do something as ordinary as walk down the sidewalk. Come on, Lace. Come for a drive with me."

His eyes reminded her of the heat lightning that flickered on the horizon on sweltering summer nights. More often than not that lightning continued dancing in the distance, hinting at relief without making any promises of rain. From now on she needed promises.

Pushing away slightly from his dusty pickup truck, she said, "April and her sister-in-law are coming over. They're probably waiting for me now. I really do have to go."

She didn't know why her heart was racing as she turned on her heel, but the need to flee was instinctive and strong. She waited until she'd reached the end of the block to look behind her. The dusty-blue Chevy was no longer idling at the curb. Noah was gone.

With a deep, calming breath, she resumed her trek toward the apartment she once again called home. She took a shortcut through the hardware store the way she used to. As she wended her way through a maze of aisles, she faced the fact that she wasn't fleeing from Noah. She was running from her feelings for him. It would be so much easier if he didn't bring out every yearning for happily-ever-after she'd ever had.

She walked around a display of box fans and past bins containing nuts and bolts, electrical wire and plumbing supplies, and emerged into the alley, two stores away from her own back door. She hadn't taken more than half a dozen steps when she stopped in her tracks.

That dusty-blue Chevy was sitting in her dad's old parking space. Noah leaned against the tailgate, his arms folded and his ankles crossed, giving the illusion that he'd been waiting for a long time.

Although the sun was still shining on the other side of the brick buildings lining Division Street, dusk had fallen here in the alley. Shadows stretched from end to end, deeper and darker in the narrow spaces between buildings, in doorways and beneath stairs.

"Where's your dad's truck?" Noah asked, letting his arms fall to his sides.

"I sold it two days ago." Her voice sounded normal. At least something functioned normally. "Noah, what are you doing here?"

Noah admitted that it was a legitimate question. The truth was, he hadn't planned to come here tonight. When he'd left the orchard after dinner, he'd assumed he had another twelve hours before he began laying the foundation for a future with Lacey. Then he'd seen her when he'd turned onto First Street. And now here he was, twelve hours ahead of schedule.

She'd exchanged her navy slacks for gray shorts that hugged her hips and showcased a pair of legs that should have been outlawed. He'd never met another woman who caused his hormones this much commotion just by walking down the sidewalk. He could see the butterfly tattoo on her right foot from here. It matched the yellow nail polish on her toes. Another tiny butterfly was hidden beneath the waistband of her shorts. He remembered it well.

Before every last drop of the blood rushing through his ears ended up south of there, he strolled closer. Lacey held her ground. Damn, she was something.

"We can't just pick up where we left off, Noah. Real life isn't like a fairy tale." She held up one hand. "Stop right there."

He didn't stop until the tips of his shoes touched the tips of hers, their bodies so close he felt her heat and she felt his. She wanted to know what he was doing here. That much he knew. He was going to kiss her. And, if he was lucky, she was going to let him.

He didn't say anything as he placed a hand on either side of her face, his fingers splaying wide in her hair, his thumbs resting lightly along the outer edges of her cheekbones. Her eyes looked violet in this light, blurring before his as he tipped her head up slightly. Slowly, he covered her mouth with his. He heard her breath catch. And then her eyes fluttered closed.

Her lips were warm and soft and wet, and tasted like cinnamon candy, her favorite. Sampled this way, it was his favorite, too. He moved his mouth over her sweet lips, again and again and again, a gentle persuasion that somehow translated into an unspoken how do you do.

It was just supposed to be a kiss, and yet it made sense out of nothing, gave rhyme to reason and changed the beating rhythm of his heart. Heat coursed through him, converging at the very center of him, tempting him to wrap his arms around her and fit her soft curves where need was demanding attention. My, was he tempted.

For what seemed like an eternity, she remained motionless, her face tipped up, her mouth open slightly beneath his, breathlessly accepting his kiss. Then he felt it, the tentative touch of her fingertips as she placed her hands over his. He offered up a silent prayer of thanksgiving for granting him this moment.

He'd kissed Lacey a thousand times, but he'd never kissed her quite like this. It might have gone down in history for its richness, its purity and its sweetness. All the while, their only points of contact were their lips, his hands on her face and her hands on his.

Muffled laughter and what sounded a little like a stampede of elephants ended the kiss. When Lacey opened her eyes, she saw those teenage boys again. They were running through the alley, trying their darnedest to keep from snickering.

They weren't the only ones taking this shortcut. A slender young woman stepped aside, quietly letting the guys pass. There was something about her that held Lacey spellbound. It was hard to tell how old she was in this light. She wore jeans and a black T-shirt. The bill of a dark baseball cap was pulled low over her forehead. Unlike the boys, she kept her head down as she hurried by.

Realizing that she and Noah were still standing toe-to-toe, her face still in his big hands, her hands still on his, Lacey finally came to her senses. She took a step back. Her arms fell to her sides and so did his. They dragged in deep breaths, as if they'd forgotten to breathe until now.

"Well," she said.

His grin reminded them both of his sore lip.

"Does it hurt?" she asked.

"What, my lip?"

Okay, the Noah she knew was back. She tilted her head abruptly and slanted him a look that spoke volumes.

Noah shrugged those amazing shoulders of his. Running his hand over his jaw, he said, "Honestly? I forgot about my lip until now. That was great therapy. I'd like to try it again."

The need to flee had returned. This time she stood her ground and said, "But we're two different people now."

"You're still you and I'm still me. It's safe to say a passion like ours hasn't evaporated into thin air."

"Now you're playing it *safe?*" she asked.

"Leave it to you to choose *that* word out of all the others to call me on."

At least sparring with him was in her comfort zone. Sharing sweet kisses that made her feel beautiful and wish she believed in fairy tales like the ones she'd read to April's twins last night wasn't.

Tomorrow she was going to the Sullivan household where she would assume the role of Joey's temporary nanny. Before that occurred, there was something she needed to say, a point she had to make. "We can't pick up where we left off, Noah. We can't go back. Nobody can."

Widening his stance slightly, he rested his hands lightly on his hips and met her gaze. "I was going to wait until tomorrow to talk to you about this, but you might as well know I have no intention of going back to the beginning."

"At least we agree on some—"

"And you're right. We can't just pick up where we left off over two years ago, or last year, either."

She drew her eyebrows down, a no-no according to the

beauty magazines. She forgot why. "Then what was that kiss?"

"That's what I wanted to talk to you about," he said, his grin slow and sincere. "Years from now we'll look back on this day. Because today is the day we began anew."

He gave her that smile again, the one that reminded her of an alley cat stretching languidly in a glorious patch of sunshine. Darned if her insides didn't stretch a little, too.

"That kiss," he said, his gaze settling on her mouth, "was the beginning of our new beginning."

There was something about the way he'd spoken that sounded like the prequel to happily-ever-after. She really needed different reading material. Nobody lived happily ever after. If people were lucky, they lived happily-sometimes-after. That brought her back to the beginning.

While she was still standing there, her heart speeding up and slowing down by turns, an Oldsmobile with an engine knock pulled up alongside Noah's Chevy. April threw the gearshift into Park and cut the engine.

Each of the Avery brood had learned to drive in that car. Although the mishaps and the wear and tear showed, it still had a few good years and a lot of miles left in it. With the youngest off to London for the summer, April's mother-in-law had assured Lacey that she was more than happy to let her borrow it. That was the kind of good people there were in Orchard Hill, in Michigan, in the world. They were "It takes a village" people—kind, thoughtful ordinary people who made others feel just a little extraordinary.

April was opening the door of the car she was dropping off for Lacey to drive, as her sister-in law pulled up in a shiny new SUV. "Sorry to interrupt," she said, smiling at Lacey and Noah.

Had everyone seen that kiss?

April's sister-in-law got out, too. With a knowing little smile that was an answer to Lacey's silent question, Gabby Avery pushed her chin-length blond hair behind her ears and opened the back of her SUV. Suddenly, Noah was there, hauling out the for-sale signs they were going to place in the tavern's front and back windows.

The man had a rangy physique—there was no doubt about it. His jeans were faded at the major stress points: knees, pockets and fly. His split lip lent the ultimate authenticity to his bad-boy persona.

"You didn't interrupt, April," he said as he carried the signs past her and leaned them against the tavern's back door. "I was leaving. Tell Jay hi for me, okay?"

"I will, Noah, thanks."

His gaze rested on Lacey for a heartbeat longer than the others. "Do you need a ride in the morning?"

Lacey shook her head and managed to say, "I've got it covered."

"Then I'll see you tomorrow."

With a swagger that made all three of them salivate, he sauntered to his pickup and got in. In no time at all he'd started the engine and backed out of his parking spot.

Gabby Avery was ten years older than Lacey and April, and had been happily married to Jay's oldest brother for eight years. Obviously, that hadn't prevented her from appreciating the view. She fanned herself with one hand and said, "What on earth was that?"

For a moment Lacey paused, on the brink of the precipice that was the rest of her life. Before her was the unknown with all its wonder and risk. She could turn her back on all of it. Or she could take the next step into the unknown. The choice was hers.

In her mind she saw herself testing for solid footing with the tips of her toes. "If I'm not mistaken," Lacey said, watching until Noah's taillights disappeared around the corner, "that was the beginning of the new beginning of Noah and me."

"Ow."

"What happened?" April asked.

"It was just my finger," her sister-in-law said. "Don't worry. I don't use that one much anyway."

The two of them were at the front window in Bell's Tavern, trying their darnedest to fasten the for-sale sign with its fancy Avery Realty logo and phone number to the window frame. The board wasn't heavy; it was cumbersome, bulky and a tad unruly. Lacey had tried to help. When it became apparent that she was only getting in the way, she'd left the installation to the experts.

"Ow." This time it was April who pinched her poor finger.

Smiling to herself, Lacey thought that perhaps *experts* wasn't the proper term. The lights were on in the tavern and the back door was propped open. After casually checking the window locks and finding them all intact, Lacey wandered to the pool table in the back of the room.

She hadn't been down here since Officer Pratt had taken a look around. It wasn't that she hadn't thought about it. She just hadn't quite gotten up the nerve to venture down here alone. She wondered if Officer Pratt had been right, and whoever had been here was long gone by now.

Far away from the thumps and thuds at the front window, she peeked under the pool table. The sleeping bag was still there, pretty much where it had been the other night. It was difficult to tell if it had been slept in, but the water bottle was gone. A partially empty bag of cashews and a half-full bottle of green tea were now beside the sleeping bag.

Biting her lip to stifle the little buzz of excitement running through her, she cast another look to the front window to make sure April and Gabby weren't looking. Confident that the coast was clear, she swooped down for a closer look at the little nest that had been created here.

A strand of hair on the edge of the bedroll caught her eye. Grasping it between her thumb and forefinger, she brought it closer for a better look. Lacey's hair skimmed her shoulders. This strand was twice that long.

Her Houdini had been back. Once again she'd come and gone without breaking a window or leaving any clue as to how she was getting in and out.

Little by little, Lacey felt as if she was becoming acquainted with her guest. Although she was still no closer to discovering her Houdini's actual identity, Lacey knew she wore pink lip gloss and had long brown hair. She didn't leave a mess, and apparently she liked healthy snacks.

She must be very brave to live as she was living. Lacey was beginning to think that perhaps she wasn't the only woman in Orchard Hill poised on the brink of beginning anew.

Chapter Six

Traffic on Old Orchard Highway wasn't heavy at twenty minutes after eight on Friday morning. The window on the passenger side of the car Lacey was borrowing from April's in-laws wouldn't go all the way up, and the seat only latched in two places, but the car started on the first try, the brakes were new and the radio got fantastic reception.

It had rained during the night. Now the sun was shining, turning the moisture on the ground into vapors that shimmered like radio waves in the distance. At the River Bridge, she slipped on a pair of sunglasses, cranked up the radio and crested a hill, leaving her stomach behind.

That might have been nerves. Or anticipation.

Before she fell asleep last night, she'd taken a personality quiz in a fashion magazine. The twenty questions were an eclectic mix of random information: How many letters were in her name? What was worse—spiders or snakes?

Did she dream in color? Had she ever had an encounter with an alien or settled a dispute using rock, paper and scissors? That sort of thing. According to the "scientific" results, she wasn't a morning person. She'd known that before sharpening her pencil, but a little validation never hurt anybody.

Being a night owl hadn't prevented her from jumping up at the crack of dawn this morning and preparing to begin her new job. Nothing could have prevented her from dreaming about new beginnings and Noah's kiss. She couldn't help wondering what the day would bring.

Just then, the orchard came into view. The first driveway followed the east property line and ended in a large clearing that bordered the stone cider house and the whitewashed bakery barn and the shed where homemade apple cider and doughnuts were sold to the throngs of people who swarmed here every autumn. Lacey turned into the second drive. Secluded and private, it led to the big Victorian house at the top of the hill.

Pea gravel crunched beneath her tires as she pulled up beside Noah's truck. She finger-combed her hair and straightened her clothes. With everything she would need to begin her new job stacked neatly in her arms, she went to the back door.

One thing she didn't have was a spare hand to knock. "Hello?" she called.

Hearing no answering call telling her to come in, she stood for a moment looking through the screen. The coffeemaker was gurgling noisily on the counter in the kitchen. A chair had been left out. It appeared to hold the spillover of baby clothes from the table.

"Anybody home?" she said softly, in case Joey was sleeping.

Of course they were home. The door was open and the

coffee was brewing and Marsh, Reed and Noah's vehicles were all in the driveway.

"Hello?" she called again.

After a little finagling to free one hand, she let herself in. Now that she was inside, she could hear faint masculine voices. They seemed to be coming from the front of the house. Leaving the bowl she was returning on the counter and her purse, camera, library books and the little gift she'd brought stacked neatly on the table, she went in search of whoever was in charge.

"Marsh, is that you?" Reed called.

Expecting Lacey any minute, Noah had been on his way to the kitchen, but hearing Reed calling, he stuck his arms into the sleeves of his clean T-shirt and cut across the living room instead. He found Reed sitting behind his desk in his home office, Joey sucking noisily on his bottle.

"I just met Marsh on the front stairs," Noah said. "Do you need something?"

"Go get him. Tell him it's important."

Noah had taken Joey's four-o'clock feeding, but the tone of Reed's voice was quickly dissolving his grogginess. Marsh must have heard it, too, because he was suddenly in the doorway beside Noah.

"An email just came in from that P.I. Sam Lafferty," Reed said. "Take a look at this."

Marsh and Noah crowded behind Reed's desk and looked at his computer screen. The three of them practically knocked heads as they leaned closer to the monitor where there were several photographs of a dark-haired woman. While they were studying the pictures, the phone on the desk rang.

Reed answered, listened intently and promptly said, "He and Noah are both here, Sam. I'm putting you on speakerphone." He pushed a button and, when Joey started to fuss, reached for the forgotten bottle and offered it to the baby once again. Joey forgave him as soon as he had the nipple in his mouth.

"The pictures on your screen are of a woman named Julia Monroe," Sam said. "She just went into a little bungalow on a tree-lined street here in Charleston. Of the six women with that name I found in West Virginia, three are in the right age bracket. This is the only brunette. If she's not the right Julia Monroe, there are more in Florida, Alabama and Tennessee. There are likely others but I'm starting here because you said she had a soft Southern accent and that she mentioned growing up in West Virginia. Is it her, Marsh?"

Marsh studied the screen. "It might be. Her hair was long when I knew her."

Marsh took a closer look at the pictures of a woman with extremely short hair. Once again, Sam's voice sounded over the speaker. "A new hairstyle can completely change a woman's appearance. Look carefully at her face, her clothes and her build, anything that might trigger recognition."

"I can't be sure from this angle," Marsh said. "Can you get a picture from the front?"

Just then Noah noticed a movement in the doorway. Lacey paused there, taking everything in.

For Noah, time stood still.

Once, a guy he knew down in Ohio told him about a phenomenon he described as feeling thunderstruck. He said one minute he'd been in a crowded airport and the next there was only him and some woman looking back at him from across the terminal. Voices muted and sound ceased and everyone else disappeared. It had happened to

Noah yesterday near the Johnny Appleseed sculpture. He felt the same way all over again.

Lacey wore blue jeans, sandals and a gray knit top that fit her perfectly. Her hair was mussed, her eyes as blue as the morning, her nose pert. He wanted to walk across the room and take her hand, just her hand, and maybe sit with her and talk.

"She's suspicious of my car parked around the corner. I'm pretty sure she was trying to get a make on me while I was getting one on her."

Oh. The P.I. was still talking. Noah came out of his trance with a start.

"She's acting nervous. People who act nervous usually have a reason," Sam said. "If I get any closer she's liable to call the cops. She's camera-shy and she's flighty."

"Is everything okay?" Lacey whispered from the doorway.

Reed motioned her in, quietly saying, "Our private investigator has a lead on Julia."

"Who's there?" Sam asked.

Lacey's eyes widened. She looked at the phone on the desk and said, "I'm the nanny."

"Maybe you want to take me off speakerphone."

Lacey took the hint and started to leave the room.

"Lacey, wait," Noah said. "She's a friend of the family, Sam."

"And completely trustworthy," Reed added.

"Completely." This, from Marsh.

"You aren't going to believe this," Sam said. "A moving van just pulled into the driveway."

"What does that mean?" Marsh blurted.

"It would appear that she isn't planning to stick around."

Suddenly all eyes were on Marsh. He'd paled beneath

his tan. His jaw was set, his lips drawn into a thin line. He looked more haggard suddenly, and a little desperate.

Sam persisted. "I can continue my surveillance then follow the moving van. If she drives her own car and takes a different route I'll have a decision to make. Or—" Sam thought for a moment. "Noah, is your plane flight-ready?"

It was Noah's turn to pale. He had a clear-cut plan in mind for today. And it didn't include flying to Charleston. Half a dozen expletives ran through his head. He glanced at Reed, at Marsh, at Joey and finally at Lacey. He only hoped she would understand.

"Mine's still missing a propeller, Sam, but I'll borrow a plane." He looked at his watch. "I can have Marsh in Charleston in three-and-a-half hours. Four hours, tops."

Marsh was already moving toward the door. He stopped suddenly and looked at the baby, obviously torn.

Lacey took charge with quiet authority. Laying a gentling hand on his arm, she said, "Aren't you glad you hired a nanny? I'll take good care of Joey. Go, both of you, before those movers get Julia's things boxed up and she disappears."

Noah opened his phone and touched the screen. Tom Bender answered on the fourth ring. Still on speakerphone, Sam rattled off a house number and street address, and told them how to avoid the construction on Highway 79. Placing the baby to his shoulder as if he'd been doing it all his life, Reed wrote the information on a notepad in his meticulous handwriting.

Lacey stepped out of Marsh's way. After Sam told them which airport was closest to his stakeout and the make and model of a rental car that would be waiting, Marsh turned around again and said, "Just don't lose her, Sam."

The gravity of the situation stopped everyone at once. Four hours from now they might very well have the answers they were seeking. In four hours they should know if this Julia was the right Julia, and if she'd left Joey on their doorstep three days ago. They might even know why.

As quickly as it had ceased, activity resumed. Sam promised to be in contact, then promptly broke the connection. Marsh went upstairs to get his wallet and change his shoes. Reed offered Joey the rest of his formula. And Noah followed Lacey into the living room. He didn't have much more than a minute and he planned to make the most of it.

"This," he said firmly, "has nothing to do with our new beginning."

She looked up at him and whispered, "Did you see the expression on Marsh's face?"

He nodded. Marsh was hurting. The man was pining for this Julia. Until Joey had arrived, Noah hadn't even known Marsh had spent a week on the coast with anyone special.

He glanced into Reed's office again. His fair-haired brother was quietly watching Joey drink his bottle. Had it not been for Joey's arrival, Noah might never have known that he wasn't the only Sullivan with a little bit of rascal running through his veins. That baby was teaching them all so much. And Joey hadn't said a word.

"You take care of Marsh," Lacey told Noah softly. "And I'll take care of Reed and Joey."

Noah's chest expanded, but before he could do more than nod at Lacey, Marsh's footsteps sounded on the stairs. He wished he had time to tell her what he'd been rehearsing since he'd left her in the alley last night. There was just no time for that now.

"It's at least a three-and-a-half-hour flight there and another three-and-a-half hours back," he said. "Allowing for driving time and surveillance time, it'll be at least six o'clock before I return. I'm afraid the next step of our new beginning will have to wait to begin until then."

"The next step?" she asked.

He nodded. The first step had begun before he'd realized what was happening. It had been a culmination of everything that had happened from the moment he'd heard that Lacey was back in Orchard Hill to the moment he'd held her face between his hands and kissed her gently last night. The only part of step one he'd planned had been that kiss. Steps two and three would be different. After all, it wasn't every day that a man got a second chance with a woman like Lacey Bell. "It's a three-step plan. I would tell you but I don't want to spoil the surprise." He smiled and watched the effect it had on her.

Her eyebrows went up in perfect arches and that attitude of hers showed in the tilt of her head. "The sooner you get going, the sooner you can put your money where your mouth is, flyboy."

There was only one place he wanted to put his mouth. Or maybe two. Or three. Hell, he could think of a dozen, all of them soft and lush and—he didn't even try to hide his groan of frustration.

Marsh joined them in the living room and Reed came out of his office with Joey, an empty bottle and the notepad containing the information Sam had given them in his hand. The next few minutes were filled with instructions and reminders and calculations and plans. And then Marsh and Noah were pulling out of the driveway and Reed, Joey and Lacey watched from the back porch.

Lacey smiled and waved.

As Noah sped away, he wondered if she had any idea what that smile had done to him. He faced the fact that she wasn't simply in his blood.

He'd known her well for ten years. He'd liked her from

the beginning. He'd wanted her, and he supposed in his own way he'd loved her for most of that time.

This morning something had changed. He didn't know how it had happened, or why, but he'd seen her standing in the doorway of Reed's office, and he fell headfirst, head-long, head over heels for her. Now he had a burning need to move to step two in his plan.

He rolled down his window. With the warm air rushing over him, he glanced at Marsh. His older brother was staring straight ahead. His arms were folded, his jaw set. Noah wasn't the only one with a burning need.

He checked for traffic and stepped on the gas. His truck shot forward. In a matter of minutes they arrived at the county airfield. Digger was already fueling Tom's twin-engine plane. It was time to get this show on the road or, in this case, in the air.

In the kitchen, Lacey poured two cups of coffee and carried them to the table. Since Reed didn't appear to be ready to relinquish Joey, she moved the child-care book aside and gestured for him to have a seat at a right angle to her. With her pen poised over a yellow legal pad, she said, "I thought we could go over my duties."

Silence.

She looked up from her blank sheet of paper and saw that Reed was staring down at Joey, seemingly lost in thought. This wasn't easy for him. She put her pen down and reached for her camera. Reed seemed oblivious as she removed the lens cap and adjusted the focus. The flash got his attention. As he looked up, she said, "What you're doing for Joey—what all three of you are doing—is a kind of good we don't see very often, Reed. I'm not sure there are three brothers alive who would have handled the situation half as well. That little boy has wrapped his hand around your hearts."

She caught him looking at his wristwatch. He was probably wondering if Noah and Marsh had taken off yet, as she was. She hoped they discovered Joey's mother's identity soon. She remembered an old Bible story about a baby claimed by two mothers. The king's solution was to cut the baby in half. She forgot how it ended, but shuddered at the thought.

She only hoped this situation didn't slice Marsh and Reed apart. "What time is your meeting?" she asked.

At his look of surprise, she motioned to his clothes. The man was dressed to the nines in tan slacks, shoes by a maker she couldn't pronounce, a sky-blue shirt and a striped tie. "Not even *you* wear a tie around home," she said, tongue-in-cheek.

There was something about the look he gave her that reminded her of Noah. It endeared him to her and reminded her that there was more to him than confidence and a keen mind.

"My lawyer and I and two other orchard owners are going to crash a little party this morning," he said. "There's a shady developer from downstate who's proposing the construction of a housing development on Orchard Highway. He's packaging it nice and pretty, but in reality it would be a glorified trailer park. There's a county ordinance a mile high and just as wide against such ventures. But you know how visions of tax revenue can dance in the heads of township and county officials. We're going to make sure no loopholes are created. Luckily, my new brother-in-law got wind of it, and told me before it was too late."

"Your brother-in-law's name is Riley Merrick, isn't it? I heard Madeline got married," Lacey said.

Madeline Sullivan had been a grade behind Lacey in school. Blonde and blue-eyed like Reed, she'd had more than her share of sadness in her life. Recently, she and her new husband had moved to Traverse City and were happily expecting their first child.

"What did Madeline say when you told her about Joey?" she asked.

Reed Sullivan had been the valedictorian of his graduating class and the president of the debate team at Purdue. If he put his mind to it, the man could have won an argument with the devil, yet this innocent question seemed to have struck him dumb. Obviously, he and his brothers hadn't thought to call their sister.

Lacey held her hands out for Joey. While she settled the baby into the crook of her arm, Reed glanced at his watch again.

"Madeline is going to have our hides," he said. "There's no sense calling her now until after we hear from Marsh and Noah."

With that decision made, he began to tell her about Joey's quirks, his likes and his dislikes, how often he ate and how much, and how he liked the new mobile on his crib and didn't like to sleep on his stomach. She jotted everything down with her free hand.

"According to this book written by a group of renowned pediatricians, babies need something called tummy time. I'll work on that. What about baths?" she asked.

Reed did a double take all over again. Evidently, giving the baby a bath hadn't occurred to them yet.

She wrote *BATH* at the top of the page. She and Reed discussed other responsibilities, such as washing baby bottles and folding Joey's laundry. When they were both satisfied that they'd covered everything, she pushed the wrapped package toward him.

"This is for all of you," she said. "Go ahead and open it. While you do that, I think this little guy needs his diaper changed."

"Lacey?" he said when she'd reached the doorway. "A word of caution. The kid's got an aim on him you wouldn't believe."

Reed tore into the wrapping paper. Rather than ask him to explain, she carried Joey into the room they'd converted into a nursery.

Wow, she thought, turning in a circle. The boys had been busy. A baby crib was in the corner where Marsh's leather sofa had been, a matching changing table and dresser opposite it where a television had been perpetually tuned to the weather. Bright-colored artwork of zoo animals hung on the walls.

She placed Joey on the new changing table and delighted in the way he stared up at her and grinned. Although something drastic must have happened to cause his mother to leave him the way she did, he seemed healthy and content and incredibly adaptable.

She unsnapped his little sleeper and removed his wet diaper. Keeping one hand on his tummy, she reached onto a low shelf for a dry disposable diaper. A fountain sprang forth, dousing everything in its path. She scrambled for the first thing she could find and threw a receiving blanket over the stream.

So that was what Reed had been talking about.

A movement at the doorway caught her eye. Reed was there. He held the photograph of Joey she'd developed, framed and wrapped in tissue paper late last night. There was a smile on his face.

The shortest-running temp job she'd ever held in Chicago had lasted three days. During those three days she'd adjusted lighting and backdrops for a photographer taking pictures of men flexing and posing for a fundraising calendar. Reed Sullivan would have been a shoo-in for Mr. July, and yet there was no pounding of her heart or fluttering of butterfly wings. There was only sweet affection.

"It looks like you have everything covered," he said.

She shot him a look she often shot Noah.

Unscathed, he said, "I'm leaving now." He entered the room and strode directly to Joey. "You be good for your Aunt Lacey, all right, buddy?"

Tears sprang to Lacey's eyes. *Aunt* Lacey. How could something so simple fill her with so much wonder?

"I wrote my cell number on that legal pad on the kitchen table," Reed said, apparently oblivious to the fact that he'd just paid her the highest compliment in the world. "Call me if you have any questions or need anything. Anything at all."

"What time do you expect we'll hear from Marsh and Noah?" she asked, still a little awestruck.

"They'll call as soon as they know something," he said.

They both dreaded the wait.

Reed left for his meeting. And Lacey gave Joey his first bath since arriving on the Sullivans' porch. It took an unbelievably long time. Wet babies were slippery and she had only watched April bathe her twins. Joey wasn't the only one soaking wet when it was over. He wasn't the only one enjoying himself, either.

She powdered him and dressed him in a little pair of pants with paw prints on the seat and a T-shirt with a puppy's face on the chest. She read him a story from one of the early-childhood-development library books she'd brought along. When the baby fell asleep for his morning nap, she laid him in his crib, turned the wireless monitor on and left the nursery.

She tackled the sink full of baby bottles, lids and nipples and folded the baby clothes somebody had piled on the table. The phone rang every half hour. It was Reed every time.

Marsh and Noah hadn't called. She could only imagine what was happening on that tree-lined street in Charleston.

The twin-engine Gulfstream Commander shimmied slightly on a patch of rough air. Marsh put his hand over the pit of his stomach and Noah put both hands on the controls. He pushed the throttle forward and pulled back on the yoke, leveling the airplane out. Shaking his hand slightly once the ride was smooth again, Marsh carefully laid it back on the ice pack in his lap.

Noah kept his expression carefully schooled as he flipped switches and checked dials on the dash. He responded to Air Traffic Control and climbed to three thousand feet as soon as he was cleared by the tower. Now that they were safely above the thunderstorm rolling across Fort Wayne, he pointed the nose due north. From there it was smooth sailing.

They were going home.

The cockpit was drafty and noisy. That wasn't the reason he and Marsh had barely spoken since takeoff. Everything that had happened during the hour they'd been on the ground in Charleston spoke for itself.

The moving van had been in the driveway when they'd pulled up in the rented car. Marsh had parked a few spaces behind Sam's nondescript sedan just as the movers closed the doors. Julia hadn't shown her face, but the movers were getting ready to drive away. While there was still time, it was decided that Noah and Marsh would knock on the bungalow's front door.

The air smelled like honeysuckle and was so heavy

with humidity that sweat trickled down both their faces as they approached the house. Marsh rang the doorbell. He was going to do the talking. Noah was along for moral support.

The door opened, but instead of the brown-haired woman they were expecting, a man as big as an ox told them to get the hell off his stoop. His head was shaved, his chest broad, his arms meaty and heavily tattooed.

Marsh, being an all-around decent guy, said, "Hello. I'm an old friend of Julia's. Is she here by any chance?"

"Who wants to know?"

"Tell her it's Marsh Sullivan."

The other man started to turn around, as if he intended to speak to someone over his shoulder. Marsh made the mistake of taking his eyes off him. Noah saw the swing coming and ducked, but Marsh wasn't so lucky. The big man's fist made a resounding whack when it connected with Marsh's jaw.

"Okay, okay," Noah had said, holding up both hands. "We obviously have the wrong house. We're leaving now."

Oxman glanced menacingly at Noah. Marsh used the momentary distraction to slam his fist into the other man's gut. Noah hadn't been trying to create a diversion at all. Not that he blamed Marsh for retaliating. That sucker punch his poor brother had taken had been low-down and dirty. Noah only hoped the grinding he'd heard when Marsh had given the jerk a taste of his own medicine wasn't the bones in Marsh's hand crumbling.

He managed to drag Marsh off the stoop and back to their rental car without either of them losing life or limb. Marsh was swearing a blue streak and both were sweating profusely.

Strangely, Sam wasn't in his car when they got there. They looked all around, but there was no sign of him. They decided to wait inside the car just in case they needed to make a quick getaway.

Sam returned a few minutes later, in worse shape than Marsh. Blood trickled down the side of his cheek and there were bits of leaves and grass on the seat of his pants and in his hair.

Sam Lafferty was in his late thirties. He stood six-four and weighed over two hundred pounds. He worked out every day and it showed. With a groan, he climbed into the backseat.

"What happened to you?" Noah asked.

Sam ran his finger along the screen of a small phone that looked as if it had the capability to launch missiles from outer space while making him a sandwich. Holding the gadget out to Marsh, he said, "I got that picture of her from the front you wanted."

It was actually a video and starred the woman they'd seen in the photographs on Reed's computer back in Orchard Hill over four hours earlier. Sam had caught her slipping out her back door. Noah could tell that she wasn't pleased he was there. There was no sound, but those lips were easy to read.

The last they saw of her in the video, she was performing a high kick that would have made Bruce Lee proud. After that there was nothing but blue sky.

Marsh handed the phone back to the private investigator. Cradling his hand again, he said, "That's not her."

"You're sure?" Sam asked.

"Positive. She's not the woman I knew. She's not even close."

That was that.

It was discouraging, but the beatings Marsh and Sam had taken hadn't been for nothing. One Julia Monroe down, several more to go. Sam was going to continue looking. He would broaden his search for Julia to the Deep South. He was also going to Texas where Reed had spent a night with a stacked blond waitress named Cookie.

Noah had driven back to the airport in Charleston. They'd turned in the rental car and now they were almost home.

Other than a little air turbulence and cabin noise, the trip back had been uneventful. The Gulfstream Commander was Tom Bender's oldest and fastest plane. It was a thrill to fly her. There wasn't anything about flying that wasn't thrilling. Noah liked holding the control loosely in his hands, and was always invigorated by the sensation of gliding a thousand feet above the ground. And yet today, he could hardly wait to land.

"Look!" Marsh said loud enough to be heard over the engine noise and air leaks in the cabin. "There's the orchard. I'd forgotten what it looks like from the air."

There it was, rows of apple trees with bright green leaves, two-track trails running between them. The metal roof on the cider house glowed like melted copper in the bright sunshine. The sprawling house with its peaks and gables and three chimneys sat away from the other buildings. Noah buzzed it the way he always did when he was coming home.

Reed and Lacey rushed outside. He saw Lacey turn Joey around as she pointed at the airplane.

If Noah could have landed in the clearing they used as a parking lot every autumn, he would have. That was how impatient he was to introduce Lacey to the second step in his master plan. He made do with tipping his wing hello.

He didn't know how long step two would last. Part of him hoped to high heaven it didn't take long. It would take as long as it needed to take. He'd rushed her ten years ago. This time, he was going to take it nice and slow.

He was almost sure she was going to give him this chance to begin anew. Only a fool would waste it.

Lacey and Reed both lifted a hand in greeting. Marsh waved back. "Noah?" he called over the cabin noise.

"Yeah?"

"In case I forget later. Thanks."

"Anytime, buddy," Noah said, his chest expanding. "Anytime."

Marsh was going home to the apple trees he'd nurtured, many of them patiently grafted with his own two hands, and the baby he hoped was his son. Noah was flying home to one very special woman.

He banked hard and turned the plane around. The instant they were headed in the right direction, he poured it on. After all, it wasn't every day a man realized that soaring through the wild blue yonder was nothing compared to the thrill of landing in the arms of the woman waiting for him on the ground.

Chapter Seven

At the end of Lacey's first day as Joey's nanny, she left him in Reed's care and, with her library books under one arm and her purse over her shoulder, walked out the back door. She was surprised to see Marsh walking toward her. She'd known that he and Noah were back when they'd buzzed the house, but she hadn't heard anyone drive in.

"I'll see you on Monday," Marsh said gruffly as he walked past. Lacey and Reed had discussed her work schedule, and since the brothers apparently had been in contact and agreed that they would handle Joey's care over the weekend, Lacey saw no reason to detain Marsh now. Cradling his right hand, he went inside without saying another word.

Noah was waiting for her in the driveway. Unlike Marsh, he looked relaxed and at ease. "Hey, Lace," he said. "Got a minute?" His voice had taken on a sleepy velvet smoothness that didn't necessarily mean he was sleepy.

Shading her eyes with one hand, she was pretty sure she was about to hear about step two. They seemed to have the same idea at the same time and, in unison, cut across the driveway to the shade of an enormous maple tree. An old-fashioned swing hung from a high branch. After giving the ropes a tug, Noah said, "Care for a push?"

She hadn't expected that, but she set her things out of the way and tested the ropes, too. "Maybe a small one."

He slipped silently behind her, and then she felt herself being drawn backward. With a whoosh, she was soaring through the balmy evening air. A little giggle bubbled out of her.

"Want another?" he asked.

"No." She laughed out loud. "This was easier on my stomach when I was a kid."

"Do you remember the first time we went out, Lacey?"

"Out?"

"You know, on our first date."

She glanced over her shoulder at him to see if he was serious. His eyes, those deep brown eyes, were trained on hers. His lips were parted slightly, the edges tilted up just enough to tell her it was an honest question.

She straightened her arms and leaned back. Her hair nearly brushing the grass every time she passed the middle, she looked up at the branches disappearing in the lacy green leaves and considered Noah's question.

Back in school, he was one of those guys all the girls noticed. Two grades ahead of her, he'd driven an old white Charger, a sweet car if there ever was one, until he wrapped it around a tree his senior year. How he made it out alive was anybody's guess. He'd been popular with everybody, even the teachers who shook their heads and threw their hands up in surrender for all the times he pushed his limits and theirs.

Lacey's path didn't cross his until a few years later. He'd grown up a little by then. He hadn't settled down, but he'd found something he loved more than driving too fast and raising hell.

Late one night after he'd returned from a vigorous year-long Airfield Operations Specialist training program down in Florida, she stepped onto the landing hoping to catch a little relief from the sweltering August heat. What she'd caught was Noah Sullivan's attention as he was cutting through the alley. To this day she remembered the butterflies that had fluttered inside her rib cage when he'd looked up at her and said, "Hey."

She'd stared down at him from the top of those steps. She might have smiled but she didn't say a word.

"Are you coming down here?" he'd asked.

Raised over the local bar, she'd learned how to take care of herself. She'd taken plenty of risks, but she didn't take chances with guys in dark alleys, no matter how cute they were. "I'm not planning to."

He'd laughed. And she was smitten.

"Mind if I sit down here, then?" he asked.

"Suit yourself."

He made himself comfortable on the third step from the bottom. After a while she'd settled on the top step. They'd talked for two hours, him looking up, and her looking down, cigarette smoke and noise wafting into the alley every time one of her dad's customers opened the tavern's back door. When Noah returned the next night, he moved up a few steps, and she moved down. Before long, they sat in the middle, side by side.

A few weeks later he took a job flying wealthy businessmen from one corner of Texas to the other. The next time she saw him she was nineteen and he was twenty-one. He came into The Hill where she'd worked as a waitress. Her shift was just ending, so she'd taken off her apron and he'd walked her home. Again, they'd wound up talking for hours. He flew off into the wild blue yonder often during the next few years, but he always came back to her.

Now he was asking if she remembered their first date. She hopped off the swing and faced him. Slipping her hands into the front pockets of her jeans, she said, "Did we go to the movies?"

"The first movie we saw was about a group of World War II fighter pilots. We walked to the Division Street Theater and you paid your own way. Not a date in my book."

"Did we go for a drive or grab a burger somewhere?"

"That doesn't count as a date, either."

"I guess I don't remember our first date," she said.

He smiled, and her heart turned over. "That's because we never went on a first date." He came closer, the swing still rocking gently between them. "All those years we did just about everything else. How could I have missed that?"

She didn't have anything to say to that.

A warm breeze ruffled his shaggy hair and fluttered the hem of her gray shirt. A car drove by, loud music blasting from its open windows. When only the vibration of the bass remained, Noah said, "Would you have dinner with me, Lacey?"

"Dinner?" Okay, she really needed to stop repeating everything he said.

His throat convulsed on a swallow. She realized this was important to him. "Yes," he said, "dinner. You and me in a restaurant that uses cloth napkins. If you say yes, it'll be our first date."

"When were you thinking we would go on this first date?"

"How about right now?" His voice had deepened again, stirring her in a way no other man ever had.

Glancing down at her clothes, she said, "I'm not dressed for dinner at a restaurant that uses cloth napkins."

"How long would it take you to get ready? An hour?" He must have interpreted the look she shot him, because he slanted her a smile he didn't overuse. "An hour and a half, then?"

There were a dozen reasons—all of them good—why she should ignore the way her heart rose up like a ballerina on tiptoe, ready to start twirling. There was only one reason she didn't, and it had everything to do with the promise in Noah's smile.

"An hour and a half, it is," she said, surprised at how cool, calm and collected she sounded. She picked up her purse and camera and books and started across the grass.

She felt his eyes on her as she opened her car door and got in. Finding her keys in the bottom of her bag, she stuck them in the ignition. *Oh-my-gosh-oh-my-gosh-oh-my-gosh.* As she drove out of sight, excitement erupted in a screech of laughter. She cranked the radio up and crested a hill, once again leaving her stomach behind.

She kept to the speed limit, but it wasn't easy. She made a left turn on Elm and then made a beeline for Baldwin Street. She had April on the phone when she pulled into her driveway.

"I need your help," she said, getting out of the car.

April met her at the door. "What's wrong?" she asked, her curly hair in wild disarray.

"I need to borrow a dress."

"A dress?"

Face-to-face but still on the phone, they both burst out

laughing. Lacey put her phone away and went in. Being careful not to step on the coloring books and matching pink boas on the living-room floor, she said, "I have a date. A first date."

"Who's here, Mommy?" a little girl called from the next room.

"It's Aunt Lacey," April answered over her shoulder. To Lacey she said, "A date with who?"

Aunt Lacey. She took a moment to savor the sound of it. Her hand settled momentarily on her abdomen. See, she thought, recalling the serious conversation she'd had with her doctor following her second surgery in Chicago. A woman didn't have to *have* children to have children in her life. With a watery smile, she said, "With Noah."

"Follow me." April spun around and led the way across the living room without stepping on a thing.

Jay and April had purchased the house on Baldwin Street shortly after they got married. Built seventy years ago when houses were small and lots were large, it consisted of a living room, an eat-in kitchen and one bathroom with a bedroom on either side. The upstairs had sloping ceilings and walls that were unfinished. It was the first thing Jay was going to do when he came back from Afghanistan. Well, Lacey thought as she followed her petite friend to her bedroom, maybe not the first thing. First, they would begin anew.

There was a lot of that going around.

April didn't ask Lacey if she'd lost her mind. She didn't suggest that going on a first date with Noah now was impossible. She was Lacey's friend, and if Lacey said she needed her help April was going to help her.

She reached to the back of the closet and started flipping through hangers. "This won't do. Neither will this. Or this. What about this?" She held up something only to put it back. "Never mind." Reaching the end, she popped her head out. "A dress, you say."

"Yes."

April looked askance at Lacey for the first time since she'd arrived. "Honey, I don't know how to break this to you, but your chest isn't going to fit into anything I own."

Lacey glanced down at the front of her shirt. Oh, dear. "Noah is picking me up in less than an hour and a half. I don't have time to go to the mall."

The twins came scampering into the room. One had curls like April, the other straight hair like Jay. Both climbed onto their mother's bed.

"No jumping," April warned.

Thwarted, the first plopped down in the middle of the bed and her sister climbed off.

"Wait. I have an idea." April bounded from the room very much the way her daughters had just bounded in. When she returned, she was carrying a garment bag.

Lowering the zipper to reveal the edge of an aqua-colored dress, she said, "I only wore this once. I was still nursing the girls, so I actually had cleavage. Jay couldn't take his eyes off me. Wear it at your own risk."

Lacey drew the dress from the bag. As light as a feather, it was sleeveless. Since she and April were both a hair under five-five, the length was perfect. The bodice over-lapped, forming a V that didn't look too low. The skirt wrapped around, held together with a tie at the side of the waist. Holding the confection in front of her at the mirror, she said, "Are you sure you don't mind loaning it to me?"

"As I said. I wore it when I was nursing, and I'm not planning a repeat performance."

Lacey could feel April watching for her reaction to her inadvertent mention of pregnancy. She'd broken it off with Noah because of her desire to have babies of her own. April knew about Lacey's ruptured appendix and the complications that had followed. But Lacey was starting anew, and that meant growth. It was spontaneous and exciting, the outcome unknown. And this dress was going to be perfect for taking a leap of faith.

"Well, girls?" Lacey said, smiling at April's adorable children. "Do you think Aunt Lacey will look good in this dress?"

The three-year-olds clapped. And April smiled again. Lacey beamed at all three. *Aunt* Lacey had a certain ring to it.

"What about shoes?" she asked April. "Will my brown sandals do?"

"Trust me, Noah isn't going to be looking at your feet. How much time did you say you have?"

Oh, my. The clock was ticking. Lacey started in one direction, stopped and started again.

"Leave the dress," April commanded. "I'll bring it with me along with everything else we'll need. Go take your shower. Make it a quick one. I'll be a few minutes behind you. Girls, go finish your chicken nuggets. We're going to Aunt Lacey's to help her get ready for her date."

"What's a date?" one of them asked.

At the door Lacey listened for April's reply. "It's like Cinderella's Ball."

"Is Aunt Lacey a princess?"

"Yes, Gracie, she is. And her prince isn't going to know what hit him."

April Avery was helping her twins down the stairs when Noah pulled into the parking space in the alley. He tossed his sunglasses onto the dash of his pickup and got out. Somewhere, the marching band was practicing for the upcoming Fourth of July parade, the drums and occasional trumpet blast carrying on the warm air. Dog walkers were out on Division Street, and two boys were being reprimanded for skateboarding on the sidewalk.

"Whoa. You don't clean up too bad, Noah," April said on her way by.

Noah liked April, and was about to tell her she wasn't so bad herself, but he happened to catch a glimpse of Lacey at the top of the stairs by her door. Whatever he'd been about to say was wiped from his mind.

That glimpse of Lacey had been fleeting, and yet he started up the stairs like a moth drawn to a flame. At the top, he found her door ajar.

"Lacey?"

Her muffled voice carried from a distant room. "Come in, Noah. I'll be right out. I just have to change purses."

The boxes that had filled the living room several nights ago were gone. There was a slipcover on the sofa and a small glass that held two dandelions on a table beside it. Propped behind the makeshift vase was a photograph of Joey. There was a similar one in a frame in the living room at home.

"Take your time." He was opening a book from the library when Lacey entered the room.

"Hi," she said.

"Hi." He caught her looking at the flowers in his hand. She caught him looking at her in that dress. The color was somewhere between green and blue. The skirt fluttered like a whisper as she walked closer. The neckline ended at a V that whispered something else entirely.

"At first I wasn't sure how this first-date idea was going to go," she said.

He met her in the middle of the room and handed her the bouquet. The flowers had been an afterthought. Witnessing the pleasure she took in them made him wonder what else he'd left out in the past. "And now?" he asked. "How would you say it's going now?"

"So far so good." It was a phrase he'd heard her use often. She was the same Lacey. Or was she?

Their gazes met, held, slid away and met again, and it felt very much like a first date, full of potential and excitement and discovery. Her hair waved close to her face, the ends resting lightly at the delicate ridges of her collarbones. Her lips were shiny, her cheeks bronzed, but her eyes stole the show. Bluer than blue, they were surrounded by lashes that looked a mile long.

"I would offer you something to drink," she said, "but I only recently moved back in, and I started a new job today, and I'm afraid I haven't had a chance to go to the store."

It was exactly the sort of comment someone would make on a first date. "We can get something to drink at the restaurant," he said. "Do you like Italian food?"

He knew she did. And he knew it was going to be a memorable first date when she burst out laughing. This was Lacey. Only better. He was himself, but he was going to be better, too.

She put the flowers in water and switched on a lamp so she wouldn't come home to the dark. Slipping the purse she'd kept him waiting for over her shoulder, she preceded him out the door.

After she'd buckled her seat belt and he'd buckled his, he said, "I just returned from a little trip myself."

He had her in stitches as he described his and Marsh's encounter with Oxman this afternoon. By the time he'd told her about the size-six shoeprint the wrong Julia Monroe had left on the private investigator's cheek, Noah was laughing, too.

The restaurant he'd chosen was one of those chains

that had popped up in college towns throughout the Midwest these past few years. Decorated in faux old-world-Italy style, it wasn't exactly five-star, but Reed had said the food was good, the waitstaff was prompt, and there wasn't a television or a paper napkin in the place.

Since it wasn't the kind of establishment that took reservations, they'd had to wait to be seated. Not long after the hostess led them to a table under a window, their waiter appeared. "Could I interest the two of you in something from the bar?"

Normally Noah's drink requests leaned toward a shot and a beer. Tonight, he ordered a bottle of the house wine, and watched as Lacey turned her attention to her menu. He put his down. He knew what he wanted. He'd already decided what he was going to order, too.

Lacey could feel Noah's gaze on her. Glad to have something to focus on, she continued to peruse the menu, still deciding between the lasagna and the baked chicken. In the back of her mind, she thought April was right. Noah was having trouble keeping his eyes off her in this dress.

April had brought a cache of products with her when she'd arrived. There were potions and lotions, makeup, perfume and jewelry. She'd helped Lacey decide how to wear her hair, and inspected her makeup when Lacey was finished applying it. Lacey had taken April's advice and applied another coat of mascara and a spray of flowery perfume, but she'd decided against wearing a necklace and earrings. The dress was enough.

The waiter arrived with their wine and took their orders. While Noah poured, Lacey studied him unhurriedly. He'd never been pretty-boy handsome, not this man. His features were too rugged to be considered classic. Pretty boys had never appealed to her. Noah had always been a little rough around the edges. Earlier she'd noticed that his belt and shoes were a tad scuffed and his chocolate-brown pants sat just below his waist as if they'd been made for him. The combination of his shaggy hair and tan skin above the open collar of a finely tailored shirt was declaring open season on her senses.

She asked him questions about his work and his travels as if she didn't know him from Adam. And he asked her about hers the same way. Their meals arrived, and they refilled their wineglasses, and they talked about anything and everything under the sun. Much of what they said was simply a refresher course, and, yet, refreshing it was. Somehow it all felt brand-new.

Last night he'd told her they would look back for years to come and remember it as the night they began anew. By the time the waiter brought Noah the check and a take-out box containing the uneaten portion of her entrée, Lacey had already forgotten much of what they'd talked about tonight. It wasn't the conversation that made the night memorable. It was the care Noah took to make sure she had everything she wanted.

She didn't miss the significant look the waiter gave Noah when he took his credit card, or the slight smile Noah gave the young waiter in return. She'd seen that kind of male communication before. It was the equivalent to the beat of distant drums and smoke signals, and it meant *go for it!*

She wasn't certain what Noah was planning, but she could tell what he was thinking by the way his gaze lingered on her mouth, and the base of her neck, and the V of her dress. And knowing sent those butterflies aflutter.

He held the door for her as she got in his truck. Now that the evening was winding down, she rolled her window down and let her hair blow in the onrushing breeze.

He rolled his down, too, and to Lacey it felt a little as if they were flying.

Flying would have explained why the drive back to Division Street lasted only as long as a blink of an eye. The mercury lights were on in the alley when they got there. The poles were spaced apart so that each circle of light ended before the next one began. Noah parked between two of them. And for the first time since the date began, they both fell silent.

She looked over at him. The little gash on his lip had healed, and his hair was windblown now, too. He was looking back at her, and it occurred to her that she didn't know how this night would end, not really. It was part of the great unknown. She didn't have to know. Somehow not knowing added to the excitement and the pleasure.

He drew in a deep breath, and said, "I'll walk you to your door."

Her chest filled with wonder. Would their first date really end at her door?

She slipped out on her side and met him at the front of his truck. They took a leisurely walk up the stairs side by side. At the top, she dug through her purse for her key. A tear sheet from a magazine came out with her keys. "I forgot I brought a personality quiz with me."

"A personality quiz?" He took the key from her and put it in the lock.

"I took it myself last night and brought it along in case we ran out of things to talk about during dinner."

He faced her. The dim yellow light beside her door was behind him, casting his shadow on her. His eyes looked darker, his expression difficult to read. "You took it, you said?"

She nodded.

"What did the results say?"

For a moment the heat in his eyes made her forget the question. In a moment or two, he was going to kiss her good-night. She wondered if he had any idea that she'd been waiting for this kiss since he'd arrived.

Sliding the torn pages back into her shoulder bag, she said, "It turns out I'm not a morning person." She hadn't meant it to sound so sultry and sensual.

"I'll take that under advisement." He placed his hands lightly on her shoulders, drawing her closer. Their mouths touched, and it felt like the beginning, like one of those childhood wishes to go back and do something over, only better, knowing now what she didn't know then.

When he'd asked her earlier if she remembered their first date, she'd told him no. If he'd asked if she remembered their first kiss, she would have said yes. It had happened after he'd finished his six-month stint flying wealthy businessmen from one corner of Texas to the other.

There was a balmy breeze tonight, but that night winter had just begun. It was three days before Christmas and it had been snowing since early afternoon. All anybody Lacey had waited on at The Hill had talked about was Christmas. She'd decorated the tree in the restaurant and another one at home, but she really hadn't been looking forward to Christmas that year.

That changed when the door opened just before closing time. The movement set off the jingle of the sleigh bells Rosy Sirrine had fastened over the door the day after Thanksgiving. The sight of Noah Sullivan staring back at her, the collar of his bomber-style winter coat turned up against the weather and snowflakes melting in his dark shaggy hair, had set off another round of chimes in the pit of Lacey's stomach.

She'd exchanged her white apron for her winter coat,

and he'd walked her home. And she remembered thinking there was nothing more still or magical than the first measurable December snow. They'd talked all the way to the back alley. She didn't recall the subject matter, but she remembered thinking that Christmas was going to come early for her that year.

And it had.

They'd been young and impetuous and more than a little wild back then. He'd kissed her at the bottom of the stairs. That first kiss had led to another, and another, and had landed them both in her bed.

It was summertime now, and all these years later Noah's kiss wasn't impetuous or wild, as their first kiss had been. Tonight, his kiss was a contradiction and a promise, so deeply etched in her memory it might have been entered in an ancient record and yet so new it seemed to have been invented just for them. Unbelievably intimate, it caused her heart to speed up and her thoughts to slow. It was thunder and lighting and a warm, nourishing rain. If it went on forever, it would be over too soon.

She wasn't sure if she swayed closer or if he did. She only knew that her body came up against his—thighs, hips and bellies. A moan escaped her at the proof of how badly he wanted her.

A groan escaped him, too, but he imposed an iron will upon himself. Drawing away gallantly, but with obvious reluctance, he pressed his forehead to hers for a moment. "Good night, Lacey."

"I had a wonderful time, Noah. I mean that."

He watched her slip out of his arms, and he waited until she'd closed the door before starting down the stairs.

Covering her lips with her fingertips to hold in her cheer, she pressed her back against the door. The lamp she'd left on cast a soft glow through the room. She took a deep breath of air scented of roses and lilies and a handful of other flowers in the bouquet he'd given her. He'd never brought her flowers. As much as she'd loved him, she'd never felt quite like this.

Elation bubbled out of her. She spun away from the door and twirled around and around, her skirt billowing like a dancer's. Stopping when she got dizzy, she stood perfectly still, waiting for the room to stop spinning. She looked around the apartment that once had been cluttered with her dad's things. She was beginning to understand what he'd meant by hidden treasure.

She'd always thought she'd wanted one thing. The night they'd broken up, she'd told Noah she wanted a house with a picket fence and a dog and children. Hiding beneath the surface now was something else.

She might always want babies, but she was starting to realize that she could have a rich and meaningful life without having children of her own. She was Aunt Lacey.

As soon as the tavern sold, she would pay off her medical bills, and she would be free to explore another kind of future. Wasn't that what Noah had wanted?

April was bringing a client to see the tavern tomorrow. Lacey thought for a moment about her Houdini, and wondered where she would go if it sold and a new owner reopened the bar. Again, Lacey wondered about the other woman's identity. She was probably downstairs getting comfortable right now.

The idea piqued her curiosity. *Was* she downstairs right now?

Where did she go during the day? And why had she chosen Bell's Tavern? How on earth was she getting in?

Lacey's silent questions led her to her door.

Opening it an inch at a time, she peered out. She knew every hiding place in the alley. She also knew which window was near the pool table. What if she tiptoed down the stairs and took a little peek inside? It was still her tavern, after all. What harm could there be in slipping into the shadows where the mercury light didn't reach?

She opened her door a little farther. It was midnight. The moon was out, spilling weak silver light onto the stairs. She turned one ear to the night. Voices and music carried from the outdoor tables at the Alibi Bar across Division Street, but the alley itself was quiet.

Lacey slipped out onto the stoop and carefully drew the door shut. She peered down into the shadows. Satisfied that the coast was clear, she tiptoed down the steps. Again, she listened intently. Hearing nothing, she crept silently from shadow to shadow. At the building, she ducked down like a cat burglar and scuttled beneath the first window where the for-sale sign now hung from the inside. Up and down she went until she came to the window in the far corner.

Her heart was racing with excitement now. Rising up on tiptoe, she looked in. Seeing only her own reflection, she pressed her nose closer. She curled her hands beside her eyes like field glasses and leaned all the way to the glass. That was better. She could see one end of the pool table. She inched to the next pane, and studied the patch of moonlight spilling onto the floor. Try as she might, she couldn't make out the sleeping bag underneath. Or wait. Was someone inside?

Her breath caught at the possibility. She had to go up on tiptoe to see better. Nobody was inside, at least nobody she could see. That had obviously been wishful thinking.

She was in the middle of heaving a deep sigh when a

hand cupped her shoulder. A big, heavy, strong, terrifying hand.

Her heart reared up and alarm bells clanged in her head. She spun around and opened her mouth to scream.

Chapter Eight

Oh-my-god-oh-my-god-oh-my-god. This was it. The moment every woman feared.

Lacey knew better than to skulk around in dark alleys, even in towns with only 25,000 people. This was the price she paid for throwing caution to the wind. How could she have been so trusting, so stupid? She would probably be murdered, her body never found. Or worse.

She spun around. Fright—stark and vivid—lodged in her throat. She couldn't even scream. Or breathe. Or think.

"It's okay, Lacey, it's me."

She blinked in the darkness. Her heart was racing so fast she thought she'd heard somebody call her by name.

"Are you okay?"

She knew that voice. A man dressed in dark pants and shirt, making him all but invisible, stood a few feet from her. She peered up at him.

Noah?

He wasn't an ax murderer. Or a rapist. Or her Houdini. It was Noah.

Her heart was racing. It wasn't a good feeling, and it couldn't be good for her. Her hands automatically went to her hips and that fighter's chin of hers went up. "Somebody needs to put a bell on you. You should know better than to scare people like that. What if I had a weapon or a black belt in karate or a bad heart? What are you doing here, anyway?"

He held up the white box from the restaurant. "You left this in my truck." There was an edge of annoyance in his voice, but he continued his explanation. "I was going the wrong direction when I remembered your leftovers. The cop I saw made me think twice about doing a U-turn, so I parked on Division Street and walked over. I think the question should be what the hell are *you* doing out here?"

She ducked her head.

Noah knew that tactic. It was a ruse to buy Lacey some time until she thought of a way to change the subject.

"I forgot all about my doggie bag," she said, gesturing to the square box in his hand. "You didn't have to make a special trip to bring it back. But thank you just the same."

Noah saw through the innocent act like a picture window. He took a step backward, putting a little distance between them. The near-darkness bleached the color out of everything, so that her pale aqua dress looked silver. Her face was pale, too. He couldn't see the expression in her eyes, but they were wide-open. Undeterred, he asked, "Why were you looking in the window?"

"Shh." She glanced over her shoulder. "She'll hear you."

She stopped so quickly he knew she hadn't meant to say that. "Why were you looking in the window?" he said again, intentionally louder.

She covered his mouth with her hand. Making a show

of looking all around again, she removed her hand and said, "If I have to tell you I'd rather not do it down here where everybody and anybody might hear."

She didn't exactly stomp her feet, but she didn't make any attempt to be quiet as she led the way up the steps. At the top she opened the door and traipsed on in. She didn't turn around until he'd closed the door firmly behind him.

In no mood to make concessions, he took the leftovers to the kitchen and stuck the foam box in the old refrigerator. After closing the door with a loud clank and making sure the handle was latched, he retraced his steps and found her still standing in the center of the room. Her color was heightened. Her eyes were large and round, her mascara smudged slightly. Something was going on, and he wasn't leaving until he knew what it was.

He folded his arms, waiting.

She raised her big blue eyes to his. She must have realized that he wasn't going anywhere until she told him the truth, because she heaved a great sigh and finally began. "If you must know I was hoping to get a glimpse of Houdini."

It was his turn to do a double take. "I thought Houdini was dead."

"What? Oh. He is."

"Since when do you believe in ghosts?" he asked.

With a roll of her eyes, she said, "Her name isn't really Houdini."

"Whose name?" he asked, louder again.

"Whoever has been sleeping underneath my pool table." She blinked, gnashed her molars together and groaned. Obviously, she hadn't meant to say that, either.

"Somebody has been sleeping under the pool table? Downstairs? In the tavern? Right below you?" His voice grew louder with every question.

She winced. She might say nothing, but she wouldn't lie. He knew from experience that she couldn't help telling the truth, even when it pained her.

"I thought you had the locks changed."

"I did."

"You're telling me somebody is breaking into the tavern? An out-of-business, closed, empty tavern? On a regular basis?" Okay, he admitted that was a little loud, even for him. Toning it down to a less deafening decibel level, he said, "And you thought, what? That you were going to catch him red-handed? You could have been killed. Did you think of that?"

"Actually, I didn't think of that until you showed up."

Failing to see the humor, he reached into his pocket and pulled out his phone. "I'm calling the police."

"Noah, don't."

He'd already pressed the nine and the one.

"I called the police," she said.

He paused, his finger on the final number. "I don't hear any sirens."

"I didn't call them tonight." She huffed as if he was really starting to annoy her. "I called them when I discovered the sleeping bag and water bottle tucked out of sight underneath the pool table."

"When was that?"

She glanced at the clock. "It's after midnight, so I guess technically it was four days ago now."

He remembered how spooked she'd been when he'd caught her unawares down in the bar the other day when he'd come over to apologize for accusing her of deserting Joey. Now he understood why she'd been so nervous. It would have been nice if she had told him then rather than risk her life by herself. But, of course, she wouldn't have told him. They hadn't been a couple then.

He had every intention of rectifying that, but first he was going to get to the bottom of this. He widened his stance a little and put his hands on his hips again. "What did the police say?"

"Maybe we should sit down."

Obviously, this wasn't going to be a short story. He glanced at his two options and chose the old leather recliner. He sank deep into the cushion. Rather than sit back, he leaned forward, his knees apart, his elbows resting on his thighs.

Lacey lowered herself daintily to the sofa adjacent to him. "Perhaps I should start at the beginning." She sat forward, too, her knees together beneath her skirt, her hands clasped. "The other day I was showing April through the tavern. She was taking measurements for the listing and I happened to notice a cue stick lying out. Then I saw something sticking out from underneath the pool table. It was a sleeping bag. I knew it hadn't been there when I swept the day before."

"So you called the police."

She nodded. "They sent a seasoned officer who checked all the windows and doors and locks. Everything was buttoned up nice and tight. Since the sleeping bag was narrow and on the feminine side, he said it was probably some young high-school or college student or maybe a runaway just passing through town. He was pretty sure she wouldn't be back."

Noah took an easier breath.

Lacey ruined that when she said, "But then yesterday I found a partially eaten bag of mixed nuts, and the water bottle had been replaced with a bottle of green tea."

He sat up straighter. Something about this bothered the back of his mind. Hell, everything about this bothered the back of his mind.

"I still don't know how she's getting in and out—that's why I call her Houdini," Lacey said. "I'm pretty sure Officer Pratt was right about her gender because there was a pink lipstick print on her water bottle and she has long brown hair."

"You've seen her?" he asked.

She shook her head once. "I found a strand of her hair on the sleeping bag last night."

He stood. "Get your things together."

"What?" She rose, too. "What things?"

"A suitcase. With a change of clothes and whatever else you need. You're staying with us."

"Noah, I'm not packing my suitcase." He opened his mouth, but before he could tell her she sure as hell was, she said, "I'm not going anywhere."

"Somebody is living in the bar. It could be anybody. A vagrant. A murderer. A lunatic. A serial killer."

"She's not a murderer or a lunatic or a serial killer."

"You don't know that. And if this person can get around the locks downstairs, she could get in up here. Pack your things."

The only move she made was to dig in her heels.

"Why are you arguing?" he demanded, turning toward her.

"I'm not arguing."

"You're right," he said impatiently. "You're flat-out refusing to see reason."

"Where is the reason? Noah, I spent my formative years in this apartment. There were far scarier people than this girl walking by at all hours of the night, shattering beer bottles, howling at the moon. Why are you worried now?"

He clamped his mouth shut so hard she probably heard it. He hated that she was right. Nobody liked to be wrong, but in this instance it was worse because it reminded him of how much he'd taken for granted.

Why was he worried now? A better question would have been why hadn't he worried about her back then? He should have been scared out of his mind. Her dad had spent every night behind the bar serving drinks to his customers. Lacey could have gone anywhere and done anything, and often did. And yet Noah hadn't experienced this brand of fear until now. It was a direct result of that headlong, head-over-heels tumble he felt himself taking for her.

"I don't want anything bad to happen to you, all right?" he said.

She smiled. And he wanted to bite through his cheek.

His groan had a lot in common with a growl. He put both hands on his head, and stood looking at her, his elbows akimbo and his hair sticking out. "Why do you want to stay here when you know somebody is breaking in and out of a locked building?"

"Because I'm not afraid."

"You're not afraid." He let his hands fall to his sides.

"There," she said, tipping her head ever so much. "See? I knew you would understand."

"You're not afraid."

Her smile brightened. "I haven't been afraid all night."

Noah faced the fact that Lacey wasn't talking about things that went bump in the dark or this mysterious Houdini wannabe anymore. She wasn't *afraid* of what was happening between them. Damn this burgeoning admiration.

Then and there he wanted to swing her into his arms and carry her to bed. He'd start by untying the sash at the side of her waist of that amazing blue-green concoction she was wearing, and then he'd move to the straps at her shoulders. He would take his time there; he would take his time everywhere.

"But if it'll make you feel better," she said, "there is one thing I'd be willing to do."

Only one? he thought. "There is?" he asked. "And what's that?"

"I could give you my phone number if you'd like. If it isn't too forward of me after only the first date."

"You're something else, do you know that?" he asked.

"Are you just figuring that out?"

She had him there.

She recited her phone number as she walked to the door. She opened it and held it. Saying nothing, she waited for him to take the hint. Hitting him over the head with a two-by-four would have been a hint. This was less subtle.

For a split second he considered grasping her hand and pulling her out onto the stoop with him. Keeping her firmly at his side, he would proclaim to the world that Lacey Bell was his.

But that was part of step three. He couldn't take that leap just yet. He owed her a courtship, dammit, so he walked out the door she was holding open. Over his shoulder, he said, "Lock that. Wedge a chair under the damn doorknob, too."

"I will, but only because I know it'll make you feel better."

On his way to his parked truck on Division Street, he looked back. Her door was closed. In his mind's eye he saw her dragging a chair from the kitchen and wedging it beneath the doorknob. She'd said she would, and she didn't lie.

He met two groups of people taking a shortcut through the alley. The first looked like a couple of old army buddies. The second was a man and woman he'd seen having drinks at the outside tables in front of the Alibi across the way. Nobody had long brown hair.

Long brown hair.

He'd lost track of how many times that description had come up in less than twenty-four hours. Marsh said his Julia had had long brown hair when he'd known her. And Lacey believed her intruder had long brown hair, too. Was there a connection they were all missing?

Four days ago Lacey had noticed the sleeping bag under the pool table for the first time. The night before that somebody had left Joey on the Sullivans' porch. Now Noah wondered if it was the same woman.

That would be the mother of all coincidences, but it didn't explain how Lacey's Houdini was getting in, or why. And if she were Marsh's Julia, why would she leave the baby with them and then stay nearby in a deserted tavern? There were a dozen whys, and just as many ifs, ands and buts. It was enough to make his head pound.

Noah dug his keys out of his pocket and started his truck. At the red light he pulled his phone out, too. He slid it open and deftly pressed the number from memory. Before the light turned green, he broke the golden rule of first dates.

"I have an idea," he said after Lacey answered.

He hadn't waited twenty-four hours to call. He hadn't even waited until he got home. That was a no-no.

"What kind of idea?" He heard the smile in her voice.

"For our second date," he said. No-no number two— never assume.

"What did you have in mind?" Had her voice always been so sultry and deep?

"Have you ever been on a stakeout?" he asked.

"Oh, Noah, that's a great idea. It so happens I know the perfect place."

"I figured you would. I'm going to call Sam tomorrow and get a few pointers. I'll call you then."

She disconnected first, but not before he heard her little gleeful giggle. Noah was shaking his head when he hung up. If anybody had been looking they would have seen that he was smiling, too.

"Today might need to be reclassified," Noah said.

Something told Lacey that Noah wasn't referring to the fact that Marsh and Reed had decided they didn't need the services of a temporary nanny on the weekend and therefore she had the day off. One hand at the small of her back, she went around to the other side of the old whiskey barrel she was filling with petunias and waited for Noah to make his point. Ultimately, his silence drew her gaze.

Bent at the waist, he stood on the fourth step from the bottom of the staircase leading to her apartment. He had a wide paintbrush in his hand. A gallon of gray paint sat on another step.

Lacey had never been accused of being particularly patient, but in this case the view gave her plenty to appreciate while she waited for him to continue. His jeans were faded, his legs long, his backside just muscular enough to be interesting. The temperature had reached eighty-six degrees today. Here in the alley the bricks and the blacktop had soaked up the heat until it felt like at least a hundred. There hadn't been more than a whisper of a breeze all evening. Noah had shed his shirt an hour ago before the sun sailed out of sight behind the tall buildings on the opposite side of the alley.

He finished painting another step, then slowly straightened up. Making a show of stretching, he cast a casual glance over his shoulder as a group of people strolled past. Lacey saw them, too. There were three men, all of them balding, and four women, all with short hair. Like every-one else who'd taken this shortcut to the Orchard Hill Theater's grand reopening a few blocks away, they seemed to have no idea that the painting and flower-planting was a cover for the stakeout Lacey and Noah were conducting.

Going down another step, Noah dipped his paintbrush in the can again. "I don't think there are two other people in the world who've had a second date like this."

So that's what he'd meant by *reclassification.* Stepping back to view the barrel now filled with yellow, lavender and white flowers next to the stairs, Lacey said, "When we first moved to Orchard Hill, these steps were open. For my fourteenth birthday I asked my dad to install the boards on the back so I wouldn't be terrified that some-body was going to grab my ankle every time I went up or down."

She found herself looking at her pointer finger poking through the hole in the end of the brand-new garden glove she'd found in the clearance bin, remembering the young girl she'd been at fourteen. "Dad bought the lumber that very day. For my birthday a week later he converted the hall closet into a darkroom. I got a decorated cake and a new camera, too."

Finding Noah still looking at her, she smiled.

"Never let it be said I don't know how to work the sys-tem."

"You're saying you don't mind this so-called date?" He gestured to their tasks, to the alley setting and the lack of privacy.

"Mind? This is the most fun I've ever had on a second date. And those steps look fantastic. April was right. A coat of paint on the stairs and these flowers next to them really helps to make the entrance to the apartment look more inviting. Hopefully, buyers will agree."

"I thought you might reconsider selling and reopen the bar," he said, moving down yet another step.

She shook her head. "That would take money. Besides, if I could be anything in the world, I wouldn't be a bar-keep."

Noah resumed painting. Noticing the play of light where the sky met the roof of the building on the opposite side of the alley, she automatically reached for her camera. She set the focus then snapped a picture. Next a petunia just opening in the whiskey barrel caught her eye. She took a close-up of it, her garden glove now lying next to it. Through her lens she discovered a ladybug she hadn't noticed before.

She was still taking pictures when Noah finished painting the last step. "Are you hungry?" he asked.

"Starving," she said, snapping a picture of him, too.

"Pizza?"

They'd been taking turns going after something one or the other of them needed. When Noah ran out of paint, she'd gone to the hardware store for another gallon, leaving him to keep watch in the alley. When she'd needed more potting soil, he'd gone and she'd stayed behind.

"It's my turn," she said. "I need to wash my hands before I go." She was looking at the soil on the tip of her pointer finger, and might have started up the freshly painted steps if Noah hadn't pulled her back.

Since she couldn't very well go out for food without washing her hands, she said, "Maybe you could go pick up a pizza."

She followed the course of his gaze to the black T-shirt draped over the railing at the top. Until the paint dried, he couldn't retrieve his shirt, and without a shirt, he couldn't go into any restaurant in Orchard Hill.

As he extracted his phone from the front pocket of his

blue jeans, she took advantage of this legitimate reason to be looking there. When she'd first met him, he'd been thin as a rail. He was one of those guys who would always be lanky, but he'd filled out over the years. His shoulders had broadened and his chest was muscled and accentuated by a spattering of dark curly hair. She glanced away because, well, because this was only their second date for one thing.

Eventually, she noticed that he'd grown silent. It occurred to her that he'd asked her a question. Since he was ordering the pizza, it stood to reason that his question had to do with that. "Surprise me," she said.

And that was exactly what Noah did.

He surprised her when the pizza arrived and he lowered the tailgate on his truck and helped her up as if he were holding her chair in a fine French restaurant. He surprised her when he asked her if she still had that personality quiz she'd mentioned yesterday. After she ran to the cab of his truck where she'd stashed her purse, and brought the tear sheets back with her, he surprised her again and again.

She gave him the quiz between bites of pepperoni-and-mushroom pizza with green peppers and extra cheese. She didn't bother asking him to explain his viewpoint about clowns, but she couldn't help peering over her fountain Coke at him about his latest reply. "Spiders are worse than snakes? Are you kidding me?"

"If I don't answer truthfully I don't see how the results would be accurate," he said.

"Fine. B. Spiders." She circled the corresponding letter. "Even though spiders build incredibly delicate, yet strong—not to mention beautiful—webs out of a substance they produce themselves. Snakes don't build anything."

He shrugged one broad, bare shoulder. If he had issues,

his masculinity obviously wasn't one of them. "I think snakes are sexy."

She made a sound of pure disgust. "There is nothing sexy about a snake."

"Tell that to Adam and Eve."

Darkness was falling fast. The mercury lights came on while Lacey's blood was thickening and her thoughts were wandering to naughty scenarios. It was no wonder it took her longer than it should have to calculate his score.

"Am I a night owl, too?" he asked, biting into the last slice.

She carried his total to the results section on the back. She read the short paragraph describing his character type then wadded the paper into a ball. He rescued it from the pizza box and smoothed it out.

Reading the explanation pertaining to his score, he smiled. "I'm morning, noon and night? You don't have to worry about it going to my head." His gaze met hers, and she knew where it was going.

Noah couldn't remember when he'd had this much fun. He admitted that Lacey was right. This may not have been a typical second date, but it was one he would never forget. It wasn't easy to take his eyes off Lacey, and hadn't been since he'd arrived three hours ago. She wore flip-flops and faded cutoffs and a tank top the color of ripe peaches. She'd been wearing a shirt over it when he'd gotten here. It was one of those little feminine numbers, so thin it was practically transparent with pearly buttons and little dots all over it. She'd taken it off about the same time he'd peeled off his T-shirt.

Three teenage girls ran by, giggling. Two of them had long hair. Only one was a brunette and her hair was extremely curly. Lacey and Noah watched them, committing their appearance to memory. So far their stakeout hadn't produced any young women with long, straight brown hair.

When Noah had spoken to Sam on the phone, the P.I. said private investigation work was ninety-eight percent sitting still. "Trust me, the other two percent makes all the boredom worth it."

Noah hadn't been bored. The fact that he'd had fun painting steps was a testament to the company he was keeping.

When they finished eating, he touched the steps with his fingertips. Deeming them dry, he went up and retrieved his shirt. He pulled it on, then stood looking down at the alley. Lacey was donning her shirt, too.

She'd worn her hair up today, fastened near the top of her head with a shiny clip. As the afternoon turned into evening, more and more tendrils had escaped, curling at her nape and around her ears. Her face was shiny, and there was a smudge of dirt on her shorts. She'd looked beautiful last night in that dress. She looked just as beautiful today.

He started down the steps toward her.

"Is that 'Moon over Miami'?" she called out of the blue.

His attention had been so intent upon her he hadn't noticed the song wafting from a passing radio. Every time a car went by the entrance of the alley, its radio blasting, they'd tried to name the title of the song. It had been Lacey's idea. She could make a game out of anything.

She'd seen their second date's potential from the beginning. There were so many things he was discovering about her. She'd always been a stickler for washing her hands. Until he'd watched her eat her pizza with a napkin wrapped around her pointer finger, he hadn't realized just how germ-phobic she was.

And she knew something about everything. She was

the one who'd told him that new owners were reopening the Orchard Hill Theater. She'd spoken about a grant the city had been awarded for a beautification project that included sprucing up the town's sidewalks, storefronts and alleys.

Noah agreed that the steps looked better with a coat of paint and the flowers, but the real beauty back here was Lacey. There wasn't anything about her he didn't like. Even her stubborn streak was adorable. Marsh and Reed would have called it the blush of a new relationship. In reality, theirs was the blush of an old one.

Gearing up for step three, he met Lacey at the bottom of the stairs, on her way to the trash can underneath them. Since her hands were full of the empty pizza box, napkins and paper drink cups, he went with her and removed the trash can's lid.

"What would you be?" he asked.

She looked up at him in the near darkness, a little furrow forming between her eyes. He wasn't surprised that she had no idea what he was talking about. What surprised him—and humbled him—was that he'd never asked the question before.

"Earlier you said if you could be anything in the world, you *wouldn't* be a barkeep. What would you be?"

He could see the pleasure his interest brought her. Since the clip was sliding from her hair, she whisked it out and shook her hair down. "I would be a professional photographer. I started photography classes in Chicago."

Of course that was what she wanted to be. He remembered the first time he saw her walking to school, her hair short and her jeans tight, a chip on her shoulder and a camera around her neck. She never knew it, but he'd had his eye on her for a long time.

"Now it's your turn," she said. At his blank look, she added, "Tell me something I don't know about you."

From out of the blue, he heard himself say, "My grandfather was a well witcher. And now I think I'd like to kiss you."

When Noah was a kid, he'd seen his grandfather find an underground spring using two divining rods he'd fashioned from pieces of wire. Somehow the electromagnetic field flowing through the water was transmitted up through his grandfather's body and out his hands, causing the rods to cross.

Until Lacey reached up and touched his cheek with the tips of three fingers, slowly letting them trail to his mouth, Noah had never understood the concept of electromagnetism. Her touch changed that. Electricity arced from her body to his, buzzing in places indirectly connected.

"A well witcher, really?" Her smile was sexy as hell. "The kissing part I already knew."

With his heart thundering in his ears and his desire kicking into overdrive, he covered her slender hand with his. Slowly, he dragged it from his lips to his chest. He wanted her to feel what she was doing to his heartbeat before he'd even kissed her.

Her lips parted in the most enticing manner. He swooped down and covered them with his. At that first melding, his heart reared up, then settled into a rhythm that grew stronger with every beat.

The staircase made their little refuge feel secluded. The shadows made it intimate. But it was the touch of his mouth on hers that made it feel like heaven.

Lacey felt Noah's arms come around her, felt herself being drawn up, folded into his embrace. Heat radiated from the entire length of his body, branding every inch of her body that came into contact with every inch of his.

She went up on tiptoe, diving into a frenzied kiss. She didn't know how he did it, how he made every kiss feel different than the last one. This kiss was rough and possessive, a wild mating of mouths and heat and hunger. As far as second dates went, tonight had been astoundingly wonderful. As far as kisses went, this one was off the charts.

Need shot up between them, the need to open her mouth and deepen the kiss, the need to stroke, retreat and stroke again, the need to look back at where they'd been and look forward to where they might go. More than anything was the need to savor Noah's heat, his passion, right here, right now.

Savor, she did. He kissed her, and she let him. She kissed him back, until she didn't know where she left off and he began. It was amazing. It was heady. It melted her from the inside out.

It might have gone on forever, had a sound from up above not penetrated her consciousness. She heard a little scrape of wood against wood. It almost sounded as if a window was being opened. She was still kissing Noah, her lips apart, their bodies in tune with a dance they hadn't experienced in more than a year.

The sound of wood scraping against wood came again. This time it was followed by a thud.

Noah must have heard it, too. His lips stopped moving against hers, and he held perfectly still.

The hollow thud of feet landing on the ground ten feet away severed the kiss in one fell swoop. She and Noah jerked apart and turned their heads. They saw the woman at the exact instant she saw them.

They all froze.

The young woman recovered first. She spun on her heel, dark brown hair nearly reaching her waist billowing like a curtain as she went.

"Wait!" Noah untangled his arms from Lacey's and started after her.

He saw her cut between the tavern and the store next door. He darted in after her, his breathing ragged, his eyes trained on the svelte creature pulling farther away. The space between the buildings was so narrow that his shoulders occasionally touched the bricks on either side as he ran. The walkway was lit only at the ends. Here in the center, he could barely make out the shape of the woman up ahead.

He was a fast runner. She was faster. Part gazelle, part acrobat, she scaled the wrought-iron gate that blocked the entry from Division Street, then bounded to the right without looking back. He went up the gate, too. From the top, he searched for a young woman with waist-length brown hair.

The Orchard Hill Theater had just let out, and throngs of people milled about the sidewalk. His gaze darted in every direction, but she seemed to have disappeared among them.

He jumped from the top of the gate. Landing lightly on his feet, he made a quick sweep up one side of Division Street and down the other. He didn't find her between buildings, in doorways or porticos. She might have literally disappeared.

It was no wonder Lacey called her Houdini. Like a siren or a forest sprite, she slipped out of buildings and scaled fences and seemed to disappear into thin air. The famous magician had used smoke and mirrors and a cape, and had taken the secret for his astonishing escapes with him to his grave. This girl's only cape was her long brown hair;

her smoke and mirrors were her speed and agility. She had no assistant to wave her arms and draw the crowd's attention, no props or publicity. Her secret remained a mystery. And so did her identity.

Noah took a different route back to the alley, back to Lacey and to what was turning out to be a very unusual, though invigorating and interesting, second date.

Chapter Nine

When Noah returned to the alley, Lacey was sitting on the steps. She stood as he sauntered closer and, with a lift of her eyebrows, asked him a silent question. He answered just as silently with a shake of his head. Their mysterious Houdini remained at large.

The alley was losing its heat to the darkness and the stars their brightness to the blue haze of the mercury lights nearby. Many of the same people she'd noticed going toward Division Street earlier had already come by again in the opposite direction. As the murmur of voices grew distant, she and Noah returned to the place the young woman had been.

"I found something interesting," Lacey said, holding out her hand.

She showed him something that resembled a credit card. Taking it from her fingers, he held it to the light. "A bus pass?"

She nodded. "It's a prepaid bus pass. It must have fallen out of her pocket when she was climbing down."

"We don't know who she is," Noah said, handing the pass back to her. "We don't know where she came from, why she's here or where she's going, but apparently she's riding the city bus to get there."

Lacey peered up at the second-story window. "Now we also know how she's getting in and out of the tavern."

"What's up there?" Noah asked.

"Nothing much. The upstairs is a big empty loft. My dad always talked about converting it into another apartment, but he never did."

"What's in the room directly below the window?" he persisted.

"The storage room. Why?"

Two stragglers wandered through the alley. Lacey and Noah took note of them out of habit as they passed. After a moment of quiet deliberation, he went to his truck and opened the passenger-side door. He rifled through the glove compartment, and returned with a slim flashlight. Sliding it into his back pocket, he said, "Did you get a good look at her?"

"I did."

"So did I. How old would you say she is?" he asked.

Lacey looked up at Noah's profile. He was studying the galvanized pipe that ran up the side of the building to the roof. It had been cut off six feet above the ground and capped years ago. It no longer served as a downspout, but the girl must have used it to climb up and down.

"She looked seventeen or eighteen to me. Not more than twenty," Lacey said.

"That's what I thought, too." A bead of perspiration trailed down the side of his face. His breathing was almost back to normal, though, his mind seemingly on the puzzle he was trying to solve. "She isn't Joey's mother." He said it so quietly he might have been thinking aloud.

Lacey felt her eyes widen. "Did you think she might have been?"

He was looking at her now. The moon and stars were competing with the mercury lights, but they were no competition for the glint in Noah's eyes as he nodded. "Her arrival coincided with Joey's, but the women Marsh and Reed are looking for are both over thirty. Something doesn't add up."

He wiped his hands on his jeans. Rubbing them together, he gave her a smile he reserved for situations involving risking life or limb or both, then reached high and grasped the pipe with both hands. He pulled himself up until he had a toehold, scaling the brick wall inches at a time. He gripped the pipe between his knees and ankles, reached out with one hand and carefully raised the window.

There was a victorious smile on his face when he looked down at Lacey. She gasped when he slipped, but he quickly regained his footing. It must have taken a great deal of concentration and agility to throw his left leg over the windowsill.

Before he could duck inside, she said, "You still think there's a connection, don't you, between the young woman we saw and Joey's mother?"

Balancing on the window ledge fifteen feet above the ground, he could have been an outlaw of old, his hair shaggy, his jaw darkened by a day-old beard, his golden-brown eyes delving into hers. "I believe in coincidence less and less every day," he said.

This wasn't the time or the place to discuss his philosophy regarding destiny, and yet she got the distinct impression he was including her in his statement. She had to admit that she felt energized by the idea that maybe it wasn't a coincidence that she was back in Orchard Hill and Noah was back in Orchard Hill. Maybe there really was a method to the universe's madness.

"I'll meet you inside," he said.

"It's a date."

He looked down again and said, "I think it's time to proceed to step three." His voice was rich and sincere, but there was something lurking behind his grin, something unknown but not quite hidden.

On the brink of that precipice that was the rest of her life again, she ran up the newly painted stairs for her key.

Lacey had the back door open and the lights on inside the tavern when she heard footsteps overhead. The sound led her to the storage room where her father used to keep boxes of peanuts and pretzels, and crates of whiskey and scotch, and untapped kegs of beer. The shelves were crude and empty now, and all that remained was a leftover wooden crate and another whiskey barrel like the one she'd planted flowers in earlier.

A ceiling tile jiggled, and then it was being lifted away from above. The next thing she knew, Noah was lowering himself feetfirst through the opening.

He dropped lightly to the floor, brushed himself off and turned toward her. "It's hot up there. I'm not surprised she prefers it down here. She let herself downstairs through this ceiling tile, but she was using two windows to get in and out of the building, this one and one on the east side of the building. She may run like the wind but your Houdini left footprints that were easy to follow."

"Did she leave anything else?" Lacey asked.

"Nothing that I could find. Where's this bedroll she's been sleeping on?"

She led the way from the storeroom to the back corner of the tavern. They both hunkered down at the far end of the pool table. The sleeping bag was still there but the snacks were gone.

"Tell me why you think she has something to do with Joey's arrival on your doorstep." She spoke quietly, reverently almost.

Resting his forearms on his thighs, Noah said, "It's just a hunch."

"What connection could she have to your situation?" she asked.

"I don't know, but the timing is right. As I said, it's just a hunch."

"You don't think she'll come back here again now, do you?" she asked.

"You know her better than I do. What do you think?"

They both stood up slowly.

A little taken aback by the fact that Noah seemed to understand Lacey's affinity for her guest, she said, "Whoever she is and whatever she's doing in Orchard Hill, she's street-smart. She won't want to risk getting caught. I almost wish we hadn't seen her. At least then she would be safe. Where will she sleep now?"

"You said it yourself," Noah replied. "She's street-smart. She'll find a safe place. If my hunch is right, and her arrival is somehow connected to Joey's, we haven't seen the last of her."

The idea chased Lacey's melancholy away. She couldn't explain it, but she felt a kinship with this unknown and mysterious young woman.

She shook out the sleeping bag. Folding it neatly, she left it on top of the pool table and added the bus pass, just in case the girl returned for either one.

Noah went to the storage room. Standing on an old

crate, he slid the ceiling tile back into place. Lacey turned out the lights. They went out together, and she locked the door.

The wind had picked up, ruffling the collar of her airy shirt and sifting through his dark brown hair. He'd surprised her so many times today. It began when he'd offered to paint her steps, and continued when he'd asked to take that silly personality quiz, when he'd raced after her Houdini and when he'd climbed up the brick wall.

He surprised her again when he took her hand, and held, just held it. "I should go," he said. "Marsh and Reed are going to want to hear about our encounter with your Houdini. Madeline and Riley have invited all of us up to Traverse City for Sunday dinner tomorrow. I want to tell Marsh and Reed about tonight before they leave. I'm sure they're going to want to talk to Sam Lafferty."

"You're not going to Madeline's?" she asked.

"I have something more important to do tomorrow." His voice had taken on a sleepy huskiness that didn't necessarily mean he was sleepy again.

"More important than visiting your sister?" Lacey noticed her voice had grown a little husky, too.

He inched closer, his hand still cradling hers. "After everything my baby sister has been through, believe me, she'll understand that what I'm planning for tomorrow needs to be my top priority."

"What are you planning for tomorrow?" she asked, her eyes on his.

"You don't really want me to spoil the surprise, do you?"

Her heart teetered slightly, because he was right. She wanted the anticipation, this prelude and, yes, she wanted to be surprised, even though waiting for surprises was almost unbearable.

"I *will* tell you this much," he said, his mouth a few inches from hers. "Tomorrow is the beginning of step three. I still have a lot to do, but I should be ready by five. Can I pick you up then?"

She nodded. And then he kissed her full on the mouth. He left her breathless and wanting, and eager to see him again.

The American flag Tom Bender raised to the top of the flagpole outside his office window every morning flapped in the breeze blowing across the tarmac. Lacey and Noah were caught between that same breeze and the warm air whirling from the propeller of Noah's newly restored Piper Cherokee.

He'd arrived to pick her up a few minutes early. His hair still damp from his shower, he'd wasted no time on small talk. "Are you ready?" he'd asked the moment she opened the door.

Ready? She'd taken a bubble bath, dried her hair, applied her makeup and changed her clothes four times. Oh, my, yes, was she ever ready. She was practically bursting with readiness.

"Where are we going?" she'd finally asked after he'd pulled onto Orchard Highway.

He crested a hill and said, "There's something I want to show you."

He was wearing blue jeans and a blue cotton shirt with buttons down the front. When he turned into the county airfield, she was glad she'd decided on jeans, too. "Is your airplane finished?"

Noah didn't blame Lacey for being curious. Patience had never been her strong suit. Waiting until Christmas morning to open her presents had been excruciating for her. There was no hiding place she didn't discover, no wrapping paper she didn't tamper with. She was being a hell of a sport. A few minutes from now, he planned to make the wait worth her while.

When they'd first arrived at the airstrip, he'd gone inside to check the computer and radar. The wind had picked up an hour ago, and was coming straight out of the north, pressing a mass of hot air ahead of it. There was a thunderstorm sitting behind it, but the front was moving slowly. It was a little after six now and, as luck would have it, he was going to have plenty of time before it hit.

Just then his sleek white airplane taxied from behind the first hangar. "My plane is finished," he said with a sense of undeniable pride, "but that's not the main attraction."

A Cessna landed on the second runway. Noah paid close attention to the engine speed and the sound of the brakes immediately after it touched down.

"Could you at least give me a hint?" she asked.

"I'd rather show you." He took her hand and led her out onto the tarmac where Digger was making another pass with Noah's plane. The Piper was a beauty, if he did say so himself. They'd finished her test run this morning, and she'd passed every inspection with flying colors. The engine hummed, the electrical system worked perfectly and so did the rudder, the propeller, the landing gear and ailerons, the beacon lights and navigational signal and every gauge on the dash. She'd been two years in the making and now she was all his.

"Is Digger going to fly the plane?" Lacey yelled. "Is that what you want to show me?"

Noah shook his head. For two years Digger had been helping Noah restore the Piper from a beat-up relic to this flight-ready beauty. All he would accept as payment was first taxiing rights after the last tweaking had been done.

Noah could see Digger inside the cockpit, an old leather cap and goggles on his head and a big old smile on his face. Digger didn't fly—not anymore. One of these days he would deal with his issues, but not today.

He finished his loop around the airfield and brought her back to Noah. He cut the engine, opened the door and climbed down.

Lacey didn't know it yet, but Noah had faced the fear that had been eating at his insides since his parents' accident. As he took her fingers in his and led her to the plane, he'd never felt so free.

He ran his hand along the Piper's left wing. Next, he helped Lacey up. When he was in his seat, too, they fastened their belts. He flipped switches and started the engine. In almost no time they were rolling forward. He made adjustments for the direction and speed of the wind, and poured on the power.

He kept his eyes on the dials and instruments on the dash, his hands on the control wheel, his feet on the pedals on the floor. Ground lights and runway markers blurred in his peripheral vision. One second the plane was barreling across the ground. The next she was airborne.

Every takeoff was a thrill. This one was special. Not because he was flying his own airplane, although that added to the excitement, but because of the woman sitting in the noisy cockpit with him, her hair windblown, her cheeks pink, her eyes bluer than the sky.

He climbed to two thousand feet before he leveled off. He didn't see another airplane in the sky tonight, but in the distance was the Chestnut River. Two miles north of it was what Noah had been working on today.

He began his descent. When he was directly over his mark, he tipped the wing so Lacey could see all the way to the ground. He knew the moment she saw it, for her breath caught and her mouth opened.

Nine months out of the year, the meadow east of the orchard was just that, a meadow. Every autumn it became a parking lot for thousands of customers who visited Uncle Sully's Orchard to buy apples and pies, to ride in a horse-drawn wagon and attend craft shows and watch the cider press in action. This afternoon Noah had transformed it into something private.

Tears pooled in Lacey's eyes. She blinked them away, but more formed. She wasn't normally a crier, and didn't know what was wrong with her lately.

"Would you make another pass?" she asked. It wasn't easy for her to speak around the lump in her throat.

She didn't look at Noah. Instead, she kept her eyes trained on the terrain far below. She saw apple trees and rooftops and roads laid out in a grid pattern. He did as she requested. And then he was tipping the wing again, and there it was.

LACEY + NOAH was spelled out in white block letters. She stared at it until they flew past it again.

"How did you do that?"

"I wrote it with the same kind of chalk they use at the ballpark. I had to promise a free flight lesson next month in exchange for the use of their machine this afternoon, but that's a small price to pay. There's more." He climbed back to a safer altitude and said, "For years I flew away from you, Lacey Bell. Tonight, I'm coming back to you."

Her breath caught all over again. "Can you land down there?" she asked over the air leaks and engine noise.

"Do you want me to?" he asked.

She nodded.

She knew that Marsh kept the runway mowed for those occasions when Noah chose to land here. It was just a track through the old pasture, but it was long enough and it was a perfectly safe runway for small planes. Although he obviously hadn't planned to land here tonight, he radioed Tom and cleared it with him, as if he would grant her any wish at all.

"With this storm moving in, you'll have to wait until the wind changes to take off again," Tom warned.

"I'll park her on low ground," Noah said into the radio. "Don't wait up."

Lacey's gaze met his.

"Ten-four, pal, and give Lacey a kiss for me."

He set the plane down lightly. Landings were always loud. Because of the grassy track, this one was bumpy, too. He brought the Piper to a complete stop with plenty of runway to spare. Directly ahead of them was Lacey's name in big white letters.

"I can't believe you went to all this trouble," she said.

"A woman like you deserves a grand gesture. I thought about having a banner made and flying it behind my plane, but you're too private for that. This is intimate, for you alone."

Lacey had always known Noah had a noble streak and a heart of gold. She'd had no idea he was sentimental, too.

"Come on," she said, removing her seat belt. "I want to see it up close."

Noah got out first. Reaching up for her, his hands went to her waist, lingering even after her feet touched the ground. The branches in the nearby cottonwoods sang in the evening breeze. There was something romantic about the sound of the wind. Romance, it seemed, was everywhere.

"If I forget to tell you later," she said, "I had fun tonight."

He leaned down. For a moment she thought he intended

to kiss her on the mouth. He surprised her once again when his lips brushed her cheek instead. Holding perfectly still, she closed her eyes, for there was something incredibly touching about the whisper of a man's lips on a woman's cheek. It was a first for her.

"Believe me, I'm planning to make tonight so memorable you'll never forget it."

It was so like him that she couldn't help laughing out loud. Noah Sullivan might have been on his best behavior, but he was no choirboy.

Thank heavens.

"You sound awfully sure of yourself, flyboy." She darted away, toward the letters in his name.

Noah let Lacey go, but he didn't let her out of his sight. He knew what she wanted. It so happened that he wanted the same thing. What an understatement. Before the night was through, they were going to make love. He'd been planning for it all day.

He'd written his message to her on the downward slope of a grassy hill. He'd flown over it twice, driving back and forth in order to tweak it to get the lettering just right. Now Lacey was walking along the lower edge of his message. Unable to contain her joy, she did a cartwheel and laughed out loud. Her arms outstretched, her hair streaming behind her like an aviator's scarf, she wove in and out of the letters in his message. The woman held nothing back. She never had. His body heated the way it had the first time they'd made love.

At eighteen she'd been a lot like him, a little beaten up by life, slightly belligerent and very bold. The guys around the pool hall used to say she was easy. She'd been an enchantress who knew her own mind, what she liked and whom she'd wanted. For some unexplainable reason, she'd wanted him. Back then he'd been so full of himself that he'd seen no reason to deny her. If he could go back and do one thing differently, he would change the way he'd taken her that first time. But he hadn't known. Like everyone else, he'd assumed she'd been experienced.

He'd been wrong, for there had been blood on her sheets, and afterward, he'd heard her crying in the bathroom. Uncertain about what to do, he'd gone in to talk to her, and wound up wrapping his arms around her. He would have been content to do just that, but she'd had other ideas. Lacey Bell wasn't one to stay down for the count.

In the past two-and-a-half years they'd been intimate on only one occasion, and that had been more than a year ago. When she'd first broken it off, he'd tried to eradicate her memory every chance he had. He couldn't remember a single face, and yet he'd never forgotten hers. He hadn't admitted it out loud, but he hadn't been with anybody since that night a year ago after her father's funeral.

"What's next?" she called.

She stood near the bottom of the hill, her hair blowing in the wind, her jeans low and her black knit shirt just tight enough to be interesting. He walked closer, his stride long and purposeful. "What I'd planned to do was have a picnic. And then I was going to seduce you."

Her chest heaved with the deep breath she took. "That sounded like past tense to me."

He heard himself chuckle. "That's because I didn't plan to land here. The grinders and drinks are in a cooler in my truck at the airfield."

He was only four feet away when she said, "As luck would have it, I had a late lunch."

His body heated a little more.

"Do you think you could kiss me now?" she asked.

"I don't think anything could keep me from kissing you."

They came together on a rush of air and joy. The kiss was an explosion of heat and need and everything earthy. His hands were in her hair, on her back, at her waist, but his mouth never left hers. Her curves molded to the contours of his hard body, and desire unlike anything he'd ever felt kicked through him at three g's.

His arms tightened around her as they dropped to their knees on the soft grass, the wind whipping her hair into both their faces. The low-hanging clouds formed an arc over their little haven, making the meadow feel secluded and exotic. They remained on their knees, their bodies tight together, their mouths connected the way solder joined metal.

The sprinkles came first. Warm and gentle, they fell from the low clouds, soaking into their clothes and dampening their hair. Too soon the sprinkles turned to rain. Then the thunder came. It rolled and rumbled, shaking the ground until they both felt its vibration in their knees.

Noah cast a look to the sky as lightning forked in the west. "It's going to get dangerous to be out here," he said, drawing her to her feet. "We'd better make a run for the house."

She looked up at the clouds and then at the rain falling to the meadow. "It's going to wash away your note."

"Only from the grass," he said. "Never from here." He pressed a fist to his chest.

"What about your airplane?"

"They're not predicting strong winds. The Piper's on low ground. She'll be fine."

They started toward the house at a jog, building to a steady run. They followed the lane through the west orchard, emerging into the clearing at the foot of the hill leading to the house, winded. It was pouring by the time they reached the back door. Although it was only seven o'clock, it seemed like much later.

The clock on the stove ticked and the rain pattered against the window. Otherwise, the big old house was quiet and empty.

Noah brought them each a towel from the bathroom downstairs. "We have the house to ourselves," he said as the lights flickered off, then on again.

"How long?" she asked, drying her face and hair.

"For a few more hours, at least."

Invigorated by the run and the landing and the storm, he dropped their towels to the back of a kitchen chair and reached for both her hands. He drew her to him and kissed her again, long and slow and deep.

The next time lightning struck, the lights went out and stayed out. It was too early to need candles or a flashlight, so, without saying a word, he led the way up the back staircase.

Partway up the stairs Lacey thought about the scars on her abdomen. Other than her doctor, no man had seen them. Noah would be the first. She would tell him how she'd gotten them, and what they meant for her future. It would be a relief to finally tell someone, especially someone who'd gone to so much trouble to tell her how he felt about her.

The back hallway was narrow, the floors old and creaky. It was their music. The rain on the roof was their refrain, and Noah's murmurs and Lacey's sighs as his arms came around her in his room was the most amazing melody.

Not much had changed since she'd been here last. His bed was on the wall opposite the window where it had always been. There was a lamp and an alarm clock and a dresser and a bedside table, too. Outside, lightning zig-zagged out of the low black clouds.

Noah quickly closed the window and drew the blinds. While nature put on a light show between the slats in the blinds, he placed his hands on her shoulders.

How many times had she seen him looking at her this way? How many times had she looked back at him, her eyes wide in the semidarkness, her thoughts gentle as she tried to commit the sight of him to memory?

She stepped closer to her bad boy turned knight in shining armor and unfastened his first button. Beneath his damp shirt, she felt his heart rate quicken. She could tell by the slow deep breath he took that he was trying to be patient and let her take her time. His patience lasted until she loosened the second button.

And then he took over. He undid them all and peeled the wet garment off, turning it inside out in the process. Her black shirt was next. His eyes were on her now. She thrilled at the way his gaze heated as she reached behind her and unfastened her bra.

He had her in his arms, a hand on her breast, his eyes closed deliriously. Moaning softly, she closed her eyes, too. Belt buckles jangled and zippers were lowered and jeans came off. Wearing only a wisp of black lace, she shivered, but she was only chilled on the surface. Everywhere else there was only heat.

He whipped the summer quilt off his bed and held the sheet for her. She climbed in, and he followed her. Between the smooth layers of thin cotton, their legs entwined.

She lay on her side now, and he lay on his. He touched the tip of her chin with the outer edge of his hand, slowly trailing to the little hollow at the base of her neck, down the center of her chest, grazing her breasts, each in turn, with the back of his hand.

He found her mouth with his lips, working magic there. And then he moved his magic elsewhere. He began at that sensitive little spot below her ear, moved to the ticklish hollow on her shoulder and, finally, to her breasts. She wound her fingers through his rain-dampened hair, along his ears, to his shoulders and the corded muscles of his back. As thunder rumbled, they rolled across the bed, lips trailing, hearts quickening, breaths rasping and deepening in turns.

She didn't tell him how wonderful it felt to be back in his arms. Instead, she showed him with every kiss, every sigh, every touch and murmur and groan and lusty cry for more.

"You're wild," he told her.

But she wasn't the only wild person in this bed. In some far corner of her mind, she was aware that he'd leaned over the side of the bed and was rifling through a drawer. He came back to her with a small foil package between his teeth.

He tore it open, and said, "I hope these things don't have an expiration date."

She didn't understand what he meant.

Until he said, "Hopefully they're good for longer than a year."

For a moment she thought she'd heard wrong. Noah had gone an entire year without making love? Her heart rose up to her throat again. She took him in her hand and said, "You don't need to use anything. I won't get pregnant."

"You're sure?"

She nodded. She thought he might question this further. Obviously he trusted her. She knew they would have to talk about this, and soon.

He tossed the packet over his shoulder, and came to her, thigh to thigh, belly to belly, breast to chest, his lips on hers. And the time for talking and for coherent thought came to an end.

She lost track of who touched whom, of who was on top, and of where he left off and she began as he took her breast in his big hand, and slowly, reverently almost, lowered his mouth to her soft flesh. His other hand wandered to her belly, and slipped beneath the lace edge of her panties. After he'd drawn them down her legs and slowly eased on top of her, and brought his mouth to hers, she only knew that whatever happened from this moment on really was the beginning of something brand-new.

Chapter Ten

Noah was sprawled on his back, his pillow mysteriously missing from the bed, a corner of the sheet all that covered him. His head rested on one arm while the other arm dangled off the side of the bed, his fingers grazing the floor. Beside him, Lacey lay on her stomach, her face turned toward him.

Night had fallen and the storm had moved on, leaving behind only a steady rain. The power must have come back on. He could feel the cool air blasting from the vent, but he hadn't turned on a lamp in here. In the black-pearl darkness, he could barely tell that Lacey's eyes were closed.

"I might never move again," he said. He was that relaxed, that spent, that satisfied. Especially that.

She made a sound deep in her throat that meant ditto.

It was no wonder they were both practically comatose, though. Three hours of sex did that to a person. Make that three hours of Lacey.

Soft and supple where he was hard and solid, she was thinner than he remembered, but wilder and lustier, and somehow freer with her passion. The first time they'd made love tonight, he'd taken his time, drawing every last sigh out of her until she'd cried out for release.

The next time she'd set the pace, and what a pace it was. When the sheets got tangled, they'd kicked them off. Thunder had rumbled and lightning had flickered, but the storm was nothing compared to the crescendo they created with every kiss and touch and sigh and moan. He'd used his hands and his mouth and every inch of his body to show her how he felt, and she'd shown him her feelings in countless ways, too.

All day he'd planned to seduce her, but even he couldn't have planned that last time. He'd been feeling pretty damn satisfied as he'd gathered up their damp shirts and jeans and carried them down to the dryer in the basement. He hadn't bothered getting dressed, and she hadn't heard him pad back up the stairs barefoot. He'd found her on her knees on the floor, looking under the bed for her other sandal. Even in the semidarkness, one glimpse of that delectable backside of hers was all it had taken. He'd had to have her again. When it was over they were both seeing stars.

Step three was off to a great start. Spent and sated and half-asleep now, he really might never move again.

"I'm starving," she said sleepily.

He made a grizzly bear sort of reply.

"Are you?" she asked.

"Now that you mention it. What are you hungry for?"

"A cheeseburger and fries and a hot-fudge sundae."

He chuckled because she'd obviously given it some thought. She'd always had a hearty appetite. Although half the time he didn't know where she put it, he liked that about her. In fact, he couldn't think of anything he didn't like about her.

Resigning himself to the fact that he had to move sooner or later anyway, he swung his feet off the bed. "Your clothes are probably dry by now."

"What time is it?" She sat up, too.

"A little before ten."

She caught him looking at her breasts from the light spilling from the hallway. Pointing to the door, she said, "Food, I need food. And The Hill closes at eleven on Sundays."

He scooped up the foil packet he'd opened but hadn't used, and tossed it in the wastebasket on his way out the door. She'd assured him that he didn't need it. Women knew their cycles, but the truth was he wouldn't have minded if he'd gotten her pregnant tonight. It had been surprising enough when he'd experienced those brief twinges that night when Joey first arrived. He'd almost been disappointed Joey wasn't his son. This was a complete change of heart. He wondered what Lacey would say if she knew. It wasn't something he could just blurt out. So instead, he said, "I'll be right back with your clothes."

Lacey waited until Noah left the room to make a run for the bathroom. As she was closing the door, she saw that he was walking away from her toward the top of the stairs.

Lacey knew that confident swagger, that attitude. She was tempted to call him back to her all over again. Hungry or not, she would have enjoyed making love again. But Noah went downstairs and she closed the bathroom door and began to freshen up. After all, they didn't have to make up for lost time or try to fit a week's worth of memories into one night. They were starting anew, and this was just the beginning.

She'd never felt so full of hope and enthusiasm for to-morrow and the day after that. The future really was wide-open.

Like so many big, rambling old houses, the upstairs bathroom had been installed long after the house had been built. Once a closet, it contained a narrow shower, a toilet and an old-fashioned pedestal sink. There was a mirrored medicine cabinet over the sink and another mirror on the back of the door.

She stood at the sink, looking at her reflection. Her hair was a mess. Since there was no saving her smudged mas-cara, she scrubbed her face clean. She found a hairbrush in an old cabinet and an old tube of Madeline's lip gloss and mascara. After applying a little of both, she glanced over her shoulder at the mirror on the door. She started to turn away. Only to stop.

For the past six months, she'd stayed away from full-length mirrors, preferring not to dwell on what was below her waist. Tonight, she took a long look at her entire reflec-tion. What she saw was a twenty-eight-year-old woman with dark hair and blue eyes, pouty lips and full breasts. There was a whisker burn on her neck and a heart-shaped birthmark above her waist. Two scars crisscrossed her belly below it. The lines had faded from red to pink in the past six months. A year from now they would lighten to the color of her skin.

She'd forgotten about them while she and Noah had been making love. That second time she would have been hard-pressed to remember her name if asked. As it turned out, it had been too dark to see them, after all. When the time was right she would tell Noah about her ruptured ap-pendix and the internal scarring that had resulted from the subsequent infection. She would tell him that the like-lihood that she would conceive a child was somewhere between slim and none. She wasn't pretending that she wasn't still sad about it. There might always be a sensitive little spot where that wish for a baby of her own had been, but her incisions weren't the only things that were fading. Hope and happiness were magnificent healers. Still, she couldn't help reflecting on the irony of it all, for the reason she'd broken things off with Noah two-and-a-half years ago was because she'd wanted children and he didn't. Fate had stepped in. Now a future with or without children was no longer an issue between her and Noah.

Placing a hand on her belly, she waited for the anguish and searing disappointment. Perhaps it was the lingering effects of euphoria following all that amazing sex, but she felt the first stirring of acceptance.

She donned her bra and panties. Hearing him moving around his bedroom, she peeked out and discovered her dry clothes right outside the bathroom door. Her shirt and jeans were slightly warm from the dryer. Still wearing that beatific smile, she left the washroom. Noah had called tonight step three.

Step three had only just begun.

The founding fathers of Orchard Hill had been a pragmatic group of loosely connected men whose families had originally emigrated from Scotland. It was said that they'd wasted nothing. Even middle names were an extravagance to them, and were rarely bestowed. It wasn't surprising that the town had been laid out just as pragmatically, the streets named for numbers and trees and a president or two. It stood to reason that they'd called the path through the very center of the grid Division Street. Intersecting streets fell away to the Chestnut River in the west and to the orchards in the east. It was only fitting that businesses lined either side of the wide avenue. Also fitting was the name of the town's oldest restaurant, which happened to sit on the highest elevation in town.

After all these years, people didn't frequent The Hill because it was aptly named. They came here because the food was always good and the gossip even better.

Decorated in early Americana diner style, the restaurant had been surprisingly crowded when Lacey and Noah arrived at a little after ten. Now, fifteen minutes before closing time, only a handful of customers remained. That didn't detract from the hometown ambiance. It did, however, make the sound of the trio whooping it up in a booth near the back audible in every corner of the room.

Lacey didn't remember the last time she'd laughed so much, or loved so much, or eaten so much, for that matter, and all in the same day. She and Noah had been tucking away the last of their burgers and fries with loads of ketchup when a large man with a shaved head stopped at their table.

Noah was completely nonplussed by the man's unexpected appearance. Ever since he'd climbed out of bed that last time, he'd been so cool, calm and collected that she doubted anything could ruffle his feathers. She was a little surprised when he introduced the man as Sam Lafferty, the P.I. Marsh and Reed had hired, but she wasn't surprised that he and Noah were friends.

Noah had friends everywhere.

Lacey liked the private investigator almost immediately. He'd told Noah about a call he'd gotten from Marsh regarding some woman named Houdini. Lacey and Noah had told him what they'd discovered. Before he followed a lead on a waitress in Texas, he wanted to get as detailed a description as possible. He was going to pay the Sullivans a visit. Marsh and Reed were due home in an hour, and Sam had decided to kill a little time at The Hill.

The P.I. was a giant and might have seemed intimidating, with his muscular arms, shaved head and pierced ear, but he'd been genuinely pleased to be invited to sit with them. He was either a fast healer or tough as nails, because she didn't see any evidence of the boot he'd taken in his face a few days ago.

From what she could gather, the life of a P.I. was solitary and messy. Sam sure wasn't lacking in entertaining stories. Most of them began with the same three words.

"There I was, minding my own business, and in walked an old mark who was supposed to be in jail."

Or "There I was with a doughnut in one hand and a pair of binoculars in the other."

Or "There I was, staring down the wrong end of a Smith & Wesson."

She didn't know how he'd had time to finish his hot-fudge sundae with all the talking he'd done. If half of what he said was true, he was lucky to be alive.

Noah's sundae was gone now, too. Free, his right hand found its way beneath the table to her knee. He squeezed her leg gently, and moved up a few inches. Heat bloomed in places not directly connected to her knee.

She kept her eyes on her parfait glass, anticipation melting her insides as if she were made of ice cream, too. On the other side of the booth, Sam launched into another tale.

"There I was," he said in his booming voice, "hand-cuffed to a headboard in my birthday suit, when in walked my date's old flame. It was a real mood breaker, let me tell you. A jealous ex-lover is more dangerous than a roomful of rattlesnakes."

"How did you manage to get out of that one?" Lacey couldn't help asking.

"Sometime I'll have to show you the trophy head-board—" Sam began.

"Hanging on his wall," Noah said.

They'd spoken in unison, and shook their heads the same way. Looking from one to the other, it occurred to Lacey that this was a side of Noah she didn't know anything about.

"How did you two meet?" she asked.

Her question launched another "There I was" story that had Lacey laughing all over again. It didn't bother her that Sam Lafferty was one part bluster and the rest Irish bull. She liked him.

She liked men, even the dangerous ones. She would be forever grateful to the women who'd taught her about the facts of life and how to hold her head high and how a knee placed just so could render a man defenseless, but it was one very special man who'd taught her compassion.

It was a well-known fact that her mom had been gone by the time Harlan Bell bought a run-down bar on Division Street. A lot of people thought her father had been too lenient with Lacey when she was growing up. She'd even overheard a few say he had no business raising a daughter when he spent most of his time pouring drinks for deadbeats and losers downstairs. But those people—her well-meaning teachers, mostly—hadn't seen the way her father had taken care of his family before they'd moved from Ohio to Orchard Hill.

They could think what they wanted, but they hadn't awakened in the middle of the night to the croon of her dad's deep voice in the next room when her mom was in too much pain to sleep. Night after night, day after day, through doctor visits and disappointments, he'd held Lacey and her mom up, and he'd gotten them all through it. So, yes, Lacey liked men, especially men like her father, a-little-rough-around-the-edges types with bawdy stories and honorable souls. If she had to venture a guess, she would say that Sam Lafferty was one of those.

The P.I. dropped a five spot on the table and slid from the booth. "Want me to tell Marsh and Reed not to wait up?"

"That's not the kind of thing you say in front of a lady, Sam," Noah answered.

"I don't doubt that Lacey is a hell of a lady. I'm just saying it's been ten minutes since I've seen your hand."

Once again, Lacey laughed out loud. Sam Lafferty hadn't earned the reputation as one of the best P.I.s in the state by being unobservant. When Noah lifted his hand, Lacey's came up with it, her fingers laced with his.

"You've been holding her hand? You've got it bad, pal." Shaking his head, Sam ambled out of the restaurant. Lacey and Noah sauntered to the front counter to pay for their meals.

"How was everything?" the tired waitress asked.

"Wonderful," Lacey replied. "Everything is wonderful."

The other woman put the money Noah handed her in the drawer and counted out his change. "Yes," she said, "I can see that."

Rosy Sirrine was tall and had sturdy hips and steady hands. As much a fixture in Orchard Hill as the sculpture on the town square, her ethnicity was a mystery. Nobody could remember a time when she hadn't been head waitress here, yet there was no gray in her black braid.

She reminded Lacey of an old nursery rhyme about a wise old owl. The more she saw, the less she spoke, the less she spoke, the more she heard, or something to that effect. "What are you doing working the late shift?" Lacey asked.

"Dora went down to the courthouse today and got married. She up and quit without any notice," Rosy said drolly. "I was planning to call you tomorrow. Are you still looking for a job?"

Lacey was aware of Noah beside her, but she kept her eyes on Rosy. "I've picked up a temporary position, but I don't know how long it'll last. What hours would you need me?"

"What hours could you give me?"

"I have a temporary job, but I could work evenings for now."

"That would be a great help," Rosy said.

Try as she might, Lacey couldn't help asking, "Who did Dora marry?"

Dora Peterson had worked here almost as long as Rosy. She had her hair washed, curled, coifed and shellacked every week at the Do-Da Salon around the corner, and batted her fake eyelashes at every man who walked through the door.

"Henry finally found somebody to accept his proposal," Rosy replied.

"Henry Brewbaker?" Noah quipped.

Lacey remembered when the old sweetheart had proposed to her.

"It was only a matter of time before somebody saw the opportunity and took it." Rosy pressed her lips together as if she'd put a tick-a-lock on them.

"Are you upset that you've lost your best waitress?" Lacey asked.

Rosy made a sound through her pursed lips.

And Noah said, "Rosy would never stand in the way of true love, Lace. It's a pity, though, if she's lost her best customer."

Rosy smiled, proving that not even she was immune

to Noah's charm. After a little more discussion regarding her hours, it was decided that Lacey would hold both jobs for the time being, thereby giving Marsh and Reed time to hire a replacement and perhaps a permanent nanny. She would begin here tomorrow night at six.

Noah took Lacey's hand again as they left the restaurant. He held her door, then walked around to the driver's side of Reed's Mustang, which he'd borrowed for the occasion because his truck was still at the airfield.

It would have been just as fast to walk to her apartment, but she enjoyed the short drive. It was as if every one of her senses was heightened. The radio hummed and the car purred and the late-night air felt blessedly cool after the rain. It was all somehow sweeter because of the man at her side.

Noah walked her to her door, but he waited to kiss her until they were both inside. All of a sudden she was in his arms again, and he was kissing her as if it had been months since he'd worked his magic on her lips.

She was coming to expect that every kiss would sweep her off her feet. This one didn't disappoint. Wet, wild and possessive, it left her breathless and opening her mouth for more.

Her head tipped back, need uncurling all over again. She glided her hands around his waist, catching in the folds of his cotton shirt along the way. He pressed his body to hers, seeking what she was seeking. And then, with Herculean strength of will, he tore his mouth from hers.

Resting his forehead against hers, he said, "Damn. Reed, Marsh and Sam are expecting me. Leaving you like this is getting old."

She brought one hand to his cheek. "Your brothers are

lucky to have you. You should be proud of yourself for everything you're doing for them."

His brown eyes widened. She was pretty sure a slap wouldn't have surprised him more. He seemed uncomfortable with her praise. Finally, he said, "It was a lot easier being the hell-raising, no-good brother."

"You were never no-good, but this feels good, doesn't it?" she asked.

A certain look entered his eyes. "Are we still talking about pride?"

She pushed playfully at his shoulders. "You have a dirty mind."

But she noticed that he was smiling. She stepped away from the door so he could open it. "I'll see you in the morning, Lace."

From the doorway she watched him drive away in his brother's Mustang. "I'll see you in the morning," she whispered into the vast night sky.

She closed the door, eventually, and wandered through the small apartment, pinching herself. It was hard to believe that only a week ago she'd stood in the smelly exhaust fumes of a Greyhound bus, three suitcases and her camera all she had to her name. It had seemed there was little hope of happiness for the future.

Now she was driving a borrowed car and living in an uncluttered apartment that smelled like the rain-freshened air wafting through the window tonight. She had friends who cared about her, and little ones who called her Aunt Lacey.

She'd lived in Chicago for more than two years, but this felt like home. She had roots here, and now she had two jobs instead of none.

Her life had purpose here. April had shown someone

else through the tavern. One of these days, it would sell, and she would pay off her debt to the hospital in Chicago.

And she had the feeling that the best part of her new life was yet to come.

Chapter Eleven

Marsh, Reed and Joey were at the kitchen table when Lacey arrived for work Monday morning. Marsh smiled absently at her after she let herself in. Moving Joey to his shoulder, he turned his attention back to Reed and whatever they were doing on his laptop.

The coffeemaker stopped gurgling while she was washing her hands at the kitchen sink. Wondering where Noah was, she poured the steaming liquid into two mugs and carried them to the table. Again, Marsh smiled absently at her.

Reed said a quick thank-you and continued typing.

She turned back to Marsh and held out her hands for Joey. "When was his last bottle?" she asked quietly.

"A little after six o'clock. He slept through the night," Marsh said.

"We never heard a peep out of him," Reed added without looking up from his screen.

"We don't know what came over him. Noah, either, for that matter."

"Noah isn't awake yet?" she asked.

"Last I knew he was still sleeping like a baby," Marsh answered.

Smiling warmly at Joey, she walked around the room with him, rocking him in her arms. Today she was going to give him a bath and then at least twenty minutes of tummy time to strengthen his back and arms. She was going to read to him, too. According to her library book, it was never too early to begin.

Gazing up at her, he studied her face so intently he didn't even blink. He was a very serious baby. She'd noticed that when he smiled, he put his heart into it. Already his eyelashes were long and dark. It was too soon to tell if his eyes would stay blue, like Reed's, or turn brown, like Marsh's.

She looked at Marsh and Reed, searching their faces for similarities to Joey. Focusing on whatever they were doing on Reed's computer, they were both clean-shaven, their hair, although different colors, clipped short. They had similar noses and builds. They would never be able to determine which of them was Joey's father through appearance alone. She didn't think it was her place to bring up the DNA test.

"How does this sound?" Reed took another sip of his hot coffee. Resting his elbows on the table, he said, "Wanted—Professional nanny for three-month-old baby boy. Weekdays from nine to five. Degree in early childhood development preferred."

"Experience required," Marsh said, lifting his mug to his mouth.

Evidently, they were composing an ad for a nanny.

"And references—don't forget those," Marsh added.

Reed typed another line then asked, "What about transportation?"

Joey grinned up at Lacey. It was as if he knew all this was for him.

"Preferably something with a good crash rating," Marsh said.

"She can't be too young," Reed said.

"Just say she should wear her hair in a bun and must smell like fresh-baked bread." Lacey, Marsh and Reed all turned as Noah sauntered into the room. Looking as if he'd just rolled out of bed, he wore his usual faded jeans and a gray T-shirt with fold marks down the center. His hair was mussed and his feet were bare.

"Very funny," Marsh said.

Noah ignored him. He hadn't taken his eyes off Lacey. She wasn't sure what he was up to, but she held still as he took Joey from her. Admittedly, it was most likely an accident when the back of his hand brushed her breast in the process. It was no accident that he noticed.

He carried Joey across the room, his fingertips meeting at the baby's sturdy back. "You can have her back in a minute, buddy," he said to the baby, "but you have to share."

Handing Joey to Marsh, he sauntered back to Lacey and kissed her on the mouth right there in the kitchen in front of God and everyone. Brief but powerful, it was a firm kiss, a possessive kiss, an I've-missed-you-and-it's-only-been-ten-hours kiss. When it was over, he gave her a cocky grin and strolled back for Joey.

Lacey saw the look Reed and Marsh exchanged. *Ah,* it said. *So that's why Noah slept like a baby.*

She was too familiar with them to mind. How could she mind, when they'd taken the news that they needed to find another nanny in stride the way they took everything in stride?

When Joey was back in Lacey's arms, Noah poured himself a cup of coffee then joined his brothers at the table. Their personalities were as different as their choices in clothing. And yet there was no denying the family resemblance. Every one of them exuded enough pheromones to be dangerous. As she carried Joey from the room to prepare for his bath, she doubted that even grandmother types would be immune.

Noah was whistling when he pushed through the back door. Letting the screen bang shut behind him, he slung his duffel bag over his shoulder and descended the porch steps. His gait was loose, his stride long and sure. He'd just kissed Lacey goodbye, and although he'd thrown a change of clothes in his duffel, he was hoping he wouldn't be gone all night. He wanted to come back and do that again as soon as possible.

For now, he was on his way to the meadow and his airplane. He cut across the side lawn where the old wooden swing swayed slightly in the gentle breeze, and started down the lane. Sam was meeting him at the airfield. From there they were flying to Dallas and what Sam hoped was a lead on the woman from Reed's past.

Noah was halfway to the meadow when he saw the ATV parked near the cider house up ahead. Not far from the four-wheel-drive utility vehicle was a pile of mangled ivy. He didn't see Marsh, though.

His brother had a vendetta against the invasive vine. Nobody knew who'd planted the damn nuisance, but generations of Sullivan men had been battling it ever since. Sometimes it disappeared for a year or two, only to sneak back up the stone exterior of the cider house when nobody was looking. It had become a test of wills, and so far Marsh and the ivy were neck and neck.

"How about a ride to your airplane?"

Noah turned around at the sound of Marsh's voice, and found his brother just off the beaten path under one of the trees he'd grafted years ago.

"I'd take a ride to my plane," Noah said.

There was something about the way Marsh strode toward him that gave Noah the impression that his brother had been waiting for him. He had no idea what was going on in his older brother's mind. Marsh was a tough nut to crack. They were alike that way.

Marsh hopped on the ATV and Noah flung a leg over the seat behind him. Within minutes, they arrived at the meadow where Noah had parked his airplane last night.

They scattered a flock of sparrows and elicited a scolding from a pair of crows. It was another warm June morning with blue skies and sunshine. The ground had softened and the grass had greened and dandelions were blooming like a thousand little suns.

As Noah climbed off the quad, he noticed that the chalk had been washed away. "Thanks, Marsh. Sam and I will let you and Reed know as soon as we find this waitress named Cookie." Duffel bag in hand, he started toward his airplane.

"Hey, Noah, have you got a minute?"

Noah turned around, his gaze taking in his brother from head to toe. Neither of them wore sunglasses and both were squinting. They were dressed similarly, too, but moisture had wicked up the hem of Marsh's jeans.

The morning was quiet now that the quad wasn't running and the birds had disappeared. Marsh was quiet, too. That was nothing new. Reed was the talker in the family.

"Whatcha need?" Noah asked.

"You've been flying us all over kingdom come for the better part of a week." Marsh slid his hand into his front pocket.

"You know me. I was born to fly. Besides, it feels good to pay you back."

Marsh wore a look of genuine surprise. "Pay me back for what?"

"Oh, this and that." Noah couldn't quite pull off a nonchalant shrug.

Marsh folded his arms, a sign that he wasn't going anywhere until Noah came clean. His oldest brother was like the damn ivy, tenacious and determined. "Pay me back for what?" he repeated.

"For giving up your future for me and Madeline when Mom and Dad died, for one thing."

Suddenly Marsh was only an arm's length away. "Why would you think I gave up my future for you?"

"Because you did."

"The hell I did. You remind me so much of Dad sometimes I can't believe it."

This was news to Noah. Marsh's genuine surprise convinced Noah that this wasn't the reason he'd put himself in Noah's path this morning.

"As long as we're on the subject, thank you. If you and Reed hadn't stepped in, Madeline and I probably would have wound up living with the judge."

Marsh grinned, just as Noah had hoped he would. "There were times I considered threatening you with that, but for your information, I didn't give up anything. Coming back to the orchard was what I'd always wanted to do. Keeping our family together was an honor and a privilege."

"All the hell I put you through was a privilege? Are you crazy?"

"All this guilt you've been carrying around has been for nothing," Marsh said. "Who's the crazy one?"

They wore similar smug expressions.

"I want to talk to you about something else," Marsh said.

"Make it quick. I've gotta pick Sam up and gas the plane at the airfield."

"You and Lacey looked pretty happy this morning."

Noah thought about the expression on Lacey's face when he'd told her goodbye a few minutes ago. Her hands full of slippery baby, she'd smiled at him through the sprinkles Joey was sending up as he kicked his feet and flailed his arms, and Noah hadn't wanted to leave.

"As soon as I get up the nerve," he said, "I'm going to ask her to marry me."

"No kidding? Good for you. That's what I wanted to talk to you about."

Marsh reached into his pocket for something. He extended his hand toward Noah and slowly opened his fingers.

Noah stared at the treasure in his brother's palm. Emotion thickened his voice as he said, "That was Mom's. Reed and I think you should have it."

All around Noah the sun-kissed meadow came to life. Birds sang and insects buzzed and the breeze combed through his hair like a mother's hand. He had to clear his throat in order to speak. "What about Madeline?" he asked.

"It was her idea."

A lump lodged in Noah's throat.

As if he knew the moment called for drastic measures, Marsh shoved his hand closer and said, "Take it already. You have a plane to fuel and I have ivy to eradicate."

Wrapping his fingers around the delicate heirloom,

Noah didn't know what to say, except, "I can't believe you thought about dumping me at the judge's."

Marsh took his time smiling, and the rite of passage was complete. He climbed on the quad and Noah climbed into the cabin of his airplane. From the cockpit he watched Marsh speed back to his orchard. The lump in his throat dissolved and his heart beat a steady rhythm.

He checked gauges and radioed the airfield. The minute he was cleared for takeoff, he raced down the grass runway. As he lifted off, he'd never been more proud to be a Sullivan.

By the end of the day they should know more about the identity of this woman named Cookie. As soon as he could, he would be flying home again. And when he did, he was going to make Lacey an offer he hoped to high heaven she couldn't refuse.

All these years Noah had been convinced that Marsh was the family man who'd given up his future for Noah and Madeline. He'd somehow believed that Reed had given up an urban lifestyle for the same reason. Now Noah realized they were all family men at heart. Wasn't Lacey going to be surprised?

The first thing Lacey did after she let herself into her apartment at nine-thirty that night was open every window. When she'd stopped home earlier to change her clothes before going to The Hill, she'd peeked inside the tavern. The sleeping bag and bus pass lay undisturbed on the pool table where she'd left them.

The second thing she did after getting home was peel off her clothes and turn on the shower. Lathering her hair and washing the day's grime down the drain helped, but the effects didn't last long in the hot, airless apartment.

The third thing she did was admit that the stuffy apartment and the fact that her Houdini hadn't returned weren't the reasons she felt so listless. She couldn't even blame her aching feet and the dull headache she'd brought home with her after her first shift serving up food to the supper crowd at The Hill.

Noah was still in Texas.

She'd known there was a possibility he wouldn't make it back until tomorrow. She'd just seen him twelve hours before. There was no reason for her to feel so out of sorts.

She padded to the living room and yawned. Holding two jobs was tiring. She should just go to bed.

She aimed the remote at the television, adjusted the rabbit ears, aimed the remote at the little black digital-converter box again and repeated the process. Even with the ball of aluminum foil on the top of each ear, only three stations came in. One was a police drama, two were reality shows and all were slightly fuzzy. She had enough reality in her life, thank you very much. She turned the TV off and looked around.

Her camera sat on the end table next to the couch. She'd gotten some great shots of the alley during the stakeout a few days ago. She could always develop them now. She even went so far as to carry the camera into her darkroom, but there was no window and, consequently, no relief from the heat that had been building inside all day.

She put the camera back where she'd found it. Next, she brushed the fallen daisy petals into her hand. With a sigh, she threw the entire bouquet of wilted flowers away. She found a brass fan in her dad's old room and plugged it in and turned it on in hers. Yawning, she flopped down on her bed in front of the artificial breeze and sighed.

She was just tired. After all, even night owls got tired.

Turning the radio on low to cover the sounds wafting

through her open window, she found herself looking up at her ceiling. She missed Noah.

There, she'd allowed herself to think it. And the sky hadn't fallen and the earth hadn't opened up and the oceans hadn't swelled, as far as she knew. She loved him. There was nothing wrong with missing him. Having him nearby this past week had spoiled her. Having him gone tonight reminded her of how alone she used to feel when he was gone for weeks at a time. She'd let her guard down, and had fallen even deeper in love with him. She prayed she wouldn't be sorry.

Heaving another sigh, she fluffed her pillow and lay back. The music played softly and the fan whirred, stirring warm air that was better than no breeze at all. Her eyes were just beginning to drift closed when her cell phone rang.

There were only three people who had her number. She hoped it was Noah but would have been happy if it was April and wouldn't have minded if it was her new employer, Rosy Sirrine. She checked the caller ID. Rats. It listed the number as unknown. Only someone who was bored and lonely would answer, right?

She slid the phone open and said a tentative, "Hello?"

"Are you in bed?"

"Noah?" she asked more loudly than she'd intended.

"How many other men call you at night and ask if you're in bed?"

She smiled in spite of herself. "I thought you were either a wrong number or a heavy breather. Whose phone are you using?"

"Sam's. Mine's dead and I forgot to pack my charger. Back to the heavy breathing."

Lacey laughed. It sounded slightly provocative and very content.

"Did I ever tell you I like the way you laugh?"

"I don't think so."

"Want to know what else I like?"

She chuckled again. "Oh, no, you don't. I'm not touching that line with a ten-foot pole."

"Spoilsport."

"You'll thank me when you don't need a cold shower." She couldn't help laughing again, though.

"What are you wearing?" he asked.

"If I tell you, that heavy breathing I was worried about is going to be coming from you. How's Texas?"

She could hear him moving around, and imagined him getting comfortable on some bed in a mediocre motel room. He told her about the flight and the lead on the waitress that turned out to be another dead end. They talked about the traffic in Dallas and a dozen other things. She told him about her first day back at The Hill, and that she'd considered developing the pictures she'd taken these past few days, but hadn't.

"I'd like to watch you do that sometime."

"You want to watch?" she asked.

"I was talking about watching you develop your film, but I'm open to watching you do other things."

"You're a real sport."

This time he laughed.

She stretched sinuously, crossed her ankles and pointed her toes. It was as if that little butterfly tattoo on the top of her foot really fluttered its wings. It set off an entire flurry of sensations up and down her body. She sighed, and smiled, and laughed when he described what he'd had for dinner. The radio played softly and the fan stirred the warm air. She burned up twenty-five of her prepaid minutes. She didn't have it in her to care.

"I wish I was there," he said.

"Put your money where your mouth is, flyboy."

He groaned as if he was thinking where he wanted to put his mouth. "I'll be home tomorrow by three, Michigan time."

"What then?" she asked, surprising herself.

"There's something I want to tell you."

"There's something I want to tell you, too, Noah."

"Good night, Lacey."

"Good night."

Neither of them hung up.

"Noah?" she asked softly.

"Hmm?"

"I'm wearing a white T-shirt you left here a long time ago."

"Anything else?" His voice had warmed at least ten degrees.

She made a humming sound that meant no. She moved her hips a little and imagined him doing the same.

Moaning deep in his throat, he said, "Make that two o'clock Michigan time."

She was smiling when the call ended. She wasn't going to be sorry she'd let her guard down and opened her heart to Noah. After turning off the lamp, she turned on her side, and was asleep with the radio playing softly and her heart amazingly full.

Chapter Twelve

It was closer to three o'clock than two when Noah finally pulled into his driveway on Tuesday afternoon. He parked between Lacey's car and a little import he didn't recognize. Patting his pocket reassuringly, he took a deep breath, rehearsed his opening line one more time and sauntered on in.

He wasted his entrance on Marsh and Reed and a chunky woman who looked as if she was about to burst into tears as she faced the stony expressions of his older brothers across the kitchen table. Apparently, the temp agency had sent over their first nanny candidate.

Feeling a little sorry for the woman, Noah smiled kindly. "Sorry to interrupt," he said to Marsh and Reed. "Where's Lacey?"

Reed motioned with his head.

As Noah left the room, he heard Marsh say, "Have you had any problems with post-traumatic stress disorder?"

Noah almost turned around. Post-traumatic stress?

He continued toward the front of the house, listening for a clue as to where Lacey might be. He hadn't gone far when he heard her voice. Following that soft croon, he paused in the doorway of the room that was now Joey's nursery.

Lacey sat in the rocking chair in the corner. She held Joey partially upright in one arm. In her other hand she held a colorful storybook.

"...and the dragon came charging out of his cool, dark cave, breathing fire. He roared. And waited for the shrieks of terror he always heard.

"A little boy with auburn hair stood looking at him from a meadow of wildflowers. The dragon roared again. The little boy smiled. And two dimples appeared.

"'Run,' the dragon growled, smoke rising from his nostrils.

"The little boy didn't run. He smiled again and said, 'Would you like to come out and play?'"

Perhaps Lacey felt Noah's presence. Or perhaps she felt his gaze. For whatever reason, she stopped reading and looked up at him.

Warmth bloomed in Noah's chest.

"You're back," she said.

"I'm back."

"Is the interview still going on out there?" she asked.

"I think it's winding down." He made a sound of an explosion and an accompanying gesture with his hands.

"The first one didn't go well, either," she said. "It's possible they're being a tad picky."

He tilted his head. "Feel like taking a walk?"

She closed the book and set it on the corner of the dresser Noah had assembled several days ago. Had it really been less than a week since they'd discovered Joey on their doorstep? Had it really been less than a week since he'd rediscovered Lacey?

Noah reached for his nephew. Settling him at his chest so that he was looking over Noah's left shoulder, he offered a hand to Lacey.

She took it, and rather than interrupting the interview a second time, they went out the front door the family rarely used. This was it, Noah thought as they stepped onto the porch. This was the pinnacle of step three. Up until this point, he had employed the circle, advance and retreat strategy. Patting his pocket where his mother's heirloom ring was waiting, he went over one last time *everything* he'd been rehearsing. He had so much to tell her about how much he'd missed her these past two-and-a-half years and how much he'd changed since she'd returned. He wanted her, and he wanted what she'd always wanted.

They started along the lane. They went west this time, away from the two-track that led to the meadow. He patted the pocket of his jeans again. When he finally spoke, it was to ask a question. "If you could go back and do things differently, would you?"

She looked up at him in the dappled shade on the winding path. Joey was content in Noah's arms, his eyes bright as he watched the world behind them.

"You mean do something the easy way?" she asked. "Who, me? Us?"

He smiled, one hand on Joey's back. "Do you remember the first night Joey was here? I pounded on your door and threatened to break it down if you didn't let me in."

"I vaguely remember that," she said drolly.

"I wanted him to be ours."

Lacey turned her head so fast she nearly gave herself whiplash. Had she heard correctly? she wondered. "But I thought you didn't want children."

"That's what I thought, too."

Lacey's heart was racing, her thoughts spinning. Noah had always looked dangerous around the edges, but he'd never looked as dangerous as he looked this afternoon, his hair freshly cut, his face clean-shaven, the truth bare in his golden-brown eyes.

The birds were busy tending their nests in the branches overhead. To Lacey's ears, their melody sounded like a song played on the piano with one finger. Duh-duh-duh-da.

"You look surprised," he said. "I don't blame you. It surprised me, too. I've been rehearsing this for hours and I haven't said any of this the way I'd planned."

They'd stopped walking and now stood in the dappled shade of an enormous weeping-willow tree. Patting Joey's back, he said, "When you were reading that story to him a few minutes ago, all I could think was how amazing it's going to be when it's our baby in your arms."

Lacey felt something under her sandal. She wouldn't have been surprised if it had been her lower jaw. Actually, it was a small blue sock. She bent down automatically. Picking it up gave her something to do with her hands and something to look at besides the naked truth in Noah's eyes.

"Noah, there's something you should know."

"What is it?" he asked, pointing to the baby bootee in her hand. Evidently noticing her stricken look, he said, "Lacey, what's wrong?"

She handed him the little sock. Turning it over in his hand, he gazed back toward the house and said, "This was where she waited."

She could hear her heart beating in her ears. It wasn't easy to hear anything else. "This was where who waited?" she asked.

"Joey's mother."

The wispy willow branches arched to the ground here, brushing the grass in the slight breeze. The tree stood between them and the house. Through the fronds, Lacey could see all the way to the front porch.

"Are you saying this is Joey's sock?" she asked.

Noah nodded. "He was wearing the other one when we found him. This one was missing. She must have waited here with him. It probably slipped off his foot before she worked up the courage to creep out of her hiding place. I saw her. When I was flying over. I saw a woman hurrying across the front lawn. After she left him on the front porch, she probably hid here until she knew Joey was safely inside."

Lacey's heart was still pounding with the knowledge that Noah wanted children. A car drove by. It was the woman Marsh and Reed had interviewed leaving in her little import.

"I've gotten off the subject." He smiled at her. When she failed to smile back, he said, "What is it?"

She shook her head. She couldn't have found her voice right then if her life had depended on it.

"I didn't plan to do this with Joey along," he said. "But now I think maybe it's fitting that he's here for this. After all, his arrival is what finally opened my eyes."

He felt his pocket again.

Unable to speak, she shook her head and backed up a step.

"Lacey, what's wrong? What the hell is it? You're scaring me."

Noah hadn't meant to speak so loudly. Too late he saw Joey's little lip quiver. The baby started to cry. Noah felt like a goddamn monster. "I didn't mean to frighten you, buddy."

Jiggling the baby, he tried to reach Lacey, too. He didn't know what was going on. What had he said? What had he done wrong? Her face had paled. And her eyes, those forget-me-not blue eyes, were swimming with tears.

She took another step back. Away from him.

At first he didn't understand what she was doing. She hiked her shirt up. For a second there he got a little side-tracked by the sight of bare skin. She hitched her shirt a little higher and unbuttoned her jeans.

"What are you doing?" he asked.

Her zipper went down. And then, with both hands, she slung her jeans open to reveal her belly.

His first thought was—

He forgot his first thought. For the first time he noticed two scars on her stomach. "What happened?" he said.

Joey was wailing and Lacey was shaking her head and backing up. "I can't have your babies, Noah."

She spun around and hurried toward the house.

"Lacey, come back."

Joey cried harder. And Lacey started running. Noah didn't know what the hell to do about either one of them. One thing he did know. He had to calm down.

As he rocked Joey to and fro, the woman he loved ran to the house. She went in the front door that not even company used. Less than a minute later she went out the back. Still running, she got in her car. And then she drove away.

Okay. This was a new low, even for Noah. He'd raised a lot of hell in his life, and he'd made people pull their hair out. He'd brought more than one woman to tears, teachers mostly. He hadn't spent a lot of time with kids, but he might have made one or two of them cry, too. He'd never made a woman and a baby cry at the same time.

He parked in the alley by Bell's Tavern twenty minutes

after Lacey had fled. He'd tried calling her. She hadn't answered. Her car was here, but that didn't mean she was home.

He'd shown the baby sock to Marsh and Reed, and briefly explained where Lacey had found it. Reed had taken Joey and Marsh took the sock.

Reed told him that Lacey had run out of the house, crying. "I don't know what's going on," he said. "But go after her."

"We've got things covered here," Marsh had insisted. "Go."

It was the best advice his brothers had ever given him. Now that he was here, the adrenaline rush that had gotten him this far lost pressure like air through a leaky valve.

He threw the shifting lever into Park, set the brake and got out. He paced back and forth in front of the barrel of petunias. He wasn't sure where he'd gone wrong, and while he didn't understand what had precipitated Lacey's reaction, the image of her scars and the echo of her voice as she'd said, "I can't have your babies, Noah," was embedded in his brain. Once his thoughts were in a semblance of order, he took the steps two at a time and knocked on her door.

Lacey was in her bedroom when she heard the pounding. She'd splashed her face with cool water, fixed her mascara and tied her hair up for work at The Hill. She wasn't surprised that Noah had come looking for her. As far as explanations went, hers left a lot to be desired. She'd definitely stuck to the facts. Or one fact. She couldn't have Noah's babies.

For the second time in less than a week, the pounding on her door got louder. "It's me, Lacey. Open the door."

Noah.

She was on her way across the small living room when the pounding got harder and his voice louder. "I'm not leaving until we've talked. If you don't open up, I'll break the door down."

She turned the dead bolt and stepped back.

The door swung in. For just a moment, neither she nor Noah moved.

Her breath caught at the sight of him. His jeans were faded, his legs long, his chest broad, his breathing a little ragged. His eyes were narrowed, his jaw set. Short hair or not, he had *bad boy* written all over him.

"Either come in or go out," she said. "You're letting in flies."

He came in. And he closed the door. He took a few steps, stopped. Heaving a great sigh, he said, "Tell me about those scars."

She didn't ask him to sit down. He couldn't have sat, and neither could she. Heaving a sigh, too, she said, "Six-and-a-half months ago, I woke up with a mild ache in my side. No big deal, right? I thought I was just ovulating, or something I'd eaten didn't agree with me. I took some aspirin and went to my temp job. By midnight, I couldn't take the pain. I went to the E.R. Emergency rooms are busy places in large cities in the middle of the night. Six hours later, I was in surgery."

"What was wrong?" he asked.

"It was just my appendix. Ninety-nine-point-nine per-cent of the time, appendectomies are routine. In, out, pa-tients are good to go. You know me. I don't do anything the easy way. There was an infection. To make a long story short, I lived. But the internal scarring damaged my fal-lopian tubes, the right one more than the left. They actu-ally took a photograph of my insides. It wasn't a pretty picture."

She went to the table and picked up a sheet of paper, with line after line of dollar amounts. "This is a little souvenir of my vacation in the hospital. It's the reason I came back to Orchard Hill. I have to sell the tavern to pay the hospital back for saving my life."

Noah had eased closer during her little speech. With every step he took, she raised her eyes a little more, never wavering from his gaze. "God, Lace. You could have died."

"I didn't. The only thing that died was my dream of having kids. Just because I can't doesn't mean you can't."

"What are you talking about?"

"You want them, Noah. You should have them. It would be a crying shame not to pass on all those incredible genes. So this is it. It's been fun."

Her voice shook a little, but not too badly.

"It has been fun," he said. The edge in his voice was sharp enough to cut steel.

Noah couldn't decide if he should wrap his arms around Lacey or throttle her. In the end, he snatched the sheet of paper from her hand, scanned it and stuffed it in his back pocket. "The goddamn fun isn't over yet," he said, on his way to the door. "Don't even think about leaving town because I will hunt you down."

"*You're* mad at *me?*"

He sucked in a breath and spun around. The floor shook beneath his feet as he stomped back to her. He slid his fingers into her hair and covered her mouth with his. He took her gasp of surprise into his own mouth.

The kiss was neither punishing nor particularly sensual. It was a brand. It was an exclamation point. It lasted only a matter of seconds, but it wasn't the end of anything.

"I'm mad at you because I love you."

As Noah left Lacey's apartment, he didn't know for sure

where he was going. He didn't have a plan. He wished to hell he did. This was no time to resort to flying by the seat of his pants. What else could he do?

One thing was certain. He would be back, and by God she had better get used to the idea, because after he figured this one out, he wasn't leaving again.

Chapter Thirteen

Waitress uniforms weren't required at The Hill. Rosy asked only that her employees show up for work on time and were clean, courteous and pleasant to her customers and each other. The busboys wore full aprons and the waitresses short white ones with pockets large enough to hold an order book, pen and tips.

At the end of Lacey's shift on her second night, only one customer remained. And he was no ordinary customer.

Noah had been holding up the end of the counter for the better part of an hour. He'd ordered a Coke, but as far as she could tell, the ice had melted and he hadn't taken so much as a sip. He was too busy stalking her with his eyes.

The other waitress was putting up chairs in the back. All Lacey had left to do was wipe down the counter. As she wrung out her cloth, she happened to glance at Rosy, who was counting money at the cash register. "Choose your battles, dearie," the older woman said.

Along with a secretive past and an uncanny habit of spouting pearls of wisdom at the precise moment they were needed, Rosy Sirrine possessed the rare ability to raise one eyebrow independently of the other. She demonstrated that move for Lacey while casting a pointed look at Noah, then resumed counting.

There was no sense wondering how the woman could have known. "Noah," Lacey finally said when he lifted his elbows from the marred Formica surface, indicating that she should clean up around him. "We're closed. You shouldn't be here."

He drank his entire glass of watered-down Coke without saying a word. But he didn't leave.

"I'll finish up, Lacey," Rosy said. "Go ahead and go."

She untied her apron and left it on the counter. Noah slid off the stool. He fell into step beside her, held the door for her, then clamped his fingers around her wrist.

"What are you doing?" she asked.

"I'm giving you a ride home." It was the first words he'd spoken since ordering that Coke.

Lacey stood looking at him on the sidewalk in front of The Hill.

There were only a few people on the sidewalk. If Lacey had chosen to scream, someone would have come to her rescue. She wouldn't scream. She wasn't the least bit afraid. She was curious and a tad nervous, but she knew Noah wouldn't hurt her.

He had something to say. He'd told her he loved her and that he wished Joey were theirs. The least she could do was listen. So she let him lead her to his passenger-side door. When he opened it, she got in.

Absently rubbing the wrist he'd just unhanded, she

buckled her seat belt and turned the tables on him, her gaze now stalking him. He caught every green light. It would be cruel of her to say this was his lucky day. It would also be a lie.

He pulled into the alley and parked next to her borrowed car. She got out. And he did, too.

"Upstairs," he said.

"Do not order me around." She raised her fighter's chin and started up the newly painted steps.

Noah followed her up the stairs. She unlocked her door, opened it and went in. He closed it quietly. She dropped her purse on the coffee table and raised her eyes to his.

"Okay," he said, as if a minute had elapsed since she'd told him about her surgery, instead of six hours. "Your appendix ruptured, and there was an infection and some scarring. What else did your doctor say?"

She made a sound of impatience then set about opening windows. She hadn't intended to end up in her bedroom, but it was too late now because he'd followed her there. He turned on a fan, rested his rear end on the edge of her dresser and settled in.

She looked beyond him at her reflection in the mirror. As usual, her hair had defied the metal clasp. Dark tendrils had escaped, framing her face and falling over the collar of her ivory-colored blouse.

"You want to know what my doctor said?" she parroted.

He nodded and crossed his ankles and arms.

Her long-suffering sighs didn't seem to faze him.

"My doctor said my appendix had ruptured several hours before my surgery began. There was an infection."

"And the infection caused internal scarring," he prodded. "How much scarring?"

She folded her arms, too. "You want a percentage?" she asked.

"Actually, I do."

"I don't know what percentage of my innards are scarred, all right? But I can tell you that my fallopian tubes were damaged, the right one more than the left."

"How much more?" he asked.

"Noah, what in the world? My doctor told me there is a ninety-two-percent chance I'll never conceive."

The fan whirred and the barest hint of a breeze jostled the blinds at her window. He uncrossed his ankles, unfolded his arms and stood up. "Just so there's no confusion," he said, moving stealthily toward her, "I would have done this if you'd told me the number was a hundred percent."

"You would have done what?" she asked.

Oh, she talked tough, but she heard the little telltale hitch in her own breathing, and she felt the flutter of hope in her chest. He took another step toward her. He reached into his pocket, and held his hand out to her.

"Would you marry me, Lacey?"

She couldn't believe her ears or her eyes. She was pretty sure Noah had just proposed. If she could have looked into his eyes, she would have known whether or not she'd heard right, but she couldn't take her gaze off the ring he held delicately between his thumb and one finger.

Her hands went to her cheeks before she could stop them. She didn't even try to check her tears. The ring, made of gold, was caught in the lamplight. On the dainty side, it contained a swirl of what looked like diamonds, sapphires, rubies and an aqua-colored stone she couldn't identify.

She finally looked up at Noah. The glint in his eyes was more inspiring than the ring.

"But, Noah, I can't give you children."

"Why do you always have to look on the negative side?"

Her chin came up a notch. "I'm being realist—"

"There's a ninety-two-percent chance you'll have trouble conceiving. I did the math. There's a good chance you will."

"You call eight percent good?"

He smiled, and eased a little closer, the ring still in his outstretched hand. "Honey, eight goes into a hundred, what, twelve-and-a-half times? That means we'll have to make love twelve times more than normal. I don't know about you, but I'm up for the challenge."

The scathing look she gave him would have brought some men to their knees. It invigorated Noah.

Lacey almost couldn't help smiling. The man was inspiring, no doubt about it. She held up one hand. "All challenges aside, Noah, there's a chance, a good chance, I won't conceive. You want children. You deserve them. I won't blame you if you walk out the door right now and find somebody who can give you better odds."

She held her breath, terrified that he might do just that.

"We'll try," he said. "We'll try hard. And if that doesn't work, we'll see a specialist. And if that doesn't work, we'll adopt, or spoil our nieces and nephews rotten. We'll be a family of two or three or ten. As long as I have you, I'll be happy."

A tear ran down her face.

Wiping it away with the pad of his thumb, he said, "I want to hear you say it."

She started. "Say what?"

"That you'll marry me."

A smile bloomed on her lips. Just below it a butterfly lit at the little hollow at the base of her throat. Below that, a thousand wings fluttered. She tipped her head to one side and studied this man who was as stubborn as she was, as wild as she was, as crazy as she was. "Fine, I'll marry you. But don't say I didn't warn you."

She was about to throw herself into his arms. Luckily one of them had the sense to remember the ring. He took her left hand and slid the ring on her finger. She had to help him get it past her knuckle. It fit her as if it was made for her, the way the glass slipper fit Cinderella in the fairy tale.

"This isn't just any ring," Noah said. "My dad gave it to my mother when he proposed. His father gave it to his bride before that. It comes down through a long line of tenacious, determined people—people with deep roots and long memories."

She sniffled. Admiring the colors in the stones, she said, "Do you think you could kiss me now?"

His arms came around her. In that moment before his lips touched hers, he said, "I can do a hell of a lot better than that."

Her arms went around him, too, and she lifted her face to his. The thing about Noah was that he kissed with everything he had. He poured everything into it, his heart, his soul, and he had a lot of both.

She drew her arms tight around him, holding him to her, and her to him. Slowly, her hands glided up to his shoulders, and back down again. She loved his back, loved the corded muscles and sinew, loved his narrow hips and rear end. Her hands went there, squeezing.

Something crinkled in his pocket. She reached in like a street urchin and brought out a sheet of paper.

She gave herself up to his kiss for another full minute. She moaned into his mouth, and sighed at his touch. His fingers went to the buttons on her shirt.

She spun around, fitting her back to his front. Never one to pass up any opportunity, he covered her breasts with his hands. He seemed to know instinctively how much pressure to exert, squeezing without hurting her, kneading until she arched her back and brought one hand to the nape of his neck.

She opened her eyes, and once again noticed the piece of paper in her hand. She unfolded it, and scanned it. It was the itemized bill from the hospital in Chicago. She'd gone over it dozens of times. The *PAID IN FULL* scrawled across the columns was new.

"What's this?" she asked.

He groaned at being interrupted in the middle of kissing her neck. "Oh, that."

Something about those two words breached the haze of her desire. "Why does it say *paid in full?*"

"Because I wired the money to the hospital a few hours ago."

"You what?" She turned around. And looked him square in the face. "How?"

"Modern technology."

That wasn't what she was asking. "This was for tens of thousands of dollars. How could you have paid it off? Even if you sold your truck, you wouldn't—"

Her breath caught. There was only one thing he could have sold for this much money.

"Oh, Noah, you didn't sell your airplane."

Noah took a deep, fortifying breath. He couldn't do anything about what was happening below his waist, but he attempted to clear his mind by blinking his eyes.

"I thought maybe we could talk about this later—" He made a little jerking gesture toward the bed with his shoulder. "But obviously you want to talk about it now."

A circle of pink appeared on her cheeks. He knew what it meant. She was miffed.

"Look, I had three offers before I took her for a test flight. I accepted the best one. There will be other planes."

"How could you? This was my responsibility. I had every intention of paying this off as soon as the tavern sells. Someone's interested in it, by the way."

"Fine," he said, adopting her favorite word and stance. "When it sells, you can buy us that house with a picket fence you've always wanted."

"You would accept that? You would live in a house I bought? You wouldn't have a problem knowing you were a kept man?"

He supposed he shouldn't have grinned, but he couldn't help it. "As long as you're the woman keeping me, oh, yeah, I'd be as happy as a clam."

It must have been the right thing to say, because she tipped her head and gave her shoulders a little shrug. "I guess we would be even then, wouldn't we?" she asked.

Darkness had fallen. The only sound in the room was the whir of the fan behind them and a moth beating its wings incessantly against the screen in its never-ending quest for the light. Noah had never understood such a quest better than right now.

"Are you done talking?" he asked.

She shrugged again, then stepped back into his arms. He curled his body around her, and said, "Can I get that in writing?"

She moaned deep in her throat. "Get what in writing? That we're done talking?"

"No, that you'll marry me—the sooner the better."

"Why don't we just elope so I can't change my mind?"

He smiled. "That's a great idea."

She opened her eyes wide. "I was being sarcastic."

"I know. You sound like a wife already. Let's do it. Let's elope."

"Now?"

He nodded.

"But how? Who would marry us at this time on a Tuesday night?"

Their gazes met, held. They had the same idea at the same time. "The judge," they said in unison.

She chortled. "Can you imagine what Ivan the Terrible will say if we wake him up?"

Imagine it? Noah had been waiting ten years for an opportunity like this. "Come on." He took her hand.

"Wait." She looked down at her mussed shirt and faded jeans. "I'm only going to get married once, Noah Sullivan. Give me ten minutes to change my clothes and fix my hair."

"I'll give you ten minutes if you'll give me one minute to do this."

He tipped her face up and kissed her.

Lacey gave herself up to the moment, a moment that lasted far longer than a minute. Somewhere, somehow, while his lips melded with hers, and his breath became her breath, she heard a clock strike midnight. Breathless with wonder after the kiss ended, she fairly floated to the closet and brought out the dress she would wear to become Noah's bride.

The houses on Jefferson Street were some of the oldest and largest in all of Orchard Hill. Noah parked at the curb and peered at the dark windows of his uncle's intimidating mansion.

He ran around and opened the door for his bride. He'd waited longer than ten minutes for Lacey to get ready, but when she'd emerged from her bedroom, a vision in that aqua cloud of a dress, her face serene, her eyes shining with anticipation and happiness, it was worth every minute he'd waited.

Hand in hand, they ran up the sidewalk. They couldn't believe they were doing this. He pressed the doorbell. From somewhere on the second floor, a yappy dog started barking. Noah stood holding Lacey's hand, fireflies flitting above the rosebushes on either side of the front door. When the barking stopped and no one came, he pressed the doorbell again.

Just as he was about to ring the bell the third time, the foyer light came on. "Who is it?" a grumpy voice asked.

"Why, it's Noah, dear." Noah's plump, gray-haired great-aunt opened the door and blinked in the bright light, a little gray dog on one arm.

"What are you doing here?" the judge groused, blinking owlishly, too.

"We'd like to get married," Noah said.

"Come to the courthouse in the morning." He started to slam the door, only to have his efforts thwarted by his wife.

"Don't you kids mind his fe-fi-fo-fumming. Come in. This is so romantic. Isn't this romantic, Ivan, dear?"

"What's romantic about being awakened out of the best sleep I've had in weeks?" He peered up at Noah, his combover sticking out, his eyes watery behind his smudged wire-rimmed glasses. He gave his great-nephew a look that usually made even the toughest, thick-skinned people fidget. Tonight, Noah held the judge's gaze unwaveringly. In that moment, something passed between them. And even though the judge heaved a condescending sigh, Noah realized it covered genuine affection. "I guess I'm awake now," the old man said. "I might as well make an honest man out of you. Maude, bring me my—"

She'd already thought of that, and came bustling back

into the room before he'd finished the command. In her hands were a worn leather-bound book and two legal-looking documents, her satiny robe and fluffy dog fluttering behind her.

"I don't remember the last time some young couple woke us up to marry them. There's just a dab of paperwork to fill out so it's all nice and legal," she said, beaming up at Noah and Lacey. "By the way, I'm Aunt Maude."

Lacey smiled so warmly even Ivan noticed.

"Why, aren't you a pretty little thing," Maude exclaimed, wetting the tip of her pen with her tongue.

She asked them pertinent questions, and filled in the blanks with their answers. And then the judge led them to the living room.

He stood with his back to the stone fireplace. And Noah took Lacey's hand.

There was no violin music, no candlelight, no flowers, no church filled with guests, or bridesmaids in taffeta and pearls. Lacey had never wanted any of those things. All she'd ever wanted was the love of the man holding her hand.

And Noah did love her. She believed it with her whole heart. She loved him, too, just as much.

As she stood waiting for the civil ceremony to begin, she thought she heard her father's voice whisper, "Didn't I tell you you'd find the hidden treasure?"

Feeling almost as light as the air she breathed, she smiled and whispered back, "Thanks, Dad."

The judge cleared his throat and began. He asked the *Do you's* and said the *Repeat after me's*. The ceremony lasted five minutes at the most. Noah and Lacey had no wedding rings to exchange. They had something greater. They exchanged promises to love, honor and cherish each other as long as they both lived.

"By the power vested in me," the judge said, "by God and the State of Michigan, I now pronounce you husband and wife."

Great-Aunt Maude sniffled. When the judge forgot the best part, she whispered, "You may kiss your bride."

Noah eased his face closer to Lacey's. And he kissed his wife for the very first time. Lacey closed her eyes and kissed her husband, too.

She forgot her camera, but Great-Aunt Maude snapped several pictures before they left. Already Lacey knew what she would write at the top when she put them in her scrapbook.

A Bride & Her Groom Before Dawn.

And just like that, the beginning of their brand-new beginning began.

Epilogue

Three days before Christmas...

Noah turned up his wool collar against the morning chill and watched as a few more guests arrived for this morning's traditional wedding ceremony. Well, he thought, sliding a hand into the pocket of his full-length black coat, this was as traditional as he and Lacey could be.

Having another wedding ceremony with his closest friends and family in attendance had been Noah's idea. Having it outdoors on a cold winter morning beneath an arbor decorated with pine boughs and holly at the orchard had been Lacey's.

But he was getting ahead of himself.

The notion to have a second ceremony had occurred to him in the middle of the night a week ago. By the time Lacey had awakened beside him at dawn's early light, he'd had an entire night to revel in the wonder that he and Lacey were going to have a baby—two, actually.

But of course there would be two! Noah's three-step plan had had a mind of its own from the start. Why would he have thought that had changed? He loved the way everything had worked out. His genes and Lacey's had found one another in a petri dish. Now, nine weeks later they were snug as two bugs in a rug inside their mother's uterus. Noah had lain awake in awe the entire night following their first ultrasound appointment.

"Our kids are going to want to know our story," he'd whispered into Lacey's ear.

She'd hummed an agreeable sound.

"We have to make sure it's a good story," he'd insisted.

"Stories don't get much better than ours," she'd answered on a sigh.

"I want to show them a photo album of our wedding and all our guests," he'd said.

That brought her the rest of the way awake. "You want us to get married again?"

"I thought you'd never ask!" He'd placed his hand over her belly, only now just starting to round. And although he couldn't feel their children, he and Lacey both believed their babies felt the love radiating from their daddy's hand. Within minutes, the plans were made, their closest family and friends were called, and here they were, a week later, about to exchange their vows one more time.

Joey, nine months old now, babbled loudly from his mother's arms behind Noah. It appeared that Charlotte, Noah's niece and Riley and Madeline's three-month-old daughter, was going to sleep through the outdoor ceremony of her *favorite* aunt and uncle. Noah had a couple of brothers and two sisters-in-law who would have disputed that particular designation. After all, the only thing the

Sullivan brothers enjoyed more than loving their wives was claiming bragging rights to uncle-ship. It never ceased to amaze Noah when he thought about the fact that all four of the Sullivans—Madeline, Reed, Marsh and Noah—had married the same year.

As if they'd read his mind, Reed and Marsh suddenly appeared on either side of Noah. "The judge is ready," Marsh said.

"Everybody's here," Reed added.

They each clapped him on a shoulder, and the girl Noah had first glimpsed climbing out the window above the tavern last June raised her violin to her shoulder. And the beautiful undulating notes of "Joy to the World" swirled like love itself to the ears of each wedding guest gathered in the meadow where Noah had written *LACEY + NOAH* six months ago.

Even Joey quieted. All eyes turned to the vision in a flowing velvet cape stepping into view from inside the cider house nearby.

Lacey took a moment to let her gaze rest on the glowing faces of her best friends, and her sisters-in-law and brothers-in-law. They all stood beaming back at her, smiles on their faces. Even the judge wore a warm glow this morning.

What a morning! Something had happened in the atmosphere overnight, and with the rising of the sun, it was as if the universe was telling her this morning was a gift for her and Noah. There was a dusting of snow on the ground and on everything—every roof and every branch of every tree—was frost so sparkling and white it was almost too much beauty to take in with only one's eyes. It was as if it needed to be felt, too, in order to be fully appreciated. It reminded her of the love she saw as her gaze met Noah's.

She started down the stone steps of the cider house as

the lovely strains of that single violin continued. She had no one to escort her to the arbor where Noah and the judge waited, and yet she had no fear of tripping. Later everyone would tell her she appeared to float down the steps and along the curving pathway. But Lacey knew she wasn't floating, for she felt the firm foundation of the earth beneath her every step.

Noah had never looked more handsome than he did at that moment when he reached out his hand, and cradled her cold fingers in his warm palm. April swooped forward and lowered the velvety hood of Lacey's cape. The music ended. And the judge began.

"Dearly beloved, we are gathered here this morning to once again join these two in marriage..."

One of the babies started crying while Lacey and Noah were saying their vows. By the time Lacey and Noah both said, "I do," the babies weren't the only ones sniffling.

Lacey's and Noah's eyes remained dry. A slight breeze wafted across the meadow, and suddenly the air was filled with bits of frost glittering like starlight in the light of day.

Noah kissed his bride, even though they'd been officially married for six months. Never let it be said that a Sullivan didn't take every advantage handed to him.

What a Christmas, she thought, slightly dizzy with happiness as she and Noah faced their family. As everyone hugged everyone else and backs were patted and babies jiggled, it felt to Lacey as if she'd been in this exact moment before. She couldn't explain it, but with Noah at her side and their children growing within her, and all these people to love and be loved, it already felt like Christmas.

As Lacey held out her hands to Joey, and Noah took Madeline's little girl and Riley's baby in his arms, and all the family gathered around them, they all knew that Christmas wasn't just a day. Christmas was the belief, the innocent trust in a misunderstood universe that something joyful was coming. It had nothing to do with what was material, and everything to do with what wasn't.

* * * * *

LET'S TALK

Romance

For exclusive extracts, competitions
and special offers, find us online:

 facebook.com/millsandboon

 @MillsandBoon

 @MillsandBoonUK

Get in touch on 01413 063232

For all the latest titles coming soon, visit

millsandboon.co.uk/nextmonth

GET YOUR ROMANCE FIX!

MILLS & BOON
— *blog* —

Get the latest romance news, exclusive author
interviews, story extracts and much more!

blog.millsandboon.co.uk